The Bean Jar

The Bean Jar

Guernsey girls.

Guernsey gossip.

Guernsey Gâche.

Jessica Leather

For Mum. For everything.

Prologue

If you're looking for an island paradise but can't quite afford the Caribbean, there's always Guernsey.

Guernsey. Sarnia, if you're being particularly old-fashioned. Tucked daintily between France and England, it's technically part of the British Isles, though its few small miles of land don't bear much resemblance to the UK. It's an island of creamy milk and golden goats, of sandy beaches and magnificent cliff walks; of rich bankers and gated mansions. Packed with wartime history, winding lanes, and a plethora of fresh-faced millionaires to reside alongside the wrinkled dairy farmers: the island is unique. The doors in the seaside cottages may be small, a relic of the days when no true Guernseyman cleared five feet three inches... but the personalities are huge.

In an unassuming corner, just off the cobbled high street of St Peter Port, sits the Bean Jar: a cosy coffee shop held in high esteem by islanders old and young. Fabulous espresso blends mix with the richest milk to make exquisite lattes and cappuccinos as far as even the most jaded coffee-addict can drink, and intriguing smells emanate from the kitchen when the charming local delicacies are being baked.

But no matter how much you try to make it sound like a tourist brochure with beautifully cheesy flowing adjectives, nothing can hide the truth of the Bean Jar: if you can't hear the choice phrases "fuck me sideways with a Guernsey tomato",

"Christ on a bicycle", or the classic "bollocks" echoing through the window… well then, either the customers are anomalously well-behaved, or the baristas are busy having adventures.

Annoying Customer of the Week, Part 1

"Hi, what can I get for you this afternoon?"

"Just a coffee."

"Sure thing, what kind of coffee would you like?"

"A coffee."

"Just an ordinary filter coffee? Not latte, Americano, cappuccino..."

"Yes, one of them."

"A cappuccino?"

"Yes. A black cappuccino."

"Um, there's no such thing as a black cappuccino, I'm afraid. A cappuccino is defined by its foamy milk..."

"All right, that then."

"OK, would you like a small one or a big one?"

"Medium."

"We do big or small, sir."

"Medium!"

And as I hit my head very hard against the coffee machine, the last shift of the year came to a close. Finally, I thought. I can get to that party before they run out of booze.

Chapter 1

"I hope you don't think you're getting paid for this," Zach grumbled.

We ignored him.

Some of us were far too hungover to be listening.

Well, technically Lizzy didn't need to be listening. He wasn't *her* boss.

Gemma wasn't hungover. But as this was still a fairly novel state for her to be in, she kept with tradition and ignored him anyway.

And Flic neither worked for him nor had the kind of hangover that required the constant presence of a bucket within a five-metre radius. But she was kind enough to join in the ignoring anyway; she was particularly good at putting a nice supercilious spin on it.

Realising he was being thoroughly underappreciated, Zach stomped off towards the kitchen, muttering mutinously to himself. I was pretty sure I heard something along the lines of "useless and incompetent" and "bank holiday" and the word "why" repeated at least twice.

I suppose it was probably a bit cheeky of us to be there. As his two best – and only – baristas, Gemma and I had bullied him into opening the Bean Jar on New Year's Day, purely so we could camp out and hide from our families. The holiday season had felt about eight months long, and I for one really didn't fancy spending my most hungover day of the year in the company of my mum and fourteen-year-old brother. I couldn't even hide with Nan; she was still in bed nursing her own head after whatever shenanigans she'd been up to with Joyce and Pat over midnight. I was still too delicate to check her Snapchat and find out what had gone on.

I needed hangover food. And ever since I started working for Zach at the Bean Jar, my hangover food had been the Retro Chicken Curry soup.

Admittedly, Gemma had allowed her sister to come into the café, somewhat negating the 'no annoying relatives' rule; but even though she at Flic were usually at loggerheads, they shared a mutual distaste for their parents after a week spent in their company. At least Flic had managed to escape to her boyfriend's family for a couple of days – they'd been together since she was fourteen, so she was almost as much a part of their family as her own. Gemma didn't exactly have that luxury, especially as she still lived in the family bungalow.

Lizzy, dutiful daughter as ever, would have stuck with her family if they had asked her. But as her mum and dad had buggered off on a cruise for Christmas, and were still happily floating around the Caribbean with a gin and tonic in each hand (probably), she had spent most of the season with me and my lot. So like it or lump it, she was coming to celebrate the dawn of the new year by stroking my hair sympathetically while I groaned, head slumped across a table, an untouched cup of cold coffee in front of me and half a bowl of soup perched next to it.

"I mean, it's not like there's anybody in town today!" Zach called from the back, emphatically clattering some unused coffee cups around. "If anyone comes in, I'll have a heart attack!"

"Shut up, Zach," Gemma said briskly, settling herself back into her seat after her third pee since we arrived, less than an hour ago. The perils of being nearly four months pregnant and only able to keep morning sickness at bay with litres and litres of Diet Coke. "So where were we?"

"You were filling in Cleo's memory lapses," Flic said in her best 'parental' voice. A couple of years older than us, she had always been disapproving of her sister's habit for rampant drunkenness and thus, by extension, of me. This got exponentially worse when she clocked my collection of heavy metal t-shirts and instantly pegged me for some kind of leather-clad, headbanging maniac (not a million miles from the truth, granted). Yet somehow, begrudgingly, as the months had passed we'd developed a strange sort of friendship. I think she enjoyed feeling like she had the moral high ground in matters of, well, everything. And she was impressed that I'd racked up quite a lot of followers on Instagram just through the occasional drunken selfie and pictures of endless cups of coffee.

Flic had had such high hopes when she met Lizzy, Lizzy being rather shy and quiet and (seemingly) docile. She'd immediately wanted to take her under her supervising wing and make her the calm, sedate little sister she'd always wanted.

No luck there, of course. I've known Lizzy since we were both eleven years old. She'd been well and truly under *my* wing for thirteen years, and there was no chance that little streak of rebelliousness I'd created could remain tucked away forever. Most of the time she kept it well under the surface, only bringing it out on special occasions, but it was definitely there.

"Never mind Cleo's memory lapses," Lizzy said sadly. "Mine were worse."

"You remember everything that happened," I mumbled, my voice muffled beneath my own arms. "You always do."

"Well, yes." She sounded tearful. I propped my head up on my arms and tried bravely not to vomit. "But I feel so guilty!"

"Oh, don't be ridiculous." I let my head drop again. "You didn't do anything wrong."

"But I kissed another man!" she wailed. "I let myself totally forget about Dan, how could I do such a thing?"

"Oh, spare me the sob story," Gemma interrupted snappishly, before Lizzy could get into her stride. "You've been broken up for *three weeks*. That's like, practically years."

"It's not," Lizzy protested. "It's so soon, we could get back together, I want to get back together."

Gemma let out a noise like an angry cat; but Flic was nodding sagely.

"Once you get a man like that, you have to hold onto him," she said. "Solvent, capable, good-looking..."

Lizzy gave a little wail.

"Shut up, Flic, you're upsetting her," I said, just about managing to pat Lizzy on the arm without vomming.

"I'm just telling the truth! You two are twenty-four, that's the perfect age to be finding your life-partners. Of course," I refused to put my head up again to see the smug smile I was sure was crossing Flic's eerily smooth face (we were sure she'd been at the fillers already), "not everyone can be like Jonathan and me."

"No, because some of us like to actually grow up before choosing," Gemma said. I could tell, even with my head buried, that she was rolling her eyes, hard. We'd all heard this before. If I'd been a bit more alive, I would have mouthed along with Flic's inevitable lecture.

"Like you grew up when you slept with... what was his name again?"

"No idea!" Gemma practically sang. She was pretty cheerful, considering the circumstances. She really didn't care that she had no idea what the father of her unborn child was called. She claimed that at least this meant she wouldn't have to try and spell it on the birth certificate – he had been either Latvian or Polish ("can't remember which, I was pretty hammered").

Flic harrumphed in a particularly horse-like manner. Bear in mind, though, she absolutely loved the fact that her little sister was knocked up without a father in sight. She'd never say it, but we all knew. She was only pissed off that, at twenty-three, Gem was too old to get a shiny 'teenage mother on benefits' badge. That would have made it far more fun to tut about, and would have further reinforced her position as their family's Shining Example of Daughterhood.

Lizzy was still looking absolutely distraught.

"What if me and Dan do get back together, though?" she whimpered. "I've kissed another man. *Properly.* Yes, I was drunk... does that still count as cheating? What if we were only on a break?"

"Firstly," Gem took a gulp of her decaffeinated macchiato and winced. "That sweet little thing you kissed last night was barely a man. Boy, at most. Certainly not up to kissing 'properly'. Secondly – fucking hell, why do I bother with this decaf bollocks? – you're not going to get back together with Dan."

Gem's voice was the ringing tone of truth, even as she was spitting her 'fake coffee' back into its cup.

After all, Lizzy had walked in on Dan with her replacement, barely hours after he'd called off their relationship of two years.

And he was very much *with* her wobbly-boobed replacement at the time, if you get what I mean.

There wasn't a trace of guilt on his face when he realised his very recently dumped ex-girlfriend was standing there staring at him with a face like a fish who'd been hit with a mallet.

How do I know this? I was right behind her, having come to their almost-new flat to help her move out. Lizzy got custody of their Christmas tree and a collection of carefully curated photo albums chronicling their relationship; Dan got a new redheaded girlfriend with boobs that could practically spin in a circle.

No, it really didn't look like the two of them would be getting back together.

Hopefully Lizzy would see it soon for herself. It had only been three weeks – but to me and Gem, that was the length of a good-sized relationship. Of course we couldn't see quite where Lizzy was coming from, just out of what we might call a two year prison sentence (it was fair to say, we hadn't been entirely keen on Dan).

Lizzy had been doing so well, that was the thing. Her rich grandmother had recently moved out of her duplex along the St Sampson seafront into a more manageable bungalow far away on the mainland. Seeing her granddaughter's predicament, she had let Lizzy start renting the flat from her for a pittance. She had had her 'breaking down in tears mid-conversation' moments and a newly-developed line in insomnia, of course she had (Lizzy, not her grandmother), but surely that's typical of the recently dumped?

All this passed sluggishly through my head while I tried not to let it move around too much. Gemma was tapping her fingers impatiently, far too close to my poor swollen brain for my liking.

"Last year really was *shitty*, romantically," she said pensively.

"Not for me," Flic put in quickly.

"Oh, shut up." I could feel the tiniest breeze waft past my head as Gem waved her hand dismissively. The breeze was quite nice; I wished she'd do it again. "You and Jonny are stagnating."

"We are not…"

"I said, shut up." Aah, the breeze again. "You two are stagnating away, Lizzy's had her heart torn up, I'm having a baby by a bloke I neither know nor care to, and Cleo's become the queen of the one-night stand."

I stuck both my thumbs up, my head still face down on the table.

"Cleo, you are far too proud of that." Flic's disapproving voice was beginning to grate; it was always far worse when I was hungover, especially when she tried to posh-up her accent.

"I bet I've had sex more times than you this year," I stuck my tongue out, before realising that as my head was still down, I was pretty much just licking the table.

"I had sex this morning, did you?"

"No. At least, not that I remember. I know I pulled… but I'd remember sex."

"Then I've had more sex than you this year. It's 2016 now, Cleo."

Gemma's tone was business-like again. "I've had an idea."

"Oh, this never bodes well."

"Shut up, Flic." Those had to be the three most used words in Gem's vocabulary. "Like I was saying; stagnation, heart torn up, random bloke and queen of one-nighters. We're all fucked."

"We are not…"

"Shut *up* Flic." This time I chorused along with her; even Lizzy attempted to join in, albeit in a rather small voice.

"What are you on about, Gem?" Flic sounded properly impatient now.

Gemma cleared her throat importantly.

I propped my head up on my hands again, blinking at the sudden brightness. I fixed my gaze on the mural Zach had delicately painted behind the coffee machine: a lovely swirly cloudscape overlaid with the words to Sarnia Chérie, Guernsey's 'national anthem'. It was beautifully calming, and made my head feel at least vaguely connected to the planet.

"We need to make 2016 a better year. With men, anyway. We need a challenge."

"No, we don't," Lizzy put in. "Unless you're challenging me to get Dan back."

"I'm bloody well not. Think what year it is."

"1996," I groaned, closing my eyes. "Can it be 1996? That was a good year. I hadn't discovered vodka yet."

"No, it's 2016. And do you know what that means?"

"If I continue the year the way I've started it I'll be dead before April?"

"Shut up, Cleo. It means… it's a leap year."

Silence met Gemma's triumphant announcement.

"Um, and that's important because…?"

"It's a leap year! There's no thirtieth of February!"

"Gem, there never is," Lizzy had the politeness to point out. "It means there'll be a twenty-ninth of February when there usually isn't."

"I knew it was something like that." Gemma waved her hand dismissively. "The point is, they have all these stupid traditions around leap years, right?"

"Oh shite, I can see where this is going." I gripped my head with my hands and willed it to fall off.

"It's the whole thing about women having to, like, propose to men!" Gemma said triumphantly. "This is our year!"

"How is it our year?" I felt the need to ask.

"That's the challenge, you see? We need to propose to men!"

"Gemma, we don't *have* men."

"Excuse me, I have a man."

"Shut up, Flic. You see, that just makes it that bit more exciting! Cleo, the thing is, I have loved being your pulling partner. But maybe it's the hormones, or maybe I've just listened to this one for too long." Gemma thumbed her sister. "I think my baby might just need a father figure. And seeing as I have no attachment to the actual daddy…"

"Or any idea of his name?" Flic butted in.

"Yeah, that too. Thanks to that, the bloke with the biology is kind of out of the question. So I feel like I should probably track a new one down. Preferably by the end of the year, before the kid is old enough to know the difference."

"You're mental," I said, hitting the table with my forehead once again.

"No, she's got a point," Flic mused. "It *is* a leap year, so it would be socially acceptable for her to ask someone. Let's face it, nobody's going to ask her."

"I'm going to pretend you didn't say that," Gem growled. "Not like Jonny's asked you, has he?"

"He will." Flic sniffed. "We're just taking our time."

"But that's my entire point," Gem carried on. "I don't want to do this by myself, it's not a challenge unless there's competition! We all have to do it, all four of us."

"You're saying...?"

"I'm saying that by the end of the leap year, we all have to be engaged at the very least, if not married. And we have to have done the proposing."

"This really messes up my 'shag as many nineteen-year-olds as I can find' plan," I said, breaking the awkward silence. "I was looking forward to it – it was going to be a scientific experiment."

"So you're in, then?"

"Oh, whatever." I yanked the skirt of my apron over my face, all the better to block out as much light as possible. "If it'll shut you up. It totally won't happen, but I'll give it a go."

"Never say never!" Gemma chided.

"Plus, I suppose it could be a kind of good idea," I mused, more to my apron than to anyone else. "You've seen my mum and her luck. Even Nan, my granddad was her third husband, and that was kind of a big deal back then. First marriages in my family just don't work. Or second ones, for that matter. It'd be a good thing to get mine out of the way quick."

"Precisely!" Gemma thumped the table with enthusiasm. I thought my head might actually come off and roll across the floor. "So come on, Flic, Lizzy?"

"Can I ask Dan?"

"No, you bloody well can't. He'd only say no, he's got Miss What's-Her-Face with the saggy boobs now. You can find a nice new man. Asking Dan is going to be strictly forbidden under clause number one in this contract."

"You're going to make a *contract*?"

"A metaphorical one. Shh. So, Lizzy?"

"Well… OK, if Cleo's in, I'm in."

"Does first past the post get anything?" I piped up from under my own arms.

"Respect," Gemma said firmly.

"Well, I'm definitely in." Flic pushed her chair back from the table. "In fact, I'm off now."

I looked up again, just in time to see her down the rest of her (skinny, decaffeinated, single-shot, why bother) latte in one.

"Why? We can hide out here for hours yet, nobody else is coming in."

"Which begs the question…"

"You're not part of this conversation, Zach!" Gemma called back to the kitchen. "Yeah, why are you off already?"

"To propose to Jonathan, of course!" Flic gave a tinkling little laugh. "See you later!"

With a swish of her coat and a slam of the door, she was off.

"Oh, that hurt," I moaned, gripping my temples as the slam reverberated through my skull. "I'm going over there." I picked myself up, feeling every bone creak, and collapsed onto the aesthetically battered brown leather sofa in the window of the café.

Lizzy and Gemma didn't bother following me; the bottom floor of the Bean Jar was so small that there was no point. We'd be well able to carry on our conversation at different tables – and Gemma would be well able to continue her cheerful abuse of Zach, who was still clattering around in the kitchen behind the coffee bar.

"Do you think she'll really do it?" Lizzy said.

"Of course she will," Gemma scoffed. "When Flic wants something, she gets it. Look how she was with that Michael Kors bag on Black Friday."

I shuddered at the memory.

"It wasn't pretty."

"They'll be married before the year is out, you mark my words," Gemma said sagely. "And so will we. More coffee, you two?"

She bustled away behind the bar to fix me and Lizzy our drinks: Lizzy's latte, my triple shot Americano with a drop of full-fat milk to cool it down (I needed it extra strong to combat the hangover, if I could ever force it down my neck – coffee was my fuel). I could hear her grumbling about having to press the decaf button as she started making herself a fresh one too; then a really attractive burp and an expectorated "fuck". Gemma had had issues with the smell of coffee almost since the line had shown up on the pregnancy test; something that depressed her greatly. Coffee may have been my fuel, but it was Gemma's essence.

As she hurtled into the kitchen for her third morning-sickness vom of the day, I pondered what I had got myself into.

The Leap Year Pact. Would I be married before the year was out, too? It was too big a thought to even comprehend. But whether it was just the hangover talking or the actual logical part of my brain, I *did* feel like it would be a good idea. Twenty-four years old: too young, in my opinion, to be settling down for life. But certainly old enough to get that all-important first marriage-and-divorce combo safely out of the way. Then I'd be able to settle down and find my real happy-ever-after and all that bollocks.

If said bollocks existed.

"Right, you lot, we're not getting any customers." Zach stamped out from the kitchen, a tea towel in one hand and his mousy hair sticking up every which way. His glasses were fogged up, and he peered owl-like through them, his blue eyes like lighthouse beams seeking out his recalcitrant staff, his voice foghorning to match. "I've washed every cup we have, and Gemma just puked all over my lovely clean sink. So now I have to disinfect the entire kitchen – unless you want a go, Cleo?"

"If you make me go near that kitchen I will vom dramatically myself."

"Then you can bugger off and go back to your own homes."

"Aww but Zach… can we at least finish our drinks first?"

"You don't have any drinks."

"Gem was just making them, can you finish them off?"

"Sod off," he muttered, but started twirling the milk steamer nonetheless with a crooked smile he was blatantly trying to repress. So easily manipulated, our boy Zach. Sometimes I had to wonder which one of us was the boss.

Chapter 2

After Gemma had rung up her long-suffering fisherman dad and bullied him into driving her the two miles to their house, Lizzy and I decided we'd have a walk back to her flat. It was definitely a better option than going back to my house; the one I shared with Mum, Nan and Charlie. Even though it was technically closer to town, it was up one hell of a hill and I just didn't think my hangover could deal with it.

Wrapped up warm against the freezing wind, we started the long walk along the sea front. Well, I say 'long walk' – it was going to take us forty minutes, with maximum dawdling. But with the wind blowing an absolute hooley, and the possibility of Guernsey's horrendous driving rain coming off the sea, it was going to be the kind of walk that certainly blew away all the hangover cobwebs.

I hoped so, anyway.

Days like that made me really love Guernsey – though I always preferred them without the hangover to be blown away in the first place.

Oddly enough, up until I was eighteen, all I wanted to do was leave. Living on an island was too cramped, too crowded, too small. I wanted to be free; to be somewhere where you could just jump on a train and be hundreds of miles away within hours, not where you had to book planes and boats months in advance and then face the issue of whether you'd end up fogged in anyway. I didn't want to walk down a high street and realise that I knew at least a third of the people shopping there, and that at least a fifth of them had seen me drunkenly attempting to pole dance round the Liberation monument.

Off I went to university... and realised how much I actually loved my little island.

Oh, I still had a great time in Manchester, don't get me wrong. I had everything I wanted there, for the person I wanted to be at eighteen. But returning to Guernsey really was a proper homecoming. I knew I still wanted to travel one day, and maybe to spend time living elsewhere in the world. But I would always be a homing pigeon, I just had to leave in the first place to come to terms with it.

You can't get a walk like that in Manchester, for a start– all the way along the seafront, rounding the headland away from town to see the long beach that stretched in front of Lizzy's house.

Of course, it wasn't looking its best on the first day of the year. The sea was grey and angry, almost lapping at the grassy headland. It didn't look like the kind of beach you'd want to sunbathe on, that was for sure, even at high tide with the sea covering the smelly piles of vraicq (Guernsey-French for a particularly disgusting type of seaweed) that would inevitably be left behind. I might have got a few likes on Instagram for a moodily-framed shot of the roiling sea, but I was far too hungover to make an effort with the filters.

Shielding my eyes from the wind and the rain, I could just about make out the tiny islands of Herm and Jethou, rising out of the mist a couple of miles away. I couldn't see Sark at all, even though I knew it wasn't far behind them. The Herm Trident boat was doggedly bouncing along the waves, determined to get to its destination even at this time of the year – I was bloody glad I wasn't on it. I've never been one for seasickness, but it looked just a bit unstable.

This particular side of Guernsey wasn't the prettiest in winter. Oh, yes, the view of the islands rising out of the waves across the bay could be spectacular, and I was thoroughly jealous of Lizzy's view of them from her flat. But in the winter, it was just grey. Grey waves, grey sky, grey beach. You couldn't even take joy in the distant view of Castle Cornet, hanging precariously off the edge of town.

But the other side of the island, around by Rocquaine, or even Cobo... that's always something impressive. In the summer it's beautiful, of course. White sand, the bays hugged by the grassy headland, clear water. Dinky rockpools with the requisite crabs and cockles present and correct. In summer, you can't walk three paces without stepping on a sandcastle.

But in the winter, when the waves beat dramatically against the rocks, throwing up spray for miles, almost drowning the ancient fishermen's bungalows clinging to the edge of the beach – it's something remarkable to see. You never realise how much power the sea can command until you watch it relentlessly battering the sea wall, or the towering totems of rocks left hanging precariously from centuries of relentless abuse by the waves.

On the worst days, the spray reaches three times the height of the houses along the shoreline, dwarfing the Martello towers still doggedly perched on the coast, even the huge German gun emplacements looking like nothing against the true might of nature. Those are the days the roads get closed and everybody whines about the sea defences, but nothing ever changes. Nothing can keep back that kind of power.

It seems entirely wild, no matter what time of year. Sometimes I'd hop on my little red scooter and, trying not to get blown into the sea along the Perelle road, drive out to the furthest corners of the island just to watch the waves breaking against the bays, or to Vazon to watch the surfers determinedly try to beat the swell.

Still, some fairly recent view-spoiling industrialisation didn't stop Lizzy's side of the island from being buffeted by the gale-force winds coming straight from France. And, therefore, it was going to do nothing to stop me almost being lifted off my feet as I tried to stagger along the seafront to Lizzy's. Blowing away the cobwebs? Blowing away my head, more like it.

"Why does it hurt so much?" I wailed at Lizzy over the howling of the wind, clutching my ears.

"Because you drank like a dehydrated fish, Cleo," she reminded me.

"I've drunk more than that before and been fine," I said adamantly. "I used to be so much better than this when I was a student!"

"Worse, Cleo. The word you're looking for is 'worse'."

We dashed across the road to the big white house where Lizzy had the top two floors. There was only one other flat downstairs, but hers was lucky enough to be twice the size, thanks to her gran renovating the building's attic back in the eighties. It was a gorgeous flat, and as I assured her many times, it was one less thing for Lizzy to mourn over after her relationship with Dan; the 'renovation project' flat they'd bought together at the arse-end of the island had been dire.

"Here, I'll find you a towel." As we got inside, Lizzy instantly went straight into hostess mode, chucking her keys on the hall table and bustling into the bathroom to present me with a crisp white towel. Christ on a bicycle, she'd been there for two weeks, half of which she'd spent at mine and all of which she'd spent in considerable emotional turmoil, and yet she was already organised enough to be ironing her towels. In three years of living away from home during my degree, I don't think I'd touched an iron once. And certainly not since moving back in with my mum.

"Anything in a better colour?" I looked at the towel, and then gestured to my dripping hair. I'd just chopped my hair off, this time to a straightened-to-within-an-inch-of-its-life bob, and changed its colour again, from red to purple. I wasn't particularly imaginative; I vacillated between the two. And at that moment in time, I was very likely to turn Lizzy's beautifully ironed towel into a blotchy, post-murder-scene mess.

"I've probably got something darker in here somewhere." She disappeared into the sizeable airing cupboard under the stairs. I shook my head sadly. I just couldn't believe how much room she had. With four of us in a thin terraced house, personal space was a luxury at my place. And I didn't even have a sea view to make up for it. The only view I had was the roof of my old secondary school. That's just not fair.

"So come on, Liz." I tagged after Lizzy into her galley kitchen, where she was pouring herself a glass of apple juice. After the previous night's Vopple Juice overindulgence – a splendid concoction of vodka and apple juice, obviously – I couldn't face it. "Any resolutions this year?"

"Other than the one we all just made to get married?"

"Other than that." I gave my hair an extra hard rub. "Totally pretending that's not happening."

"Already?"

"Already." I nodded firmly. "I'll think about it tomorrow. Or whenever. So come on, resolutions?"

Lizzy considered, sipping her juice. Although she'd been pretty rough that morning, she already seemed to have recovered from her hangover, her creamy pale skin already having lost its grey tinge. Lucky cow. "I just want to be happy, really."

"Aww, bless," I scoffed. "Come on, I'm sure you've got something else up your sleeve. Something a bit less dull."

"Well." She coloured slightly. "I'd... well, this year I'd like to be a little bit more like you."

"What, drunk and slutty?" I nodded again, ponderously. "I'm sure that can be arranged."

"Don't call yourself that." She belted me with a tea towel. "Not quite as drunk and *friendly* as you. I just... well, now that Dan's gone," she paused to sniff dramatically, "I'd like to learn not to care so much."

"Thanks."

"You know what I mean!"

"I'm a cold, unfeeling bitch?" I stuck my tongue out. "Charming."

"Oh, no, you know..."

"I know what you mean." I patted her on the arm. "For what it's worth, I think behaving like me is an excellent resolution." I gave what had to be an evil grin. "We're going to have some fun..."

"Next resolution though – don't get in any trouble!" Lizzy added hastily. "I don't want to end up arrested or anything-"

"Elizabeth Wyatt, have I ever been arrested?"

"Not that I know of... but who knows what you got up to behind my back at uni?"

"I was a saint!"

"How many one-night stands was it, again?"

"Pah." I waved my hand dismissively. "One does not count such things, it's unladylike."

"Well maybe *one's* resolution should be to start!"

"What, start counting? God, no." I groaned dramatically. "I was never the best at maths."

"Go on then, what are your resolutions?" Lizzy took another dainty sip from her apple juice.

"I don't know, I was hoping to get inspiration from yours." I pondered. "Everyone always says 'lose weight' so maybe I'll join in."

"Why?"

"Lizzy, I look like a pot-bellied pig."

"No you don't, you look like a normal-sized short person with a pair of boobs." Ever the pragmatist. "If you lost weight you'd be bony. Well, maybe not bony." Lizzy corrected herself. "You'll never quite make Gem-levels of skin and bone."

It was true; technically, both Lizzy and I really could stand to lose a pound or two. Out of the three of us, Gemma was the only one you could properly call skinny, even with the miniscule baby bump she was just about starting to show. It came from living on a pre-pregnancy diet almost exclusively composed of coffee and cigarettes, supplemented with the occasional slice of Guernsey Gâche if she felt peckish. Now, of course, having been forced to replace both of her staple fuel sources with industrial vats of Diet Coke, she was finding it difficult to even survive.

"If I dropped a few pounds, it'd be perfect." Lizzy sighed. "Maybe that should be my resolution, then Dan might... ow."

The rest of her words were cut out by me pummelling her with my already-purple-stained towel.

"Don't be thick." I punctuated my pummelling with words. "God, you still have a long way to go."

Just because Dan had gone straight from Lizzy to her near-exact physical opposite, hardly meant that Lizzy was the creature from the black lagoon. Despite our moaning, neither of us have ever really bothered that much about our weight, having quite the shared love of fine cuisine.

Well, family bags of Malteasers and Galaxy Counters at any rate.

Anyway, there was certainly nothing wrong with her to look at: she was curvy and cute, with her freckles and heart-shaped face, and the kind of long blonde hair most women would kill for.

Of course, she could hardly see that herself, but who can?

"Maybe I'll just start going to the gym, then," Lizzy mused. "I could go after PE on Thursdays, we take the whole lower school to Beau Sejour for trampolining."

"Beware – you know who lives in that gym."

I was, of course, talking about Flic. If she wasn't sweating on the gym equipment of Guernsey's only leisure centre (or contorting herself in its yoga studio), she was in its spa, nattering to her stream of perfect work colleagues. Funnily enough, she never brought them to the Bean Jar, even though they all worked in one of the accountancy firms just down the road... funny that. You'd almost think she was ashamed of us.

Not, of course that she'd have any reason to be ashamed of her little sister and her friends. Oh, never. We'd *never* been on a night out with her and got off with one of her co-workers (me and Gemma, that is; we both liked the look of the bloke so had a turn each). Then of course *none* of us had puked copiously on the pavement outside the Barbados nightclub (that might have been me). And we *certainly* hadn't blanked the poor guy in question when he came into the Jar the next day (to be fair, neither of us could remember what he looked like in the harsh daylight).

Nothing to be ashamed of at all.

"You're perfect already, Liz," I said, giving up on trying to dry my hair before my hungover head fell off and deciding to give Lizzy's ponytail a quick rub instead. "You don't need any resolutions other than to get over that man."

"I'll try my best," she said in a small voice.

"If I puke one more time, I'm going to kill myself!" Gemma wailed dramatically.

Gone was the calmly logical, cynical Gemma of New Year's Day. We were supposed to be serving up lunch to Guernsey's grumpy office workers, on their first day back at their desks. Today's soups were an ordinary creamy chicken and a spicy Indian vegetable – despite these cheerful concoctions, nobody seemed to have a smile on their face.

I was the cheeriest person on the island. I was paid to be, after all. And my hangover had finally dissipated.

It was somewhat satisfying to see their grouchy faces. It was a constant sore point that they all seemed to get a good two weeks off work over Christmas while those of us working in food or retail had to slog on through the season and pretend to be festive about it. Their misery upon their return was somewhat comforting.

Plus, I hated other people to be happy when I'd been up since six making toast, bacon butties, and an entire day's worth of bread rolls to go with soup.

Five days a week a lovely lady came in and made all our bread and cakes for us. Every morning, rain or shine, Mrs Machon came in for a couple of hours and created a veritable smorgasbord of baked goods to keep the hungry masses happy.

I'm lying.

Oh, not about the bread and cakes, or that Mrs Machon made them. No, I'm lying about the 'lovely' part.

Mrs Machon. Zach's grandmother. Not a single 'lovely' bone in her body, she struck fear into the hearts of better people than me.

I would regularly arrive at the Bean Jar in the morning to be faced with her wrath.

"Why has the soup kettle not been cleaned?" she'd bellow. "Which one of you closed up last night? Hmm?"

Or: "Who's taken the special knife I use to measure out my currants? One of you moved it, didn't you? Get to Creasey's and buy me another one!"

Or occasionally even: "*If you don't make my cup of tea in the next thirty seconds I am leaving and never coming back!*"

Believe me, when that's hollered at you by an elderly six-foot harridan with arms like a boxer, you want to get that cup of tea made with speed. Especially when she's in a kitchen that contains very sharp knives. Sometimes I just wanted to leave her to it. But then I'd remember that if I did and she carried through her threat to bugger off, it would be me having to bake a three-foot stack of bloody bread rolls every day for the rest of my life.

Without Mrs Machon, we'd be left without one of our best sellers: traditional Guernsey Gâche. Gâche is a sweet buttery bread baked with raisins and sultanas, and try as I might to make it myself, I've never been able to get it right. Mrs Machon was the absolute master, and the smell of it wafting through the Jar would get me through the day on many a hungover morning.`

Now she was pregnant, Gemma was absolutely no use around the breakfast buns or the cakes, which was hardly helping my mood. When Mrs Machon made Bean Jar, the traditional Guernsey stew that Zach had taken the name of the café from that, while cooking, smells like warm farts, poor Gem had to take the day off to escape the smell. She could just about serve soup over lunch, if she could turn her head away and pretend she was somewhere else. And, of course, the smell of coffee was liable to set her off if she wasn't careful.

"This isn't meant to go on this long!" she was wailing, in an uncharacteristically un-Gemma-like way. We were in the kitchen: I was getting another massive jug of soup out of our giant soup kettle, while she was standing in the carrier-bag-and-paper-coffee-cup cupboard clutching a Tupperware container in shaking hands.

She paused to dryly retch in the general direction of her Tupperware.

"I'm sixteen weeks pregnant," she moaned. "I was supposed to get over this weeks ago!"

"There, there." I patted her awkwardly on the back with one of my heat-proof rubber gloves. The normal Gemma would never allow such an affectionate gesture, but she just looked like she'd rather I just gave her a hug. I had to blame the hormones – either that, or the sheer stress of spending weeks on end not knowing whether she'd be able to keep her breakfast down.

"Why don't you just go home?" I tried. But she was having none of that.

"And leave you all on your own? It'll pass in a second and I'll come back out." She burped again.

I made a speedy exit from the kitchen, almost flinging my jug of soup into its big pot.

"Right, who's next?" I picked up a ladle and bellowed at the surly-looking queue of bankers and office workers.

There was a bit of a surge. The Jar hadn't half got popular in the past few months; queues had been known to actually reach into the street. We'd been relatively quiet when we just served coffee and cake, but once Zach had decided to introduce bespoke soup to the mix as well, we'd found ourselves a bit inundated with lunchtime customers. Zach was thrilled.

Of course, I'd be thrilled too – if Zach would deign to come in for the lunchtime rush.

Don't get me wrong, usually he was an excellent boss. We only really needed two of us in at any one time, one to serve and one to race around up and down the stairs clearing tables. As I technically had the job title 'assistant manager', there would always be someone with a semblance of authority to whine at if there was the odd overlooked crumb. Most of the office workers took their lunch away anyway.

With Gemma's morning sickness, though… it would have been nice if Zach could magically materialise and give me a hand, instead of just sauntering in at about three o'clock, putting an apron on over his t-shirt and jeans and half-heartedly making a few coffees.

Then, of course, he'd have a little whine that the steam was fogging up his glasses and he was urgently needed in his cupboard of a back-office to order us another box of paper soup cups.

"No, you can't have bread with your soup, I ran out ten minutes ago. Sorry, if you're that upset, get yourself down to the Co-op and buy some. Four ninety-five, please. No, I can't deduct anything, the bread would be extra anyway. No, I won't make an exception. Bye, see you again soon!"

The grumpy bloke in a suit stamped out of the café, mumbling to himself. I had a little mumble of my own, largely consisting of the word 'twat'.

"Who's next, please?" I hollered.

"Hi, um, sorry, you do takeaway coffee, right?"

"Sure do!" I put my best barista grin on my face. I tried not to get irritated at the fact that this idiot couldn't have missed a similarly besuited person just leave clutching a coffee in a paper cup.

"Great, I didn't know if there was anywhere I could get a decent one, I thought I'd have to just get a boring…"

"What can I get for you today?" I widened my smile. Painfully.

This one wasn't too bad though, as customers went. He was young, and tall. Definitely not a Guernsey native, then. Tall Guerns are a rare species, I'm the perfect short-arsed example of that. He had a shock of blonde hair that despite his tidy grey suit was messy, curly and untamed. Not bad, not bad, I thought, scanning over his wide-set blue eyes and strong jawline. Not my usual type, of course – I preferred my men long-haired and greasy, preferably with a few piercings. But there was scope with this one. The Leap Year Pact was fresh in my mind.

"Are you new around here, then?" I said, as I rolled the steam arm to get the somewhat-hot suit's predictably boring latte the perfect temperature and consistency. "I haven't seen you in here before."

"Yeah, fresh off the boat." He grinned. Was that a hint of a Welsh accent I could hear? Hmm, I wasn't averse to a nice accent. The Guernsey one was so dull. The real Guernsey accent is limited to far too few people, having been mostly replaced by the clipped tones of the rich bankers who moved over to conquer tax-haven living. It all sounds too southern, too posh. A bit of variation was a pleasant surprise. "I just started at Barclays."

"Great!" I didn't think this was particularly great, as a matter of fact. As a rule, bankers are wankers; that's my hard-learned motto. "Well I hope you enjoy it, and make sure to come back again!" I leaned forward and gave him a wink as I handed him his coffee. "My favourite customers get free drinks."

I'm nothing if not brazen.

He looked a little surprised. But hey, if you're not totally shameless about these things, you don't get anywhere.

It only took him a second to recover, and I got another bright-eyed grin. "I'll make this place my regular."

Then with a cheerful "see you!" from me, he was off.

Not bad at all, I mused. Worth sowing some seeds, at any rate.

I turned to my next customer, a woman in a twinset who didn't look all that impressed by my little bit of flirting.

"Eurgh, right, I'm back, I'm better." Gemma came wearily in from the back, re-tying her tight ponytail. Her long hair, mousey brown and uncontrollably curly, reached almost to her bum, and she was in a constant battle with Zach (and Health and Safety laws) over whether she should have to wear a hairnet for work. "Next, please, and be nice to me!"

"What can I get for you?" I put on my second-best sparkle for Twinset.

But before she could even start her order, the door crashed open, and a force of nature scattered the six or so soup-seeking suits waiting to get their lunches.

That force of nature was Flic.

"LOOK!" she shrieked, in a very un-Flic-like manner. "Just LOOK at it!"

Oh, hang on. There was some definite crowing going on here. And why was she waving her left hand in the air? Waving it so violently she was nearly walloping one of the suits in the head.

"I'M ENGAGED!"

"Oh, bollocks." And so Gemma puked into the barista sink.

Annoying Customer of the Week, Part 2

"Hiya, what can I get you this afternoon?"

"A motcha please."

"Um... sorry?"

"A motcha!"

"A mot... oh! A MOCHA, do you mean, with the coffee and chocolate together?"

"Yes, a motcha."

"Of course, I'll just get your MOCHA for you. What size would you like?"

"Medium, please."

"We do big, or small."

"Medium."

At least it wasn't quite as bad as 'expresso'. I got that at least once a day, sometimes twice. One day, I was going to screech "eSpresso with an ESSSSS!" very loudly across the café and have a mental breakdown to boot.

Chapter 3

"Are you guys having your summit tonight?"

"Yep." I groaned and gave the milk steamer a far more enthusiastic blast than was probably necessary. "She's going to bring us up to speed with all her plans so far."

"You sound chuffed to bits." Zach raised his eyebrows and leaned on the bar next to me.

The lunchtime rush had just cleared out and we were having a brief moment of peace – just one elderly couple relaxing on the sofa with their lattes (peering out onto the damp high street with great disapproval at the rain) and a suit with a laptop hiding upstairs.

After Flic's dramatic announcement earlier that week, we called an official emergency summit for Friday evening to get the full story. Flic had been all set to just blurt out the whole lot there and then, but we wouldn't give her the satisfaction. Plus, our gang of waiting suits would probably have been less than thrilled with the situation.

Even Gemma had refused to listen to her sister's story until the summit. She claimed it made her too nauseated just to think about it, let alone hear about it. As a result, she'd temporarily set up camp in Lizzy's spare bedroom with her Tupperware vomit container and enough clean knickers to last the week. The De Carteret parents were overjoyed, apparently, and every third word in their house was 'wedding'. Gem and Flic's dad was even threatening to deck out his fishing boat with bunting and bring Flic around the island on it on her wedding day, "for that Insta thing you like so much". Apparently that had been the last straw, and Gem had fled with a sicky burp.

Zach didn't mind us using the Bean Jar after hours, as long as we left the place in a decent state. And as long as we didn't make him stick around and brew us our drinks.

"Ahh, I'm happy for her." I shrugged and crossed my arms, thumping back against the wall. "It's not like we didn't all see it coming. But bloody hell, she's going to be insufferable for the next – how long are people engaged for?"

"No idea." Zach shrugged too. "Couple of my mates from school have been engaged for about three years now and I don't think they've even set a date yet."

"Oh shit." I drooped down the wall. "She could drag this out for three years?"

"Or even longer." Zach grinned. His smile was always crooked, dimpling right into his left cheekbone. From the right side, even when he was smiling, he looked almost stern. Of course, he was one of the least stern people I'd ever met, no matter how hard he tried.

The door clanged open, and I tried to un-droop myself: then sank all the way to the floor with near professional speed.

I should have expected her, really.

"Good afternoon!" With a rustle of capacious flowery skirt, she bustled in.

Mrs Doubtfire. Or, as she should be called to her face, Joan. None of us had ever heard her real surname, but from the moment she first determinedly stomped into the Bean Jar, she had been known as Mrs Doubtfire. Because yes, she looks exactly like Robin Williams dressed in drag as an old lady.

Only louder. And more annoying.

She'd been a great devotee of the café at the top of Creasey's department store, a café that probably featured in the Book of Martyrs, it's so old. It has lovely views across the harbour; it's further along St Peter Port's main street than the Bean Jar, so there's a much clearer view of Castle Cornet.

Mrs Doubtfire, apparently, used to love the place. She'd go there with her best friend (the Jean to her Joan) and they'd sit at the best table, drinking extra-weak lattes and sharing a piece of cake between them.

Then came the 'Great Schism'. Otherwise known as 'Jean meeting a spry old fart at the local Age Concern and starting to step out with him'. Mrs Doubtfire got jealous, and refused to socialise with the toothless lothario (something to do with him not paying her the proper respect; in other words, buying her a ticket to the Liberation Day tea dance when he bought one for Jean). Ever since then, Mrs D had been on a boycott of both Creasey's Coffee Shop and Jean, and had sought other sources of exceedingly weak coffee.

We, at the Bean Jar, were the lucky recipients of her custom.

Oh, she wasn't a malicious old bat. She didn't actively try to make our lives hell every time she came in. It just kind of... happened anyway.

Zach kept reminding me and Gem that she was just a lonely old woman who wanted some company. "Be patient, be polite," was his motto. But good lord, it was hard to keep your patience with her around.

Nothing was ever good enough for her. Pick, pick, pick. The food, the drinks, the other customers. She even hated the mural behind the coffee machine. Apparently we weren't being 'patriotic' enough with our homage to Sarnia Chérie, and we should have been honouring Guernsey's connections to the UK instead with the lyrics to God Save the Queen and a lovely picture of Her Majesty. Bleurgh.

The moaning, apparently, was the joy of her life – when Gem finally broke and suggested if she hated it all so much, she just go elsewhere, Mrs D looked utterly confused.

"But this is my favourite teashop!"

We weren't a teashop. There was no telling Mrs D, though. She'd been my Annoying Customer of the Week for about twelve weeks on the trot, before I realised she'd won the lifetime award and nobody else would ever have a chance if she was in the running.

As Zach said, she was harmless, she was lonely. You just learned, after a while, to nod and smile, and just agree with everything she said. Then she wouldn't pull Zach aside and have a 'quiet word' about your 'bad attitude'.

There would be a queue of suits almost out the door, Gemma puking in the back, and Zach gesturing furiously at me while his glasses steamed up over the espresso machine, and Mrs Doubtfire determinedly telling me why I shouldn't even think about getting any more tattoos because they'd give me diseases and I'd never get a husband. For the third time since she'd arrived, half an hour previously.

We'd see her coming, and it was an automatic groan. Nothing would get done for at least an hour, and we'd be bored stupid.

Out of all of us, Zach was the best at putting on the Doubtfire Friendly Face.

"Lovely to see you, Joan! A latte?"

"Of course, my love. Half a shot, please. And extra hot." I could hear her crackly perm tossing in derision. "I can't be having those cold coffees!"

"You sit down, Joan. I'll bring it over." Zach stepped over me to get to the coffee machine, flashing another grin at me sitting on the floor at his feet. "Bit short-staffed today, I'm afraid."

"Oh, my love, have those girls deserted you?"

"Yep." Zach smirked down at me. I gave him the finger and stuck my tongue out.

"Well, I've always said it, haven't I? Feckless. *Feckless*. Running around all over the place, getting intoxicated… you know that Cleo girl was talking the other day about something called a Jägerbomb, and how… well, Zachary, I wouldn't want to worry you, but I think she was talking about…" Mrs D's voice dropped to a piercing whisper. "The way she was talking about them, I'm not sure they're legal." There was a screech as she pulled her chair across the floor, which luckily covered up my hysterical snort. "I don't think anyone who drinks things like that should be trusted running a teashop, Zachary."

"I'm sure she doesn't drink Jägerbombs while she's at work, Joan." Zach was trying very hard to keep in his laughter. "What she gets up to at the weekends really isn't any of my business. And I'm the one who runs the place – OW."

"Are you all right, Zachary?"

"Quite all right, Joan." Zach finished steaming the milk for Mrs D's latte, manfully not leaping into the air at the stab to the leg he'd just received, courtesy of me and a fork somewhere around his ankle. "Just a… cramp."

"I know *you* run the place, of course," Mrs D was still chuntering merrily on. "Though you did call that Cleo 'assistant manager', didn't you? I'm not sure that was sensible…"

"No, neither am I, to be honest." Zach aimed a kick at me while he put Mrs D's latte on a tray. I dodged easily, and prodded his other ankle. "Oh whoops, hang on, Joan, just dropped the sugar!"

He dropped to his knees and snatched the fork out of my hands.

"I'm going to stick this somewhere in a minute and it won't be your ankle," he whispered, his hair flopping into his face as he feinted the fork towards me like an épée.

"Bite me," I whispered back, giggling.

"You realise you've got to stay here till she leaves, right?"

"Oh… shit."

* * *

"But I want a winter wedding, I've always said so!"

"Yes, but March? You seriously think you can organise all that bollocks you want in eight weeks?"

"I don't want to have to wait until next year! And December's too close to Christmas, I don't want my wedding overshadowed by Christmas trees. And I don't want to have my anniversary presents mixed up with my Christmas presents for the rest of my life."

If it was anyone else, you'd think they were joking. But no, it was Flic.

The three of us shared a brief stunned silence, then returned to the assault.

"I am not being pregnant for your wedding," Gemma growled, taking tentative sips of her decaf macchiato. I leaned over the bar with Lizzy's latte and a slice of Guernsey Gâche.

"Yeah, what if she's still puking? Jesus in the biscuit barrel, that won't be good."

"Exactly! And I bet pregnant-person bridesmaids' dresses cost more than normal ones."

"They're called 'maternity' dresses, Gem," Lizzy reminded her.

"Aah, shh. I hear the word 'maternity', I think 'smock'. I'm not wearing a smock."

"Or dungarees, you could wear those," I put in helpfully. "They're even getting quite fashionable!"

Flic gave an angry snort. Oops, we were neglecting her hasty wedding planning.

I'd had to stay marooned underneath the coffee bar for a full hour while Mrs Doubtfire strung out her latte and riffed on my failings as a human being to Zach. Bless him, he did try to defend me, though that might have been through fear I'd find a knife next.

I could only get some respite when Mrs D trundled off to the toilet, and I could pretend I'd just arrived: at which point she switched to dissecting Gemma's flawed morals instead. Zach swanned off soon after she did, leaving the Jar to me to clean up and wait for the others to pitch up at closing time. It was after half past six, and so despite the occasional person wandering sadly past and gazing in the window with a longing expression, we weren't letting anyone else in.

Technically I was supposed to be cleaning up while we had our summit. Mrs Machon's morning session at the baking bench needed forensic preparation, after all. But we had more pressing problems.

"Anyway, never mind the wedding, we'll get to that later," I called across the café to where Flic had installed herself regally in the centre of a sofa. She visibly blanched at the phrase 'never mind the wedding', and I carried on quickly before she could publicly disown me. "You still haven't told us the juicy bit. Didn't you ask him right after you left us on New Year's Day?"

"Well, I was going to," she said, derailed from her March madness. "That was the plan. But when I got back to the flat, he was so flustered. He was trying to finish a big project, it's a really important one. He was sitting at the computer for hours. He didn't even want me to make him any dinner!"

I'd experienced Flic's cooking before; we all had. None of us had volunteered for this 'privilege'. Whatever she 'cooked' was usually assembled after much Pinterest research and couldn't be eaten until it had been photographed and hashtagged with buzzwords, preferably '#cleaneating' and '#fitfood'. Of course, this meant that most of what Flic served up was inedible rabbit food but hey, it made for a colourful Instagram feed.

I stared determinedly at the mural of Sarnia Chérie painted behind the coffee machine. The cloudscape wasn't only pretty, it was also nicely soothing: it certainly helped me restrain myself from telling Flic precisely what I thought of her 'cooking'. I wanted to hear the end of the story, after all.

"I realised I'd have to wait until after his meeting on Monday morning, when the project was due." At least Flic had stopped trying to interest us in whatever boring accountancy things she and Jonny got up to. Only Lizzy had ever tried to look politely interested, and even she couldn't manage it for long. "He came home at eleven – his boss was so impressed, he gave him the rest of the day off after his presentation. I'd got John at work to give me the morning off too, I told him I had something *particularly* important to do." She paused to preen a little, patting down her highlighted, carefully straightened hair. Those of us with jobs where you couldn't just waltz off mid-shift – in other words, the teacher and the two baristas in the room – bristled just a little bit. I stared even harder at Sarnia Chérie.

Gemma rolled her eyes. "Continue."

"I was waiting for him when he got back. I had spread a blanket on the living room floor, pulled the blinds and lit some scented candles."

Gemma gave a tiny pukey burp.

"I made a little picnic, just a few homemade sandwiches and pieces of fruit," she said proudly. Yeah, because it's the world's most difficult thing to make sandwiches and chop up fruit. She'd probably got the lot from the big Waitrose near her flat anyway. Right down to ready-sliced strawberries.

"Then when he sat down to eat, I made an excuse and slipped into the bathroom. I had the ring, you see." She gave another smug grin. "I bought it that morning. I had it in its little box, and I put it under one of the sandwiches. And I made sure that by the time I came back from the bathroom… Jonathan had found it."

"You bought your own engagement ring?" Gemma's face was already an incredulous picture.

"What was his reaction to that?" I had to ask. I mean, come on. Surely you'd be a little confused. And Jonny's not the sharpest pencil in the box as it is.

"He asked me what it was, and I said, 'a ring of course!'" Flic gave her best tinkling laugh, something she'd clearly been practicing for years. "I explained to him that now is the perfect time to get engaged, that it's the Leap Year and so I was asking him to marry me. And that I love him, of course. And that if he felt the same, to give me the ring!"

"And so he did?"

"Obviously!"

"Well, er, congratulations, of course!" I tore my eyes away from the lovely calming mural and threw one of her favourite low-fat blueberry muffins across the bar. Lizzy leaned over and gave her a hug. Even Gemma smiled, though I could tell she was still trying her hardest not to vom dramatically over the bar at the tweeness of it all. I could just picture it: Jonny obediently shoving the ring across the picnic blanket. As requested, all present and correct.

"It was so romantic." Flic allowed herself a single dreamy sigh. Then she looked down at the muffin I'd chucked her and gave a gasp, literally shuddering. "I can't have *this*, Cleo!" She pelted it back at me with such force I ducked. "No, no, no. It's action stations now, I've really got to up the healthy eating game. I can't have dairy, I'm steering clear of gluten…"

As one, the rest of us just blinked in silence as Flic reeled off a list of foodstuffs that were now toast (ha) under her self-imposed ban. Then, of course, it was back to business. "So yes, a March wedding. It's what I'd love…"

This time, though, Lizzy had engaged her brain and managed to cut Flic off before she could really get going.

"I was thinking, you want a winter wedding – but why? Yes, having white fur capes and things would be lovely… but you work so hard at keeping yourself in shape." Flic nodded pensively. "Why go to all that bother if you're going to cover up completely on the most important day of your life? You should have a summer wedding, really, then you'd get to show a bit of skin." Lizzy paused, clutching her slice of Gâche like a defensive weapon. "In a tasteful, sophisticated way, of course."

"You might be right," Flic mused. "And we're not even guaranteed cold weather in March…"

"It might just be super windy and grey, and you'd end up with your fur cape blowing off towards France and all your photos looking like a funeral," I put in wildly.

"And if Dad does do the boat thing," Gem paused to grimace, quite possibly being a tiny bit sick in her mouth, "you'd have one hell of a shit time in March. Dad's boat in a squall, with a wedding dress on? Good fucking luck."

The next thing we knew, the wedding – if we were to keep to the pact, the first of four – was to be at the end of August. Eight months to plan a wedding… well, it was better than eight weeks.

* * *

I fell through the door a couple of hours later and was instantly hit by the smell of burnt toast. Excellent, Charlie was home. I had a lovely evening ahead of listening to incomprehensible 'indie' music wailing angstily up through my floor.

What had the world come to? It was a Friday night, I was twenty-four years old – in the prime of my life! – and instead of spending it in the local nightclubs dancing like a loon while off my face on Vopple Juice, I had to sit at home with my family.

I missed Gemma. Pre-pregnancy she was such a good pulling partner, always up for a night of debauchery. But if the smell of coffee made her queasy, the smell of alcohol made her almost pass out. She'd just about managed to get through the New Year's Eve party we'd been to, but only because it had been largely in a freezing cold garden, so she could get as much icy fresh air as she needed. To her sadness and mine, a crowded club would be a bit more difficult to negotiate.

Quite often I could bully Lizzy out – and now she was single again, I knew she'd be far more up for regular nights staggering round town (usually me doing the staggering, and her keeping me upright). While she was with Dan, she'd practically become a hermit. Those days had to be over.

But I hadn't counted on the endless piles of marking faced by a primary school teacher. Seriously, how much schoolwork do eight-year-olds do? It's ridiculous. But, as she said, if she got it all done on the Friday night and Saturday morning, we'd be able to go out and get trashed on Saturday night and she wouldn't even have to worry about being too hungover to finish it off on Sunday evening.

Of course, I was supposed to worry about being too hungover to work on Sunday morning. But hey, the Sunday shift was only a short one. Admittedly a horrible one, as everyone on Guernsey seemed to save up all their twattishness during the week and let it all out on a Sunday when they stormed into the Jar after a posh lunch at Moore's or the OGH. And it was Mrs Doubtfire's favourite day to visit: she'd usually be in for the entire shift. But still, we were only open for four hours, and even during the worst hangovers I could manage the coffee machine for that long.

"Mum, Nan? Are you in?" I called up the stairs.

"In the lounge, Cleo!"

I hauled myself up the stairs.

I loved my childhood home, even though sometimes it could get to feel a bit like a prison. It was one of those tall, thin terraces, leftover from when a huge Victorian mansion got sliced into three separate houses, with what could sometimes feel like ninety-six flights of stairs. In reality, there are only four floors – the ground floor, with the kitchen and the dining room, then the floor above with the big open-plan living room (which usefully prevented me from sneaking boys upstairs when I was a teenager; Mum had a knack of sitting in there at just the right time to catch me). Then came the floor with Mum and Charlie's rooms, then the attic conversion, where Nan and I lived.

Of course, you'd think it was somewhat cruel to have a seventy-nine-year-old woman – *post* hip replacement – marooned at the top of a building with her wayward (ish) granddaughter. Making a lady of that age climb all those stairs is surely elder-abuse of some description, so you might concur.

Like hell. Not with Nan! At seventy-nine, she was fitter than me – especially since she'd discovered the Senior Aerobics classes at Beau Sejour leisure centre.

"Osteoporosis is for old people," she was fond of saying. "I'm the Bionic Woman with this new hip," was another favourite. After the hip surgery, Mum had offered to convert the dining room into a bedroom for her – the kitchen would be big enough for us to eat in, just about. But Nan just looked at her like she was speaking in tongues and told her to sod off.

I bloody hope I'm like my Nan when I'm old. Not only energetic and sprightly, but nuts. Somewhat reminiscent of that famous poem. "When I'm an old woman, I shall wear purple." Though if it had been written about Nan, it would have started "When I'm an old woman, I shall wear leopard-print and sequinned yellow shoes."

I clumped up the stairs in my giant New Rock platform boots (all the better for riding my scooter, not to mention giving me an extra couple of inches so people could see me over the coffee bar) and collapsed onto the sofa beside Nan. Tonight, she was wearing a fetching ensemble consisting of a leopard-print cardigan and a long flowery skirt, accompanied by sequinned fluffy slippers. For once, she wasn't wearing a hat: a rarity.

"Hello, my love." She leaned over and gave me a kiss. "Good day at work?"

"It was all right. Flic's well and truly engaged, we got the full, sick-making story."

"Well, we knew that was going to happen, didn't we?" She turned back to the TV.

Mum gave me a wave from the other side of the room, where she was ninety percent occupied with the Daily Mail. She looked far more like an old lady than her mother: dressed head to toe in Per Una with a conservatively dull hairstyle. If we didn't have the exact same (small and somewhat upturned) nose and (rounded, chubby-cheeked) jawline, I'd say I was actually Nan's child and not hers. Personality really does seem to skip a generation – maybe I shouldn't have children at all, if they're going to turn into my mother.

"Get this – Flic wants us all to go to London on a department store crawl to find bridesmaids' dresses."

"She's asked you all, then, already?"

"Yeah. And some dull Denise from Jonny's work, I think they were all at school together. Flic's just disappointed none of us have any cute kids to be flower girls. I think she's contemplating hiring some from a catalogue. Where's Charlie?"

"Upstairs," Mum waved her hand vaguely towards the ceiling. "With Adam and Tristan."

"Ugh." I groaned, settling further into the sofa. My brother's friends were his Hollister-clad clones – no other way to describe them. Rugby obsessed and much as I hated to admit it, leaning towards the 'braying'. I'd had such high hopes for my brother when he'd been small: I thought I could turn him into my tiny, naughty sidekick, even with a ten-year age gap between us and the fact that Mum spoiled him something rotten.

But then he'd hit eleven and headed off to his posh boys' school, and fell in with the wrong crowd. Rich, rugby-loving rahs, as stuck up as they come, in an interchangeable mass of designer shirts and floppy hair. Adam and Tristan were the two head clones in Charlie's crew, and sometimes I couldn't actually distinguish between the three of them, particularly when they were all wearing their matching rugby shirts.

Somehow, despite going to the girls' version of Charlie's school (in other words, one of Guernsey's three independent schools rather than one of the normal secondary schools) I seemed to have escaped the 'rah' influence. I'd gone out of my way to avoid it, in fact. No Jack Wills tracksuits for me, not a scrap of Abercrombie and Fitch in sight. The closest thing to a designer label you'd find on me was a New Rock boot or two. And maybe my ancient Criminal Damage jeans, if you could count them. They had a label on them that wasn't 'New Look', anyway.

I wouldn't say I was a Goth. Not any more, anyway. I probably fit the bill a lot better when I was younger, definitely when I was a student. No, nowadays I was probably just more of a metalhead.

I tried to immerse myself in whatever it was my relatives were watching on the television, but it was too dull for words. Nan clearly had the right idea with the hip flask I could see just peeping from the folds of voluminous skirt: I couldn't see myself managing the programme without alcohol. So I retreated to my bedroom and played Karin Cluster's latest album until Charlie banged on his ceiling with a hockey stick and pleaded for mercy.

* * *

I would like to point out now, that even though it looked like my life was stagnating away, it wasn't. Not really. Yes, I was on a tiny island, yes I still lived in the family home, yes I was only a barista ('assistant manager' actually, to Mrs D's eternal horror). But I loved my life. I had all these grandiose plans, of course I did. I wanted to live abroad, I wanted to travel, I wanted to have sex with a different man in every country, so on and so forth, etcetera. For the moment though, I was content enough.

The wonderful thing about having no rent to pay was of course that I could save up my wages (those that I didn't blow on nights out, anyway). And whenever life looked to be getting a bit too dull... I could use my stashed funds to escape. Just for a little bit, just for a break. It was starting to look like one of those times.

I don't know whether it was Flic's engagement, or Gemma's crazy Leap Year Pact, or just one Mrs Machon rant too many, but I needed a break.

Behind the bar, working the coffee machine, my smile was starting to get just that little bit too forced.

Plus, I'd got through quite a large percentage of the decent men on the island. I had a couple of irons in the fire, yes, like that blonde suit who was starting to become a regular fixture in the Jar. But the fact remained I was probably on my second go-round of Guernsey men and I needed a bit of variety.

If I was going to get this Leap Year Pact fulfilled, I was going to have to widen my net a little bit.

Speaking of the net, I was in bed idly browsing it.

Karin Cluster had a tour coming up.

And, of course, the buggers weren't coming anywhere near me. I didn't know what problem they had with the UK, but it had been ages since they'd come anywhere near. I knew, of course, they'd never come to Guernsey, it can be a bit of a musical wasteland. There are hardly any venues, for a start; certainly no buzzing heavy metal community.

And I love a buzzing heavy metal community.

When I moved to Manchester, a brand-new student, it was a revelation. Other people like me! People who liked the kind of music I did! Other people who liked to dye their hair odd colours, other people who liked to clomp around in giant boots, other people who liked music filled with feeling, meaning, and psychosis! It was beautiful.

That was when I got into Karin Cluster: a German metal band that not many people had heard of, back then. I heard their dreamy, symphonic keyboard layering over a pounding bass while I was in a grotty metal bar one night, and I fell in love.

Granted, that happened fairly often with a few beers in me.

But this time it was for real.

Of all people, It didn't take long for me to convince Lizzy that she liked them too. Even though I'd tried very hard, back at school when I was first getting into the likes of Nightwish and Within Temptation, I hadn't been able to drag Lizzy's taste along with mine. But something in Karin Cluster's balance of symphonic film-score type music with heavy metal drums and growls managed to get right into Lizzy's psyche, and she developed a passion that nearly rivalled mine.

I loved them. Quite obsessively, to be honest. There wasn't a playlist on my Spotify that didn't have them on there somewhere. As I rode my little scooter around the island, Karin Cluster was always my first choice to bellow obnoxiously into my helmet, shocking pedestrians as I whizzed by making one hell of a tuneless racket.

And yet I'd still never seen them live.

Annoyingly, they still weren't huge in the UK. They had become pretty popular among the European metal community: long-haired headbanging Scandinavians loved them. As did high-pitched Spaniards and pushy French people (I'd been to see a couple of other bands in Paris; four broken toes later, and I *knew* the French were pushy). Their touring schedules always seemed to coordinate perfectly with a time when either I was a student in the midst of important exams, or when I was absolutely stony broke. Or on one memorable occasion, when I was waiting for my new passport to be delivered and couldn't make it out of the country on time. It was a bugger.

Then all of a sudden, they stopped coming to the UK at all. Rumours abounded online about their guitarist and an English girl, or something to do with the lead singer and an explosive rivalry situation. Nothing was ever confirmed, but the British gigs just dried up entirely, even as their record sales started to grow. It looked like I'd lost all my chances to see them.

But now… I had a little bit of money put away, all ready to be blown. I could totally hop across to Europe for a little touring action. If I bullied him enough, Zach would let me have the time off work. Karin Cluster were going all over Europe – I could have my pick of European men to perve on! I'd always fancied Finland, or maybe Denmark. Somewhere a bit chilly, maybe even with a chance at seeing the Northern Lights.

And who knew? Word on the street (well, on the internet) was that the Karin Cluster guitarist was single again, or at least in the process of some messy break-up. And they were bound to have a support band. The Leap Year Pact could get fulfilled in a truly spectacular manner.

With thoughts of celebrity Las-Vegas-style weddings and full-page spreads in not-entirely-existent glossy metal gossip magazines crossing my mind, I happily fell asleep.

Chapter 4

The next morning, I decided to wait a little while before proposing my gig ideas to anyone else. After all, I needed a buddy to come with me. I wasn't going to parade around Europe without company – 'company', of course, meaning 'someone to prop me up when I was about to fall over in European gutters'. I'd ask Lizzy, of course, but she was still rather less than stable, after the great Dan-departure. She needed some time. Plus, right now Gemma was a bit too busy growing a human in her uterus to be up for any madcap dashes across the water.

Besides, two weeks later, my mind was quite sufficiently distracted from my plans of escape.

Saturdays were always crazy in the Bean Jar, just like every other coffee shop in the world. Usually, one person had to be absolutely glued to the coffee machine.

Zach had really been quite smart when he painted the cloudy mural of Sarnia Chérie behind it: rolling your eyes towards it as if it represented the actual heavens was particularly cathartic when the place was filled with rampaging families and irritating teenagers making eyes at one another over their Guernsey Gâche.

I'm sure that mural had actually saved Zach a lot of money, as without it he'd probably have had to bail Gem and I out of prison several times a month.

This particular weekend, it was even busier than usual. Because, drumroll please... it was the end of the January sales.

Of course, in Guernsey, this isn't quite the big event you'd see elsewhere in the world. I'd lived in Manchester; I'd briefly worked in the Trafford Centre during sales season. It had been like a zombie apocalypse, only more bloodthirsty. But it was still a big enough event in Guernsey to warrant some... concern.

Oh, not just that every person in Guernsey seemed to be milling around town, in a desperate search for bargains. No, I'm talking about their way of advertising these 'bargains'.

I don't know why shops can't just give out flyers. Or maybe put up some banners. A nice poster in the window, that would work.

No, they have to go for balloons. Handing them out to little kids, putting them up in daft arches over the doors. I can pretty much guarantee you won't have even noticed them. If you're 'most people'.

Most people don't have a problem with balloons. But I've grown up with Lizzy. When we met, aged eleven, I'd never heard of anyone who was scared of balloons before. And when the first girl in our class to turn twelve had a birthday party, I laughed just as much as all the other kids when the chubby little blonde kid with glasses and braces started to cry – we'd been batting balloons around the church hall's improvised dance floor, and someone had just popped one.

We all thought she was a freak of the highest order, especially when her mum had to come and pick her up because she was full-on hyperventilating with tears streaming down her face.

As the only kid from my junior school having moved up to the posh girls' secondary school, I was eager to fit in, and I laughed along with all the rest of them.

I realised soon enough that the prissy, stuck-up girls in my class with shiny faces and designer clothes were never going to be my friends: my determined 'new start' at secondary school didn't last all that long and soon enough I let my true colours come flying forth. I got my reputation as a pain-in-the-arse off to a good start before the first year was out, and one of the first steps was making friends with nervous, impressionable Lizzy. Within a year, I had 'rule-breaker' practically tattooed on my forehead, and poor Lizzy was always swept along somewhere not far behind me.

It took some getting used to, the whole balloon-phobia thing. Because, as I learned, it actually *is* a true phobia. There was no attention-seeking to it, no over-exaggeration. If a balloon popped near her, she would burst into loud, sobbing tears. She tried to battle through it and still turn up to parties (those she was invited to, anyway), but she'd always end up getting sent home in a damp, weepy mess. And of course, becoming her best friend within a matter of weeks, I loyally stuck with her. If she was going to have to avoid the parties, well then, so was I.

Far from getting better as she got older, it got worse.

Instead of bursting into tears – well, sometimes as well as bursting into tears – Lizzy would faint. Exposure to a small child playing with a balloon for any length of time left her dizzy, and the pop... well, she was on the floor.

"It's my defence mechanism," she'd told me, the first time that particular reaction had happened around me and I had heroically panicked for Guernsey. "My body hears what it thinks is danger and just shuts down. I can't control it, and, to be honest, I'd rather be unconscious anyway than see everyone staring at me."

In recent months, it had become apparent that something had to be done. Lizzy's a teacher; in the primary wing connected to our old secondary school, no less. She had a whole class of Year Four girls under her wing, all of whom were delighted to participate in the balloon race at the school sports day.

Let's just say, it hadn't been the best day for Lizzy. Though at least the elderly man she'd fainted on hadn't sued when she knocked him to the ground, and his hip had only been bruised, not broken. Poor bloke had only gone along to watch his granddaughter in the egg-and-spoon.

After that particular incident, Lizzy was finally on the waiting list for some kind of talking therapy. Having supported her since we were eleven, I personally didn't have much faith in it. I really didn't see how just discussing the problem was going to help at all. She'd talked about it enough to me, anyway. But she was willing to try anything by this point. She didn't want her pupils to lose respect for her; and one day, she wanted kids herself. She didn't exactly want to have to ban her own children from going to birthday parties, or pass on the fear herself.

I suppose the point I'm trying to make is that usually, on sale days and holidays, Lizzy stayed as far away from town as she could; if she really had to come in for any reason, it was with earphones rammed firmly into her ear canals, Karin Cluster blaring so she could shut herself off from the crowds.

But this particular Saturday, the last day of the January sales, Gemma and I had an issue.

Zach had called in sick.

Well, 'called in sick' is taking it a bit far: Zach never 'called in sick'.

He'd come into work with tonsillitis more than once, and had been known to lie flat behind the bar with a migraine rather than leave us unsupervised on such a busy weekend – but Mrs Machon had got wind of the bout of flu from which her grandson seemed to be suffering on this particular occasion. She'd more or less tied him to his bed, and was playing Cerberus in front of his bedroom door, thrusting a specially-prepared traditional Guernsey Bean Jar into his protesting face at regular intervals.

On such a busy weekend, I knew that Gemma and I couldn't cope alone. She was mostly getting over her pukiness, now she was approaching her twentieth week of pregnancy, but there was still the possibility of it setting off if she got too close to a particularly smelly customer. She'd still been having the occasional moment each day where she had to go in the back and dramatically clutch her Tupperware container, just in case.

Plus, the Bean Jar was spread across all those stairs. The ground floor, like I've said, was tiny – you could sit on the coffee bar and maintain a conversation with the person sitting in the window seat at the same time, possibly while cleaning the coffee machine, if you were so inclined. The next floor up contained Zach's tiny office and me and Gemma's equally staffroom, and the third floor had a couple of toilets and a storeroom piled high with mops and cleaning products. Then the top was the real beauty: the whole floor was a bright, open seating area, with a wall-to-wall window looking out over the harbour.

It had cost Zach a fortune to get that all converted from the dingy attic it used to be, but it was worth every penny. Customers loved it. We'd never made any effort to publicise it, so its existence became known just through word of mouth; it seemed like quite an adventure, following the little 'more seating upstairs' sign all the way to the top of the building.

Of course, Gemma and I didn't feel quite the same about all those stairs to tackle. Especially now Gem was pregnant. Hoiking her belly up all those stairs wasn't entirely going down well, especially loaded with trays of cups and bags of rubbish.

We really needed three people around, on a Saturday at least. One to serve, one to work the coffee machine, and one to run around like a maniac clearing all the mess customers tend to leave behind.

With just two of us expected to work on one of our busiest Saturdays of the year... we were in trouble.

And what do I do when I'm in trouble? What have I always done when I'm in trouble?

Call in Lizzy, of course.

I'd drafted her in that morning, and she was resolutely clearing the tables when the disaster happened.

A child with a balloon.

Just a toddler, happily clutching his free orange balloon between his be-mittened hands while his parents queued up to order coffee.

I saw it first. I hoped like hell that it would be leaving soon; that the parents were ordering coffee to go and would be out of our hair before Lizzy could see it. It had to be the moment she was in the same room, as well; clearing up the almighty mess another family had left around the big brown sofa in the window, wet-wipes and snotty tissues aplenty.

But, of course, mid-afternoon was not the typical time for people to be getting their drinks and buggering off. The two parents ordered themselves lattes (unimaginative) and a couple of pieces of cake, and started to scan around for seats, the little boy following them all the while, balloon clutched to his chest.

"Oh, can you bring us our lattes over for us?" the mum said to Gemma. "I can't manage them with all this." Both she and her husband had straining armfuls of shopping bags.

"I'll grab it," I called over to Gemma, trying to side-eye the balloon without Lizzy noticing. Gemma, of course, didn't have a clue what I was eye-gesturing about.

"Nah, I'm fine, I'll do it." She gave a bit of an eyebrow-raise in the direction of the oblivious parents, expertly rolling the jug of milk to get the proper silky latte consistency.

Meanwhile, Lizzy had finished cleaning the sofa – and the balloon-accompanied family were heading for it, leaving her trapped between the sofa and the coffee table.

"Buggeration," I hissed to myself, as Lizzy froze.

Nothing more to it than that, to the unpractised eye: she just froze, almost as if she was about to do a really dramatic sneeze and had to mentally prepare herself.

However, I knew better. I knew that under her wide-eyed statue impression, she was starting to panic. If you looked closely, you'd be able to see her hands starting to sweat and shake, her breath starting to come in gasps, desperate to search for an escape route but unable to take her eyes away from the perceived threat.

All because of a balloon. It was absolutely ridiculous; but what phobia isn't?

Ignoring the bloke who'd just stepped up to be served, I dodged out from behind the bar, in front of Gemma, ready to haul Lizzy free from behind the coffee table and out of the door if I had to.

But right at that moment, the toddler, still clutching his precious orange balloon, slipped.

He'd just caught the edge of a wet-floor sign, left there by the conscientious Lizzy after the last chaotic child had spilled a drink.

The toddler's oblivious parents hadn't even seen the sign, and he'd had no warning to slow down or stop.

With a tiny little shriek, he tripped.

And landed flat on his balloon.

It made a surprisingly loud bang. There was a brief moment of silence, then chaos broke out.

With a tiny gasp that I could see more than hear, Lizzy dropped. Her knees just gave way, and she landed almost gracefully onto the sofa. She was getting pretty practised at this whole fainting malarkey by now.

Gemma, however, wasn't quite so graceful. She hadn't seen the balloon before that moment. I didn't know whether it was something to do with the pregnancy hormones, or whether she'd always been susceptible to such sudden shocks, but something in her gave way too.

With the clatter of a tray, and the crash of two large lattes tumbling to the ground, Gem gave a groan and fainted too.

The café erupted into noise, and the tiny space seemed to get even smaller. The elderly couple sitting near the bar were both on their feet, squawking in horror. There were thundering footsteps from upstairs as a group of teenagers came clattering down to see what all the noise was about. The oblivious parents with all the shopping were trying to work out why there suddenly seemed to be a woman slumped across the sofa where they wanted to sit, and what had happened to their lattes. All the while, the poor small boy was screaming.

I had to judge the situation quickly.

"RIGHT, you lot! EVERYBODY OUT!" I hollered, bending down to Gem. I judged her unconsciousness was the more urgent case, in this situation. At least Lizzy was used to it. "Come on, bugger off! Don't look at me like that, can't you see I've got a medical emergency here? OUT!"

The two elderly people beat a hasty retreat, as did the parents with all their shopping, scooping up their wailing child as they went.

"But our coffees," the dad started to protest as they got to the door.

"Come back later." I practically pushed him outside and span around. "You lot too!" I yelled towards the stairs, trying to budge Gemma away from the shards of coffee cup at her feet. "Come on, get out!"

"I'll shift them," said the bloke who I'd just been about to serve.

"Yeah, thanks," I said, not looking at him.

At least when she'd fainted, Gemma hadn't managed to scald herself with the coffee, most of it splashing onto her apron (and the floor). And by the looks of it, she was already starting to come round, with her eyes flickering, and mumbling under her breath something that sounded suspiciously like "fuck".

"Gem?" I said – well, more whimpered – as the troupe of teenagers was hustled loudly out of the shop. "Are you awake? Are you OK? Do you need a doctor?"

"Do you need me to call for an ambulance?"

Having loudly slammed the door, the customer-bloke was back, squatting down next to me at the side of the coffee bar. I sighed, and glanced up at him.

Oh. It was the somewhat-hot-suit, the one who'd come in for coffee for the first time just after New Year. He'd been in a few times since then, and I'd been starting up a campaign of flirting, mostly via the method of giving him the occasional discount on his coffee (I hadn't decided whether he deserved free ones yet). The rest of the time I'd always been scurrying round mid-rush so couldn't exactly stop and have a proper flirt, much as I was warming to the idea. It was the first time I'd seen him in anything but a suit, and the pink and blue rugby shirt he was wearing somewhat clashed with the fetching coffee-spatters from getting caught in the crossfire of Gem's faint.

"Er, I don't know…" I bit my lip, trying to work out what to do.

"I don't need a fucking ambulance," Gemma growled, groggily.

"Gem? Is – are you all right?"

"I'm fine, I'm just a bit dizzy… let me move."

She was already trying to get to her feet.

"Oh no you bloody well don't." I gave her a gentle shove back down again, trying to remember my primary school first aid training. "You need to lie still, you need to lie on your left so the blood gets back into your heart or something."

"Bring her over here," came Lizzy's voice, suddenly. Oops, I'd kind of forgotten about her, in the shock of the 'sturdy' one crashing inelegantly to the floor. I had neglected to remember that Lizzy herself was probably in need of some TLC. She was already sitting up, though, and was shakily smoothing out the sofa cushions.

"You sit tight, I'll be sorting you out in a minute," I said as sternly as I could manage.

"No, she'll be best lying down on the sofa. I'll... I'll just come over here," Lizzy said, tentatively getting to her feet and flopping onto a spindly wooden chair, then nearly toppling off it.

"Be careful!" I squeaked. "Stay still! And you, oi, you can keep still too!"

"Here, I'll grab her," said Somewhat-Hot-Suit, scooping Gemma up in one swift movement before she could get to her feet herself.

"Hey, put me down you fuck..."

Thankfully, the Bean Jar is so small that it only took seconds for Somewhat-Hot-Suit to gently plop Gemma onto the recently vacated sofa.

The pair of us stood over her, nervously, while she properly came round. Lizzy had her head on the table next to us, trying to recover from her panic attack. I stroked her hair, knowing that it was best to let her use her well-practised breathing techniques to get back to normal. Gemma, however... I was still worried. Her eyes were slightly unfocussed, and she swore several times more, then seemed to notice Somewhat-Hot-Suit bending over her and looking concerned. "Who the fuck are you?"

"Hi." He smiled warmly at her. I felt a brief pang of jealousy. Gemma could find her own gullible idiot to induct into the Leap Year Pact. This one was *my* gullible idiot. "I'm James."

"Who the fuck are you, James?" Gem spat, clearly heartily annoyed to be making introductions three seconds after being prostrate on the slate floor of the Bean Jar. Usually that only happened on the sticky floor of Folies (Guernsey's premier awful nightspot), after quite a significant number of alcoholic beverages.

"I'm Cleo's customer," James said. I preened a little bit. *Cleo's* customer. I had a customer all of my own, and a rather pretty one at that.

"Well then, *Cleo's* customer." Gemma shot me a woozy look. "Now you've dumped me on the sofa, are you going to help me get back up, or are you going to stand there all day?"

"Oi, you're not getting up," I jumped in. "What if you landed on the baby? We really need to get you to a doctor."

"I don't think so." She gingerly felt her bump. "Feels the same as ever."

"Are you sure? Why did you faint in the first place? Surely that's got to be a sign of something bad."

"Shut up, customer. Yeah, feels fine. Look, I've been getting dizzy on and off since this thing took up residence."

"You've not fainted before though, have you?" I said. "I'd have noticed!"

"Nah, but I keep telling you, I'm fine. We're fine. Doctor reckons I'm anaemic, I've probably got some lovely iron pills coming my way. I've got my scan on Wednesday, though. I'll get them to check it out, make sure the thing's still kicking in the right direction."

"Gem, you can't keep calling it *the thing*."

"Can if I want." She shrugged. "What am I supposed to call it, the bubba? The ickle bubz? Urgh." She made her puking face. "The *thing* will do until I know what it is."

"Are you going to find out on Wednesday?"

"I might. I might just wait and be surprised. It'll be a girl though. I've decided."

"Like you could possibly *decide*," I scoffed, accepting one of the two glasses of water James had just poured out, tapping Lizzy gently on the arm to get her to drink it.

"I'm a girl, so she's a girl, I can't picture anything else. I'm getting very feminine vibes," Gemma was saying.

"Maybe it's a boy and he's gay," I pointed out.

"What, like this one?" Gem thumbed James.

"Erm, I'm not gay," he said, raising his eyebrows.

"Your hair looks gay."

"Oh, shh, Gem, hair can't look gay," Lizzy piped up weakly. James seemed to notice her for the first time.

"Hey, are *you* OK? Why did you pass out, is this place full of unstable pregnant women?"

"No," I said hastily. "Just Gem. Lizzy's just... she just fainted."

"I'm fine," she said weakly. "Just give me a minute."

I took her hand, feeling her pulse. Yep, going like the clappers. Poor Lizzy. I really hoped this whole therapy thing would come through for her, she didn't need any of this.

"But why…"

"That's none of your business," Gem put in cattily. We both knew how embarrassed Lizzy got about her phobia, and I knew that even in her semi-conscious state, Gemma didn't want to make it worse for her. Still, I didn't think she needed to be quite so bitchy about it.

"Calm down, you, and drink your water," I said. Trying to be stern with Gemma never got anyone anywhere, of course, but it was worth a go.

"So… Gemma, the pregnant one, she'll be fine too? Only, I really should go, but I can stay if you need me."

"Honest, I can look after her. She'll be fine." I gave James my best effort at a comforting smile. I probably looked more like I had wind.

"Yeah, she will be," Gem put in. "I'm right here, you know. Sod off, will you, so I can enjoy this break I've had forced on me?"

"If you're absolutely sure you don't need an ambulance or anything…"

"Just go, James." I kept my smile firmly fixed. I hoped it was at least vaguely 'winning'. A hard thing to achieve, with Gem trying to reach over and blatantly poke me in the ribs and Lizzy starting to hiccup from somewhere below me. "Look, you've been really helpful today. Your coffee's on me for at least… well, until the boss makes me start charging you again."

"Aww, cheers!" With a grin that actually *was* winning, James left the shop with a clatter of the door and his little man-bag satchel.

"Well," Gem puffed, practically blowing a bubble in her cup of water. "He's a cute little Welsh thing, isn't he?"

"What does him being *Welsh* have to do with anything?"

"He probably plays rugby." She shrugged. "And he might be able to sing. I don't know. Whatever, he's cute. I think you should marry him." This was far too matter-of-fact for my liking, especially for someone who'd recently passed out in the middle of the shop.

"Can I at least shag him first?" I started to remove Gemma's coffee-covered apron from around her neck.

"That's probably a good start," she mused, batting me away. "Have you ever seen him in town at the weekend?"

"No, I think I'll have to actually ask him to come out so I can pounce."

"Good girl." Gem nodded. "Take the direct approach."

"No, no, I mean I'll ask him to come out and *then* I'll pounce. I'm not going to just say 'by the way, come to Folies on Friday so I can pounce on you!'"

Lizzy gave a feeble giggle. "Why not? I'm sure it'd work."

"Oh, now *you* can shut up and drink some water."

"I'm just going to the loo, actually." Already with a lot more colour in her face, Lizzy got gingerly to her feet.

As she made her careful way up the stairs, Gemma turned back to me.

"By the way, are you coming with me to the scan on Wednesday?"

"Um… was I invited?"

"Yeah, of course you are!" Gem snorted. "I don't want Flic coming and getting all pious, you know what she'd be like." She put on a very passable impression of Flic's over-exaggerated 'posh' accent, all evidence of the long Guernsey vowels fully erased. "'Oh yes, doctor, she doesn't know who the father is. Do you need to do any extra tests in case the baby is *diseased*?'"

"What about your parents?"

"What use would they be? They've just about accepted that I'm pregnant, but I don't think they could deal with the hard evidence quite yet. Dad's spending more time out on the boat than ever, and he's supposed to be semi-retired. I'm not sure he likes looking at me right now." A flash of sadness passed across her face before she could mask it. I hadn't realised her parents had been even remotely difficult about the pregnancy: the impression I'd had was more that they'd always expected their youngest daughter to do something like this, that it was only a matter of time. Maybe they'd actually been a bit more deluded.

"He'll come round." I risked a pat on the shoulder. Christ, things must have been tense: Gem didn't even bat me away. "So you want me to come with you instead?"

"Yeah, aren't you getting that yet?" Gem tutted and raised her eyebrows. "I want you to be my birthing partner, too, by the way."

I must have looked absolutely repulsed.

"Why the face? It's not like you have to deliver the fucking thing. Just hold my hand and listen to my screams."

"But it'll be… gross."

"Like you give a shit! Believe me, I want you firmly at the head end. But I need someone there, and I think you'll do."

In Gemma-terms, that was practically a declaration of love. I was touched.

Chapter 5

"Oh do shut up, the doctor said I can come, so I'm fucking coming!"

"I'm warning you now, if you puke on my dress, I will punch you squarely on the nose, baby or no baby!"

"Hey, last person to puke on anyone's clothes was *you*, on *me*, remember your birthday?"

"No."

"Exactly."

"Will you two stop bickering for two seconds, please?" Lizzy was somewhat exasperated. "It's hard enough to do your foundation anyway, Cleo."

"I've got a massive face, I've got a massive face!" I howled, burying my face in a cushion. Lizzy winced. It was her cushion. And her foundation, actually. Yes, I used plenty of make-up myself, I owned enough eyeliners to re-draw the Mona Lisa. But I stuck to the kind of stuff you can find on a three-for-two in Boots, and Lizzy's mum had given her a huge package of designer make-up for Christmas. Gemma and I had fallen on it with wild abandon.

"You don't have a massive face," Lizzy chided, hauling me up by the hair and inspecting the damage to her brand-new beige cushion. "You just don't keep still."

"No, it's massive." I inflected as much tragedy into my voice as I could manage. "Huge. Forty-two chins and cheeks like a chubby child."

"You have a round face, deal with it. Not everyone can have *her* cheekbones." Lizzy thumbed Gemma with a fake glare.

"I'd do anything for a fag," Gem muttered, manically painting her own eyebrows into thick, dark arches that made her look even more acerbic than usual. "This is the moment, right now, between eyebrows and eyeliner. I'd have one while I waited for the setting gel to dry…"

"And thank goodness those days are over," Lizzy chirped. "Don't you feel better now, less, less… smelly?"

"I was never smelly!"

"You were a bit."

"You two are mean tonight, you know that. I should have stayed at home and watched One Born Every Minute again."

"You were making yourself nauseous with every episode."

"It's preparation." Gem nodded grimly, pressing her lips together. "I know it's got to happen to me sooner or later, I just have to steel myself."

Gemma's scan that Wednesday had changed her attitude in a radical way. She'd gone from going-with-the-flow and kind of pretending the pregnancy was somebody else's problem, to seeing that little baby-shaped lump on the screen and realising it was actually going to come out of *her*.

It helped that, as Gem had confidently predicted, the scan had revealed that the baby was a girl. Knowing for sure that she was carrying a miniature version of herself, as opposed to a miniature version of whatever she'd shagged, had really bumped up the old enthusiasm levels. She'd found every episode of birthing programme One Born Every Minute online and was watching at least two every day.

Even though I knew I was going to be there for the big event, I couldn't quite bring myself to watch the programme myself. I'd heard the howls of the woman in the intro, that was enough for me. Sure, I'd be there for Gem. I'd be a good friend. But I'd rather let everything else come as a bit of a surprise, thank you very much.

Though apparently we had 'Parent Craft' classes looming. And I'd be required to be there, too.

I was putting that out of my head. Firmly.

After all, tonight was Operation Shirley Bassey.

Not my choice of operational names, I would like to add. I would have gone with Operation Tom Jones, but Shirley Bassey was the first Welsh person Gemma came up with and the name stuck.

I was out to snare a Welshman.

This, of course, involved preparation that would rival a military campaign. We were a threesome for the night: Flic had been invited, and apparently strongly considered coming, but chose a yoga retreat instead – says it all really. We had assembled at Lizzy's to get ready and, in two out of three cases, drink a fair bit of alcohol before hitting the bars. And, of course, in the other case, moan like hell about not having any vices left.

Flic hadn't totally abandoned us, though. When I'd attempted to mine my wardrobe for old clothes I'd worn at uni, like a Tolkien-esque dwarf but seeking synthetic fabrics instead of precious metals, I'd come up with nothing. Absolutely sod all.

I don't know what it was about Somewhat-Hot-Suit – sorry, *James* – but I had a bit of a tingly feeling in my fingers whenever I thought about him. Maybe he was the fabled 'One'... well, the 'One' for the Leap Year Pact, anyway. I wasn't going to start calling anyone the 'One' until I'd had a good few rounds of bedroom trampolining with him.

Yeah, I'm definitely *not* one of those 'no sex before marriage' types, in case you didn't guess that already.

Whatever this feeling was, whether it was the possibility of some kind of future or just the not-so-innocent tingling of lust, it felt a bit special. A bit different.

Usually when I fancied someone, the feeling came about in a club, after a fair bit of Vopple Juice, and most often in the middle of a pounding song while throwing some ridiculously uncoordinated shapes on the dance floor. There was never really the chance for much plotting... it was just a case of see a man, like the look of him, do a bit of grinding, then wake up in his house a few hours later.

Slutty? Probably. But why put a label on it?

This time, with it being that little bit 'special', I decided I should *look* special, too. At the very least I should try my best, which involved wearing something a bit out of my ordinary repertoire. I wanted all eyes on me. Something that would make me stand out above all the rest. There are some good-looking girls in Guernsey, I hated to admit. I didn't want to fade into the background.

My 'ordinary repertoire' didn't stretch very far. In my 'day wardrobe' (the pile of clothes that lived on my floor until, every few weeks, Mum threw a hissy fit and folded them all up), I had enough skinny black jeans, clingy vest tops and band t-shirts to keep me dressed for several months. All well and good, but going-out clothes were an entirely different matter.

I had a black lacy dress, with a purple lining and just the one long sleeve. It was short, probably too short for decency, and went very well with my one pair of giant black platform heels.

Then there was the black dress with dungaree-style straps, and a silver zip down the middle (Gemma had always liked to unzip it in the middle of Folies when too far onto the fun side of intoxication).

Then there was the black and leopard print strapless dress, with the built-in corset, that Nan had bought for me. She loved a bit of leopard print, and I had a sneaky feeling she'd originally bought it for herself but couldn't manage to squeeze into it. But that one was *definitely* out – even though I wasn't bored with it yet, I'd put on a few pounds over Christmas. I'm sure it would look lovely… if I could ever do it up again.

I had sighed in despair, looking over the same tired old selection of dresses. The one with the shoulder out was my standby dress, but it was starting to look a bit shabby. And with me having put on a bit of weight, it made my boobs a bit… shelf-like. The dungaree-style one had what appeared to be a Vopple Juice stain right across the chest; I hadn't been able to touch it when I took it off in the early hours of New Year's Day, thanks to the smell making me want to vomit dramatically, and I'd forgotten to sort it out since then.

Plus, they were all so *samey*. Black, black and more black. Yes, I'm a metalhead, but that doesn't mean I have to be entirely shrouded in darkness all the time. Metalhead, not Goth. Not any more, anyway.

I'd updated my Instagram story with a melodramatic black and white shot of my expansive floordrobe, captioned in a particularly exuberant fashion.

"Fuck this for a bag of biscuits, I HAVE NO CLOTHES."

Within about five minutes, the cavalry had arrived.

"I don't care what Zach says, on your lunchbreak tomorrow, WE ARE GOING SHOPPING."

Flic really seemed determined not to be the only one going down the aisle on the Leap Year Pact: she wanted bridal company.

"You want to marry this man," she kept saying as we marched around town (I'd have gone for a gentle amble, but she was insistent on not letting her FitBit down: my short legs struggled to keep up). "So we're not going too revealing."

"But I love revealing!"

"You reveal yourself every bloody weekend." Flic's perfect eyebrows twitched. "I've seen you at that Liberation Monument."

"I don't dance round it *every* weekend."

"Come on. In here."

I was frogmarched into Dorothy Perkins and came out twenty minutes later feeling surprisingly pleased. Flic had scanned the shop in about thirty seconds and instantly homed in on a dark purple skater dress. It wasn't low-cut in the slightest, but the entire top half of it was covered in wine-coloured sequins that caught the light and sparkled. I tried it on, and of course she was right; it was perfect.

"You look gorgeous," she said, and for once she didn't even sound condescending. At least, for a few seconds. "I'd rather spend the extra and get the Miu Miu version, of course, but on your salary…" She trailed off with a tinkly laugh.

Oh well, it had been fun while it lasted.

"It's not too dressed-up, is it?" I asked for the ninety seventh time, trying not to flinch while Lizzy pumped up my eyelashes with several layers of designer mascara.

"No, it's perfect," Lizzy said firmly. "Right, you're done."

I peered into her hand-mirror. "Are you sure that's enough eyeliner?"

"It's more than most people wear," she pointed out. "If I put on any more, you won't be able to hold your eyes open."

I peered at myself in the mirror and couldn't help feeling rather happy with myself.

My hair, still a pretty vibrant purple, was shiny and swingy after a good go with the GHDs, and I had let my favourite Deathly-Hallows-shaped studs go for the night in favour of some silver dangly chandeliers, donated by Gem. They jangled rather pleasantly in my ears every time I tossed my head and did my Disney princess impression.

I just had to try hard not to get them tangled in my other earrings: the stud in my left tragus, and the industrial bar across the top of my right ear. I still sorely missed my eyebrow bar (taken out on Zach's request in case it fell in someone's soup; I couldn't be arsed taking it in and out every day and so let the hole close up) but at least one of my tattoos was on display: the thorny rose on my left shoulder was under the dress, but the chain of musical notes twining round my right ankle was out. With my black platform heels, the dress was just the right length to make my legs look like they didn't belong to a stumpy child.

Yes, I was quite proud of how I'd turned out for the night.

Though I was far more proud of how my friends had turned out; we weren't a bad-looking bunch.

Gem was standing in front of Lizzy's full-length mirror, alternately peering critically at herself, and squinting through the window into the darkness, trying to see if it was raining or not. She'd just spent the past several minutes wiping curl-taming gel into her hair, trying to de-frizz the unruly poodle that she could almost sit on.

"If I get caught in the rain and get all frizzed up, I'm going to scream," she announced through the comb she had trapped between her teeth.

For someone carrying another person inside her, she was looking pretty damn good. From the back, you wouldn't even know she was pregnant; twenty weeks in and she was still as spindly as Guernsey tomato plant, apart from the perfectly round bump and the slightest indication that she might, finally, be getting some boobs.

I, for one, wouldn't be wearing her dress on a normal day, let alone a pregnant one. I count myself as a pretty confident person... but not *that* confident. It was bodycon, pale grey with long sleeves and cold shoulder cut-outs. There was a big strip of pink slashing across her stomach, and more cut-outs in the 'bandages' of the bodycon at her waist. She looked sexy, in the kind of way that I knew would thoroughly confuse any men perving on her.

She fastened a pair of huge silver hoops into her ears while she waited for her hair gel to set in, and eyed Lizzy's glass of wine with no little envy.

"Only twenty weeks to go," she sighed. "Oh, listen to me, I'm a proper pregnant person now. I've started talking in weeks instead of months."

"Twenty weeks, five months, they both sound years away." I waved my arm dismissively. "We have a lot of shit to get through before that baby girl has to come out so here's an idea – let's not think about it."

"I can't help it!" Gem whined. "I want wine. Well, I want JD and Coke. Or vodka. Mmm, vodka. And fags..."

"Right, before you start to cry, I'll drink my wine." Manfully, Lizzy took a giant gulp of her drink. "I'm going to need it for Operation Shirley Bassey."

Before she'd attacked my face (and stood over me until I'd brushed my hair enough to make it shine) Lizzy had sorted herself out with terrifying speed. Speedy for someone with long hair, anyway – I was always amazed that people with hair past their shoulders managed to get ready at all, let alone with any kind of speed. I couldn't bear it myself, and chopped it off myself every time it even threatened to touch the bottom of my neck.

Unlike Gemma, who was doing something complicated involving a hair clip to get hers to lie across one shoulder instead of down her back, Lizzy liked to leave her hair to fly free when she was on a night out. What had been a bit of a blonde afro when we were teenagers had over the years been tamed into a sleek, wavy mass that tumbled down her back in a heavy curtain. The array of hair products in her bathroom to achieve this effect nearly rivalled Gemma's, but it was clearly worth it. She had to tie it up for work, which is a shame, but it meant it looked truly spectacular when she let it free.

She hadn't dressed quite as revealingly as me and Gem, of course. Lizzy never has done; even though she's always had more than enough going on in the chest department to be proud of. She's far too modest to let it out in quite the quantities that me and Gem do – though, technically, Gem has always been more about the legs than the boobs.

No, Lizzy had a bit of reticence left, which I suppose is a good thing. Someone's got to. Plus, she's always freezing. She was wearing a black denim dungaree dress with thick black tights and heels, and a tight white crop top under the dress to hug her curves. Just the tiniest flash of skin. Lizzy always managed to look understated, the kind of pretty that creeps up on you over time and before you realise it, you're half in love. If I was that way inclined (and if she wasn't rather a lot taller than me), I'd want to pick her up and put her in my handbag to take her home and keep her safe.

How she'd been dumped quite so horribly, I had no idea.

"Go on, put your contacts in!" I commanded, gulping down a good-sized glass of Vopple Juice in one go. "Your glasses will only get all steamed up in Folies."

"I'll take off my glasses when Gem takes off the lipstick," Lizzy said, sticking her tongue out.

"What?" Gem acted affronted. "Just because I like pink…"

"You can like pink as much as you want," I chimed in. "But frosted pink lipstick belongs in the nineties."

"Metalheads." Gemma shook her head good-naturedly, pouting into her phone for a quick succession of selfies.

"Come *on*." I banged my fist on Lizzy's dressing table. Whoops, it was possible I might be a tiny bit tipsy already. We *had* already been through a bottle of wine which, considering only two of us were drinking, and we'd only been at it for an hour, was relatively impressive. And I had progressed to the Vopple Juice already. "I want to go."

"OK, wait, wait, hang on." Gemma gave me a little smack on the back of the head with her phone as she let her chosen selfie upload to Instagram, and plonked onto Lizzy's bed to slip into her shoes – flat purple ballet pumps. At nearly six feet tall, Gemma has always shunned heels. She's always claimed they'd prove too much of a liability when she's drunk, if nothing else. "We need a plan of action for Operation Shirley Bassey."

"Ahh, no." I put my hands over my eyes. "I don't like proper plans of action. Not for bloke stuff, anyway... it'll curse it!"

"No, it won't," said Gem firmly. "It'll mean you have a clear objective, a mission. You'll know where you have to be, and when you have to be there. You'll be prepared. And when you've drunk your own bodyweight in Vopple Juice, I'll be there with the plan in my horribly sober head, all ready to get you back on track."

"Thanks for the support," I said drily. "Why did you never join the army?"

"Not enough men, I'd shag my way through in a week."

"Ahh yes, now I remember."

"I'm with Gem on this one." Lizzy sat herself next to Gemma on the bed. I felt like they were about to give me a job interview. Or make me do a French oral exam.

"If you don't go in with a plan, you might get distracted," Gem continued. "You've already established contact, right?"

"What, I've met him? Obviously."

"No, as in about tonight."

"Oh, yeah, when he came into the Jar this morning I asked if he would be out tonight. I believe his exact words were 'yeah, Folies'. Is that 'establishing contact' enough for you?"

"I'd rather you just gave in and added him on Facebook, but yes, I am satisfied with that." Gem had put on the voice of a moustachioed American colonel with a buzzcut. "Now the next step is to work out your pulling strategy. I know you, your normal one is just aim and fire. But you want to marry this man."

"Steady on, you're as bad as your sister. I haven't decided on that yet." I took another big gulp of Vopple Juice – maybe a bit more booze would help me reach that decision a bit more quickly. "I just want to pull him and see if he's any good. Honestly, I don't think I need much strategy. I manage it most weekends."

"And we've all seen *what* you've pulled."

"Gem, be nice," said Lizzy, taking a delicate sip of wine. I think she was trying to avoid having to start knocking back the Vopple Juice.

"She's right, though," I said. "It's Folies, there are a lot of trolls in there. We're all bound to get them occasionally... *all* of us, Gem."

"Hey, I do better in Barbados," she said, referring to one of Guernsey's other clubs – even grimmer than the famed Folies, and even stickier of floor. "Remember," she patted her belly, "I like the Latvians."

"Last week you were saying he was Polish," I reminded her.

"Ahh, whatever. I like a man with an interesting accent."

"So do I..."

"You've got your 'I'm dreaming of a Welsh accent' face on," Lizzy teased. "Come on, we need this strategy!"

"Give me another drink." I reached for the bottle of vodka, strongly considering swigging from it straight.

These two were really angling for a wedding they'd enjoy (we all knew that Flic's would be an episode of pure Pinterest torture) and apparently I was going to be their best chance at it. Oh well, at least I had some support.

"Right, I think you should start at the upstairs bar..."

* * *

A couple of hours, half a camera roll of daft group selfies and quite a few drinks later, we had made it to Folies. It had of course been raining when we'd left the house, and blowing enough of a gale that we nearly got drowned by a wave over the seafront getting into the taxi, but I am happy to report that Gemma's hair had survived without turning into a frizzball.

We'd made short work of a round or two in a couple of town's more presentable bars, then were ready to move onto the main event: Folies. Or, to give it its full title, 'Les Folies d'Amour'. Appropriate, no?

"Don't eye up that bloke," Gem chided as I watched a rather buff young man wander past where we were queuing at the bar.

"Number one, he's got to be eighteen at the very most. Number two, Operation Shirley Bassey!"

"What, where?"

"No, he's not here yet. I'm just reminding you!"

"Pah, I wasn't looking for *me*. I was looking for Lizzy!"

"I don't want you to look for one for me," Lizzy said primly. Uh oh. By the look on her face, she was already getting into the 'maudlin' part of her evening. "And I'm not drinking anything else. What if Dan comes in? And I'm hammered, and make a mess of myself? No, I'm drunk enough. I'll keep myself in check." All this with the air of a martyr.

"Nope, not having that!" Just at the opportune moment, the barman turned to me and asked for my order. I quickly procured a nice selection of bottles, and presented Lizzy with two. "Drink up, dear. And here's a J2o for you, madam."

"Ugh." Gem grimaced. "It just tastes wrong without vodka in it."

"I can't drink these, I just told you!" Lizzy was still wearing her martyred expression. It really didn't go with her pretty outfit and shiny hair. "I can't!"

"Yes you can, here you go." I more or less forced a bottle of pear cider into one hand and a WKD into the other – what can I say? I felt a nice teenage chaser would bring us some luck. "There you go, you have a choice. Would you rather I drank all four of them and ended up unconscious before Operation Shirley Bassey can even come into action?"

"I don't like either option, thank you very much!"

"Stop bickering, you two!"

Lizzy and I looked around to try and work out where the hell Gemma had disappeared to, then both jumped at the same time. Gem appeared to be leaning over the balcony... not something she usually did unless she was incredibly drunk and overbalancing on her (flat) shoes.

We had of course picked the most useful place of Folies for people-spotting – and Welshman spotting, of course. The club, one of the oldest in Guernsey, was set over two levels. On the bottom was a bar and a sizeable dance floor; at the top, another couple of bars, a cloakroom, and a convenient balcony where you could squint down at the people dancing below.

That balcony could be bloody dangerous, I'll tell you now. Oh, not because you could fall off it (though I've come close). But because that's where people took pictures. Including sponsored club photographers, who prowled around St Peter Port on a Friday and Saturday nights, taking 'official' photos. They had them in the UK as well, of course – don't get me started on the incident with the 'I Am VIP' photographer in Fifth Avenue, Manchester (it ended badly and that camera cost me a lot of money).

I swear, those photographers were purely out to capture debauchery, with the single aim of posting it on social media to shame you (i.e. me) the following, hungover day. And they liked to hang around the balcony at Folies, waiting to capture the most incriminating moments they could.

You might have just been a blur of arms and legs in the corner of the photo, but you could guarantee that *someone* you knew would see that picture, and somehow manage to identify both you and your conquest, with whom you were inevitably having a bit of a grind against a pillar. It was never pretty when that happened; it was one of the occupational hazards of living on an island of only sixty-five thousand people.

Of course, after a few drinks, you tended to forget the photographers were there.

It's one of the reasons I tried to stay away from Facebook, as a general rule. If I couldn't see what people were tagging me in, then clearly it didn't exist.

But the balcony was also incredibly useful when you were hunting someone out. Most people I knew seemed to gravitate up there as soon as they arrived in the club, to have a little peer and see who they wanted to go and dance with – or who they wanted to avoid. On that particular night, I was more in the mood to just hop straight on the dance floor.

Gem was in her 'strategic' mood, though. I had been emphatically placed on the balcony, so that if Somewhat-Hot-Suit followed everyone else's general pattern and came up to the balcony bar first, we'd 'coincidentally' run into him. And if he didn't come straight up to the balcony, we'd see him on the dance floor and be able to… 'coincidentally' run into him.

"A fool-proof plan," Gem had said, this time in the voice of a James Bond villain. She really needed to get out more.

But now she was hanging off the balcony, almost.

Oh, all right, her impending peril was probably a bit intensified by the volume of alcohol flowing around my system. But at the time, it looked like she was about to fall – or jump – to her death.

Lizzy and I rushed forward, ready to dramatically pull her back from the brink of doom… but then we noticed something. She was laughing – laughing so much there were tears running down her cheeks, and she wasn't even trying to stop her eyeliner from making a mess of her face.

"Oh look, just *look*," she cried, barely able to breathe. "Ooof." She clutched her belly. "Oh, it's making the baby laugh too, I swear. Look!"

We looked.

And then we started to laugh too.

You'd think, having been working at the Bean Jar for just over two years and Guernsey having a social scene the size of a postage stamp, we would have run into Zach on a night out before. And we had; but only in pubs. Before clubbing – before all that much drink had been taken. Certainly before any dancing was to go on.

"This is possibly the best thing that has ever happened." Gem was shaking, she was laughing so much.

Bless him, Zach really wasn't the world's best dancer. It's something we could probably have predicted, if we'd ever even entertained the thought. He was hardly the most graceful person on 'dry land', as it were, let alone on a dance floor.

By the looks of things, he'd dressed up for the occasion; instead of his usual uniform of 'jeans and t-shirt' or, on an exciting day, 'jeans and Harry Potter t-shirt', he had put on an actual shirt with his jeans – a purple one that was fairly crumpled.

I was impressed that he'd managed to get it on without Mrs Machon flying at him with an iron – though, I reminded myself, she didn't actually live with him. She just followed him round far more than most grandmothers consider necessary.

I did have a quick scout around, just to make sure she wasn't secreted in a corner with a glass of sherry, keeping an eye on her grandson.

That was the extent of the aforementioned 'effort', of course: Zach was still wearing the elderly Converse he threw on for work every day, and his mousy brown, floppy hair was still the same as ever. No gel or styling for our boss, just a not-quite-sensibly cut mess flying round his head as he bopped away happily, a beer in one hand and his glasses just the tiniest bit wonky.

"We've got to go down there!" Gem squealed. Honestly, it was like all her Christmases had come at once. I could see it in her eyes; being the only sober one on a night out where our boss was off his tits could have some excellent bribery and blackmail potential.

"But what about Operation Shirley Bassey?" Lizzy put in, sounding anxious. "I thought that was the main goal of the night!"

"Yeah, but there's also 'Operation Embarrass Zach'," Gem said. "Come on, we can't let this opportunity get away from us!"

Without another word, Gem grabbed me by one hand and Lizzy by the other, and, completely ignoring the fact we were both struggling to balance in our high heels, dragged us down the stairs.

Zach clocked us before we had quite reached him. I couldn't stop grinning by this point: a combination of the lovely warming cider and the endearing sight of Zach waving his arms like a windmill were both giving me a giddy glow.

"Oh hell, it's you lot." Zach blushed bright scarlet, all the way from his neck up to his ears – I wondered if his glasses were getting hot. I wouldn't be surprised, he looked so embarrassed. I felt a tiny bit sorry for him.

But then, surprisingly, he grinned. Not his usual slightly nervous, crooked smile – a proper ear-to-ear grin that lit up his face and practically pushed his glasses off his ears.

"Ahh, come on, let's all dance together!" He grabbed me by the wrist and pulled me into his circle of similarly-dressed friends, tugging Lizzy and Gemma behind me.

It was a short while later that Operation Shirley Bassey found me, instead of me finding Operation Shirley Bassey.

I was just starting to lose myself in the intensely cheesy dance music (largely thanks to a nice round of drinks bought by the clearly already rather intoxicated Zach), all of us dancing in a circle like we were at a school disco, when I felt a tap on my shoulder.

"Hey, Cleo!" I felt someone getting right up close behind me; quite possibly a bit too close for polite social intercourse. I turned around ready to give whoever it was quite the earful, and nearly head-butted Somewhat-Hot-Suit in the chin.

"Hiya James!" I cooed. "How are you, *James*?" I gave Gem a surreptitious nudge (probably not so surreptitious, now I think about it).

"Great, I hoped I'd see you out tonight!" His smile was very white: very intense. His lips were very red, for a man. Quite delicate, almost girly, yet somehow making his chiselled jawline and smattering of blonde stubble that bit more masculine. Very nice. Even nicer than he'd seemed in the Bean Jar. "I saw you from the balcony. I just got a round in, want one of these?" He proffered what transpired to be a vodka and orange. Not my favourite drink, but in the circumstances, it'd do.

* * *

The rest of the evening seemed to just whirl by. That tends to happen when you're rather on the drunk side, you see.

It was after James's second round (a man who insists on buying the drinks; something I'm always keen on) that things started to get a bit blurry around the edges. Not New Year's Eve levels of drunkenness, but definitely the far side of sobriety.

Some things stuck in my mind, of course.

Being in the toilets with Lizzy and Gem, giggling happily over how well my night was going...

Trying to restore my cat-like eyeliner flicks to their full glory and making a right hash of it...

Dancing to some very cheesy nineties pop with James and trying to make up our own dance routines...

76

Dancing to some very cheesy eighties pop with Zach until James cut back in again...

Dancing to something very slow and sway-y with James and putting my arms around his neck...

Kissing James rather furiously in the middle of the dance floor...

Kissing James even more furiously against the wall by the bar...

Kissing James in a taxi on the way back to his house at Vazon...

And, of course, finally, being naked as a naked thing in James's bedroom.

Annoying Customer of the Week, Part 3

"*Good morning, what can I get for you today?*"

"*I'll have a tea and an Americano, please.*"

"*Of course, would you like them small or big?*"

"*Medium, please.*"

"*We do big or small – see, here are the cups. Small, and big.*"

"*Medium.*"

"*I tell you what, I'll get you a large. Anything else I can get for you? Pastries? Sure. Altogether that'll be seven eighty, please. Thank you very much – your drinks are on the side!*"

"*Where's the skimmed milk?*"

"*Oh, I'm really sorry, but we appear to have run out of skimmed milk. Is semi-skimmed OK, if it's just for a drop in your tea?*"

"*WHAT? No skimmed milk? Oh my goodness. But I can't have semi-skimmed milk! Fat! Think of the fat! That's almost full-fat! Semi-skimmed! Can't you see I'm watching my figure? Oh, I can't believe you've done this to me. I just don't know what to do. Oh my goodness.*"

While the rather scrawny-looking woman desperately tried to come up with a solution to her world-breaking problem – semi-skimmed milk or soy milk, oh, the humanity – I just smiled behind the bar. Smiling in my own happy place in my head. The smile of a well-laid woman.

Chapter 6

"I can't believe you've been so stupid."

Another day, another Bean Jar conference. It was less than a week since the Operation Shirley Bassey incident and Flic had decided to grace the Jar with her presence, to see how the rest of us were faring with the Leap Year Pact. I was pleased to have something to report.

"It wasn't stupid, it was fun!" I stuck my tongue out. "Besides, you're the one who was encouraging me to marry him last week. You practically bloody dressed me!"

It was just gone four o'clock, and Flic had taken the afternoon off work. Gemma was pretending to clean tables around where her sister had installed herself, and I was wiping down the bar. Zach was supposed to be in his office, but was eavesdropping at every opportunity. His tufty brown hair kept appearing over the bannister under particularly spurious pretences: I was almost certain he didn't need my approval to order an extra box of cardboard cups. Considering he'd been in Folies at the weekend and had seen exactly what I'd got up to with James, it wasn't like he needed to poke his nose.

Sadly, Lizzy was still stuck at work, supervising a drama club for the kids in her class. So instead of her, we had Jonny to contend with; Flic had started dragging him everywhere she went, even to the point of making sure he had the same 'spontaneous' afternoon off work as she did. It was a little... odd. A cynical voice told me she was trying to keep him away from someone at work, but really, when I thought about it, she probably just wanted him exposed to as much wedding planning as possible. It did seem all she could talk about; I was glad that my shenanigans were giving us all a break.

"No, Cleo, it was just stupid," Flic was saying, sanctimony dripping from her hair to her yoga pants. "Yes, you looked lovely in that dress." She snorted. "I chose it, of course you were going to look good. But it was supposed to intrigue him. Make him want to know more. Keep a bit of mystery. He's not going to marry you now you've given it all up on the first night!"

"And what decade are we living in?" I resisted the urge to punt my sanitiser spray at her head. Gem appeared to be resisting a similar urge from behind her sister's back.

"You'd be surprised." Flic shook her head sadly. "I see it more and more nowadays, even in my office. Girls are falling in love with these men they meet for one-night stands, and it never ends well!"

"I'm not setting out to fall in love with him," I scoffed. "I just want to see what happens."

"She's just looking for some fucking fun, Flic. Something you'd do well to find yourself." Gemma leaned over the arm of the sofa and ruffled Jonny's sensibly-cut hair. "This one here's not exactly the life of the party, are you love?"

"Be nice, Gem," I chided, as Jonny mumbled a very faint protest.

"I am being the life of the party," Flic said sternly, ignoring Jonny's attempts to dodge another violent ruffle of his hair from his future sister-in-law. "It's about whether you can see yourself with this person for the rest of your life. And you can't work that out from a one-night stand!"

"How would you know? Not like you've ever had one." Gem stopped tormenting Jonny and patted Flic on the head. "Unless you were at it *really* young, and I think I would have noticed."

"Oh, shut up." Flic batted her sister away. Jonny was practically puce, presumably at the thought of his fiancée shagging off with someone else. Not that she ever would;

everyone knew that Flic would never besmirch her 'perfect' reputation in such a way. She wouldn't be able to put it on Instagram, after all.

"Listen, Cleo," Gem said, with the air of great wisdom. "As long as you had fun, it's all good. Sex is sex, and in my opinion, everyone should be having more of it." She gave a 'significant eye' to her sister and her fiancé.

I didn't really want to think about their sex lives, to be honest – I had the feeling it would either be horribly boring and once-every-six-months, or that Jonny had some disturbing secret kink that had to be fulfilled before anything could happen.

"You see, it's all about the chemistry," Gem carried on. "It doesn't matter whether you're emotionally compatible, or any of that bullshit, as long as you're *sexually* compatible. If you feel that fire from across the room, if you can picture him naked from the first moment you see him, feeling like you could just rip off his clothes and, and, and, *take* him…"

"Gem, have you been at Nan's bonkbusters?" I rolled my eyes. "The maid being 'taken' by the lord of the big house, very corset-y and frilly dress-y?"

"Ah, shut up," she said. "My hormones have kicked in, big time, and nobody wants to shag me!"

Jonny, by this point, was absolutely bright scarlet. As was the lone actual customer sitting at the far table, trying to finish his extra-hot latte as quickly as he possibly could. Bless him, I was pretty sure he'd be straight up to the PEH as soon as he left, crying for the burns unit.

"Follow your own advice, then, find someone next time we're out," I urged, eyeing the glass cake dome speculatively and wondering whether it needed a trip through the dishwasher.

"I can't!" Gem howled. "You can't get that same feeling when you're sober, especially sober and fat."

"You're not fat, you're pregnant," I said automatically, giving the cake dome a quick wipe and leaving it on the counter.

"Actually, Gem, you should probably start with yoga now while you still can." Flic turned a critical eye on her sister. I had a sudden urge to remove all sharp objects from Gemma's line of sight before Flic got a fork to the eye. "Being pregnant is no excuse to let yourself go all saggy. You're not too bad now, but wait until the stretch marks set in!"

"Bite me, bitch," Gem growled. But before she could start a full-blown attack, the door clanged, heralding a new customer.

Oh shit on a biscuit, I groaned in my head. Not today. I couldn't cope with Mrs Doubtfire today.

"My latte's not waiting on the bar, Cleo, you should be ashamed of yourself!" Mrs D gave a laugh that was supposed to show her comment wasn't seriously meant. I knew, though, that she really *did* mean it. After the time Gem had seen her coming from out of the window and had rushed to make her drink, in the futile hope that she'd not waste our time chatting at the bar while we made it, she'd fully expected her extra hot, half-shot latte to be ready and waiting on the bar for her when she got in.

Preferably, she'd like to sit down and have it brought to her, with no charge whatsoever. Sadly, when Zach was around, he still actually did it. No matter how many forks I stuck in his leg.

Gemma had a theory that Mrs D might be an old friend of Mrs Machon, and Zach had been ordered to keep her sweet. He denied it, but he was blushing all through said denial.

"Hiya, Joan, I'll have that for you in just a second!" I said as brightly as I could, reaching over to the coffee machine. I didn't bother charging her; I didn't get much choice in the matter, as she made a beeline for her favourite table. Gem rolled her eyes, still perched on the arm of the sofa next to Flic. I rolled mine back at her.

As I carefully carried Mrs Doubtfire's boring, scalding almost-coffee over to her, I was pretty much resigned to another long ramble about her hip replacement, dead husband, or the 'Jerry Bags' who used to shag the Nazis during the Occupation. At the very least, I was expecting to have to seriously tone down our conversation, seeing as the Jar was so small she'd doubtless become a part of it.

But thankfully, at the exact moment I put the ('medium') cup in front of Mrs D, Lizzy chose to come crashing into the shop in a very undignified, un-Lizzy-like manner.

"Cleo!" she gasped, pulling off her bobble hat and throwing it onto the sofa before practically collapsing into my arms. "It's happening! The very best thing is happening!"

"Karin Cluster are coming to Guernsey?" I said.

"They've found a wonder drug to make labour painless and dignified?" said Gem.

"They're un-cancelling Firefly?" Zach stuck his head over the bannister yet again.

"You're getting married?" said Flic.

"Shut up, all of you!" Lizzy almost sobbed, her face aglow. "I've just spoken to Dan!"

There was a collective facepalm around most of the room. At least, Gemma and I facepalmed, as, I believe, did Zach, halfway up the stairs. Jonny tried to join in but his hand was smacked away by Flic. Mrs Doubtfire just perked up her head like a meerkat at the sound of some gossip.

"I'll get you something to drink." Gem leapt up off the sofa (in as much as a woman with a five-month-old baby bump can be said to 'leap') while I led the very emotional Lizzy to a chair.

"Come on, then, what's going on?"

"I think he wants me back!"

"Christ on a bicycle." I put my head in my hands, sitting down on the chair next to Lizzy.

"Thank heavens!" Flic gave a little cheer and threw her hands in the air.

"Tell us what's actually happened." Gem was busily trying to get the latte milk to foam at high speed. "Has he come crawling back along the ground outside your classroom? Was he crying down the phone? Please tell me the little scrote was crying."

"No, no, nothing like that!" Lizzy's smile was rather shaky, but huge. "He just called me up, when I was leaving after drama club. He was all, like, 'how are you?'. It was just... kind of ordinary?"

"Like when a distant relative phones you up and you're obliged to make polite conversation?" Jonny piped up, strangely perceptive for once.

"Well... kind of like that, but *more*." Lizzy gratefully accepted her latte. "You know, because we'd been together so long. It was... natural."

"Of course it was!" said Flic encouragingly, while Gem made puking faces behind Lizzy's head.

"He just wanted to know how I was, asking if I was OK. It was like he really wanted to know, you know? Like he actually still cares. I can tell when Dan's being insincere, I really can." Lizzy nodded furiously. "And he wasn't."

"Was that it? He just rang you up and asked how you are?" I was cynical. I'd known Dan nearly as long as Lizzy had, and I knew full well he could put on a front. And Lizzy had been blinded by her feelings for him long before now.

"No, of course that's not it!" She snorted. "If it had just been that I'd be... well, I'd probably still be happy, but I'd just think he was trying to be friends or something. No, he also... well, he sort of asked me out."

"Sort of?"

"Yeah, sort of." Lizzy blushed.

"Oh, shitbags, he asked you for a shag, didn't he?" Gem smacked her forehead, loudly. "Every fucking person in Guernsey is getting laid except me. Why won't anyone fucking well..." Mrs Doubtfire, about three feet behind her, looked mildly shocked as Lizzy swiftly interrupted.

"No! Honestly, no. Well, I think I mean no."

"That means yes, then," Gem groaned.

"No! He said that he really needs to talk to me, that he's got something really important that he wants to discuss. That he can only talk about it with me. He wants to come over to mine to do the talking, and said it can only be *a week on Sunday*."

"What's so special about a week on Sunday?" Gem asked, almost drowned out by Flic's overdramatic squeal.

"A week on Sunday is Valentine's Day, dear," put in Mrs Doubtfire. Nobody asked you, I thought, but OK. The point was made.

"So..." Lizzy looked up shyly. "I can't help but think something's going to happen. Something of the getting-back-together variety."

"Of course it is!" Flic was practically jumping up and down on the sofa. "Valentine's Day! A big discussion! You know what... I bet he's going to propose. It's so romantic. He's seen the error of his ways and he's going to make a big speech. Can you try and film it? Oh, I bet it'll be perfect."

"Ooh, dear, it sounds lovely," said Mrs Doubtfire, leaning over from her table to poke her nose firmly into our business, as a group of sixth formers from Ladies' College peered through the door. They rather speedily decided against coming in and joining our café-wide conference, and scarpered. "I can see you in a big white dress, in St Stephen's, walking down that aisle…"

"Normally I'd disagree but, you know…" Lizzy's grin was pretty huge. "Why else would he want to have such a serious talk on Valentine's Day? And he knows how I am with balloons – that'll be why he wants it to be at my flat, in case there were balloons in a restaurant. It makes so much sense…"

"Come on, Liz, don't get too excited." I couldn't help myself; I had to wreck the party. "Remember the Horrible Day? Remember what he was doing? With that girl?" I felt rather mean. I could see the pain cross her face, thinking about Dan happily humping away with someone else. "I'm sorry, Lizzy, but you know what he's like. You can't trust anything he says."

"And after everything he's done to you, even if he is trying to get you back, if I were you I'd bloody well say no," Gem added.

"There's a first time for everything," said Flic. Gem responded with a hiss.

"She's right," I said, rubbing Lizzy's arm. "He could be wanting to talk to you about issues with the old flat. Or some… some furniture you left behind. It could be bloody anything, not necessarily the 'relationship'." I made little air-quote signs with my fingers. "I don't want you to get your hopes up."

"I'll try not to," she said bravely – a lesser woman would have flounced out of the café, claiming to be nothing but right. But I've been bossing Lizzy around for half her life. She doesn't really have much choice other than to listen to me. "But one thing. Don't book our husband-hunting trip to Finland just yet." I could feel Mrs D blanching at that from the change in the air alone. "I might not be needing it after all. And," she continued, raising her eyebrows as my phone buzzed on the table between us, James's name clearly flashing on the screen, "you might not be needing it either."

Chapter 7

Things with James were... well, I'm not going to lie. I won't start using rainbows and butterflies and flowery metaphors to describe how things were going.

A few days before Valentine's Day (for which Lizzy was preparing like a hurricane was about to blow down her flat), mere weeks after the original trip to Folies, things were going swimmingly. Peachy. Absolutely fine.

To be honest, I was a tiny bit bored.

We'd been WhatsApping pretty much non-stop since that first, happy, drunken fuck on the Friday night. I still didn't add him on Facebook – I wanted to get the measure of him a bit better before letting him see my whole history of drunken photos – but I grudgingly followed him on Instagram. It was no use for stalking, mostly moody shots of scenery and the occasional selfie with a bunch of interchangeable mates, but mine wasn't much more exciting and he'd followed me. Only polite to reciprocate.

Then came the next Saturday night, where I happened to be going out again with the girls. Of course, James just 'happened' to be going out with the lads from his work, as well.

Things progressed as might be expected, with me once again waking up on Sunday morning to the sound of rain and sea spray lashing against the curtainless windows of James's bachelor-ish bedroom.

He lived in one of the tiny little cottages on the edge of Vazon Bay, I think they used to belong exclusively to fishermen. They're charming little places, battered by the wind and the sea for most of the year. James's was one of the ones at the very front, just near the road, so the long garden was almost perpetually flooded in the winter, and the cottage was actually held up on short stilts.

It would have been a lot nicer, of course, if James had it to himself so we'd be able to shag happily all over the interestingly-proportioned rooms. Sadly, he had to share with his friend Alex, another banker (not half as pretty as James, nor as friendly – more of a silent seething spectre on the other side of the sloping bedroom wall).

I liked to think that Alex's grouchy presence, a few feet away at all times, was the reason why James was so... well, not quite lacklustre in bed, but certainly vanilla. All very sex-by-numbers. It wasn't bad at all, it wasn't like I felt let down by the whole experience or anything... it just felt like something was missing.

It's hard to describe, without going into either proper pornography territory or sounding like a scientific journal.

It was almost as though James had read some kind of manual, entitled 'How to Please a Woman'. I don't know, maybe they hand out leaflets in Welsh schools or something. Complete with handy diagrams. Press this here, rub this here, do this in a circular motion, one-two-three orgasm. Something like that, anyway.

I was starting to have the horrible feeling that the problem might actually be me.

I'd had a similar feeling with the last guy I'd slept with; maybe he'd read the same handbook. Like it was all a matter of pushing buttons. Maybe I'd been jaded by too many one-night stands, maybe I was a bit fed up of normal sex. If this was going to go with James for much longer, I was starting to think I'd need to introduce him to a little bit of kinky stuff. Nothing too extreme, of course, just *something* to liven things up a bit.

You see, although it was a tiny bit dull in the bedroom, he was lovely with it. Very considerate, a definite option for this actual relationship I was supposed to be pursuing. And now here he was, asking me on an actual date. A posh dinner. Just before Valentine's Day. I didn't yet know whether this meant that he didn't want to see me on Valentine's Day itself, or whether he was prepping me for some forthcoming uber-romantic evening.

I did, of course, have the same old dilemma when it came to getting ready for the date. What should I wear? We were going to a swanky Japanese place on the edge of town, which proudly proclaimed to have a chef who used to cook at Nobu. Far more upmarket than my usual stamping grounds.

Normally, I'd bring out my standard date outfit: black skinny jeans, as usual, and a somewhat slutty top. Reinforced, of course, by the fact we'd probably end up drinking in town once we'd finished the 'date'. I needed something versatile, and the restaurant wasn't so posh I'd be thrown out for wearing jeans. I'd just stick some heels on with said jeans, and it'd all be fine.

But of course, Military Marriage Bitch One and Military Marriage Bitch Two (Gem and Lizzy) had other ideas.

"It pains me to say it, but Flic's kind of right." Gemma had certainly changed her tune. "If you're going to do this whole Leap Year thing with him, you need to start coming across as more than just the girl he fucks when he gets drunk."

"Exactly." Lizzy had nodded dreamily. "If you do, we might be able to have a double wedding."

The upshot of this was that I ended up wrestled into a combination of clothes pilfered from Lizzy's wardrobe, she having been deemed the most 'marriageable-looking' of the lot of us, in a unanimous vote.

"It's still winter, so you need to look like you care about the cold," Gem had said firmly, ripping my black vest with cut-outs out of my hands, and replacing it with something red and woolly.

"And you can't have everything hanging out, just a hint," Lizzy urged.

I sighed, and gave in. With, of course, a sneaking feeling that if James wouldn't fall for me in all my slutty-clothed glory, he wasn't going to fall for me at all. Or at least, we'd end up happily married and divorced within a week, when he realised exactly what I was really like.

So there I was, standing at the front door, desperately trying to hitch up my dress a bit while avoiding both Mum and Nan. I didn't really want to explain what was going on in my love life until I was sure of it myself. Plus, Nan would be very ashamed at the lack of sequins or leopard print in my outfit.

The woolly dress wasn't as bad (or conservative) as I'm making out, of course; it was just far more *Lizzy* than it was *me*. Knee length, knitted, in a dark, rather lovely shade of red – the kind of colour I wasn't averse to in my own clothes, to be honest, though I'd rather it wasn't so woolly. I felt a bit like a tea cosy, or one of those things that old ladies use to cover up their toilet rolls.

It was a very thick knit, for a start, and had a high neck, and tiny capped sleeves that just about covered my shoulders. With my leather biker jacket on top and thick black tights, I was barely showing an inch of skin.

Very unlike me.

I was particularly concerned that the high-neckedness was giving me a bit of a bosomy shelf, instead of individually proportioned boobs. I had even been bullied out of my New Rocks, and pushed firmly into Lizzy's grey suede ankle boots, with a kitten heel, that were a size too big for me. I felt like I was going to topple over at any second.

Thankfully, neither of the Military Marriage Bitches had remembered to tell me to tone down my eyeliner, so I was, as usual, wearing so much of it my eyelids were weighed down. I liked to pretend that when my eyes got that 'hooded' look at around three in the morning, it wasn't because I was too drunk to keep my eyes open, it was because my eyeliner was too heavy. Honest.

I'd also layered on the foundation, particularly over my neck: for some reason I had convinced myself that I was growing quite a large Adam's apple. Hideously unsexy, though the girls claimed not to be able to see it at all. I bloody could, though, and I wanted it well disguised.

"Where are you off to, then?"

I nearly jumped out of my skin. I'd thought I was well hidden in the shadow of the staircase, but apparently not. Charlie had appeared as if from nowhere, precariously balancing a towering plate of cheese on toast. He'd had another growth spurt recently and was practically looming over me: lucky sod definitely got his

English dad's height genes, instead of the short-legged Guernsey ones I'd been landed with.

"Just off with a mate," I said quickly. "Are Adam and Tristan here?" I eyed the toast.

"Nah, just me." He grinned. "A 'mate'? Why are you dressed up like that then? He must be special."

"Oh, shut up, Charlie." I tried to grab a slice of toast, but he dodged.

"If you're going on a date, you need to save your appetite!" he teased. "Is this 'mate' the same reason you haven't been coming home at the weekends?"

"I told the bloody lot of you, I stay at Lizzy's," I sighed. Well, it was partly true; most weekends I was much happier getting over my hangovers in Lizzy's flat, rather than listen to Mum whining about how irresponsible I was being (and how much I was harming my liver, which I didn't want to hear – it was probably all too true).

"Yeah, you've got a bloke." Charlie's grin became impish. "I can see the signs."

"How the fuck can you 'see the signs'?"

"Me and Adam and Tristan are thinking about starting our own YouTube channel, actually." He gave his floppy blonde hair a toss. "We're going to be Guernsey's resident love experts."

"Love experts?" I scoffed. "You're not even fifteen yet! You don't have a love life. Unless..." I took on an impish grin of my own. "Holy shit on a biscuit, you do! You've got a girlfriend, haven't you? Yeah, that's it... you've got a girlfriend of your very own!"

"Maybe I have, and maybe I haven't." He tried to stick his nose in the air, but he was going red. Love expert, my arse. "A master of seduction never reveals his secrets."

"Except on his YouTube channel with his spotty mates?"

"Shut *up*, Cleo."

I gave an evil cackle, just as I noticed a shiny car pull up outside. Excellent.

"See you later, Charlie, don't wait up!" I gave my blushing baby brother a little pat on the head, and swished as best I could out of the door and into James's waiting passenger seat.

* * *

"No, no, it was lovely," I insisted.

"Doesn't fucking sound it," Gem said, eyes narrowed as she knocked back half a bottle of J2o in one swig.

It was the same night; several hours on. After our meal, James had made the suggestion that we go to Folies and join all our various friends, as I'd fully expected. I had no objection. No objection at all. It was a Friday night, at the end of the day.

"Can I just take this off and dance in my bra?" I whined, tugging at the red dress in front of the mirrored wall of the ladies' loo. "It's dead itchy. Liz, I don't know how you wear this."

"I usually wear it over a long-sleeved shirt," she admitted from her position sitting on a sink, swinging her legs. She was also sipping at a J2o – she didn't want to get drunk and do anything she'd regret before her big night with Dan. Even though it was well over a day away. "I've never noticed it being itchy, maybe you're allergic to it."

"Or allergic to James," Gem said wryly. "After tonight, anyway."

"Oh, come off it," I scoffed. "It wasn't that bad! Just, you know… not that good either."

The restaurant had been lovely. The food was absolutely divine, and there were beautiful views towards Castle Cornet. All the ingredients for a perfect, romantic night – especially if you add in the gorgeously sweet plum wine that I was determined to put a dent in from the get-go.

That was the problem. It was the first time we'd been alone, stone cold sober. Even in our morning-after moments, we'd still had plenty of alcohol coursing through our veins. If nothing else, we had hangovers to compare.

It just seemed to be kind of hard to find a topic of conversation, when we weren't boosted by booze.

It didn't help, either, that there was some kind of party going on with a group of ten people, on the other side of the restaurant. They just didn't shut up, and their braying laughter was quite disconcerting. Sure, they were happy, you can't complain that someone's being too happy, blah blah blah. But I didn't particularly want to hear it quite so loudly while I was negotiating my chopsticks. Though at least there was loud, discordant jazz music to try and drown them out. Great.

I fucking hated jazz.

Though it meant at least there was something else to focus on during the awkward silences.

"So you don't think you're going to stick with him?" Lizzy asked.

"I don't know!" I wailed, layering on more eyeliner. "It wasn't bad. I guess we just need to get used to one another while we're not hammered."

"So, not something you'll be starting tonight, then?" Gem raised her eyebrows at the large bottle of cider I'd bought within seconds of getting into the club.

"Well, once I got started on the plum wine, nothing was going to stop me." I shrugged, leaning over to drain the last dregs from the cider. "That stuff is beautiful. I'd drink it every day if it wasn't so damn expensive. Plus, drinking filled conversational gaps."

"It just seems so weird," Gem pondered. "How he kept clamming up like that. Most guys I've been out with never stop talking about themselves."

That was the oddest thing. I could see both of us clearly trying to keep the conversation going; I know I was trying, and James certainly seemed to be.

Well. Ish.

He manfully quizzed me on my university days, on my childhood, on whether I had any ambition... but every time I tried to reciprocate, he clammed up. Quickly. It was down to one-word answers, or just mumbled nothings, or suddenly staring down at his phone. A lot stranger – and more awkward – than any of the times we'd been flirting over the coffee machine at the Bean Jar. Or even any of the times we'd been lying in bed together, talking about random shite in a post-sex haze of sleep and booze.

I was starting to seriously consider breaking my Facebook embargo just to find a topic of conversation or two.

Thankfully, things seemed to perk up once our main courses arrived and we could focus on eating, instead. And there was a lovely ready-made conversation opportunity, of course, what with comparing what we were eating, and what we were drinking, and what everyone else in the restaurant seemed to be eating and drinking.

But all in all, it was hard work. And I wasn't sure whether I was ready for the full-on romance of a Valentine's meal.

Not that I'd been asked for one yet.

Slightly grim meal aside, though, I'd be damned if I wasn't going to get laid. All that effort, and not even any sex? No, thank you.

I tried to take another gulp of cider before I realised the bottle was empty. I was already finding it a bit hard to keep my balance as I stared at myself in the mirror, determinedly trying to make my eyeliner flicks balance out. Maybe tonight, things wouldn't be quite so sex by numbers. Maybe tonight, I could achieve a sexual Van Gogh.

"I've just had a message from Flic asking if James proposed over dinner." Lizzy gave a nervous giggle. "What should I tell her?"

"No, obviously." I rolled my eyes. "Fuck. You've made me screw up my eyeliner. And I need it to be supersonic sex-proof."

"Supersonic? Really?" Gem leaned back on the sink with her arms crossed.

"Supersonic." I nodded firmly and earned myself another thin line of liquid eyeliner down my cheek. "I'm pulling out all the stops tonight, girls. I'm going to liven this thing up if it kills me."

* * *

Huh. Supersonic sexual Van Gogh my arse. More like sexual Rothko – a big blob; colourful, calming, but not exciting in the slightest. No matter what I did, no matter what tricks I pulled out, James kept on with his button-pressing routine. No major complaints, of course. But surely it couldn't be a good omen when I was already getting a bit bored after a mere matter of weeks?

It wasn't looking good. Especially as I left the little cottage at Vazon the next morning with a hug, a little kiss, and no invitation for a Valentine's Sunday roast.

Oh well, I thought, stepping onto the pavement on the seafront and taking a deep breath. Now *this* was the impressive side of the island. As usual for February in Guernsey, it was raining – just a bit of a drizzle, but with the ever-present sea breeze, it felt a bit like being lashed in the face. James lived right in the middle of the bay, where the wind felt at its most fierce.

It was still breath-taking. The sea looked evil: grey and angry, beating its way to the wide beach. In summer, this place would be full. Hundreds of families would spread themselves across the beaches, here and the neighbouring Cobo, thanks to their golden sands and long shoreline. And, of course, the prevalence of ice-cream kiosks.

Now, all the kiosks were shut. Early on a Saturday morning, nobody was around bar a dog walker dragging his protesting hound towards Fort Hoummet, and a lonely surfer paddling towards the frightening waves. He could keep them.

I walked along the low granite wall towards the bus stop. The bluffs at Fort Hoummet looked like they were about to be shorn naked by the wind and, to be honest, I was a little concerned for my own attire. The wind really was going straight through the knitted dress: so much for it being warm. Why wasn't it acceptable to bring giant Karin Cluster hoodies on dates? I couldn't even steal a rugby shirt from James, just in case I never saw him again.

Oh, I was being melodramatic. I knew I'd see him again. In the Jar, if nowhere else. And, I thought to myself, why am I thinking about this like it's a break-up? We'd just had a dull date and some less-than-fabulous sex. That didn't mean things wouldn't get better and carry on in a more positive direction; on the other hand, we'd not made any actual commitments to one another. I didn't even have him on Facebook. If I did want to break things off, now would be the perfect time to do it. Before things got... messy.

Speaking of messy, I had to find out what was going on with my little brother at home, to find out who this girl was, making him blush so much. And apparently giving him enough action that he thought himself qualified to run a 'love expert' YouTube channel. Ridiculous.

It had been a good few years since I'd considered Charlie anything other than a toast machine with annoying friends and a bit too much of an investment in rah culture.

I looked out over the wall at the beach. At low tide, Vazon was paradise for little kids, and Charlie and I had been no different. I could remember summer sunshine, running up and down the beach with Nan while baby Charlie tried to toddle after me. I was just getting to the age where I didn't want to be hanging out with my family any more; I wanted to go off with Lizzy and sit on the sea wall, throwing chips at Grammar School boys and flirting. But my cute baby brother kept me around; with his blonde curls and chubby cheeks, it was hard to say no when he begged for one more sandcastle. He used to think I was the best person in the universe, staggering after me with an adoring grin.

I wasn't sure when that changed. Probably around the time his dad left, and Mum started treating him like a junior Messiah. By then I was far too cool to be hanging out with a little kid; then I went off for uni and came back to an entirely different younger brother, a spoilt private school kid who played rugby and thought the world owed him everything.

Still, it was interesting to see him growing up now he was right in the middle of puberty's grip, turning into a sea of over-confident hormones before my eyes. Of course, the slightly bad-big-sister part of me always found it fun to see him blush absolutely bright red. I could see some great opportunities for sisterly teasing, coming right up.

But before that could happen, I had a shift in the Bean Jar to get to. Thank goodness Zach was in baking all the bread already, or else I'd be in quite a lot of trouble... especially as the bus really didn't seem to want to turn up.

Annoying Customer of the Week, Part 4

"Hi, how are you today?"

"Fine, thank you love. Can I have an... expresso, please love?"

"An eSssspresso?"

"Yes, love. One of them."

"Are you sure? It's just the small, strong coffee, just this big, you could have a latte or an Americano..."

"Oh no, definitely that, love. The one that's one pound fifty, eh my love?"

"OK, no problem, would you like single or double?"

"What, love?"

"Single or double? Small, or big?"

"Oh, just medium please love."

"That's coming up for you, just on the end, and that'll be one pound fifty please!"

"Thank you love."

...

...

"Sorry, love? I don't think this is mine, love. It's tiny, eh my love?"

"Sorry, sir, I did tell you, espresso is the small, strong coffee, and I showed you how big it is..."

"Oh. Oh. Could I have it in a bigger cup then, love? And, maybe some milk?"

Every week. Every single week. It might be a different person each time, sometimes it was even the same one coming in every week. But there would always be one with no idea what 'espresso' actually meant. And don't get me started on macchiatos...

Chapter 8

"You haven't heard anything from him?" The shift might have been a busy one, but it didn't mean there was no time for Gem to give me a good quizzing over the coffee machine. Even if it left a fair few grumpy customers practically shrieking for their flat whites.

It was finally Valentine's Day. The most romantic day of the year – allegedly – and Gemma and I were stuck in the Bean Jar. Late. Zach had decided we were going to keep the place open until seven, so that people whose boyfriends had been a bit too dim to book a table for dinner could bring them in for a conciliatory bowl of soup instead.

It had worked, that was for sure. The ground floor was full of couples alternately staring goofily at one another over their chicken chilli soup, or eyeing one another frostily over a piece of cake. From upstairs, we could hear the dulcet tones of at least one hissed argument.

Lovely. *Festive*.

Zach had buggered off; he hadn't deigned to tell us where. Neither of us were under any illusion that he was off with a woman – it was more likely that he'd be taking Mrs Machon out for her Sunday lunch.

Flic, of course, was at a swish restaurant just down the road, probably boring Jonny senseless. Or being bored by him. When the pair of them had dropped by the Jar, about ten minutes previously, neither of them looked particularly happy – Flic sniping about missing her yoga class because Jonny had made such an early reservation, while Jonny just stared sadly at the floor. Flic only took a break from moaning to be smug about my lack of James-communication, and to express her hope that Lizzy's evening would go well.

Lizzy had dropped into the Jar too. Jittery as all hell, she seemed under the impression that this was going to be the most important evening of her life. She'd been tearing around town trying to find something new to wear, new make-up, new shoes... just like me before Operation Shirley Bassey, in fact.

Only she was firmly under the impression that this night was going to lead to a proposal.

Cynical bitches as we were, Gemma and I couldn't disabuse her. Even with Dan's track record and the fact we knew full well he was a certified dickhead... well, her enthusiasm was infectious and we couldn't help but catch that tiny spark of hope. And let's face it, one of us needed to get some leap-year-related luck.

"I've told you a thousand times, he hasn't even texted," I sighed.

"Ah, I thought you were just putting it on to annoy Flic." Gem hauled herself around the other side of the bar to pick up two discarded bowls of soup, as a 'happy' couple fled the Jar – well, the guy fled, the girl in hot pursuit. It looked like he was crying. Bless. "Or maybe just keeping some awful argument quiet in case you ruined Lizzy's mojo."

"Nah, it's just nothing. He hasn't even been in here. Unless he was in before my shift?"

"Nope. If he's come in at all, it'll have been when Zach's been in on his own. Oof." Gem paused to rub her stomach. "I tell you what, this thing's fluttering away in there now."

"It's not a thing," I chided. "It's a girl! Remember?"

"Yeah, I know." Gem put on a very un-Gemma-like goofy grin, then grimaced. "But it makes it all seem far too real."

From being obsessed with One Born Every Minute, Gem had gone to being terrified of it. Her hormones were sending her into horrifying mood swings, and she'd dramatically taken against her 'favourite' TV show. I believe it was an episode featuring someone in labour shitting on a bed that was finally her undoing.

Her emotions seemed to be hurtling between 'Yay, I'm having a baby' to 'Shit, I have to push this thing out of me'. The father still never seemed to cross her mind. Flic liked to have a little bitch about it, when she couldn't think of any other moans, but we were all used to it. Not an eyelash batted between the lot of us.

"Are you up to anything tonight?" I asked. "Any offers?"

"Nah." Gem waved her arm dismissively. "The Minger from St Martins still keeps on at me, but I will ignore him until I die."

"Not going to use him for the Leap Year Pact, then?" I teased. The Minger from St Martins had gone to school with Flic, and took a fancy to Gem about a thousand years ago. Every so often, usually around Christmas or Valentine's Day, he'd get in contact with her on Facebook and try his very best to get her to go out with him. Gem couldn't stand him; no matter what was going on in her life, she always said no: though in her last brief venture onto Tinder, she accidentally swiped the wrong way on him and gave him hope, buying herself another ten years of daft messages for sure.

"Fuck off," she growled. "Aren't you going out to Vazon to demand James throws you down on his bed and ravishes you?"

"Ha!" I threw a paper cup at her head. "Maybe I should. Just waltz in there, lock Boring Alex in a cupboard, dim the lights – actually, I won't bother with that, I have no shame – take off all my clothes, pin him to the bed and… and… and…"

I ground to a halt.

"And what?"

I had stopped right in the middle of a lewd hand gesture.

Because James himself was ambling past the window.

"Look!" I hissed. "*Look*!"

"Holy shit." Gem stopped in her tracks, on the way back to the bar, and stared out of the window. "*Who the fuck is that*?"

"I have no idea," I whispered.

James was not alone. Clinging to his arm, struggling to manage the cobbled street in impressive heels, was a woman. A tiny, blonde, uber-skinny woman – not really all that much shorter than me, even without the heels, but about half my weight and chubbiness. She appeared to be giggling rather coquettishly and peeping up at James through her fringe. He was laughing too, far too happy to notice me and Gem gawping out of the window of the Jar.

"What. A. Bastard," Gem said slowly.

* * *

And so, when we finally chucked out our last happy couple sometime after seven, I trudged back up the hill and stomped back in my own front door. No soppy Valentine's meal for me; no enthusiastic Valentine's shag, either. Just me, Mum and Charlie, all parked in front of the TV watching mindless rubbish. Nan was out on a date, having bullied some poor toothless sap from her favourite coach tour group into taking her out. We'd been told not to wait up, with a gloriously lewd wink that made Mum's perm twitch in horror.

"Your girlfriend doesn't want to go out tonight then, Charlie?" I said bitchily, helping myself to one of the Pringles that Mum had insisted went into a bowl, on a plate, on the table in front of the sofa where I was parked, alone.

"What girlfriend?" Charlie said quickly, shooting me a proper dagger-glare and side-eyeing Mum.

"Be nice to your brother," she said on auto-pilot. Either she was choosing to ignore the fact I'd used the words 'Charlie' and 'girlfriend' in the same sentence, or she was whole-heartedly pretending that he'd never ever do such a terrifying thing as fall in love.

I rolled my eyes. Nothing like a night in with the family to get me back in the proper teenage mood again.

About half an hour later, Mum got up to go to the loo, and Charlie was across the room like a shot.

"Actually, for your information," he hissed. "I bunked off maths and had lunch with my girlfriend on Friday and we're going out properly next weekend. She's got coursework."

"Ooh, like I care!" I stuck my tongue out. "Hang on, coursework? Doesn't that mean she's doing her GCSEs already? Have you got an older woman?"

"That's none of your business." Charlie smirked, sauntering back to his armchair, where he was pretending to do some homework.

I shook my head sadly. Even my baby brother had a better love life than me.

"Have you started your 'love expert' YouTube channel yet?"

"Like I'd tell you!"

"I'll find it, you know." I tried to sound vaguely threatening but I just didn't have the energy. "I'll find it and send Mum a link. She'd probably have a stroke."

Mum came back into the room and I was forced to shut up. Charlie carried on smirking behind his biology textbook.

Suddenly, there was a crash from downstairs. A *loud* crash. We all jumped.

"Is that... Nan?" whispered Charlie, a tremor in his voice.

"It can't be, she's got her key," Mum whispered back, just as unsurely. Whoever had made the crash was clearly hammering on the door. "It's half past ten! Who *is* that?"

"Oh, stop quaking in your slippers, you wimps, I'll go and see," I sighed, hauling myself to my feet. I clomped down the stairs, grabbing Nan's abandoned walking stick from when she had her hip replacement. Well, you never know, do you? "Who is it?" I bellowed at the door, which was practically rattling off the hinges now.

My only answer was a faintly muffled sob.

Oh, shit. It was Lizzy.

"Shit," was all I could say as I flung open the door. To put in the kindest possible way, Lizzy was a mess. Her hair was wild and tangled – I gathered it had started raining outside, again – and there was eye make-up running all down her tragic face. There was what appeared to be red wine staining the gorgeous white lace dress she'd spent the afternoon buying, and she was barefoot.

I quickly checked the road behind her just in time to see the retreating light of a taxi. Thank goodness, she hadn't walked all the way from St Sampson in such a state. Or attempted to drive.

"Come on, Liz." I took her gently by the shoulders and propelled her into the house. "Come on, let's go upstairs and get you sorted out."

She was sobbing far too hard to notice me shoving her as gently as I could up the stairs. Mum and Charlie looked aghast as I thrust her quickly through the living room.

"Charlie, cup of tea?" I gave him a meaningful look, and obedient for once, he scampered off down the stairs. I carried on pushing Lizzy upwards until I could finally heave her into my room and push her down onto my bedspread.

Probably not the 'pushing down onto the bedspread' that either of us had been imagining for Valentine's night, but you know what, it had to do.

"Come on then, Liz, calm down. You're getting hysterical. Calm down and tell me what's happened."

It took quite a while for the anguished sobs to turn into hiccups, largely helped by the arrival of the cup of tea. Somehow I managed to manoeuvre her out of her beautiful (stained) dress and into a pair of my (never-used) gym tracksuit bottoms and a fluffy 'University of Manchester' hoodie, gone bobbly from the wash.

"It was... it was horrible," she said in a small voice, through the hiccups.

"I'm guessing he didn't propose, then," I said, as gently as I could manage. She was going to have to get used to bluntness; I could predict how scathing Flic would be like when she found out that things hadn't exactly gone swimmingly.

"No." Lizzy gulped back another sob. "The opposite." The opposite? He broke up with her again? Before I could even start to process it, she broke down once again, hugging my pillow against her chest.

Finally, one and a half cups of tea later, I managed to coax the whole story out of her.

Dan had turned up bang on time, knocking on Lizzy's door at exactly eight o'clock. She'd been preparing for hours. Her flat was immaculate, there were fresh flowers everywhere, candles burning ("they're not still burning, are they?" was my first, urgent question), and even a photo of Dan and Lizzy at their happiest restored to pride of place on the mantelpiece. Ugh.

Lizzy herself was looking stunning: her ethereal new dress reinforced with the kind of underwear that could hold up a building, her shoes the perfect height so she wouldn't tower over short-arse Dan. She was even wearing the earrings he'd given her for their two-year anniversary, not all that long before the great break up.

Dan, on the other hand, didn't appear to have made the same level of effort. He'd obviously come straight from the gym, still in a sweaty tracksuit with unkempt hair. He hadn't even bothered to splash on a bit of aftershave, let alone shower. However, he was clutching a bottle of wine, which boosted his useful-points rather a lot, in my opinion.

He hadn't told Lizzy whether to cook or not, so she'd been to trusty M&S and got herself a ready-made appetizer selection, Flic-style. I'm willing to bet that if she'd had more time, she would have baked the lot herself from scratch. As soon as Dan came in, he plopped himself onto Lizzy's sofa and started throwing mini-quiches down his throat, whining about how difficult his day had been. According to Lizzy, this was exactly what he'd been like when they were still living together, and she took it as a hopeful sign. My poor misguided idiot.

She danced attendance for a little while, like a good little housewife, then Dan implored her to come and sit down so they could 'talk'.

Of course, this pretty much meant so *he* could talk.

It started off with the usual stuff; work, how hard he was working, how much his family were annoying him, how much people at work were annoying him, work. Standard Dan. Before too long, both of them had had a couple of glasses of wine – Lizzy somewhat more than Dan, seeing as she was supposed to be listening, not talking. What with the fact she'd been too nervous to eat all day, and the steadying shot of vodka she'd had before Dan's arrival (on my WhatsApped insistence), the room was starting to get the tiniest bit fuzzy around the edges.

That's when things, apparently, started to make very little sense.

"You see, Lizzy, you know me better than anyone else in the whole world," Dan had said, gripping her hand with sudden passion. Lizzy went a bit starry-eyed. "I need your advice with this, I don't know who else can help me through this. It's about Lucinda."

"Lucinda?" Lizzy had queried. Perfectly reasonably.

"Yes, Lucinda." Dan at least had the nous to blush. "I... I think you met. Once." It was clear to Lizzy then that Dan was talking about her infamous wobbly-boobed replacement. I remembered the day well, having been right behind her at the time. Dan claimed they'd only met after the break up, but none of us had been convinced. Lizzy had plenty of evidence to suggest otherwise – which I'd had to go to great lengths to remind her, every time she'd been convinced there had been something wrong with *her* in the relationship.

"Yes, I remember."

"Well, you see... Lizzy, I'm in love with her. She's so special. I think you'd really get on."

Lizzy was shaking her head at this point, trying to clear it. Where was her big romantic moment? Why wasn't Dan proposing?

"The thing is, I need your help. We were so close, you and me, so close to, you know, being together. Forever. What did you think was going to happen next? What did you *want* to happen next?" Dan squeezed her hand eagerly. "How should I propose to Lucinda?"

"How should you... propose to her?" Lizzy whispered, barely able to speak.

"Yes. I want to be with her for the rest of my life and, well, Liz, you know me best. How should I do it? How can I make her want me as much as I want her?"

Lizzy claimed not to remember what happened next. But red wine got spilt, things got shouted, and it seemed that at one point, Dan had attempted to fling a quick kiss across the lines and woo Lizzy into bed. For 'one last special night', or something along those lines. Sleazy. As. Fuck.

Then Lizzy ordered him out of her flat, vommed up her wine, and flagged down a taxi.

I quite fancied a bit of red wine myself. A 'bit', a 'bottle', either way. I really didn't know what to do.

Sure, Gemma and I had originally had a bit of an inkling that something like this would happen. And we'd had a brief conversation about what we'd do if it *did* turn out badly… but our suggestions both involved the other person being there, preferably surrounded by bottles of vodka. Then that little spark of hope had caught us and we'd started to think that maybe, finally, things would come good for our Lizzy.

And instead she was in pieces. It was breaking my heart to see her like that.

I'd really hoped this was all in the past now, the worst part of the heartache. But apparently not.

Lizzy couldn't take any more of this bullshit. I had to think of some way to divert her, some way to cheer her up.

Having stuttered out the story of her evening in fits and starts of sobbing, she was currently retreating into a shame-cocoon in my duvet, clutching her empty mug tightly.

"I can't believe I thought he was going to propose," she whispered, shakily. "I just can't believe I was so stupid."

"You weren't stupid," I soothed. "Come on, what else were you going to think? He wanted to see you on Valentine's Day, of all days."

"He said he would have talked to me earlier, but he's been so busy at work, today was the only time he could come round." Her voice was flat. "I'm pretty sure he'd been with Lucinda all day and could only sneak off to see me after his usual Sunday gym-trip."

"Ooh, that's rough."

"Tell me about it."

"But that's the point, if someone says they're coming round to talk to you on Valentine's Day, it usually means something romantic is going to go down. And, Christ on a bicycle, who goes to their ex to ask advice on their current girlfriend, anyway? When they haven't deigned to speak to them for months?"

Seeing Lizzy's eyes well up yet again, I cast around for something vaguely positive to say.

"But at least you know now, I suppose? Like, you know he's not going to come back now. Ever." Oh, this wasn't helping. "It means you can get over him, properly. You were doing so well before, this can just be a blip. Just a tiny blip in your recovery. Now you have that certainty, you *know* you're all right on your own. And he's done this in such a stupidly arsey bollock-faced way, you've seen what he's really like." Even more than when he was shagging this 'Lucinda' before your metaphorical bed was even metaphorically cold, I wanted to add, but refrained. "You're not going to want to go back to him now, are you?"

"Well…" She gulped. "It's shown his true colours, I guess."

"Ugly colours," I supplied, trying to rile her into some form of anger.

"Yeah…"

"You'll never pine for him again," I said, probably a touch too grandiosely for the situation.

"I wouldn't go that far." Lizzy smiled – a wobbly smile, but a smile nonetheless. "Oh, I need to stop. This isn't the end of the world." Well, this was better than last time. Admitting it wasn't quite apocalyptic-levels of disaster was the first step. "I've been so stupidly wrapped up in this, I've not asked about you at all!" That's my girl. Already she was wiping her eyes and making brave attempts to stop her lip stop quivering. "Have you heard anything from James yet?"

"Not as such." I put on my own best brave grin. "We saw him going past the Jar this evening with some blonde."

"Some blonde what?"

"Some blonde woman, Liz."

"What?"

"Yeah." I shrugged. "Looks like he found someone else to spend Valentine's Day with. I clearly didn't pass the romantic date test the other night."

"Oh, you poor thing!" Suddenly, Lizzy was across the bed with her arms around my neck. Bless her, I could tell she was trying to be supportive, but wearing her like a necklace didn't half hurt. I disentangled her gently.

"No, honestly, it's not like that." I gave a little laugh, rubbing my throat. "I'm kind of relieved. Now I don't have to marry him!"

"But I thought he was a proper possibility?"

"Ahh, he was. For about five minutes. But we never really, you know... clicked. And," I remembered suddenly, "we were never even in a relationship! I don't know why we're acting like this is a break up. It most certainly is not."

"Don't you feel a bit... bad? Even though it was only a sex thing?"

I shrugged again. "Nah. I can get another 'sex thing' any time I want." Well, maybe not 'any time', but I'd probably be able to find something if I was in a pickle. I'd never gone wanting before James, I surely wasn't going to start going without now he seemed a bit of a useless prospect. "And he wasn't all that great in bed, anyway."

"It's been ages since I last had sex." Lizzy heaved a deep sigh. "Months. Oh, heck, I haven't had sex since last year."

"It's only February."

"Still. Me and Dan hadn't exactly been at it like rabbits right before we broke up."

"Hey, you said that without even a wobble! Lizzy, I'm proud."

"I'm proud of myself." She grinned. A proper grin, this time, despite her face still being streaked with eyeliner and mascara stains.

"You know what, we need to get you back on the horse." I clapped my hands with relish. "I've been saying it for bloody ages – we need to get you a new man! Even just for a night..."

"Oh, come on."

"OK, I don't mean right away, I don't mean pounce on the nearest bloke in Folies this Saturday. Though, you know, that'd work. But soon."

"Maybe."

"Not maybe, yes!" I exclaimed, warming up to my theme. "You know what this means? We can get the plans rolling again! Karin Cluster!" I bounced off the bed and threw up the screen on my laptop. "I'm sure they're off on tour soon, let me have a look."

"I can't just run away to Europe," Lizzy pointed out. "I can hardly take random days off work."

"Book it anyway and call in sick."

"I couldn't do that!" Ahh, that's my Lizzy. Still not exactly thrilled to break any rules.

"Well then, don't your kids have Easter holidays? We'll time it by that. Come have a look at this."

Lizzy hopped over on the bed to peer over my shoulder.

"Ooh, I'll have to think about this." She bit her lip. "It's going to be expensive, for a start. And it looks like most of the dates are nowhere near the school holidays."

"Yeah, but what about this bit? Little mini-tour in Finland. Promised land of heavy metal." I clacked my nail against the screen. "What do you think?"

Well, it distracted Lizzy at least. A couple of hours later, we'd booked ourselves tickets to see Karin Cluster on their mini-tour in the far north. Tickets to the Helsinki gig, our first choice, had sold out. But we worked out a cunning plan involving flight transfers and buses – and decided on our destination. A small city called Oulu. In just a few weeks' time.

Chapter 9

"And breathe. And then in through the nose… and breathe out…"

"This cannot be bloody real!" Gemma hissed through her teeth.

We were about ten minutes into our first 'Relaxation in Labour' class. We'd already been to the first of the 'Parent Craft' classes, which consisted mostly of scientific diagrams of the cervix and warnings on why epidurals might not work. With some scary statistics in mind, Gemma had had another last-minute shift in her mood and decided that we should also attend the more 'alternative' of the birthing preparation classes.

"Just in case it all goes tits up," she'd justified. "I want some backup in case my cocktail of drugs fails dramatically on me."

So far, we had learned how to breathe.

Like we didn't know how to breathe already.

I mean, we'd been doing it perfectly well for over twenty years apiece.

"Seriously, I was more relaxed than this when I was getting tattooed," I muttered. "Surely this can't help while your bits are opening up like a fucking… *tulip*."

"Quiet at the back, please." The woman leading the class was shooting us daggers from across the room. She was a tiny little woman, a nurse at the hospital, and probably the furthest from an earth-mother type I'd ever seen. Hair like iron, grey and straight, in a boring bob with no texture whatsoever. Her glasses looked like they'd been made from her hair, and her steely grey eyes were the exact same colour. I'd never seen such a pointy nose on a woman: I hoped Gemma wouldn't have her peering up her business end mid-labour. The baby would be put off coming out in case she got impaled and Gem would be in labour forever. No matter how much breathing she did.

As many people would expect, we were the only pair of women in the room; the other six couples were married men and women. Or, if not married, in the kind of happy relationship where a baby was probably planned out with thermometers and fertility apps and months of trawling through Mumsnet forums. Nightmare.

Just Gem's luck not to join a class full of unmarried teenage mothers. She'd been absolutely convinced she wouldn't be the only one minus a bloke – she'd been positively blasé about it, in fact. Then we turned up for the first Parent Craft class (with the same group of people) and it turned out to be full of Couples with a capital C. Even Gem's ego had been slightly dented.

Of course, we weren't mentioning anything like it to Flic. If she asked, everything was beautiful and Gem was having no wobbles whatsoever. Flic was being her most annoying self – having known about the whole issue with James almost before I had.

While Flic and Jonny had been having their posh, romantic Valentine's meal, who should walk in, but James. And his girlfriend.

Oh yes, she was his girlfriend.

Proper and committed and all that.

They'd been seated at the table right behind Flic's, and she'd eavesdropped for most of their conversation. Of course, James had no idea who she was; she could listen in on them in perfect secrecy while poor old Jonny sat there and twiddled with his fork.

Yep, James had definitely brought his actual, bona fide girlfriend out for a posh Valentine's dinner. They'd been having a good old reminisce about their life in Cardiff, and discussing whether the girl was going to move over to Guernsey, whether she could deal with moving to such a tiny place in the name of good old fashioned love. Puke.

I didn't like it revealed that I had, actually, been the 'other woman'. He hadn't been cheating on our semblance of a relationship; he'd been using me to cheat on his actual relationship.

But then again, maybe it meant I had absolutely no reason to feel guilty. I'd had a fling with a guy who already had a girlfriend once before, and although he had pretended everything was over with the girlfriend, I'd known full well that they were still together, if long distance. He probably knew that I knew too, but we just steered clear of the subject. I'd vacillated between cripplingly guilty feelings, and defensive 'well he's told me they've broken up, how am I supposed to know better?'. It had been exhausting, but the sex had been so good I'd been willing to overlook it.

In this case, though, I really did have nothing to feel guilty about – though I was kind of kicking myself that I could probably have avoided all the bother by just adding James on Facebook when I'd first met him. But I genuinely hadn't known about his girlfriend, and I certainly wasn't the kind of person who would march up to her (if I ever saw either of them again) and tell her what her boyfriend had been getting up to while pretending he was free and single.

It was James's problem. Not mine.

And the girlfriend's, I suppose. But I didn't even know her name. Nothing I could really do, even if I wanted to.

Mean? Probably. But you know the old adage: once a man-whore, always a man-whore. If she didn't know what he was like already, she soon would. I'd let her live in blissful ignorance a little while longer. If she'd been my actual friend then yes, I would have told her. But I just wasn't bothered enough to start causing a fuss.

James needn't think he'd be getting any more free lattes from me, mind you.

I couldn't help myself from having a sneaky look at my phone while Nurse of Steel wasn't looking. Nope, no messages from James. There hadn't been since our boring pre-Valentines date, and I was pretty sure I'd heard the last from him. Whether he'd guessed that I'd twigged about his relationship, or he somehow intuited that we'd run our natural course, I didn't know: but I was just the tiniest bit sad that I wouldn't have the chance to have a go at him about his general dickishness without actively seeking him out.

And I certainly wasn't bothered enough to do any active seeking-out.

Meanwhile, Nurse of Steel was extolling the virtues of water births.

"Of course, I run an entirely separate class devoted to the birthing pool," she was saying. "There's only one at the PEH though, so if you want a go of it, you might have to wait your turn!"

"I wouldn't get in one of those fucking pools if you paid me," Gemma whispered. "I've seen One Born Every Minute. When you poo, it floats around and someone has to catch it in a fishing net. That person would have to be you."

"Fuck a duck, spare me!" Catching someone else's shit in a sieve? Ugh, no thank you.

The man-half of the couple in front of us turned around at our whispering and gave me a smirk. Gem brazenly winked at him.

I dug her in the ribs. I'd seen that wink before.

"His wife is right next to him," I hissed as he turned back. Uh oh. Gem had that gleam of acquisition in her eye, the gleam I only usually saw when she had consumed enough JD and Cokes to floor an elephant with elephantitis.

"I'm just window shopping," she hissed back.

"Quiet in the back there, please!" Good lord, Nurse of Steel had ears like a bat. I hoped Man-Half hadn't heard Gem's 'window shopping' comment, too.

I hoped his wife was also blissfully unaware of it. We didn't need any more of that going on.

∗ ∗ ∗

After hours in the Bean Jar a few days later, Gemma was sitting regally above us all on the arm of the sofa, regaling Lizzy and Flic with tales of the Parent Craft classes.

"And then, if you haven't already shat yourself, there's more indignity to come!" she was saying with relish.

Lizzy groaned and put her head in her hands. "I don't want to hear all this! Not yet! I've got years to wait yet!"

"I can't believe you didn't even know you poo when you're having a baby." I prodded her over my bowl of beef stew. "Everyone knows that."

"Everyone *does* it, apparently." Gem nodded sagely, giving her now-considerable bump a friendly rub. "Good thing I have no inhibitions anyway. Anyway, yeah, once the pooing part is over and you've shoved the baby out your chuff, there's more fun! *Stitches*."

"Come on, be fair," I said, as Lizzy went white. She's never been a massive fan of needles. "Not everyone tears."

"Yeah, but apparently when they do, it's gruesome!" Gem was enjoying this far too much. "Some people go all the way from front to back, if you know what I mean."

"Oh, don't!" Lizzy wailed. "I can't take much more!"

"Then follow Aunty Cleo's advice – always use a condom. Forever. Until death."

"Hey, I used a condom with what's-his-name!" Gem put in. "Well, I think I did. Possibly not. Possibly not properly, anyway. And now my punishment is to have my fanny rip like an envelope all the way down to my arse and leave me incontinent for the rest of my days."

She didn't seem particularly shaken by this prospect. In fact, to the outside eye, she seemed downright cheerful. Probably because Nurse of Steel had been careful to reassure the (pale, twitching) pregnant women that this only happened quite so gruesomely a tiny percentage of the time. Lizzy didn't know that, though, and Gem was enjoying tormenting her.

Flic, on the other hand, sitting on one side of the sofa clutching a herbal tea, didn't look bothered in the slightest. Unless you call 'sulky and horse-faced', 'bothered'. For once, she'd come in without her permanent accessory (Jonny) and looked rather pissed off about it. Well, I assumed that was why she was pissed off. He'd apparently had to work late.

I was sure there was something going on with Jonny and work, sure of it. I didn't know whether he had a girl there or what – he didn't really seem the type, but then neither did James. Either way, Flic always seemed grumpier when he was at work and she wasn't. Even on lunches, she'd taken to marching into his office with a couple of low-fat, gluten-free soups from the Jar, and sitting at his desk with him while they ate.

Something really wasn't right. I mean, she'd always been possessive, but at least she used to let the poor bloke eat his lunch unsupervised.

"And then when the placenta comes out, looking like a piece of diseased liver…"

Lizzy shoved her beef stew to one side.

"Do we have to hear all this?" Flic said suddenly, her face like thunder. "It's revolting and we're trying to eat. I have far more important things to worry about than your future continence!"

"Oh?" I said, perking up.

"Yes." All of a sudden, Flic was fully animated again. "The hen night. I've been thinking. I want it tasteful, I don't want any of these strippers and, and, *debauchery.*"

"So… you don't really want a hen night, then?" Gem flopped down onto the sofa, rolling her eyes. Clearly, there wasn't anything worrying Flic. Nothing major. Just the fact that attention had been diverted from her for at least fifteen minutes.

"I do," Flic insisted. "It's all over Instagram – some people are even having fully dry hen parties now."

The rest of us stared at her with horror at the word 'dry'.

Flic quailed slightly. "Well, I might not go all the way 'dry'. I just don't want you lot ruining it with your antics!"

"What antics would those be?" Gem turned to her sister with innocent eyes.

"Well, for a start, you won't be pregnant anymore," Flic pointed out. "You'll be drinking again. And we all know we can count on Cleo for a bit of metaphorical dancing on the tables."

I raised my coffee cup in a salute. "Metaphorical? Literal, please."

"Exactly! If there was a stripper, one of you would sleep with him. Almost certainly."

"I'd be pleased to fulfil that bit, if you do the dancing on the tables." Gem leaned over and solemnly shook my hand.

"Are there even any strippers in Guernsey?" Lizzy asked.

"Fair point." Gem nodded slowly. "We should really look into this."

"I'm sure we could rustle one up," I said. "I could probably train one, there's this one lad I went to school with..."

"Don't start!" Flic had put on her best big sister voice. "There's not going to be a stripper. I wouldn't want that anyway! Greased-up male buttocks gyrating around in my face..." She gave a theatrical shudder, while Gemma and I shared a look of over-exaggerated lust. Lizzy giggled.

"Go on then, what do you want?" I asked.

"I want a tasteful hen weekend," Flic started again.

"Hang on, weekend?" Gem interjected. "It was a night a minute ago!"

"That's the thing," said Flic, her face more lit up than I'd seen it in a while – she must have been due her Botox. "It has to be an entire weekend. There's this lovely hotel I've looked at, with a spa, a Michelin-starred restaurant, a pool, a yoga studio, high in the Tuscan hills, where it's totally peaceful."

"Hang about, Tuscan?" I raised my eyebrows. "As in the same Tuscany that's in Italy? There's not some Tuscany up Torteval I haven't heard about?"

"Of course Italy." Flic laughed with derision. "Where else? It's *the* place for relaxing hen weekends. We'll fly out on the Friday afternoon, have a chilled-out night in the hotel, then get down to spa treatments in the morning."

Gem's face was a picture of disgust. "Spa treatments? People I don't know rubbing smelly stuff all over my body while I'm supposed to go 'ooh'?"

"Sounds like a standard weekend for you." I poked her across the table.

"Oh, shush you. You know what I mean. Plus, remember?" Gem glared at her sister. "Some of us are going to be mothers by then. Remember this?" She gave her belly a somewhat aggressive rub. "I'll have Little Miss Mini-Me kicking and screaming. I won't be able to jet off for a weekend in Italy when my kid's only a few weeks old!"

"Come on, Mum will have the baby, for sure," Flic said in a patronising tone. "And it's not like you're going to be breastfeeding, are you?"

"I might!" Gemma actually had previously said 'I'd rather have sex with John Gollop than suffer cracked nipples', but I wasn't about to remind her of that. "Maybe once she's out I'll go all earth-mother. And then what am I supposed to do? Have the kid hanging off my tit while we're in some Italian hot tub? Take her into the sauna?"

"You'll work something out." Flic waved an arm dismissively. "Now, have you thought about those dresses I WhatsApped you?"

I hadn't even looked at the message. Or the other one. Or the one that came after that. I'd looked at the very first one that arrived – briefly. The 'bold, fashion-forward' bridesmaids' dresses (cream with a pattern of giant poppies) would have made me look like a recently reupholstered armchair. Or possibly a lampshade. I couldn't bear to look at what else Flic had dragged up from the depths of the internet.

"I don't like any of them," Gem said flatly. "I can't picture myself without a bump any more, and all of them would look awful with a baby attached."

"I quite liked that goldish coloured one," Lizzy piped up diplomatically. "The one with the halter neck? I think that's most likely to suit all of us."

I was impressed that the others had even looked at the dresses. The thought of them just made me feel a bit ill.

"See, I would have thought the turquoise would have suited all your colouring," said Flic, wrinkling up her nose.

I wrinkled mine, too. Turquoise! Ugh. Especially if my hair was still purple by that point – though of course it could have changed colour several times by then.

By the looks on Lizzy and Gemma's faces, they felt similarly. Was it a law of nature that brides were not allowed to let their bridesmaids wear what they liked?

"Anyway, those weren't the exact dresses I want, they were just ideas," Flic was saying. "I've been playing with mood boards, of course I have, but I haven't even decided on the whole colour scheme yet – I don't know whether to go for blues and greens, shades of pink, or maybe some transitional autumnal colours."

"Transitional autumnal?" Gem mouthed at me. I shrugged back, just as perplexed. Maybe it was a Pinterest thing.

"But never mind," Flic carried on. "We'll find the perfect dresses when we go to London!"

"Oh, not this again," Gem groaned.

Flic was fairly determined that we'd all be taking a little trip to London before the wedding, to go on a department store crawl in search of these all-important dresses. And she was insisting that we go before Gem's baby was born – "There'll never be time to have them altered if we go after!". There was clearly a lot of faith in Gem losing her baby weight, then.

"I've told you," Flic said. "We're going, and that's all there is to it. I want to go to John Lewis, and Harvey Nichols, and Selfridges, and Harrods – just for inspiration of course, I'm not putting you lot in anything from Harrods."

"Cheers." I infused my voice with as much dryness as I possibly could. "Remind me, why do you want us to be your bridesmaids, again?"

Even Flic looked stumped for a second.

"You're my best friends, of course," she said, the tiniest tremor in her voice. I felt a little bit guilty – just for a second. "I couldn't picture myself walking down the aisle without you three behind me." She paused. "And Denise, I suppose."

After I'd apologised, and she'd left ("Jonathan will be finishing work now, I must go and meet him") Gemma came up with a different explanation.

"We're the only people she knows who she can walk down the aisle in front of, and not be outclassed," she said, taking a cynical sip of Diet Coke. "Have you seen those skinny bitches she works with?" She had conveniently forgotten that, when not pregnant, she was the very skinniest of skinny bitches. "They're stunning. They should be, I think they all live in the gym, and they're all vegan fruitarians, or whatever 'hashtag clean eating' thing Flic thinks is cool this week. I mean, we're not bad. I don't know about this girl from Jonny's work who's been roped in, and at a push, the three of us scrub up pretty well. But still, Flic knows she'll definitely be the most polished person walking down that aisle."

"The lady makes a good point." I nodded as I started to haul chairs onto tables.

"I've got a better one," Lizzy said, getting up to help. "I think she's just asked us because we're the only people she knows she can boss around."

"Ooh, look at you getting all cynical!" I leaned over to pat her proudly on the head. "It's taken me long enough, but you're finally getting there."

"Oh, I'm not being cynical." Was Lizzy blushing? She was definitely avoiding my eyes, staring fixedly at Sarnia Chérie over the coffee bar. "I just don't think Flic's deep enough to need many reasons."

"Right, come on, you two." I clapped my hands in my best schoolteacherly manner. I gave Lizzy a look, but she seemed to have composed herself again. I'd have to ask her some other time. "I have an exciting night ahead of watching telly with my family. Woohoo for me."

"Isn't it Charlie's birthday soon?" Lizzy asked when we were outside in the cold air, linking arms with me as we headed towards North Beach car park, where I'd left my scooter and she'd parked her car – Gem was heading off to the bus station, on the other side of town. We'd both donned as many layers as we could possibly get on; in more civilised nations, the end of February was supposed to signal the first whispers of spring. Ha, not in Guernsey. We were still being buffeted by fierce sea winds, threatening to blow us all along the seafront. I wasn't quite sure how I'd manage to ride my scooter back along that bit of seafront to get home without becoming a very small red aeroplane.

What's more, we were getting fog. Dismal, dreary grey fog, rolling in off the sea and hanging in the air like a damp duvet. You'd have thought the wind might have gone some way towards dispersing it, but Guernsey fogs are as stubborn as its natives. The foghorn, perched on its rocks at the edge of town, was a constant background noise, hooting away in its melancholy, beached-whale wail. Planes were grounded by the fog, and ferries were marooned in the harbour thanks to the wind. Even Gem's dad couldn't get his fishing boat out of St Sampson, most mornings. We really were living on a tiny, island prison: our trip to Finland couldn't seem further away.

"Yeah," I said. "The big one-five. The way he goes on about it, you'd think it was his eighteenth and twenty-first all rolled into one."

"Ahh, remember when we were that age?"

"I remember *your* birthday." I grinned. "Didn't we go to the Bird Gardens? I tried to kidnap an owl so I could pretend I was at Hogwarts and train it to send post. Remember Katie Marlowe letting off party poppers on that big helter skelter slide and you having a panic attack?"

"All part of my mum's desensitisation programme." Lizzy smiled ruefully. "If they try that when my therapy starts, I might have to run away."

"At least it was more exciting than my fifteenth – was it my fifteenth? It might have been my sixteenth. When we went swimming at Beau Sejour with Holly and Lucy, spying on Daniel and Mark and their mates?"

"Yeah, that was your fifteenth. Your sixteenth was the one where we had the daytrip to Jersey and bought the stripy tights."

"God, we were cool. Charlie's been going on and on about this massive house party at Tristan's – you know it's his birthday the day after Charlie's? I was trying to eavesdrop at his door to get some info, and I'm sure I heard them recording for their YouTube channel." I snorted. "I can't find it online yet but I'm going to try, it's bound to be ridiculous."

"What did you say they wanted to call themselves?"

"Last I heard, some riff on love experts."

"Like the trolls in Frozen?"

I barked a laugh. "More like the trolls in the comments section on Vice. Ugh." I rolled my eyes. "What the hell do they think they know about love? You can't judge anything about love until you've done a few rounds in Folies and weeded out the horrors. Though, saying that, I think they're working up to it – I'm sure they're shipping in booze to this party. And who knows what else."

"Really? At fifteen?"

I shrugged. "They start earlier nowadays. Well, some of our lot started that early, if I remember rightly. We just weren't part of that crowd."

Lizzy grinned widely. "It's hard to believe that once upon a time you were one of the innocent ones."

"Tell me about it." I rolled my eyes, then pouted. "Now we're the proper cool ones. Karin Cluster, excuse me?"

"How many of the old school crew do you think can say they've flown all the way to Finland to see a heavy metal band?"

"Well, to see a heavy metal band and to husband-hunt," I reminded her as we approached the car park. "Think of the Leap Year Pact. What happens in Finland might not stay in Finland, if you know what I mean."

Annoying Customer of the Week, Part 5

"Hi, are you all right there?"

"Yes, thank you, just looking at your drinks menu. You know you do a latte?"

"Yes..."

"How many shots of coffee does that have?"

"Two. That's for both small and big, so the small one is actually a bit stronger."

"Do you do it in a medium?"

"No, we do small or big."

"OK. Do you do... decaf?"

"Yep."

"And skinny milk?"

"Of course. Where doesn't?"

"OK. Can I have... did you say the big will be weaker?"

"Yes, because it's a bigger cup with the same volume of coffee, but more milk. I can change the number of shots, though!"

"OK. Perfect. Can I please have a big decaf skinny latte, with just one shot of coffee, please? Actually, can I have it with half a shot of coffee?"

"Um. Yes, of course."

"Oh! And extra hot, please."

"Of course, madam. Two twenty-five, please. Thank you. If you want to take a seat, I'll bring that over for you."

"Thank you!"

As I walked over to Gemma at the coffee bar to deliver the order for one 'Why Bother' aka 'vaguely coffee-flavoured milk, tastebuds-scaldingly hot', I shook my head sadly. That wasn't coffee. That wasn't coffee at all.

Chapter 10

"I've found it! I've only gone and fucking found it!"

"Oh, thank goodness." Zach popped his head over the bannister. "I can't believe you pulled the bloody knob off the milk steamer in the first place, I wasn't going to fork out a tenner for a new one…"

"No, not that." I waved my arm dismissively, staring at my phone screen. I was sitting on the counter in front of the Sarnia Chérie mural, swinging my ankles against the coffee bar. Probably a health and safety nightmare, but at that moment, I really didn't care. "I've found Charlie's YouTube channel!"

"Can you at least look for the steam arm knob?"

"I have." I waved my arm again. "I think it went in the bin."

"*Cleo.*"

"Ahh, shut up Zach. I'll give you the tenner myself." I couldn't tear my eyes from the screen. This was… this was gold.

Ridiculous gold, of course.

But gold nonetheless.

I was going to have a field day with this. Oh, it was definitely not something Mum would ever wish to lay eyes on. If she could even work YouTube at all – and she was the only woman her age I'd met who couldn't or wouldn't even manage Facebook – she'd certainly pass out with horror at the fact her youngest, best-beloved child was running a channel called 'Guerns Gagging For It'.

The potential for blackmail was a deep well, too deep to see the bottom. Splendid. And I hadn't even watched it yet.

If only I hadn't. I couldn't call it 'gold' for long.

"Go on, then." There was a thump as Zach pulled himself up onto the counter next to me. "Let's have a look."

Luckily, it was mid-afternoon, and as usual, the Bean Jar was pleasantly empty. I could turn the volume up all the way, so I could really appreciate the sheer daftness of my little brother.

"Welcome to Guerns Gagging For It," said spotty Adam on the screen. The three of them, Adam, Tristan and Charlie, were sitting on what I recognised as Charlie's bed. "We're just three ordinary teenage boys living on a small island, and we're here to document our quest for true love."

"Aren't they fourteen?" Zach stared at the screen with a look of sheer incredulity "Quest for true love?"

"Fourteen." I nodded. "Nearly fifteen, but still."

Adam finished talking and it was Charlie's turn. "I'm Charlie, and I'm our panel's resident expert." I rolled my eyes as he visibly preened. "I've been going out with my girlfriend for two months and we're very happy. I'm here to give these two tips, and help them on their own personal journeys."

"Oh, this is so stupid." I threw my phone on the counter with a clatter. "It's too cringey. I can't watch."

"I can." Zach picked up the phone with his most evil grin. Charlie was still talking.

"I'm hoping to coach my friends here, and our first big test is coming up at the house party to end all house parties next week, where we're hoping Tristan here will finally get his first kiss..."

"And Charlie might be going one step further..."

"We're going to talk about an age-old conundrum today," Charlie said. "First base, second base, third base. We all know the definition of a home run, but what about the rest? As the most qualified member of Guerns Gagging For It, I'll be explaining..."

"Put it away," I wailed, wrestling the phone back out of Zach's grip. "I just can't." I firmly closed the YouTube window. "This is my little brother. I don't want to know. Eurgh."

I threw the phone across the café so it landed on the sofa.

"I'm starting to see why the steam arm has lost its knob."

"If you don't shut up about that bloody knob, Zachary, you'll lose yours."

"You're such a Slytherin."

"And you're such a Hufflepuff." I hoisted myself off the counter, leaving Zach smiling crookedly as he perched above me. "I feel like I need to wash my hands. I feel like I need to *shower*."

"I might subscribe. Pick up some tips."

"Don't encourage them." I picked up my phone from the sofa, gingerly checking to make sure Charlie's smirking face had been wiped from the screen.

"I thought you were going to use this to your advantage?"

"I still will, if I can," I said. "Like, if Charlie particularly pisses me off I'll make Mum watch it. Then she'll finally see just how innocent her perfect little prince really is and with any luck, I'll get a break from being the family disgrace."

"You're not a disgrace." Zach paused. "Well, unless you count the way you treat my coffee machine. I don't know what it ever did to you, but the poor thing doesn't deserve quite so much abuse. Still, I wouldn't go as far as *disgrace*. Mild irritant, maybe."

"You weren't there the time Mum caught me vomming on her rose bush out of a taxi window."

Zach blinked. "Yeah… I'd think you were a bit of a disgrace if I saw that, too."

"It was a long time ago. I haven't been quite that bad in ages." I waved my arm dismissively, and pottered back behind the bar. Zach hopped off the counter and made for the stairs.

"I'm going to start preparing for the stocktake."

"Don't mention it." I shuddered. "Bloody stocktake. It's not until next week, right?"

"Right. But I might as well get it prepped now while I've got chance."

"Suit yourself. I'd rather eat the wooden stirrers one by one. Then watch Charlie's video again."

* * *

"Four bottles of caramel syrup, four of vanilla, five of hazelnut, and eight of chai. *Eight*? Shit, Zach, you need to stop ordering this stuff. Nobody likes it!"

"But chai is awesome! We just need to advertise it a bit better, try suggesting it to people when they're moaning on about decaf."

"Chai is caffeinated, you dope." I resisted the urge to smack Zach on top of the head with the official stocktaking clipboard (strictly kept in the office for the first Friday in every month).

"Eh, is it? But it's lovely," Zach said, blinking through his glasses, his usually bright blue eyes somewhat bloodshot from all the counting. "I'm sure you can get a decaf version, might look into it, could be a good alternative to decaf coffee. Nothing beats cinnamon."

"Lots beats cinnamon. Like coffee. Good old-fashioned caffeinated *coffee*." I rubbed my own eyes. Counting the individual packets of artificial coffee sweetener had made them itchy. "Come on, we'll liven things up. You take the Earl Grey bags and I'll take the peppermint. First to finish wins."

"I did them already." Zach stuck his tongue out. "What do I win?"

"Respect." I thumped my chest emphatically. "Except technically you finished before the race started, so it doesn't count. So the respect goes to me."

"Not everything needs to be a competition, Cleo."

"Pah, I just like to make things a bit more interesting. How much more have we got?"

"Ugh." Zach made a very sad sound. "Big paper coffee cups, small paper coffee cups, big coffee lids, small coffee lids, stirrers, coffee sleeves, coffee carriers, small soup cups, big soup cups, soup lids, carrier bags, cake boxes…"

"Oh, shush," I groaned. "I always forget about the fucking packaging. I want to go home."

"Well, you can't." Zach gave me a companionable slap on the back. "Come on, we'll have a coffee before we attack the cupboard."

By 'the cupboard' he of course meant the cavernous space that sat under the coffee bar and housed all our spare coffee paraphernalia. From there, we'd have to move onto 'the other cupboard', which had all the carrier bags and stuff for soup. Considering we'd already been counting for a good two hours after the Jar's closing time, we were both getting fed up.

But at least like periods and hangover-free weekends, it only happened once a month.

Being stuck with Zach for a few hours wasn't too bad, really. He at least knew how to take the piss occasionally, far more than when he was in the café most days. Especially when both Gemma and I were at work, he seemed to think he needed to put on the 'I am the boss' face when there were customers around. Even though neither Gem nor I took any notice of his frantic commands when it got busy, sometimes we deigned to pretend. Just to make his ego feel good, you understand.

Though, you know, we really should have had a bit more respect. Zach had given up a lot for the Bean Jar. Not all that long ago, he had been one of the very suits we mocked on a daily basis: working in an office, doing incomprehensible stuff with a computer screen full of numbers. Banking, accountancy, something along those lines. Altogether very, very dull.

Guernsey being Guernsey, despite not coming from the most well-off of families, he'd made quite a bit of money. He'd been good enough at his job that he was offered promotions left right and centre, according to Mrs Machon – forever her grandson's biggest cheerleader.

Promotions, money, whatever. Zach was only working in that soul-sucking hellhole (his words, not mine) so he could save up enough money to fulfil his proper, actual dream. He wanted to open his own coffee shop, on the island he'd always loved. He'd had the spot picked out at the edge of the cobbled street for years, apparently: it was fate when the building became available for lease, just as he reached boiling point with the world's most boring job.

And so in a storm of angry words and papers thrown on the floor (I found that hard to believe but again, his words, not mine) Zach quit his job and snapped up the lease. He did up the place practically on his own, painted the gorgeous mural of clouds above the coffee bar and did an impressive job of overlaying it with the lyrics to Sarnia Chérie, totally freehand. He'd always been keen on art at school but it had never been encouraged, because he'd been so good at maths too.

He persuaded his grandmother that she wanted to spend her retirement baking, went on a course to learn how to make perfect coffees, and hired the first person that wandered past the window to be his assistant manager (me). Well, technically I had an interview. But I was the first person who showed up to be interviewed, and Zach had never done an interview before – he'd only just finished the mural when I came in, and he was both utterly professional and covered in paint. When he spotted the Harry Potter studs I had in one of my ear piercings, he nearly leaped off his chair with joy and started babbling on about our respective Hogwarts houses. He told me the job was mine while the next person was still waiting outside the door. Bless. As soon as we started to get some customers, he hired Gemma, and the rest is history.

What I mean, I suppose, is that what he did takes guts. He chucked in security, prospects, all that guff, so he could follow his dream. Schmaltzy, but true.

Yet sitting in front of me on the Bean Jar sofa, sipping almost nervously at a cappuccino with four shots of espresso while chewing on a piece of nearly-stale Guernsey Gâche, he really didn't look like the 'following dreams' type. He looked more like the 'sits in front of his computer and plays World of Warcraft for eighteen hours a day' type.

OK, that's mean. Not *that* nerdy. Though definitely on the same wavelength. So skinny that you'd think he never ate, instead of running a café and spending half his life sampling its wares; eyes a bit blinky behind his thick-framed glasses – even when we weren't counting every single packet of butter in the shop; mousy hair sticking up in all directions, no matter how often Mrs Machon unexpectedly flew at him from behind the walk-in fridge with a comb. Typically accentuated with a fetching milk-moustache from all the cappuccinos, of course.

I got the feeling he'd always been the same, even back when he was at the Grammar School. It was actually hard to believe he was twenty-seven – if you caught him in the right light (and when he'd just shaved), he could probably pass for about eighteen.

"What do you think about the pie idea?" he was saying, finally wiping the cappuccino foam from his lip. "It seems to work in some of the chains on the mainland."

"Yeah, I think the suits'd really go for it." I nodded. Zach was planning to start serving hot pies and mash at lunchtime, as an alternative to soup, as soon as he could find somewhere he could bulk-buy packets of Smash that we could throw in our soup kettle. The suits would never know the difference, he claimed.

"That's what I think," he said enthusiastically. "We'd have to squeeze in a holding oven, though. And some takeaway boxes for them."

"Ugh, more to count." I pretended to bash my head on the table.

"Ahh, shut up, you'd get to eat them. The pies, not the boxes."

"Good point. Very good point. I'm not averse to a pie or two."

"That's what she said."

"How does that work? Zach, you're shit."

"*You're* shit."

"Get your own insults." I yawned. "Christ on a bicycle, I could just fall asleep right now. Why do we have to count things? Can we just not and say we did?"

"I'm the boss, remember?" Zach practically puffed up. Then suddenly deflated. "Oh, hell, I have to go and compare the clipboard with the computer. Why do I put myself through this?"

"To make sure me and Gem aren't eating all your profits?"

"Yeah, that."

"After all, you never know. Gem might have started craving wooden coffee stirrers."

"I'd love to see that." Zach pulled off his glasses and rubbed his eyes. "Come on, drink your drink. We have work to do."

"Good thing you're bloody paying me for this," I grumbled, taking an obnoxiously loud slurp of my Americano.

"How was your little brother's birthday, by the way?"

"Ahh, fine." I waved my arm. "Cake, too many presents, Mum having a little cry about how 'grown up' he's getting. The usual." I rolled my eyes. "She doesn't know the half of it, between the secret girlfriend and the YouTube channel. *And* he's off at his mate's house tonight, having a 'nice quiet birthday sleepover' if you ask my mum, or the 'house party to end all house parties' if you ask the 'Guerns Gagging For It'."

"I went to one of those once." Zach got a little misty eyed. "A house party to end all house parties. Best night of my life. At least I thought it was, when I was – what was I? – sixteen?"

"Grammar School house parties weren't really my style." I waved my hand loftily. "I was more of a 'Bird Gardens and a burger' kind of girl."

"I was more of a 'let's all play on the PlayStation and talk about hobbits' kind of guy."

"I'd never have guessed." I gave my coffee one final gulp, then got to my feet with some kind of energy. "Right, the caffeine's kicking in. I think."

"That or the four sugars."

"Yeah, that. Whatever. Let's keep counting before I lose it!"

God, stocktake was dull. One of us counting whatever crap it was we had to count, while the other had the honour of writing it on the clipboard (not always Zach; sometimes I'd scowl at him until he relinquished it, with the special pen that wasn't allowed to be used for anything else). We got into a kind of rhythm, boring but somehow deadening the pain in my knees from crouching in front of dusty cupboards.

"You really should give that a clean."

"Shut up, Zach. Clean it yourself."

"I'm supposed to be above all that." Zach put on an overly sanctimonious expression, then grinned. "I'll get a duster. You start on the soup lids. Then – is that it? We'll be done?"

"Yep!" I gave a sigh of relief. "Give me that clipboard, I'll finish up. Do you want a backer up the Grange?"

Zach lived in a little attic flat in one of the tall terraced houses at the top of the Grange, one of Guernsey's larger hills leading out of town. I was very familiar with that hill. To get home, I had to go up it every day, unless I was staying at Lizzy's, but at least I got to zip up it on a scooter. As much as you can 'zip' in Guernsey traffic, anyway. Zach, however, walked up and down it every single day. He didn't have a car; driving was a sore subject with someone who'd failed his test four times, and the distance hardly justified one anyway.

"Yeah, that'd be good," he said, sticking his head out of the 'cleaning cupboard' (under the stairs) and giving me a crooked grin. "Do I have to wear the girly helmet?"

"Well, you're not having my red one just for one measly trip up the Grange."

"Ah, mean. Hang on, I just need to go and whack these numbers into the computer. Give me the other sheets, I'll leave you the clipboard for those last lids."

As Zach clomped up the stairs to his office, I settled down in front of the cupboard, a neat stack of soup lids in front of me. I hummed a Karin Cluster song to myself while I counted, my tongue between my teeth.

Suddenly, I realised I was humming *along* to a Karin Cluster song. 'Night Owl', to be perfectly precise. My ringtone: my phone was ringing.

I looked down at it. Mum. Probably wondering when I'd be home. Ah, it wouldn't be long. I'd see her soon enough.

I let the call go to voicemail. But within seconds, it was ringing again.

Just Mum being her usual paranoid self, that or asking me to bring home any leftover Victoria sponge.

But when the phone rang for the third time, I decided I'd better answer it. For a start, I was sick of the first thirty seconds of 'Night Owl'.

"CLEO!" Mum hollered the second I pressed the green button on my screen. "Answer the phone when I ring you! Oh, I don't know what to do, I don't know what to do!"

"Mum?" I started to say, but I couldn't really get the word in. Shit, she was practically hysterical.

"The sleepover, it wasn't a sleepover, well it was but it was a party, oh... Cleo, you need to get back now, we need to go to the hospital."

"Slow down Mum, what? Hospital? Who? Charlie?"

"Yes, Charlie! I just got the call from the PEH, he's been taken in, they won't say why. He's broken his neck! Or been stabbed! Oh, he's been stabbed, somebody's gatecrashed his sleepover and stabbed him! Or drugs, maybe it's drugs, oh, my baby..."

"Calm down, Mum. I'll be right there." Already, I was scrambling to my feet, cursing my dead legs. And my (possibly dead – surely not?) brother. It would be nothing, surely it would be nothing. Mum was getting all hysterical over nothing. Right?

Shit, maybe it really was serious.

I ended the call with a curt "I'll be there in a minute, all right?" and tore up the stairs. Surely nothing *really* bad had happened?

Though hadn't I been saying it to Lizzy only the other day? We were so much more innocent when we were kids. So innocent compared to all the stories I was seeing in the news; *proper* sex, drugs rock and roll. The kind of stuff I was getting up to when I was way older than fifteen – well, a couple of years older at least. Oh, what if it was drugs? I'd never been interested myself – one slim little joint and I thought I was going to cough up a lung. Clearly, drugs didn't go well in our family. Charlie would have overdosed for sure.

Or maybe Mum was right with the stabbing thoughts. Didn't every teenager carry a knife nowadays? Even in Guernsey, you never knew. Maybe even the boys from Charlie's posh school – their knives were probably just gold plated. And they were hated by the kids in the other schools, who (rightly or wrongly) thought they were all entitled snobs. What if the party really had been gatecrashed? There could have been a fight, Charlie could have been in it. It needn't have been a knife, it might have been a broken bottle.

Oh shit.

By the time I'd thrown myself up the steep staircase to Zach's tiny office, I was out of breath and my head was swimming from all my crazed imaginings. As I flung open the door, I was practically planning my funeral outfit, and what I'd say to the Channel News reporters when they asked me how I felt about knife crime and gang culture.

"Wow, the soup lids are that difficult?" Zach said, not turning round from his computer and long list of numbers. "Give me a minute and I'll finish it off if you're that bothered."

"Zach – brother – hospital – party – now!" I must have made some kind of sense, because Zach went quite a funny colour and shoved his chair back, jumping to his feet.

"Shit, Cleo. Don't worry, calm down. I'll call us a taxi and we can go straight to the hospital." He was already dialling. "The taxi rank will be way too busy on a Friday night. I'll get them to send one to your Mum's as well, we can meet her at the PEH." He turned to me for a second, phone in hand. "Here, sit down." He firmly grabbed me by the shoulder and propelled me onto his desk chair. "Breathe. He'll be fine. Calm down." He carried on gently rubbing my shoulder while he spoke briefly to a local taxi firm.

"How long?" I managed to get out.

"Five minutes," he said, putting the phone down. "We'll wait outside, come on."

"Aren't you going to…?" I gestured to the pile of papers and the computer, the screen still burning brightly with the spreadsheet.

"I'll finish it in the morning. It's fine, honest." Zach grabbed his coat from the wall and whacked the 'off' button on the computer monitor. "Go and get your stuff sorted, I'll lock up."

It's times like that you have to be grateful for a sympathetic boss. I'm sure there aren't that many people who *wouldn't* let their employee rush off early when they're convinced their brother has just been murdered, but there really aren't many who would accompany said employee all the way to the hospital, then let their hysterical mother sob all over them when they arrived.

The two taxis drew up at the hospital at practically the same time. Mum almost fell out of hers, so desperate to be the first through the doors of A&E. Nan stepped out at a more leisurely pace, ever dignified. Seeing her stopped my panic almost at once. She was so calm, it was contagious. All the way to the Princess Elizabeth Hospital I'd been shaking. Zach had grabbed hold of my hand across the backseat, claiming my jitters were setting him off.

But seeing Nan was what really calmed me. All it took was one roll of her eyes in Mum's direction, and I realised how stupid we were both being.

Of course Charlie wasn't bleeding to death in a hospital bed. Of course he hadn't taken a fatal drug overdose.

For a start, it was only quarter past ten. Fatal stabbings and drug overdoses surely only happen in the darkest hours of the early morning. At quarter past ten, you get broken ankles from falling down the stairs. Or suspected appendicitis.1

Or, in the case of my little brother, alcohol poisoning in teens who really don't know their limits.

Apparently, the 'most epic house party in the history of epic house parties' was going to be quite that level of 'epic' because the house in which the party was to be held was to be empty.

As in, empty of parents.

Tristan's entire family had buggered off to a wedding in, of all places, Alderney – Guernsey's neighbouring tiny island. Tristan himself had his Grade 7 piano exam on the Monday, and had promised to stay behind and practise thoroughly for it like a good boy.

Ha. I don't know quite how stupid Tristan's parents actually were, but I could hazard a guess. Who leaves a teenage boy alone for the weekend, the weekend after his birthday? Hell, who leaves a teenage boy alone for the weekend *ever*? Mental.

Half the island's teenage population turned up at the offer of 'free house'. The unholy trinity (Tristan, Adam and Charlie) thought they were the absolute business when they had sixth formers turning up – not to mention *girls*. Charlie might have been the only one of them to have a girlfriend, but she'd come up with the goods and dragged half her year along.

Of course, this necessitated much showing off from our boys. Tristan's dad had kindly left him with two four-packs of cider to last the weekend, surely feeling like a very cool, responsible parent (after all, his friendly neighbour was going to look in and make sure no 'shenanigans' went on). Sadly, Tristan's dad also left his wine rack conveniently full, as well as a nice bottle of vodka in the kitchen.

You might be able to tell Tristan was the eldest child in the family. No precedent.

My mum might have been in the process of spoiling Charlie rotten, but she'd been through enough with me to know there are some things you just don't do if you want your house to still be standing after a birthday weekend.

A few bottles of wine, cans, and vodka wasn't enough for the whole party, of course, but hey, Tristan had said to bring alcohol on the invite that had been Snapchatted around most of Guernsey. I had to assume they all obliged.

Not that Charlie needed it. Having been more or less smothered by Mum all his life, he'd always had everything he wanted. This included any booze he fancied trying; except, having it in reach, he'd never particularly had the urge. But with the pressure to join in at the party, and of course with Charlie being Charlie and wanting to show off as the 'experienced' one of the 'Guerns Gagging For It', he started drinking Tristan's dad's vodka and pretty much didn't stop.

A mere couple of hours later, and my dear brother was puking dramatically into Tristan's kitchen sink (a proper vintage Belfast sink, apparently, and the pride and joy of Tristan's mother). His girlfriend had been there and found it so disgusting she joined in and threw up on the draining board, before fleeing the party with her best friend and screeching that she never wanted to see Charlie again.

This was all very funny until he passed out on the kitchen floor, and all the kids started to panic. The music was getting louder and louder, more and more spotty schoolboys were turning up, and Tristan and Adam couldn't do anything to stop them. They'd had quite a bit to drink themselves, which only led to confuse them even further.

"The last thing I remember is Adam whimpering for his mum," Charlie later said, rather too self-satisfied for my liking.

Thankfully, the day was saved by Tristan's considerate neighbour, who was supposed to be 'keeping an eye out' for precisely that situation. He busybodied in, expecting to find an illicit game of strip poker and a crafty can of cider being passed around. Instead he found a house full of rowdy teenagers, and in the kitchen a posse of terrified just-fifteen-year-olds gathered around my brother, who was pretty much entirely unresponsive by this point.

The neighbour called the police, and an ambulance. The police went to work breaking up the party, and the ambulance carted my brother off to the PEH.

When we were finally let into his grim, curtained hospital cubicle, still in A&E, he was looking rather sorry for himself. He'd already been revived at this point, and was sitting up with a cardboard tray in front of him, his eyes varying between "honest Mum, I'm fine, look how awake I am" and "shit, I'm going to puke", with a bit of "I'm going to pass out again" for good measure. He had a cannula in the back of his hand attached to a drip, and Adam staring at the floor in the chair next to him. Poor Adam had what appeared to be sick on his trousers. I didn't want to know which one of them the sick belonged to.

"Mum and Nan and Cleo," Charlie slurred. "Look this isn't what it looks like honestly it just got out of hand I'm not really drunk..." So clearly going for the 'I'm sober, honest' route, then.

It might have worked a bit better, had he not had to stop mid-sentence to retch into his cardboard tray and have a good groan.

"Oh, my baby!" Mum flung herself across the cubicle and had her arms around Charlie's neck within seconds.

Charlie showed his gratitude for this selfless act of maternal love by vomiting a tiny string of bile down Mum's sensible blouse.

I nearly puked myself, in either sympathy or disgust, I wasn't sure. Luckily Zach was right there to catch me as I nearly spun into the next cubicle in horror.

"Shall we go and get a cup of tea?" he said diplomatically, as Mum realised what that lovely warm feeling was, running down her back.

"Good idea," Nan said crisply, gathering up her sparkly red handbag and straightening the black trilby I'm pretty sure she'd nicked from my wardrobe. "We shall leave them to it."

"Where's the other one?" I had to stick my head back into the cubicle to direct a quick question at Adam. "Your buddy with the free house?"

"Tristan's still at home," Adam said, still staring at the floor, his face very red. "They're trying to get hold of his parents. I don't know what'll happen to him."

Poor Adam's eyes seemed to be filling with tears. Bless. Despite his rugby-obsessed muscles, his YouTube channel, and his carefully styled hair, he was still just a kid. And he was going to be in a hell of a lot of trouble when his parents arrived.

Chapter 11

Whether I was working or not, I was starting to become an actual permanent fixture at the Bean Jar. Even more than usual, I mean. It was starting to get to the point that customers didn't know what to exclaim at first: the gorgeous hand-drawn Sarnia Chérie mural, or the not-so-gorgeous statue of a rather short woman slumped in the corner with a cup of coffee glued to her hand.

The atmosphere at home was toxic, to say the least. Nan was not remotely fazed by Charlie's little incident, of course, taking the time to have a good reminisce about a few scandalous incidents from her own youth. Nothing I hadn't heard before – she'd brought them out many times when I was younger to counter Mum's 'drink alcohol at your peril' line.

"And, of course, there was that time in the Fairy Ring at Pleinmont, when that young Ferbrache lad brought over a crate of beer he'd lifted from his grandfather..."

I could recite them in my sleep.

Mostly, I was pleased that Charlie was OK, and felt it was only right that he had had the hangover from hell the next day as punishment (he hadn't even been kept in overnight).

Of course, it wasn't entirely pleasant trying to get in the bathroom when he was groaning and retching all over it in the morning, but it seemed like karma to me.

Mum, on the other hand, had not taken it quite so much in her stride. Of course, she spent most of that night smothering Charlie to within an inch of his life; holding his sick bucket, clutching him tightly to her bosom wailing about 'evil influences', claiming she'd never let him out of her sight again.

Then, satisfied that her youngest child wasn't going to drop dead in the next couple of hours, she went to bed. And as we all know, everything looks different after a good sleep.

She woke up fuming. I'd not seen her that angry since she caught me with Tyler Le Prevost hiding naked under the desk in my bedroom at the age of sixteen (her face had actually turned purple).

I had the privilege of witnessing the first outburst, Zach having given me the day off. Although he'd seen Charlie's lack-of-death for himself – and had even escorted us home and paid for another taxi, ignoring Charlie's sicky burps – he'd firmly expressed that we were all bound to be suffering from shock, even me. I was not to come into work at all, and if Zach saw me anywhere near the building he'd chase me away with a milk jug.

Fair enough, I thought. Having got over my 'shock' nice and quickly, I just planned to enjoy my unexpected lie in.

Not so. When Mum's door slammed early in the morning, I knew something was going down. I was up like a shot, perching on the stairs between me and Nan's attic and Mum and Charlie's bedrooms. I wasn't surprised to see Nan hovering there too, having beaten me to the best ringside seat: the step with the best view of Charlie's bedroom door.

"How dare you embarrass me like that?" Mum was hissing, standing in the doorway like a centurion, hands on hips. "Barbara from bridge works in A&E, what if she'd seen you?"

"That's what she cares about?" I whispered to Nan. She shook her head and put her finger on her lips.

"She's only getting started."

"You have been so selfish! You know how much you mean to me, you're my special little boy!" If I'd been hungover myself at this point, I would have vomited. "To put yourself in such danger! And I don't know what I've been doing, blaming Tristan. And

Adam! Poor little Adam. He wasn't half as bad as you were, and I wouldn't put it past that father of his to take a belt to him!"

"Probably a bit dramatic, Janet love," Nan murmured.

"I don't know, I've seen Adam's dad, he's like a bloody wrestler."

Mum was still shrieking. "To put it bluntly, Charlie Weeks, you frightened me half to death last night. And your grandmother, and even your sister! This is the kind of behaviour I'd expect from her, not from you!" Oh, thanks Mum. Nan gripped my hand. "Don't try and interrupt me, young man. You've had this coming to you for a long time! I can't believe I've spoiled you so much."

I practically cheered. Nan pinched me to keep me quiet.

Mum closed on an ominous note. "Things are going to change around here, Charlie. I haven't decided what your punishment is going to be," I'd have thought the strength of his hangover would be punishment enough, but Mum clearly had other ideas, "but rest assured. It's going to be good."

With that, Mum slammed Charlie's bedroom door and stalked off downstairs.

I could only imagine the effect that had on his hangover.

For the next week, Charlie was on lockdown.

No rugby, no trips into town with the boys, no going round to Adam's to 'study' (and definitely not to Tristan's).

There was no way any 'Guerns Gagging For It' videos were going onto YouTube – not when all three 'love experts' were practically under house arrest. Mum caught Charlie attempting to film a quick explanatory video on his phone, and she took it away. Worse than anything else, she put a password on the WiFi and practically had to be threatened with murder to even let *me* near it.

Mum was barely talking to Charlie, at all – I couldn't work out whether she'd finished concocting punishments or if she was still only revving up. She was taking the whole thing very hard. And I wasn't sure she had it in her to keep being so frosty.

To me, yes. I'd seen that before. But I wasn't so sure about Golden Boy.

Mum had always been a bit 'special' about Charlie. Any amateur psychologist could tell it must have been something to do with our fathers – mine buggered off before I was even born and was never seen or heard of again, whereas Charlie's stuck around for a while and still stayed in sporadic contact. Out of the two, it had to be admitted that Charlie's had probably been the better bet.

Of course, I'd known Charlie's dad fairly well: Brian had not only been the stepdad who stuck around the longest out of Mum's few and far between relationships, but he was definitely the coolest. He was a tall, handsome pilot, ex-Army, and incredibly well-paid. Sadly for Mum, his career meant he had a built-in excuse to zoom off for days at a time with what turned out to be a long string of pining women. But at least when the inevitable divorce was done, when Charlie was four and I was fourteen, he kept in touch, and even sent decent maintenance payments.

Charlie had been his spitting image since the moment he was born: lanky, blonde and with a cheeky grin. I've always looked like a younger version of Mum with eyeliner and a better haircut, but Charlie might as well not have been part of our family, as resemblances went.

Mum must have liked being reminded of her dashing ex-husband a lot more than she liked being reminded of herself. Or, more to the point, how I might look like her but that was where the family resemblance firmly ended.

It made an interesting change not to have her tiptoeing around the house, picking up every dirty sock Charlie left behind and practically wiping his arse for him.

The problem was, she was instead stamping around like a bona fide black cloud (if black clouds were dressed by Per Una), glaring at anyone in her path. None of us were immune. Instead of taking some of her misplaced Charlie-affection and spreading it between me and Nan, she just got worse, snapping at pretty much everything we said instead of just the usual sixty percent of it.

Nan took to spending most of her time with her cronies – her Lizzy and Gemma, two old ladies called Joyce and Pat who could give Nan a run for her money in the 'bonkers' stakes.

And Mum was far too preoccupied with potential punishments for Charlie to pay much attention when Nan decided her chosen branch of the Women's Institute was getting a bit tame for her liking.

"Crochet!" she expectorated, marching into the house in high dudgeon one evening. I was microwaving a Pot Noodle in the kitchen, trying to make myself as small as possible to avoid Mum's ire as she noisily washed up at the sink.

"Um... crochet?" I raised my eyebrows.

"Yes, crochet." Nan flung her sequinned blue beanie onto the kitchen table and started unwrapping the leopard print scarf from around her neck. "They're trying to get me to crochet."

"Crochet is lovely," Mum piped up fiercely. "I thought you loved that tea cosy I crocheted for you?"

"It was beautiful, Janet, dear," Nan said, rolling her eyes at me. "You were eleven, though. They're trying to make me join their crochet circle and I tell you, it's just so dull!"

"Sounds it," I put in, pulling out my steaming pot of e-numbers.

"A circle of old dears nattering about the war and making doilies. Half of them weren't even here for the war, and the rest of them were barely children. They tried to have a sing-song of Sarnia Chérie today, but nobody knew the words past 'Sarnia Chérie, gem of the sea'. Amateurs." Nan stomped over to the microwave and gave my noodles a sniff. "What are these, dear? Are there any left for me?"

"Have these, I'll do a fresh pot." I grinned at her as she slumped into a chair like a sullen teenager and started spooning noodles into her face.

"The quality of biscuits has gone right down in that place too," she said through a hot mouthful. "When it's my turn I bring Bourbons, or Custard Creams. *Fig Rolls* we had today. Fig Rolls! Ugh."

Suddenly, Charlie poked his head around the door. I hadn't even heard him come downstairs – he must have been practising his 'I'm a sorry waif who never has fun' waft around the house.

"Mum," he began, his voice high-pitched and childlike. "I was wondering about tomorrow, with the match at Grammar..."

"No!" Mum barked, flinging a plate into the sink with unnecessary vigour. "I told you, no rugby!"

"But it's really important..."

"I said no!" She chucked the tea towel on the worktop. "Have you finished that essay? No? I thought not."

She dragged him back up the stairs, grumbling all the way.

"She needs to be careful with that boy." Nan shook her head slowly, jingling slightly from the heavy silver chains around her neck. "They're going to end up with a very twisted relationship at this rate." She shrugged and went back to the Pot Noodle.

"So what are you going to do about the WI?" I put my new Pot Noodle in the microwave. "Are you going to try another branch?" That's what she'd done the last time she got bored.

"No, they're all the same," she sighed. "They're all as bad as one another."

"You could always start your own."

I'd meant it as a throwaway comment, but Nan sat up straight, her eyes sparkling.

"I could, couldn't I?" She narrowed her eyes and gave me a contemplative stare. "We could have sherry at the meetings. Or Prosecco. And we could have club nights!"

"As in…?"

"I'm bored with tea dances and cake mornings. I want to dance to Rihanna!"

"You could always just go to Folies."

"No, no." She shook her head decisively. "I think the shock might finish off Pat once and for all. But if we organised it ourselves… yes."

"Actually this could be kind of fun." I thought for a moment. "Instead of making jam, you could make gin!"

"Perfect!" Nan smacked the kitchen table in delight, nearly sending her Pot Noodle flying. "And no more of those sad bingo afternoons. Poker nights!"

She shoved her chair back from the table and stalked away up the stairs, abandoning her Pot Noodle. I shook my head and started eating my own. With anyone else's grandmother, this would just be a passing fancy that never got realised… but I doubted it with Nan.

While Nan spent her days being important and organisational on the phone to every old bat in her extensive Old Bat Network, I retreated to the Bean Jar.

My caffeine intake was getting so high, if you sliced open one of my veins you'd probably be able to drain pure espresso.

It came as a bit of a shock when, one day, minding my own business with a slice of Guernsey Gâche at the table hidden practically behind the stairs, something rather odd happened. I wasn't working: I was just escaping the clouds of gloom permeating my house, and it was too cold to be zooming off around the island on my scooter.

I'm pretty sure Gemma had forgotten I was there; she'd just got through the afternoon tea rush, and she was dealing with the bar while Zach raced around clearing the upstairs tables. She didn't even think to look at me when Man-Half walked in.

Man-Half. He'd been part of the Pregnant Posse we'd run into at the Parent Craft classes; the one who'd found our messing about at the back of the class somewhat amusing. One half of a couple; a very pregnant couple.

I raised my hand to wave to him, then quickly put it back down again. He was alone: definitely no woman-with-bump trotting in behind him. And he had a purpose. He wasn't dawdling in the doorway, looking for a coffee. He was marching up to the bar, ignoring the queue so he could lean over the coffee machine and say something to Gem in a very low voice. No matter how much I strained, I couldn't hear what he was saying, but it looked... urgent.

And was she blushing? *Gemma*?

The people in the queue looked irritated as Man-Half whispered a stream of – something – in Gem's ear, while she went quite a funny colour.

Then just as suddenly as he'd appeared, he was sweeping out of the door again, just giving me two seconds to catch a look at him as he struggled to haul the door open against the windy day outside.

I'd not really looked at him before; why would I need to? He was just a bloke. Man-Half. Part of a clearly committed couple – committed enough to be having a baby, at any rate. I wasn't exactly attending Gem's Parent Craft classes to make friends, after all. I was there to support her, and laugh at Nurse of Steel.

Man-Half wasn't bad looking. Not my type... though he did appear to have a tribal tattooed sleeve which automatically scored him a point or two. He wasn't wearing a coat, despite it being categorically fucking freezing, for March. He had quite a big head, though it probably just looked bigger because it was shaved. If it really was a big head, and it was genetic, I felt bad for Woman-Half.

No, he wasn't bad looking in the traditional sense. The face underneath the shaved head (and two sizeable ear tunnels, maybe another point scored there) was distinctly chiselled, a smattering of stubble emphasising his defined jawline. His eyes were narrowed against the wind as he stepped back onto the high street. Maybe this was what made him look a bit – dodgy.

Or maybe it was just the story I was maniacally concocting for him in my head. But something about him, *something*, just seemed a bit... bad.

I'm sure most people would automatically say that about *my* ideal men. Usually covered in tattoos, long hair, pierced up to the eyeballs... metal types. Though other than the tattoos and tunnels, this one didn't seem like a 'metal' type. He just seemed like... something else.

I wasn't going to let it lie. As soon as Gem had cleared her (huffing) queue, I was over at the coffee machine in a single bound.

She nearly jumped out of her skin.

"Shit, I forgot you were there," she said, clutching at her chest dramatically. "Do you want another drink? Americano?" Without waiting for my answer, she turned to the coffee machine and started busily pressing the espresso button. "I'm out of ceramics, dishwasher's on the blink again, you'll just have to put up with a take-out cup. You know, I've had about ninety old ladies this morning go for my neck because the dishwasher can't cope."

"Shut up, Gem," I said briskly, putting my hands on my hips. "What's going on with you and Man-Half?"

"Who?"

"You know who! The man-half of Parent Craft couple! The bloke who just came in ten minutes ago and made you blush!"

"Oh, him." Give her her due, Gem wasn't blushing now. Admittedly, she was staring very hard at that coffee machine. "Well, you've been too busy to come to the classes with me lately..."

"I had to work!"

"Yeah, I know, whatever. But while I've been on my own, I've gone and sat with him and his wife. He's called Aaron, actually, and his wife is called Meredith. They're very nice people."

"So what was that all about then, just now?"

"He's been having some problems, that's all." She shrugged, still maintaining careful eye contact with the coffee machine. "Him and Meredith."

"Oh, shitting hell," I groaned. "You've shagged him, haven't you?"

"No," she protested, finally actually looking at me. Then she dropped her gaze. "Though that's not to say the thought hasn't crossed my mind."

"Gemma! Married man! Baby on the way! Talk about 'alert'!"

"I know, I know, that's why I haven't said yes!"

"He's actually *propositioned* you? What exactly has been going on?"

"OK, OK, I'll tell you." Gem looked around shiftily. "Just make sure Zach's not listening, OK? I don't exactly want everyone to start, like, judging me." She thrust my drink at me then huffed and puffed around the bar, leading me back to my quiet table under the stairs and picking up my discarded Gâche for a nibble. "The class before last, Meredith couldn't come – it clashed with her flower-arranging exam or something. Aaron was supposed to be taking notes for her, but we ended up just chatting through the class. Then he started WhatsApping me."

"How did he have your number?"

"Meredith had it." She waved a hand. "Nurse of Steel made us all swap numbers so we'd all have a 'mummy hotline'." She rolled her eyes. "Bullshit. But yeah, we started talking, just on WhatsApp, no big deal. Just, like, chatting. Then he asked me to go for coffee, so we did. Not here, obviously, we went to Costa."

"Traitor."

"Shut up. We just talked for ages and ages, it was like we'd known one another for years. He confided so much in me... you know, he's not one hundred percent sure Meredith's baby is actually his. They had a 'break' a few months back, she pissed off to India or, I don't know, like, Tibet or somewhere to 'find herself', came back, then the next thing he knew, two lines on the piss-stick."

"This all sounds remarkably fishy." I raised my eyebrows. "All 'my wife doesn't understand me' kind of shite."

"I don't know, Cleo," Gem said slowly. "I kind of... I think I kind of believe him. Meredith just seems the type. Like the kind of person I'd get along with and go on nights out with if we weren't both knocked up. So yeah, we had this coffee, and this long chat, and then... he kissed me."

"What?"

"When we were leaving. He thanked me for being such a good listener." She snorted. I understood why; 'good listener' isn't usually high on the list of her personal qualities. "Then he came to hug me, and I let him, then he went to kiss me on the cheek. Then it kind of turned into a proper kiss."

"Christ on a bicycle." I groaned again.

"Since then we've been talking a lot more, we've been Snapchatting, and he's asked me to come away with him when he next has to go to the mainland for work. To be honest, I'm kind of considering it."

"I can't believe you're even letting this guy come near you, Gem," I said. A married man with a baby on the way? Had *her* baby eaten her common sense?

And the way she'd been blushing! Something he'd said had clearly got to her. Or something about him. Gemma really wasn't the blushing type – she was far more likely to kick a guy in the balls before she'd let him make her cheeks go red.

"I know, I know." All of a sudden she looked fairly wretched. "I've been talking to the guy for what, two weeks? And I'm considering, like, running away with him? What's fucking wrong with me?"

"And he has a wife and a foetus," I reminded her.

"Well, yeah. But when has that been a particular impediment?"

146

"I thought the point of you starting this whole Leap Year Pact was to get you a decent father figure for your baby?" I pointed out. "Surely you don't want to go running off with someone who's clearly being a shit father to his own kid before it's even born."

"Yeah, but like I said, it might not even be his. He really doesn't trust Meredith, apparently she's been going all crazy."

"Gem, *you've* been going all crazy. It's called being pregnant. She's probably done absolutely sod all wrong, he's just being a dick."

"You don't know him... oh shit, what am I saying?" Gem dropped her head into her hands. "*I* don't know him. I have no idea what I'm doing, but you know what? I like him." She lifted her head up with a defiant glare. "I really do. I'm going to see what happens. Maybe I'll go away with him, maybe I won't. I'll think about it. You only live once."

With that admirably clichéd sentiment (at least she hadn't said 'YOLO'), she got to her feet and marched back over to the coffee bar (it would have been more dramatic if she hadn't had a customer waiting impatiently for someone to turn up and make their latte).

Right. I took a contemplative sip of my Americano.

It looked like I'd be needing to keep a bit more of an eye on Gem, make sure she didn't do something incredibly stupid.

This Aaron sounded like an arse to me. Come on. Who in the world still falls for the whole 'my wife doesn't understand me' thing? 'I don't think the baby is mine' is surely the next stage up from that. He'd just seen a rather attractive younger woman, was having some kind of crisis with the missus, and decided he'd go after said attractive younger woman. Possibly using her rather vulnerable situation to try and worm his way into her maternity knickers. A predator, that's what he was.

Right, that was it. I vowed that from then on, I would make more of an effort to get to every one of Gem's Parent Craft classes and pretend to be a fierce lesbian.

Chapter 12

"Ooh look, a snow castle! Cleo, look! Snow castle, snow castle!"

"A what? What the fuck is that?"

"It's a hotel made of ice! And snow! It's all made of snow!"

"Will you two give it a rest?" Gemma sighed, leaning back on my bed.

For once, we were doing our pre-drinks at my house instead of Lizzy's. We fancied a change. And, more to the point, Gem fancied a nose at the ongoing Mum-and-Charlie situation – yes, still ongoing, despite nearly a month having passed since the great alcohol poisoning incident. It was bizarre. Charlie was looking increasingly more horrified by the day, panicking that things were never going to return to normal and he'd actually have to pick up his own socks for the rest of his life.

It had been a busy few weeks.

Lizzy, of course, was blissfully free for a change. Yes, it was the start of the Easter holidays, and Lizzy's class of little monsters (or angels, to hear their parents talk) had been let loose upon the world.

To celebrate the season, Lizzy had started her anti-balloon therapy. Or, to give it its proper title, cognitive behavioural therapy: quite a serious business. She was spending much of her holiday locked in her flat contemplating the ins and outs of her mental health. Fun stuff, apparently.

She was so sick of it she'd practically cried demanding to be let out for a night out – I don't think she realised that she was allowed to keep living her life while therapy was going on. I was only glad that Dan seemed to have got the 'bugger off and never come back again' message when Lizzy threw him out of her flat on Valentine's Day. He hadn't been seen or heard of since, and Lizzy had been doing so well at rebuilding herself.

For all we knew, Dan was probably off having a cosy little foursome with wobbly-boobed Lucinda, and James and his little blonde girlfriend. Since Valentine's Day, he'd also vanished off the face of the planet. The girlfriend must have decided Guernsey was the place for her after all, and James needed a clean slate. Or she'd found out what he'd been up to in the dark recesses of Folies and had dragged him back to Wales. I couldn't really find the energy to be bothered, to be honest; he hadn't even shown his face in the Bean Jar and I was pretty sure he'd blocked me on Instagram.

Lizzy might have been free (ish), but the rest of us didn't have half as much luck. With the Easter holidays upon us, the Bean Jar was as busy as the front door of Purgatory. If you came in over lunchtime, you were lucky to find a spare corner to stand in, let alone an entire table.

Thanks to the schools kicking out, the Jar had been overrun by families. Zach had been forced to squeeze a couple of extra high chairs into the building, just to stop the parents from whining. Not a day went by when I didn't have to evict some curious small child from trying to climb into the milk fridge, and it seemed like I spent half my life in a comical dance around the café, dodging prams, feet, and screaming toddlers throwing tantrums.

Utter bliss.

Note the sarcasm.

Oh, the joy of being one of those cafés that appeals to all ages. Zach kept coming out of his office and blinking at his flourishing business with joy, proud of what he had achieved. Of course, this pride only ever lasted for a few minutes, as one of us would spot him and drag him down to the bar to do some actual hard labour.

I'd hardly had any time to talk to Gemma, and I definitely hadn't been able to get to the Parent Craft class and pretend to be a lesbian. I hadn't seen Aaron since that day he'd marched into the Jar and made Gem blush, though that wasn't to say he hadn't been around. Every time I got the chance to even mention him to Gem, she just clammed up.

All I could get out of her was that yes, they were still in contact and yes, she was still considering his offer.

My only consolation was that Gem was getting huger and huger by the day. With only two months to go until her due date, she was a veritable garden shed in size, and people kept patting her and asking her if she'd gone overdue and when she was going to be induced.

It was never a pretty situation when those questions came up.

But hauling around a bump the size of a hot air balloon and the associated annoyances and discomfort seemed nothing but a good thing to me. It meant she was less and less likely to hop across to the UK with Aaron for a weekend of unbridled passion, or whatever the kids are calling it these days. She definitely didn't feel sexy.

Getting ready for our night out, in my tiny attic bedroom, she'd abandoned all her sultry bodycon dresses of a couple of months back, though she was still far from giving in to the maternity 'smocks' she hated so much.

"Nothing suits me at this size," she moaned, holding up her phone for a selfie and pouting critically at her own face. "I'm a whale and there's nothing more to it. In fact, even my skin looks like it's growing barnacles." She prodded the cluster of spots that seemed to have sprung up around her chin overnight. "It's going to be a super-strength foundation night, that's for sure."

"Tell me about it," I said softly, running my hand almost unconsciously over my lumpy neck. Was it my imagination, or was my 'Adam's apple' still getting bigger? Was I actually turning into a man? Would I have to start calling myself Leo instead of Cleo? I'd have started to panic if I'd started getting hairier, or if my voice had been getting deeper, but it actually seemed like I was going a bit high-pitched and hoarse every so often. And that lump... I was noticing it more and more often while I was putting my make-up on. I briefly wondered whether I should be worrying about it, then remembered that worrying isn't my style.

"At least it's not like when you had the morning sickness," said Flic, who had graced us with her presence for a change. She wasn't even pretending that she was coming out with us for fun; she admitted she wouldn't be there if Jonny wasn't going to be in town too, on a night out with some work mates. "Your skin was the colour of a whale's then too. You know, you're lucky really. Some women get the sickness all the way through their pregnancy."

"Maybe I'll get even luckier," Gem growled. "And when you get pregnant, you'll be one of them."

"Of course not!" Flic shuddered. "Heaven forbid."

I could see the horror on her face. I knew she wanted kids with Jonny one day – the perfect two point four children to go in the perfect house that came with the perfect job and the perfect marriage, of course.

However, I don't think she'd realised quite how gross pregnancy could really be until the day her beloved sister dropped a Tupperware container full of sick at her feet, tripping over on the way to the bathroom.

"Please, please don't start talking about poo and tearing again," Lizzy begged, nearly drawing a line of silver eyeliner down her face. She'd managed to tear herself away from the website showing the Kemi Snow Castle. We'd established it was too awkward for us to get to on our holiday without hiring a car, sadly, but it was fun to look at the pictures.

"Nah, I don't want to think about it right now." Gem grimaced.

"Ooh, that reminds me!" Flic perked up no end. "I found this website that does the most gorgeous designer clothes for you to wear in labour."

"Designer clothes... to wear in labour." Gemma raised her eyebrows so high they nearly vanished into her hairline – which would have been a shame, as she'd just spent nearly half an hour and several different products making them beautifully 'on fleek'. "Have you not been listening when I've told you what's going to happen to me?"

"No, no, look." Flic whipped out her iPhone and started tapping madly at it. "You can get customised hospital gowns. They're beautiful material, and so convenient! There's a hole in the front so they can get a monitor set up, and they're cut low in the back for an epidural, if you're going to go for that."

"I am," said Gem, at the same time I firmly said "she is." The more drugs the better, in Gem's opinion. If Nurse of Steel had taught her nothing else, she'd taught her that.

"Well then, these are perfect! Look." Flic brandished the iPhone, and we all leaned in.

"Good – God," said Gem after a second.

Lizzy and I just laughed.

"Can you see Gem in one of those?" I snickered. "She'd look like she was lost from, from… Victorian pornography!"

"Aww, I quite like it." Lizzy giggled. "It's sweet."

"But they're so… floaty." I snorted. "Listen to this – 'I want to be pretty in all situations'. Seriously?"

"What's so funny?" Flic asked, frowning. "Surely it's not beyond the realms of possibility to look good while you're having a baby?"

"I was watching some birth vlogs," Gem admitted. "And, like, 'what to pack in your hospital bag' videos. Just for inspiration. And some of these daft cows take make-up and straighteners with them!"

Flic blanched. "Why wouldn't you? Don't you realise there's going to be photos?"

"I love Instagram as much as the next person." More, some might say, having witnessed the sheer number of selfies on Gem's camera roll. "But the thing is, with all the blood and poo and fucking medical professionals with their hands up my chuff, I'm really not going to give a shit," Gem explained, flatly.

"Come on, it's not going to be that bad…" Flic began.

"It is," the rest of us chimed in together.

While Gem launched into a repeat performance of the blood-and-guts Tales From The Abyss (literally), I whacked down my laptop, shutting off all the beautiful pictures of Finland, and started getting ready myself.

I was back to my standard black and purple lacy dress, the one with a single sleeve. All the dresses with zips were starting to get a bit too tight for me, really. I didn't really know why. I hadn't been eating any more than usual, not that I'd noticed, anyway.

Lizzy, on the other hand, seemed to have weight falling off her. If the break up and failed reconciliation with Dan had done one thing it had sparked up her enthusiasm for her own body and she was taking better care of herself than she had been in years.

She was braving the gym a couple of times a week – even with Flic's domineering presence hanging about, occasionally threatening to become her personal trainer or drag her bodily into the yoga studio – and claimed to just not fancy chocolate very often. Strange woman, but it was showing. Her skin was glowing and rosy, and her curves were becoming way more defined, a proper hourglass instead of an apple.

She had such a spark to her, if I didn't know better I'd say she was in love.

Well, we'd soon fix that, I thought, mentally rubbing my hands together with glee while I slicked on the liquid eyeliner. We'd find a nice Finnish man for her in Oulu and they could have beautiful blonde babies happily ever after.

"Hurry up," Gem moaned, Flic having dispatched herself downstairs to collect some more wine; quite possibly to escape Gem's tales of mucous plugs and placentas. "I want to go out dancing before I run out of energy." She hauled herself up off the bed, steadying her bump as she went. "Baby Girl is dancing already, look." She hitched up her dress in a way that would be fairly obscene if we weren't her best friends.

It was so weird. If you looked closely enough at Gem's bulging belly (a few reddish stretchmarks only just starting to appear; according to Nurse of Steel she was immensely lucky not to be covered in them, having been so skinny) you could just about see the skin shifting and stretching when the baby moved about. Apparently before too long we'd possibly be able to distinguish hands and feet. I couldn't imagine it; far too creepy.

"You have to start thinking of names, you know," Lizzy said. "You can't call her Baby Girl forever."

"Though 'Baby Girl' is far better than 'the thing'," I pointed out.

"I've had a few ideas," Gem said, pacing backwards and forwards across my rug, trying to reactivate the dead leg she had from sitting down for too long. "I want it to be original, you know?"

"Then don't call her Olivia, for the love of God," I said, blinking away my stray mascara clumps. "Every other little girl who gets dragged in the Jar seems to be called Olivia."

"Or Lily-Rose," Lizzy put in. "I've got one of those in my class, well, nearly, her parents banned the hyphen."

"I kind of liked the name Lily, but you're right," Gemma said. "Too boring. I want something interesting. Like... like... Cinnamon! Or Nutmeg!"

Lizzy and I looked at one another for a second, then chorused "No."

"Why not?"

"Those are things you put on a cappuccino if you're too 'adventurous' for chocolate," I commented. "Not names."

"But they're cute! Or how about... Lexie! With an 'e' on the end, of course. Or Lacey..." Gemma wandered over to where a skylight had been cut out of my ceiling, peering out at the St Peter Port sky with an air of contemplation. "Though maybe they're getting a bit too popular, too," she mused.

"Yes," I agreed with her quickly. "Very much so."

"You could use Lexi, if you make it short for Alexandra," said Lizzy. "Names that are actually nicknames just look wrong on a birth certificate, you should use a proper classic then just shorten it every day."

"Ugh, but 'Alexandra' is just so boring."

"No, it's classic. Can you imagine a high court judge called Lexie? She'd have to be a stripper," Lizzy said sternly.

"Harsh," I felt the need to point out.

"Oh, all right, maybe not that extreme. Then again, we've got the total opposite in my class. None of them would be able to be a stripper if they wanted to. Let's see, who have I got? Clementine, Wilhelmina – never allowed to be shortened, by the way, her mum came in and made an official complaint when the poor child's friends dared to call her Will – Harriet, Claudia, Lavender, Hermione..."

"Much as I love her, JK Rowling has a lot to answer for," I said.

"Too right." Lizzy grimaced. "You should hear the boys' names they've got down at Beechwood. Honestly, who looks at their newborn baby and goes 'yes, that's it, he's a Neville?"

"It could be worse, just think, Nan's generation had the likes of Norman and Walter," I pointed out.

"Oh, I know a Walter!" Lizzy rolled her eyes. "He's about three months old, my cousin's third baby. Disturbing."

"Yeah, definitely not going for an old lady name." Gemma shook her head firmly. "I like the name Angel... ooh, or Honey. Or Sugar."

"Stripper, Gem, stripper," I sighed.

"Well, she's got me as a mother, if genetics are anything to go by she won't be far off."

"Speaking of which – little bet for the night, Gem?" I waved my glass in a way that I think was supposed to be enticing (a couple of drinks in and it was hard to be sure). "We haven't had a 'who can pull the most randomers' competition in ages."

"And we won't," Gem said sternly. "Number one, I'm wearing a tent and have a belly the size of a beach ball. Number two, I'm not drinking, which gives you a major advantage. No more pulling contests until Baby Angel-Cinnamon is out, thank you very much. Then I'll be very happy to go full-on stripper with you."

"Not *full-on* stripper, I don't think Folies could take it."

"Your grandmother is making sequinned purple sashes." Flic came slowly back into the room, balancing two bottles of wine and a bowl of nuts. "Should I ask?"

Bless her, Flic had really tried to fit in with us for that night out. Instead of her favourite muted designer outfits, she'd been shopping especially to find something more 'high street' to go in her wardrobe. Her raid on St Peter Port culminated in of a pair of black sequinned high-waisted hot pant shorts, and a cream vest with studs on the shoulders. I was proud, actually. If I was as skinny and toned as she was, I'd wear something similar.

Of course, it didn't really go with her expression: vacillating somewhere between excitement at a good girly night out and complete and utter disgust that she was being forced to go to Folies. With her little sister.

"Nan's forming her own branch of the WI," I explained, helping myself to one of the bottles of wine. "Except the WI won't have them so she's making up her own rules. And a uniform. So far it just consists of the sashes, but I have a horrible feeling there are hats coming."

"OK…" Flic nodded slowly, trying to work out if it was below her middle-class sensibilities to judge Nan for having more of a life than she did. "What were you saying about strippers?"

"Your sister is trying to work out which stripper-name to call your niece," I said, very matter-of-factly. Flic's expression turned to full-on disgusted.

"Oh good lord, please tell me it's not going to be something like Tutu or Christmas or, or, *Poopoo*…"

"Ooh, Flic, Christmas would be such a good name!" I wasn't sure whether Gem was being serious or not. It was very hard to tell. "After all, she was conceived not long before then, she could be Chrissie for short."

"No." Flic thumped the wine onto my desk and glared sternly at her sister. "Don't you bloody well dare. It's very in vogue to go for older names, old fashioned ones. You don't want her left out when all her classmates have popular names, do you? You want something like Edith or Ava or Ida."

"Edith or Ava or Ida?" It was Gem's turn to look disgusted. "I'm giving birth to a baby, not a ninety-eight-year-old woman."

"How about a family name, then? You could call her Davina, after Mum. Or Daisy, after Gran. Or Felicity, after me!"

"Like that's going to happen."

"It's actually a very nice name, thank you very much."

"Will you two stop arguing and start drinking?" I interrupted. "At least, Flic start drinking. Gem, drink your Diet Coke and shut up. I want to get out."

* * *

It was the first time any of us had been out with Flic in quite a while – quite possibly since that infamous occasion where Gemma and I both pulled the same one of Flic's colleagues. It was definitely the first time since she and Jonny had officially got engaged. It was quite a revelation.

She was wearing that rock on her left hand like it was a weapon of war. It took quite a while before Jonny and his group of mates managed to gravitate to Folies, so we were just an average (ish) group of girls for a while. And, of course, when average groups of blokes see average (ish) groups of girls, they have one thing in mind: chatting them up. This little phenomenon is, of course, greatly increased when one member of the group of average (ish) girls is wearing sequinned hot pants and no tights.

We were inundated. Their curiosity got piqued by the rather large pregnant woman wearing a tent-like leopard print dress (cinched in at the waist with a handy little gold bow, just to prove it was a pregnancy-belly and not just alarmingly localised weight gain), and said curiosity got hooked by the sequinned hot pants dancing next to her.

Me and Lizzy only had to look at one another to know we were both making the same silent vow: if we ever wanted to pull again, don't let Flic wear that outfit.

Especially as, ninety percent of the time, she really wasn't appreciating all the attention. She spent the first half of the night leaning against the wall, her face sulky as a spoilt child's, her arms crossed in front of her with her engagement ring in full view. It didn't stop every local troll in the club from trying it on with her, though.

This, of course, was typical Flic behaviour. We didn't expect anything more, or anything less. We were just happy to chat to her reject blokes, when they weren't too revolting.

It was after a few more drinks that things started to get weird.

Not with every man – of course, there were still a fair few trolls knocking about – but with some of them, Flic was being nice.

Dare I say it, Flic was flirting.

Not in the brazen way her sister did it (or I did it, for that matter), but in a very subtle, eyelash-batting kind of way, she was definitely having a flirt. Looking down at the floor then looking up at the bloke through her eyelashes, shy smiles, the occasional tentative touch of the arm, all that kind of thing.

Gem and I exchanged a look of no small alarm when we realised, at one point, that Flic was actually keeping her arms crossed the other way, so her engagement ring was hidden, tucked firmly under her elbow.

Hang on. This wasn't what was supposed to be happening: she was supposed to be waving said ring in every bloke's face and proclaiming her 'future Mrs Jonny'-ness to the whole of St Peter Port.

"This really isn't right," Gem murmured in my ear. "We're going to have to step in."

"I know, but somehow I just can't take my eyes off her," I mumbled back. Lizzy was busy being chatted up by one of Flic's rejects, a creature with a massive head and truly enormous sideburns, who should by rights have been sitting under a bridge shouting at some goats. Bless her, I could see her struggling with her endless dilemma – be nice and polite and listen to his bullshit, or send him on his way with a timely punch to the ribs. Unlike me and Gem, she had enough politeness in her to take the former option. We would have sent the poor old troll packing aeons ago.

Flic, meanwhile, seemed to be almost leaning in to her current suitor; a guy on the right side of good looking, mercifully sideburn-free and suitably tall and hunky. Which was all completely irrelevant, considering that Flic was supposed to be in a serious relationship. And yet here she was, *leaning in*. As in, the kind of 'leaning in' you do when you're about to do a full face-on-face mashup.

"FELICITY!" Gem bellowed suddenly. Flic jumped backwards in shock, nearly head-butting the conventionally handsome bloke in the chin.

"What? What's happening? What's going on?" she said in a rush, her face turning redder and redder.

"I'm feeling a tiny bit faint, would you be a love and go get me a water, please?" Gem requested sweetly. "Cleo'd do it but she's… busy."

"Yeah, um, I'm very busy. I'm about to go and… have a wee." With that, I bolted, grabbing Lizzy by the wrist and dragging her away with me (she didn't exactly mind, it was practically a mercy mission). I'd let Gem have the pleasure of dealing with her sister.

Thank God, I thought, as we headed towards the toilets. A familiar figure was just trotting happily into the club, surrounded by sensibly dressed cronies. Jonny had arrived.

"Lizzy! And Cleo!" he cooed, his face veritably lighting up on seeing us. Bless him, Jonny seemed hammered. His sensibly-parted hair was all ruffled up, and there was a rather large stain on his half-tucked-in shirt – I was willing to bet it was beer. Flic usually had him drinking low-calorie wine, like her. I bet he was loving his rare night of almost-freedom with his mates. "It's so good to see you!" He flung his arms around Lizzy in a haphazard hug. She giggled and propped him up.

"You all right, Jonny?" I grinned at him. Bless. Honestly, it made a nice change not to be the drunkest person in the room.

"I'm fine," he bellowed. "More than fine, I'm happy! Happyhappy."

"Good for you, mate," I said. "Flic's over there, by the way." I thumbed the pillar at the back, having a quick glance back there myself before Jonny could focus. Ahh, excellent. Flic and Gem were on their own again. Having a row, by the looks of things, but hey. Nothing new there.

"My wife," Jonny said solemnly. "The missus."

"Nearly," I pointed out. "Not quite, yet."

"She might as well be," he said, his voice dropping. He clung to Lizzy, looking like he was about to fall over. I wasn't quite sure how he'd got past the bouncers; he was absolutely off his face. Wasted.

"Are you properly all right, Jonny?" I said, giving him a funny look.

"I'm fine," he protested.

I looked around again for Flic; Lizzy looked like she was having a bit of a job holding up poor Jonny. He was leaning on her, heavily. She was kind of patting his shoulder nervously – I could tell she was getting worried, particularly about the risk of him vomming dramatically on her pretty silver dress.

Hang on. I did a proper double take.

I've mentioned it before: Folies was otherwise known as Guernsey's premier den of sin. Friday and Saturday nights, the club was full of debauchery. Couples making out in every corner;

usually having met for the first time approximately twenty minutes previously. I should know. I was usually in one of the aforementioned corners. Possibly in more than one of them, actually, depending on how much alcohol had been consumed throughout the course of the evening, and what the ratio of troll to human happened to be in the club that night.

You'd look over, from the balcony or just the other side of the dance floor, and by about one o'clock in the morning everywhere you looked there would be a different couple. After a while, some of the faces started to become familiar; that's why after a while, I seemed to instinctively home in on tourists. You tended to get the same people in week after week – hence why we sometimes mixed it up the tiniest bit and went to the Barbados club instead. I suppose if we hadn't done that, Gem would never have got pregnant.

It kind of pains me to say it, but I reckon by this time, I'd become one of the familiar faces myself, seen in the same corners with a different bloke week after week. Well, weekend after weekend.

I rather enjoyed my slutdom – after all, it wasn't like I slept with every single one of my random pulls. A considerably low percentage, in fact, if you looked at the big picture. But I'd regularly found myself eyeing some reasonably hot bloke on the dance floor, catching his eye… then realising I'd already pulled him a couple of weeks before.

Hell, I'd been living in Guernsey so long, I was probably on my second go round. At least I'd had the three-year break of university to get a bit of diversity in there.

I was used to the dark corners of Folies. I knew what went on there, and I generally knew who was in them, at least to the point of recognising the faces (definitely the backs of their heads). For example, I'd seen the tall ginger guy many times before, the one next to the DJ having a good suck on the face of a curly-haired brunette. If I could get a good look at her face, I'd probably realise I'd seen her before, too. Then there was the guy in the tatty blue jumper, nose to nose with a tiny redhead in a sequinned dress over by the stairs. That pair had been around before, in the same combination – and the same jumper – over and over again, and yet they still acted like it was the first time they'd ever met. Maybe they were that drunk, they truly thought it was.

But there was a couple right in the middle of the dance floor who I'd never seen before. No, these two certainly hadn't been around. I would have noticed. I *really* would have noticed.

The girl was pretty generic, to be honest. She could have been one of a thousand girls who were in Folies every week. Average height, long straight hair that could have been almost any colour under the lights. Thanks to the situation I couldn't exactly see her face all that well, but I quite liked her outfit; a short red dress with a low cut out at the back (again, I wasn't exactly in the position to see the front).

The guy, however, was not generic.

Even with his eyes closed, his glasses askew and his hair more mussed up than ever, I knew him. Because it was Zach.

Annoying Customer of the Week, Part 6

"Hello? Hello? Are you serving?"

"Yes, sorry. I was just doing a bit of cleaning down here. What can I get for you today?"

"Just a tea please."

"Big or small?"

"Medium, please."

"We do big or small."

"OK, big then please. Do you have Darjeeling?"

"No, sorry, we have English Breakfast, Earl Grey, chamomile, green tea, peppermint tea and wild berry tea."

"No Darjeeling? My goodness, what is the world coming to? No Darjeeling… and you claim to be a teahouse!"

"No, actually, we claim to be a coffee shop. Which one would you like?"

"Humph. All right then. I'll have Earl Grey."

"That's one seventy-nine then, please."

"Here you go."

"Here's your tea!"

"Thank you. Is this milk?"

"No, it's Irish Cream. I have a problem."

I probably didn't need to be quite so snappy with the woman, but hey, I was in a bad mood. Plus, the milk jugs were labelled so clearly only a moron could miss them. And I'm sure there's a law somewhere that says you're allowed to be snappy with morons.

More to the point, I had to be at the airport in just over two hours, and I hadn't even packed yet.

Chapter 13

"Maybe we should sing a song. Doesn't singing keep you warm?"

"Like fuck, Liz. You know what'd keep me warm? Vodka."

"If you even mention the word 'vodka' again I will throw up on your New Rocks."

The fact that there was a snow castle just a matter of miles up the road should have been my first clue.

You know, to the weather.

Finland in April might not be quite the darkened world of ice and snow it would have been if we'd turned up in January, but we'd really underestimated quite how bloody cold we'd be up in Oulu. It was sunny, oh yes, very sunny. So sunny that the snow was almost, but not quite at the point of melting.

Why yes, there was still snow on the ground. Last time we'd thought to check, it was minus five degrees. And the sun was glinting off the snow so beautifully. So beautifully that my hangover was crying out for mercy.

Lizzy and I had arrived in Finland. We'd been there less than two days, and by my estimation we'd been drinking on and off for about twenty-four hours. It had started in Helsinki airport, waiting for our flight up to Oulu. We'd spotted some kind of Finnish berry cider next to the sandwiches in an airport café and hadn't really stopped since.

We'd made sure to arrive in Oulu the day before the Karin Cluster gig, just so we could have a little bit of time to explore – and husband-hunt, of course. By all the deities, Finnish men are gorgeous. I hadn't seen one yet who wasn't tall and chiselled, with baby-hair so fine it whipped around like a halo.

And there was a lot of hair being whipped around because, wonderfully and miraculously, we found a heavy metal karaoke bar. Let me say that again: a *heavy metal karaoke bar*. Possibly the most beautiful words to be combined in any language. After an afternoon of wandering round the pretty little waterside city, it had been the first drinking hole we'd come to.

It was rather a large bar – definitely bigger than any of the poky metal bars I'd been in while I lived in the UK. It did of course retain its dark, gloomy metal-type atmosphere; it wouldn't have been a heavy metal bar if it didn't. The most beautiful thing about it, of course, was the clientele. Gorgeous Finnish metal fans, as far as the eye could see. Tattooed women with immaculate eye make-up and sulky faces. Men with hair down to their waists and pierced septums.

I, of course, was in my element. I had been bad enough when I thought it was just a bar. But then my eyes actually lit up the moment I saw the little stage in the corner of the room – a drunken Finn already perched upon it, howling out a HIM song.

It took me about half an hour and a couple of shots of vodka to get her up there, but eventually I managed to drag Lizzy forcibly onto the stage and belt out our first Nightwish song of the night. Hey, they're Finnish. It felt appropriate. Of course, Lizzy had never heard the song before, but it was a stellar effort nonetheless. After the song finished I immediately took over for a good growl of a Children of Bodom song, which I did as a solo effort, and held the stage for a Sonata Arctica album track that should have far more of a following, in my opinion. Then we climaxed with a fabulous Karin Cluster duet.

By this point, we had quite an audience. Lizzy can just about hold a tune, if forced – I'm more of the type who can't even carry one in the proverbial bucket. Put the two of us together, and it's probably something akin to two foxes mating. Or possibly two tomcats in a sack. It didn't help that in the middle of the Sonata

Arctica song I decided that the keyboard solo had gone on far too long and called loudly for the keyboard player to "get a fucking move on, mate, I've had shags shorter than this". Whoops.

However, there must have been a novelty to two drunken British women bellowing out European metal on a stage. We'd found in our daytime wanderings that the Finns were pretty reserved to their tourists; friendly, yes, but not overly so. There was nothing fake about them. If they weren't interested in you, they politely ignored you. Even if you were quite blatantly out of your comfort zone, arguing loudly over which one of you was holding the map the wrong way up, they wouldn't approach you unless you directly appealed to them for help. Then, of course, they'd be lovely and polite and helpful. But only if you asked.

This, of course, was while they were sober. While drunk – and while drunk metal fans – things were entirely different.

We couldn't ask for more potential New Best Friends. All of them, curiously, men. The women didn't seem to like us half as much. Quite possibly because we were unashamedly flirting with the men they regarded as rightfully theirs. Well, at least, I was: Lizzy was being rather shy. Still accepting the free drinks though.

Such lovely people. Such lovely drinks. There was one in particular, a spiky-haired guy with glasses who looked a bit like the Finnish version of Zach, only with a devil-horn beard; an absolutely charming chap who I took quite a fancy to. He kept bringing over White Russians. And those buggers weren't cheap.

Of course, the lovely drinks only lasted so long before the suggestion was made that we needed to try something traditional and Finnish – something that you couldn't get anywhere else.

This 'something traditional and Finnish' was Salmiakki Koskenkorva. A word of advice: if you ever happen to be in Finland and somebody offers you a shot of Salmiakki, say no. Say no and start running. Beware, sometimes they call it Salmari. And it also comes in the form of sweets. Beware of it all.

It's an interesting drink, that's for sure. I think it's made of liquorice, and definitely some kind of alcohol, and who knows what else. It's black, anyway, pure black (except when you only have a tiny bit of it left in a shot glass, when it looks kind of brownish and sludgy – not nice) and it tastes it. It's the kind of sharp, burning taste that makes you shudder, physically shudder. The first shot I had of it, I rather wished I'd done it standing over a toilet, and I could see Lizzy had had the same reaction.

But then the feeling hits. That burning taste turns into a smoulder, pushing slowly down your throat and properly warming your heart as it tunnels past.

God, I hate to think what that stuff looked like, coated on my intestines, but man, it felt nice while it got there.

Unfortunately, it's also rather strong. We'd been doing the occasional normal vodka shot as the night had progressed, but somehow it was the Salmiakki that was our downfall. Well, mine at least. Lizzy had refused a couple of the White Russians, so she ended up being the one to haul me back to our hotel at the end of the night. A couple of the lovely Finnish men had offered to give her some support, but she fought them off.

Apparently I had a little kiss with one of them, but I can't remember it so it doesn't count.

I woke up at approximately five in the morning, slumped on my hotel bed with my hair matted over my face. Lovely.

I then had to stumble as quickly as I could to the bathroom, head spinning, to vomit black sick. Even lovelier.

"Never again… awful… Salmiakki…" I managed to get out a couple of hours later, upon waking up for the second time. This time, instead of being slumped on the bed, I was slumped on the bathroom floor. Lizzy was prodding me to make sure I was still alive.

"Yeah, I feel a bit rough myself," she admitted. She looked it. You could have used the bags under her eyes as hammocks. If she was that bad, I dreaded to think how horrific my reflection would be if I could bear to look in the mirror. "When do you want to start queuing for the front row?"

"Oh shitbiscuits. That." I dry-retched in the direction of the toilet. "I can't do it. No, wait! Yes I can. I have to. It's Karin Cluster. We have to be on the front."

"We do," Lizzy wailed wretchedly. "I just don't know how."

"Right." I grabbed hold of the towel rail and pulled myself to my feet, wobbling so much I nearly fell into the bath. I was only a tiny bit surprised to see I was still in my outfit from the night before. "Here's what we'll do. You go down to the breakfast buffet. No, I don't mean eat anything. I definitely can't." I suppressed a sicky burp. "Get cucumber. Get as much as you can carry. If we put it on our faces for a bit, the puffiness will go down."

Yeah, so my mind was definitely functioning on half-power. Which was about twice as much as my body. But it was working just enough to remember the weird savoury selection at the breakfast buffet, including what appeared to be an entire salad bar. A potentially useful salad bar.

"Can't you go? I'm going to look like an idiot, carrying a bloody cucumber out of there."

"I can't do it." I rolled into the bedroom and collapsed face first onto my bed. "You'll have to go. Bring me cucumber!"

Obediently, Lizzy stumbled out of the room and trotted down to breakfast. It felt like she was only gone thirty seconds; I must have fallen into a quick hungover nap. The slam of the door as she made her triumphant return seemed to reverberate around my skull like a shotgun blast.

"Urgh," I moaned into my pillow.

"Come on, roll over, I've got cucumber!"

If a little green man had drawn up to the window in his spaceship, somehow deciding that the Oulu Radisson Blu was the ideal place to observe ordinary humanity, he would have been somewhat shocked at the strangeness of the human race. Was it normal, he might have thought, to spend the start of the day laying completely still, like a laid-out corpse? Maybe these *were* corpses, he could have considered. Maybe this was how humans arranged their dead: on hotel beds, bedecked with green vegetables.

While Lizzy daintily pulled apart the packet of cucumber slices she'd sneaked up her top – an entire cucumber, wrapped in a napkin – I reluctantly got myself out of my party clothes and into a vest top and pyjama bottoms. Every movement made my head feel funny. I flopped back onto the bed and set about strewing cucumber all over myself. I thought it might have a bit more benefit if I put the cucumber everywhere. Everywhere exposed, anyway.

Eyes, cheeks, forehead, chest, arms… I think I had the deluded idea that the cucumber would somehow absorb all the toxic chemicals seeping out of my skin. Maybe it would actively suck them out, leaving me blissfully hangover free and ready to face the day. Plant power! Maybe this was the kick I'd been waiting for to healthy-up my life. I'd go vegan, and post about it on Instagram every third minute.

Or not.

My skin did feel beautifully fresh.

Sadly, the rest of me didn't.

I recognised this hangover. This was a hangover of New Year's Day proportions.

Potentially, it was worse.

It took a little while for us to get ourselves into the kind of state where we could get up and function like vaguely normal people. I say 'vaguely' because we still resembled a pair of ambulatory zombies.

But we somehow managed to dress ourselves in our carefully planned gig outfits. In my case: my skinniest black jeans, New Rocks, and a low-hanging loose red vest top with an embossed black and grey skull floating across my boobs, little silver studs spiking out from the straps. Lizzy was going for thermal leggings, a yellow long-sleeved shirt, and a black denim pinafore dress.

Of course, at this point we still had the hangover sweats. We didn't realise quite how absolutely fucking freezing it was out there. We thought we were being sensible by adding a couple of layers to our ensembles; in my case, a Manchester University hoodie and my leather jacket, and in Lizzy's, her dark blue parka with a furry hood.

We seriously thought that would be enough.

I thought I was well-versed in heavy metal queuing. I'd been to quite a few gigs while I was at uni, after all. I'd also been stalking the Karin Cluster fan club forums on the internet. I wasn't part of any of them myself – come on, I have self-respect and a social life – but it was good to have an occasional snoop, just to see what the scary superfans were up to. And, in this case, how to avoid them and kick their arses at groupiedom.

There was one forum thread in particular that I'd been really interested in. The one about queuing up for gigs.

Karin Cluster had recently done a pretty big gig in Hamburg, their local 'big city' (most of the band actually came from a little island off the coast of Germany called Fehmarn; I've always felt some affinity with them as fellow island-dwellers). By 'pretty big', I of course mean 'populated by a metric fuck-ton of uber-fans'. Most of their German fan club turned up, there were banners, people dressed up in cosplay representing certain songs, the works. I'd seen the videos on YouTube.

Some people had camped out for more than twenty-four hours, just to ensure their place on the front row. In February. In northern Germany. That's true dedication, right there.

From the stories on the thread, though, I gathered that the queuing experience had been an epic time for the people who were there. A proper bonding thing, despite the cold. They all sang songs, shared their junk food, told bragging stories about being groupies – all the usual heavy metal activities.

I kind of wanted to be a part of this. It seemed like such a community, like so many friendships were being made just from sitting on a concrete floor for hours, waiting for your favourite band. You never know… it might be the perfect place for husband hunting. At least we'd have a common interest.

And, of course, I wanted to be on the front row.

Come on, I hadn't come all that way for second or third.

It was imperative to get out of the hotel, and soon. As soon as my legs would work properly, anyway. Sure, it wasn't exactly the notorious Hamburg gig; we were unlikely to find anyone who'd been sleeping outside the concert hall. But still, we might have competition.

The venue was quite a bit out of town, tucked away on an industrial estate; at least, that's what Google Maps had told us. I was unprepared for the reality of the place, when we finally dragged ourselves to the hotel reception, ordered a taxi and fell into it. To get to the door of the venue and, thus, the queue, the taxi had to take us through seemingly every little back alley in the entire industrial estate. I started to think we were being

169

kidnapped for our passports or some other horror story you read in trashy magazines – surely not in Finland?

Finally, we were taken down a gritty dirt road, past a lot of warehouses and abandoned-looking buildings, and dumped in a car park. A cold, gravelled car park, next to what appeared to be an industrial chimney. To me, it looked like a building site where the builders had vanished on an eternal tea break. Or Salmiakki break, seeing as we were in Finland.

And at the far end of this building site was the venue. Well, the entrance to it anyway. A little stack of about ten concrete steps leading to a double door: simple.

We knew that it was the venue, because it had the name of it above the door in massive letters. We couldn't be mistaken.

The thing was, there wasn't a queue.

Not a single other person.

We were the first people there.

After the taxi driver disappeared, leaving us unsure as to whether we'd ever find our way back to civilisation, we had a quick Google of the venue, of the date of the gig, of the band, of everything we could think of. We checked the band's official website, their Twitter and their Facebook. Even their very neglected Instagram.

Nothing about the gig being cancelled.

We had to accept – and enjoy – the truth.

We were the first people to arrive.

Our places on the front row had to be guaranteed.

* * *

This seemed to be wonderful. Joyous news. Brag-worthy news. Have-a-little-dance-despite-your-hangover news.

For a while.

We sat at the top of the concrete steps with proper smug victory faces. We were in the right place, on the right day, and we were first. Ha, take that, fan club groupies!

But then our hangovers, which had kindly kept quiet while we were busy gloating to ourselves, decided to return with a vengeance. We were both happy just to huddle down onto our concrete step and try to have a little nap, passing a bottle of water between us in silence and pretending we didn't feel like we were going to be sick.

But oh, the cold. It was bitter. Across the car park, there was still snow on the cinderblocks. Despite the bright – too bright, far too bright – sunlight, it was still cold enough for the snow to resist melting. And said sunlight was shining right in our faces, unless we buried our heads fully in our hoods – which, yes, I was doing, my hoodie so zipped up that all you could see of my face was eyeliner, and lots of it.

Lizzy was shivering nonstop next to me. It felt a bit like sitting next to one of those vibrating massage chairs you see in service stations, even through our layers of clothes. I thought I was too cold to even shiver. The cold was going right through to my bones; it felt like if you sliced me open, you'd be able to have bone marrow ice cream. Salmiakki-flavoured, obviously.

For at least an hour, we sat at the top of the concrete steps, just freezing in silence. I don't know about Lizzy, but my head was starting to pound. Before, I'd just felt sick, and dizzy, and all stomach-crampingly twisted. Now, though, between the pervasive rays of the sun and the biting cold, my head was clamouring for a look-in at the hangover party. I could almost feel my pulse reverberating between my skull, my dodgy stomach, and the concrete step.

But with the headache, my ability to talk seemed to return. As did my ability to whine.

"I just don't think I can cope with this cold. We need to find a blanket. Or another coat. Or something."

"Where do you think we can find a blanket around here? We're on a building site!" Lizzy shook her head slightly beneath her furry hood, then winced. "Why didn't I bring my bobble hat? And I'm worried now. It's almost midday. And it's like... this." A pale hand appeared from underneath the parka and waved at the empty car park. "You're sure nothing's popped up about the gig being cancelled?"

"Definitely not. I've got push notifications. I'd buzz."

"What time do the doors open again?"

"Eight," I groaned. "Oh bollocks, we've got eight hours yet. And that mural of Jar Jar Binks is staring at me."

"That... what?"

"Over there!" I attempted to point with my hand still rolled up in my hoodie pocket. "See, that wall over there."

I thought it was part of the venue; at least, the whole L-shape around that side of the car park was painted the same colour. There was a door in the orange-ish wall, and a small fenced-off area with an outdoor heater and a couple of benches. Lizzy had made the canny assumption that it was a smoking area, for either the bar or for the backstage area, we couldn't agree on which was more likely (or whether anyone would notice us stealing the heater). Next to this, I was convinced, was a mural. A mural portraying a character from Star Wars: Jar Jar Binks.

It looked so much like him. Darker orange than the rest of the building, a kind of brownish colour. It definitely had a face. And that had to be a kind of floppy, duck-bill type mouth. Yes. I was sure.

"It's just mould and dirt on the wall," Lizzy said.

"No, it's definitely Jar Jar Binks," I insisted, stubbornly squinting into the sunlight. "When have I ever been wrong before? Can't you see it?" I pointed out where I thought the eyes and the mouth were, and how it went into the body in what was definitely a Star Wars-y outfit.

"I... I think I'm starting to see it," Lizzy said, leaning forward and narrowing her eyes behind her glasses. "Yeah. You know, you might be right."

"I totally am right," I said firmly. "You never know how weird things are going to be in Finland. It just happens that this particular venue has a mural of Jar Jar Binks on the wall. And the point is... it's staring at me and I'd quite like it to stop, please."

"I don't think you can make the mural stop staring at you, Cleo."

"Then I'm going to sleep."

* * *

I didn't have much luck with the whole 'going to sleep' thing. Have you ever tried sleeping across a couple of concrete steps? My arse was starting to feel as bad as my head.

I kept having a very persistent vision that would not go away. Almost a hallucination: maybe I'd fallen asleep after all. It was a marvellous vision, of Zach. Oh, no, not like that. Honestly, why would I think of *Zach* like that? No, in the vision he was clutching two steaming hot coffees, smiling that big goofy grin of his and presenting them to me and Lizzy while making some nerdy quip about ice planets. Then he took off his huge coat, wrapped it round me, pulled me into a hug and…

Anyway.

I wasn't having thoughts like that. Stupid vision.

Thankfully, at about one o'clock, someone else finally turned up to distract us from our various pains. Two German women, proper devotees of Karin Cluster who followed them everywhere. They entertained us for a little while with their tales of hanging around outside tour buses and getting autographs and photos, before offering to save our places if we wanted to go and get something to eat. Apparently, joy of joys, there was a McDonalds only a fifteen-minute walk away.

I was starting to get a bit peckish. After all, I'd puked up all of last night's dinner early that morning, and I'd used breakfast as a cleanser, not a foodstuff. McDonalds seemed like an excellent idea.

McDonalds was not an excellent idea. After a rather painful fifteen-minute stagger, which at least warmed us up a bit, I was hit by a wall of French fry smell. It didn't make my stomach feel happy. In fact, it made my stomach feel very unhappy indeed.

If it made my stomach feel unhappy, it seemed to make Lizzy's feel positively tragic. I strode bravely into the McDonalds, Lizzy trailing nervously behind me, clutching herself around the middle. After a brief exchange, I had a chicken nugget Happy Meal gripped in my ice-cold hands. But Lizzy shook her head furiously and silently parked next to me while I determinedly forced the chicken nuggets into my face.

They were working, I was starting to feel a teeny tiny bit better.

Lizzy, however, was not so lucky. At my admonition, she chewed nervously on a French fry.

For thirty seconds.

Then she had to clamp her hand to her face and rush to the toilet.

Thankfully, we'd parked ourselves at the tables closest to the loos. We hadn't been rendered entirely stupid by all that alcohol.

Some might say we were entirely stupid in the first place for having got so drunk at all. It was that third shot of Salmiakki that did it, I was adamant. Nothing to do with the fourth. Or the vodka. Or the White Russians. It was all about the third.

I managed to get through the rest of my Happy Meal, determined that it would stay down. Lizzy, upon her return from the grimy bathroom, refused even another single bite. She didn't look quite so much like a corpse any more, though.

Neither, for that matter, did I – at least, I didn't feel quite so much like one. Surprising how a few fries and some processed chicken can really boost the metabolism, far better than the slices of cucumber. Not that I'd eaten them. Maybe that had been the problem.

We trotted back to the venue feeling a bit more lively. As we settled back onto the concrete steps, promising to guard places for the two Germans who headed off to the McDonalds themselves, I remarked that if it wasn't for the cold, I'd be positively enjoying myself.

"Why?"

"Because it's nice, you know." I gave Lizzy's arm a squeeze. "Just the two of us. Having an adventure. Husband hunting."

"I haven't seen anyone here yet I'd marry."

"I could marry half of that karaoke bar."

"I couldn't. Not if I had to drink Salmiakki all the time." She gave a little hungover hiccup.

"I'm sure they wouldn't make you drink it every day," I said, snuggling a bit further into the hood of my hoodie. "Maybe just on weekends."

"I couldn't cope with a hangover like this every weekend."

"You practically do anyway," I pointed out. "After Folies."

"I don't go every weekend, not any more. And I'm never as hammered as you and Gem."

"More than Gem nowadays."

"Well, obviously. But I know she'd be drinking if she could. And we needn't think she'll be calming down any more when the baby arrives. She'll probably get worse."

"Probably."

"You know…" Lizzy squinted. "Now the hangover's clearing, I'm pretty sure that mural isn't a mural."

"It totally is! We've been through this," I sighed. "See where the mouth is, and the nose, and the duck bill whatsit? It's Jar Jar Binks!"

"I think it might just be mould."

We were too busy bickering about the mural-cum-mould to realise that a large blue coach, a double-decker, appeared to be trying to reverse into the car park. It was pulling a huge trailer.

"Honestly, it's just a dirty patch of wall!" Lizzy was saying when I finally peeped through my hoodie and clocked the bus.

"Look!" I interrupted, elbowing her in the ribs. "*Look*!"

"Oh. Oh!"

"We have got to go and talk to them." I started to twitch maniacally. "We've got to! It's like the law of heavy metal or something. Or the law of groupies. We have to talk to them!"

"Karin Cluster are in there," Lizzy squeaked. "I'm actually shaking."

I was shaking too, somewhere deep inside my hoodie. The bus attempted to turn around in the limited space, backing practically right up to the steps where we were sitting. A tall guy in a hoodie and jeans jumped out and started beckoning to the driver, guiding the trailer up to a big shutter just off to the side from the steps. I tucked my legs further into myself; it looked like the big blue bus was about to back straight over us. *Karin Cluster had to be just feet away*.

We both held our breath as the blue bus stopped dead. A door in the middle opened and disgorged a trio of long-haired, gritty-looking men who ignored us and started fiddling with the big shutter in the wall.

"They must be roadies," I whispered. "The band will be going to a hotel or something, they had a gig in Seinajoki last night and must have just arrived from there."

"Or maybe they have another entrance to avoid people like us," Lizzy whispered back.

Well, that theory went out of the window in about thirty seconds, as a small, bleached-blonde woman leaped from the blue bus, just feet away. She twisted her tiny body into a feline stretch, yawning violently and cracking her arms behind her head, ruffling her pixie cut into a tousled mess.

I knew who this was.

Mellina – Karin Cluster's bassist. One of the few women in metal who played bass rather than singing. Her older sister, Yasmin, played keyboards for the group... and was stepping delicately from the tour bus after Mellina, leaning against the side of the bus and lighting a cigarette.

"Oh... shit," I hissed. Lizzy merely squeaked.

I'm sure cooler people than us would have been a lot less excited to see their favourite musicians alighting from a bus three feet in front of them. After all, they're only people, right? Nothing to be intimidated by, they're just a bit more talented than the average mortal. Maybe some people could even be blasé about it. Wander up, introduce themselves, have a little chat.

I'd thought I'd be that person, I really did. I'm cool, after all. I'm confident. Nothing could bring down my self-belief, I thought.

Thought.

In reality, I was absolutely struck dumb by the sight of two of the most talented women in metal, just a few feet in front of me – one of them (Yasmin) having what appeared to be a rant in German, the other (Mellina), nodding away with a little frown puckering her forehead.

My secondary school German seemed to be kicking in slowly, but it seemed to me that Yasmin was moaning about Finnish people, and their obsession with drinking, and something to do with drums. From her tone of voice, Mellina was trying to placate her, but I couldn't quite catch what her sweet, high-pitched voice was saying.

All of a sudden, Mellina shot aside to avoid a large body tumbling down the steps of the bus.

"Fuck," he said, his voice a bass that seemed to reverberate through the concrete steps. He shook his head and rubbed his eyes, steadying himself against the side of the bus. "Was sagst du, Min?"

"Max." Yasmin sighed and shook her head, stubbing out her cigarette on the side of the bus and hauling herself back up the steps.

Yes, the man who looked, frankly, just as hungover as me and Lizzy, was also part of the band. Max Wolf, the drummer. A lanky blonde in his forties, he looked older and (allegedly) acted younger. Up close, his face was ravished by pockmarks, but was still handsome – even with his long beard, tied into a tentacular mass of braids fastened at the ends with beads. His starting-to-silver hair was tucked into his belt, and it looked like he'd slept in his outlandish pink-fringed jeans and grey shirt. He'd just come off a tour bus; he probably had.

He stretched, like Mellina had, but a lot less elegantly. Then he had a little look around – and noticed me and Lizzy.

Instinctively, we huddled closer. I could feel Lizzy's shaking through my layers, and this time I knew it wasn't due to the cold.

"Wow," he said, starting towards us. "Er... Suomalainen?" I knew that that meant 'Finnish', in Finnish. "Deutsch?"

"No, we're British, actually," I managed to get out. I started to struggle to my feet: Max was a tall bloke, and it was a bit intimidating to have him looming over me. I could feel Lizzy give a tiny squeak as I left her on the step alone. "I think we misjudged the queue."

"Just a little bit," he barked, with a grin. "English people, huh? What the hell are you doing in Finland?"

"We feel neglected!" I grinned, albeit shakily. "Are we ever going to get another UK tour?"

"Maybe one day." Max looked shifty. "I understand the promoter was a bit of a bastard last time... we don't hate you!" he added rapidly, turning a bit red. "We just had some problems in your country." His gaze shifted infinitesimally towards the bus for a second. Hmm. Intriguing.

"Who don't we hate?" Mellina skipped over in a bound.

"These two are English," Max announced, grandly. "They've come all the way from England!"

"A bit further, actually," I said, as Lizzy shot to her feet and gripped me on the arm. "We're not English… hardly even British, really. We come from Guernsey, it's a little island in between England and France."

"Island people!" Mellina squealed. "Like us!"

"Yeah, kind of," Lizzy said, managing a wobbly smile.

"I bet you're freezing," Mellina said, the little pucker appearing on her forehead again. "You can't be used to such cold in… where was it?"

"Guernsey."

"It must be almost tropical compared to here!"

"Just a bit," I said, my grin getting even wider. "We have palm trees at home. Look at Lizzy's fingers." I grabbed Lizzy's hand and pulled it out of her sleeve. "Blue! Practically dead. It doesn't help that we're hungover." Yes, I was babbling. Lizzy was still struck down with awe.

"Same as me." Max smiled ruefully.

"Max, you're always hungover," Mellina put in, giving him a little poke. "Minnie's going to throw you off the bus if you keep this up."

"Aah, I'll go with the Finns, they like a drink," Max waved a muscled arm. "We've borrowed some roadies and man, they know how to drink."

"It's so cool you're here!" Mellina chirped. "We sometimes see some English people in France or Germany but never in Finland! You've come so far!"

I was starting to feel like I was the cool one here, not the two rock stars matter-of-factly having a little discussion with us.

"Well, we've always wanted to come this far north." I shrugged. "What better excuse than seeing you lot?"

"Oh, I really hope we do you justice now." Mellina frowned again. It looked unnatural on her tiny, pixie-like face. "I'd hate to disappoint you."

"I'm sure you won't, believe me." My grin was enormous.

"Well, Minnie – Yasmin – is in a bad mood today," Mellina said solemnly. "She's not a big fan of Finland."

"Yeah, after last time, we were supporting a Finnish band," Max said with a rather lascivious wink. "There was a thing, the guy who played keyboards, looks a bit like a hamster..."

"Oh Max, it's not because of that!" Mellina cut him off. "No, everything is good there. I'm sure."

Lizzy and I exchanged a look. More intrigue! I do love a bit of intrigue.

"As long as she's not too grumpy tonight. I don't want anyone ruining the party."

"It'll be fine, we've got enough beer! And that weird Finnish stuff... Salmari?"

Lizzy and I exchanged another look. One of alarm.

"That's Salmiakki, right?" I ventured. Mellina and Max both nodded, Max with a rather happy grin.

"It's splendid," he said cheerfully, a veteran of many tours. "Not as strong as I'd like, but a good starting point."

"It's the reason we look like shit." I gestured at Lizzy, who looked a tiny bit affronted. "The reason for our hangovers. The reason Lizzy had to puke in a McDonalds." Lizzy looked a tiny bit more affronted.

"So you don't want any more of it, then?"

"Actually, I'm taking as many bottles home as I can get in my suitcase." I shrugged. "Can't say no."

"Would you like some tonight?" Max did his best over-exaggerated leer. "We have a day off after this gig. There's going to be a bit of an afterparty if you want to join us."

Chapter 14

There's nothing I can really say about the Karin Cluster show. Honestly. Flashing lights, booming bass, powerful music pounding into my heart and almost physically lifting me up...

You know, the usual.

A couple of thousand heavy metal fans leaping around, banging their heads, punching the air. The insanely talented band members almost flying around the stage, floating on the exhilaration you can only get from a room full of devotion.

We were, of course, on the front row. Come on, could we be anywhere else after being the first people at the front door? We didn't get to hang out with Max and Mel for much longer after we got officially invited to the night's afterparty; they were summoned by an irate Yasmin back to the bus, which was going to take them to their hotel to chill out before soundcheck. We did, however, get told to go up to the guy working on the merchandise stand as soon as the show was over. He, apparently, would have something for us called 'triple A passes'.

I almost forgot about this while the show was going on, of course. The passion, the intensity... just the beauty of the whole occasion. Even though Max, topless and sticky and covered in sweat, couldn't exactly be counted as 'beautiful', he did toss me one of his drumsticks with a wink at the end of the set.

Yasmin was quite scary, smashing at a keyboard like it had personally insulted her, and Mel running around with her bass wasn't exactly *beautiful*, either – the instrument was far too huge and heavy, a massive contrast to her little blonde pixiness – though the other two members of the band seemed pretty breath-taking, to my still-slightly-hungover eyes.

Luka, the guitarist (and writer of all the songs) was something rather special. I'd seen my share of long-haired heavy metal men, but among them all... he stood out.

His dirty blonde hair was held back by a black bandana, letting it swing around his shoulders when he headbanged without blocking his view. He wasn't wearing a shirt with his skinny jeans, just a shiny grey waistcoat, which was hanging open to display his chest – rather toned, unlike poor Max, who was sagging more than not.

Occasionally Luka's dark eyes would flash up at the crowd, laced with smudged eyeliner, smouldering all over the place.

I knew that fangirls across the world were obsessed with him, fantasising all over the internet... I kind of got it. There was an intensity to him that took your breath away every time he deigned to glance in your general direction. But then, he *was* very surly-looking. Sure, I'd heard rumours of break-ups and affairs and all kinds of drama in his life – but even Lilly was putting up a good show of being happy onstage, and she probably had the biggest excuse to be grumpy out of all of them.

Lilly, the lead singer of Karin Cluster, spent the entire show grinning beatifically upon the audience at her feet, striding around liberally dispensing blown kisses and the occasional hand-touch while she bellowed out the songs. She really was beautiful – her unnaturally red hair streaming behind her in billowing curls, the corseted white dress clinging to her curves as the flashing lights glinted off a sequinned belt at her waist. Absolutely stunning.

Of course, when all the shit had gone down in the band, a while back, she'd nearly been thrown out on her arse. She and Luka had long ago been in some brief semblance of a relationship, I think, and after they split up, she'd got jealous over another girl. Rumours on the internet seemed to suggest she had had a meltdown and started trashing things. Including Luka's new relationship, apparently. There had been something with their old manager, too, if the online rumour mill was correct, and someone had had a rushed marriage and divorce; though about half the comments on the band's Facebook page consisted of a raging argument over who exactly had done said marrying and divorcing.

Still, when Lilly and Luka stood together during the bows at the end of the show, arms around one another's shoulders to do a graceful lean forward, they looked spectacular together. Sure, when the band left the stage it appeared that Lilly went off one way and the others all went the other – but I could only imagine how the two of them had looked when they had been a couple.

I only had to look at Lizzy at the end of the show to see how she'd found the night. She looked exhilarated. Her hair was all over her face, she was sweaty and shiny, and her shirt was all bunched under her arms. We just looked at one another and laughed, the adrenaline-fuelled laugh of the end of a gig.

"It's not even over yet," I pointed out, over the sounds of many many metal fans being herded from the room. "We have our triple As to find!"

We hung around the bar area for a while. The merch guy, who we were supposed to be approaching, was rather busy, it being the end of the gig and all. He and his team had swarms of long-haired Finns descending on them, ready to spend a hell of a lot of money on t-shirts and hoodies and sweatbands.

Let's face it, in ordinary circumstances, me and Lizzy would probably be the first ones in the queue for as many tacky souvenirs as we could get our hands on. I certainly would be. I lived in band t-shirts, and I wouldn't mind a couple more to add to my collection.

But hey, we had more important things to be doing. Like drinking. The hangovers, long left to just a whisper of their former selves, had been blasted firmly away by a few hours of headbanging like maniacs and jumping up and down. We were ready for more booze. And, more pertinently, for some Dutch courage (or Finnish courage) to give us a bit of a boost before the afterparty. We hoped Mel and Max would remember us, after the gig... though Max giving me his drumstick, and his wink, and Mel's massive grin at us during the bows, kind of indicated we hadn't been forgotten.

Plus, of course, taking armfuls of merch to a band's afterparty? So uncool. This might only have been our first groupie experience, but we didn't want to blow it with one misplaced overenthusiastic display of fangirl-ism. Even when Lizzy timidly suggested that she buy a photo for them all to sign, I shot her down.

"Don't be ridiculous!" I rolled my eyes. "Going round asking them to sign stuff? No. We're there to make friends, not to stick our heads up their arses."

"You're the one who was claiming Luka's songwriting talent made him godlike, last week," Lizzy pointed out.

"Shut up and drink your Jägerbomb. And no repeating that!"

We were sitting on stools at the crowded bar, having fought our way through the throng of fans. I was gulping back my second Jägerbomb at speed, enjoying the fizz of the Red Bull already starting to tingle through my veins. Along with the lovely dusky taste of the Jägermeister, of course. Lizzy was still demurely fighting back her first, it not being one of her usual drinks. I was determined to have at least a bit of a buzz going when we got backstage. I didn't want to clam up and find myself standing awkwardly in a corner.

"Are you two my British girls?" Suddenly, a large man appeared, looming in front of us. By large, I mean *large*: he was about six feet seven, and nearly as wide as me and Lizzy put together. Plus, of course, he seemed even huger thanks to his enormous bushy brown beard. The merch guy, of course he was: we'd had him pointed out to us by Max earlier, though we hadn't been introduced. "I'm Udo. These are for you."

With a triumphant motion and a massive, yellow-toothed grin, he whipped out a sheet of paper. He pulled two large pink stickers off it, emblazoned with 'AAA' for 'Access All Areas', and cheerfully stuck one onto the sleeve of Lizzy's t-shirt. He paused, considering the non-existent sleeves on my vest top, and then slapped mine triumphantly onto the leg of my jeans.

"Just give us about half an hour, then come to the stage door, OK? Should be a good party, we've got one of the old bands we used to support coming over, bringing some friends." He gave us brief directions (which turned out to be to the door in the wall near Jar Jar Binks) and then rushed back to his merch stand, where his cronies were just starting to fold up the mess. Security guards were starting to shunt people outside, away from the bar, but when they saw our giant 'AAA' stickers, they left us alone. The barman even started to pour us more drinks.

"I'm never going to a gig without these again!" I announced grandly, taking a very proud sip of my new Jägerbomb. A group of Finnish girls slunk past, escorted by a bouncer, glaring at us. They were sticker-less, no accessing all areas for them, and they were most certainly not allowed to stay at the bar. Ha. I'm pretty sure I'd seen the same group of girls fighting over a discarded guitar pick earlier in the evening – they weren't keeping their cool particularly well.

Lizzy and I, however, were perfect ice queens. We didn't even squeal to ourselves when the time came to go to the stage door.

But we had a bit of a shock when we got there. It was a little bit mobbed. A hardcore group of fans were clustered around the door, eagerly waiting for their idols to come out.

"I'm not sure how to get in," I admitted to Lizzy, who was following me. Of course, I was going to have to do all the talking, at least until Lizzy's alcohol kicked in. "Do we have to wait with all this lot, do you think, or do we get to just wander in? Do you think the door's locked?"

"Let's knock on it and see," she suggested, giving me a little shove forward. I nearly collided with a rather large German boy wearing a beanie pulled low and glaring furiously at anyone who so much as looked at him.

"OK." I took a deep breath, and two steps forward, and banged on the metal door. All the fangirls held their breaths.

"No," said the German boy immediately, grabbing me by the wrist. "It is rude to do that! They will come out when they are ready."

"Eep," I squeaked, as the rather mountainous teenager loomed over me.

"Cleo! Lizzy!"

Oh, thank heavens. Just in time to stop me getting possibly eaten by a hefty German (with Lizzy for dessert), Mellina had appeared. There was a bit of a surge forward as her face appeared in a tiny crack in the doorway, calling our names as she retreated back behind the door.

"We're here," I announced, breaking gratefully away from the German and shoving my way forward through the little crowd, towing Lizzy behind me.

"Here, get in quick," Mel giggled, grabbing me by the wrist and tugging me into a dirty-looking corridor. "I don't know why Udo didn't just send you in over the stage, they're manic tonight out here!" She chuckled affectionately. "Luka had to turf a couple of girls out of the men's toilets, they were lying in wait."

She was leading us down the corridor, where various long-haired men were scattered around chatting, bottles of beer in hand. There was Luka having a murmured conversation with Yasmin, who was swigging directly out of a bottle of wine. I recognised Udo, who saluted us with the two beer bottles he was clutching in one huge hand.

We followed Mellina into a large room with a green linoleum floor, sparsely furnished with a couple of saggy sofas and some precarious-looking wooden chairs. There was a TV in one corner that looked like it hadn't been used since roughly 1994. Nobody was paying much attention to anything other than the bar, of course: a trestle table that I'm sure had been housing the merch about twenty minutes previously, stacked with shot glasses and bottles, and a fridge humming slightly underneath it.

"Mel, *komm her*!" I noticed Lilly calling Mellina from where she was regally stationed on one of the sofas.

"Just get whatever drinks you want, girls." Mel turned to us and grinned. "Mingle. Enjoy yourselves. I'll be back in a minute, just going to see what she wants." She turned back and shimmied over to the sofa, parking herself on its arm and starting to talk animatedly in German.

I looked at the bar, then looked at Lizzy. She seemed shell-shocked by the sheer prevalence of long-haired heavy metal men. I thought it would be wise to get another drink into her, quickly.

Of course, we're British. Well, from Guernsey, but it still just about counts. Even though Mel had told us we could get drinks, I still kind of didn't want to. It felt a bit wrong. A couple of guys were staring at us with no small hostility: from their jackets, I could see they were crew members. I felt like it would be a bit rude to just start drinking their drinks, without having someone of metal importance to drink them with.

But just in time, Max came to the rescue.

"It's the English girls!" I nearly jumped out of my skin as he appeared out of nowhere behind us, wrapping us both in a massive hug. "Did you like my drumstick?"

"I did." I grinned up at him. "I put it down my top as soon as you gave it to me. Not having anyone else stealing it!"

"Is it still there?" He looked confused in the general direction of my chest.

"Yup." I gave it a little poke from underneath so it popped up from my capacious cleavage. "I've been going to gigs for years, but this is my first souvenir!"

"I'm very proud to be the one to give it to you." Max grinned back at me. "Come on, let's get you guys some drinks!" He leaned over to the bar and reached for the nearest bottle: luckily, Jägermeister, and not Salmiakki. "Everyone likes a bit of this! We need to get this party going, everyone's being fucking boring tonight!"

* * *

A few shots later, and Max had his wish. The party was livening up. Luka and Lilly had briefly gone out to sign some autographs and keep the fans happy.

"I'll go out if they ask for me," Max groaned, waving his hand regally. "They don't usually know who I am. Always the problem, being a drummer." He fist-bumped a startlingly blonde man who had been introduced as a fellow drummer as he pottered by on his way to the smoking area.

As soon as the fans outside had been placated, the party really got underway. They had the room until half five in the morning, then they been told they were being thrown out. Standard practice, apparently.

Everywhere I looked, it seemed like beautiful people were drinking. Well, not all of them were beautiful, not in the conventional sense. But they were beautiful to me. Heavy metal men, with leather and studs, and hair cascading lankly down their backs, tattoos aplenty... oh, it was even better than the night in the karaoke bar.

I soon lost Lizzy. As soon as her first couple of shots hit, she regained her confidence, and I left her happily chatting to a couple of Karin Cluster roadies, proudly showing off her secondary school German. I chatted to Max for a bit longer, explaining the difference between being English and being from Guernsey, then being told increasingly ruder and ruder jokes, until he went off for a smoke and I was briefly left alone.

I was quite happy, just for a short while anyway. My head was starting to get a little bit swimmy with all the shots, and I was happy just to observe for a little bit, and soak up what was going on. I was at a real heavy metal afterparty, backstage pass stuck to my jeans, drinking Jägermeister, surrounded by people who had, only days previously, been as distant as film stars. Not any more, I giggled to myself, watching one particular local Finnish musician take off his jeans and insist on swapping them with a pass holder who, I was assured, was not his girlfriend.

You can't really hold someone on a pedestal when you've seen something like that.

All the time we'd been in there, Luka had mostly been on his own. On my way to the loo at one point I'd seen him still in the corridor, watching everything that was going on with a cool stare, a beer in one hand. How aloof, I thought to myself. How obnoxious.

I'd been on my own for about five minutes when he suddenly appeared out of nowhere at my shoulder, a beer in each hand.

"Would you like a beer?" he said simply. As introductions it wasn't hugely eloquent, but it'd do.

"Thanks," I replied, taking the bottle and giving him a tentative smile. God, he was tall. He hadn't seemed anything more than average sized while he was jumping around in front of me on the stage, but up close, he was nearly as tall as the bear-like Udo; but nowhere near as densely packed. He was lithe, almost lanky-looking until he shrugged off the jacket he'd been wearing, revealing his muscled, toned arms.

Zach was lithe and lanky too, but I was pretty sure he didn't have this kind of musculature.

Hang on, why had Zach popped into my head? Bugger off, Zach.

Luka had a strange tattoo on his right bicep: two black towers on a gated wall, above a thrashing black sea. I couldn't think how the tattooist had done it, it was so subtle, but when the light hit them, the towers looked like they were bleeding.

"What is that?" I blurted out, nodding my head at his arm. I couldn't help myself, I was intrigued.

"Can I join you?" He didn't answer my question immediately, but waited until I'd nodded assent to his before he sat down next to me. How polite. He took a large sip from his beer. "It's adapted from the crest of the island I come from. It's supposed to be in colour, but I wanted it to represent... a bit more darkness." He turned his dark gaze on me, and I noticed for the first time that his eyes were actually a slate shade of green, not grey.

As his eyes locked onto mine, I felt the first stirrings of something.

Of course, it might have just been the Jäger firmly kicking in.

I fumbled opening my beer; of course I did. In the presence of the coolest people I'd probably ever meet, I couldn't get the bloody bottle top off, even with the bottle opener I had handily attached to the end of my belt for such occasions.

"Here, let me," Luka said, reaching simultaneously for my beer bottle and a bottle of sparkling water that someone had innocuously left on the sofa behind me. In one swift movement, he had the beer bottle gripped firmly in one hand, the water bottle hooked under the top. With a quick jerk of his wrist, the bottle top flew into the air with a click. I caught it in one hand.

It was only a quick movement, but there was something about it – something about Luka's firm grip – that made me twinge in places I hadn't thought about for quite a while.

"Thanks," I said, my voice inadvertently husky. I took a quick gulp of beer to disguise it.

"The others tell me you've come all the way from the UK," Luka said, twiddling his own beer between his fingers. His voice took on a strange stilted quality, almost like he'd rehearsed for our conversation. "I like that country, it would be nice to go back there. Where... where is it you come from?"

"Guernsey," I said eagerly, leaping on one of my favourite topics. "It's a little island in the middle of the English Channel. I don't know how it compares to the one you're from, but it's an island anyway."

"Really?" Oddly enough, Luka sounded a bit disappointed. "I thought you might have met some people I know from the North. North East."

"Probably not," I admitted, a little bit puzzled about where this was going. "I went to university in Manchester, never been much further north than that... and you know, even in Guernsey there are people I've never met, let alone the whole British Isles."

"Oh." He took a contemplative sip of his beer, looking at the floor. His expression was one of utter devastation, to be honest. It was like I'd just told him that someone he loved was dead. There was a brief, awkward silence. Great. What had seemed like a promising few seconds had been just a ruse to see if I'd run into his mates – though, from the weight in his eyes, it was more than just a 'mate' he was missing. Quite intriguing.

Fuelled by rather a lot of Jägermeister and a few gulps of beer, I reached out and touched him gently on the arm. "Whatever it is, and I have no idea what it is, it can't be the end of the world."

"To use a very British phrase, what bollocks." But at least he was smiling; the first time I'd seen him smile since he'd been on the stage. It was rather a lovely smile. It lit up his entire face, making him seem nowhere near the sullen piece of granite he'd been before. "But thanks for the thought."

"Yeah, I'm probably one of the worst people in the world to come to with any sort of depression," I confessed, taking another gulp of my beer. At least he was still on the sofa with me: he hadn't stormed off in a rage at my clumsy sentimentalities, stripping me of my triple A pass as he went. "I'm no good with the advice. My solution to everything is to get drunk and pull someone."

"An admirable sentiment." Luka nodded, still smiling at me. "I will certainly drink to that." He leaned over and grabbed a passing pair of beers from the hand of Udo, who was taking them towards Lizzy and the roadies. He didn't even notice their disappearance. "We'll take these for the future and see where the drinking gets us, yes?"

* * *

Oh come on, I couldn't make it any more obvious where this was going. Even with little Mellina bouncing around determined to talk to her two new favourite Brits, and Max trying to capture me to road-test some more dirty jokes, I was always going to be Luka's for the night.

That something I'd just glimpsed while he was onstage, the surly sex appeal that attracted fangirls in the thousands, was far more obvious up close and in person. Something in the graceful way he moved, something in those intense eyes, the same green as a moss-coloured slate…

It made such a change from thinking about blue eyes.

NO, I told myself. I wasn't thinking about blue eyes. Why would I be thinking about blue eyes? Not like someone I knew had a pair of piercing blue eyes that could indicate severe displeasure even across a busy coffee bar…

No. Anyway.

There was even something in the contours of Luka's jawline, where his skin was so tightly stretched, his artful stubble failed to hide the subtly skeletal edge. On any other man it might make him gaunt, but with his eyeliner and his pallor, he was more like a Tim Burton hero, without the creepiness. The bashful smile he gave when he made me laugh, the eagerness in his expression, just seemed such a contrast to his carefully constructed serious-rocker image. All of it together made a quite exceedingly beautiful package.

Yes, I was well and truly sucked in. And when he suggested moving onto the tour bus to have a quieter drink, I was up for it.

I had some conflicting ideas in my head of what a tour bus should be.

On the one hand, I thought it should be impressive: decked out in high-tech gadgets and full of musical instruments and shiny surfaces.

On the other hand, it was being used by a heavy metal band and their crew. I expected it to be covered in horror – beer stains everywhere, dirt, mess, overflowing toilets, general disgustingness.

I was pleasantly surprised, though. It was neither: no intimidating shininess, but no gross piles of washing either.

We were just about to step onto the bus when we were leaped on by one of the crew members, a short man with wild curly hair and an impressive beer belly, wielding an industrial flashlight.

"You're going on the bus?" he barked. I wasn't sure if he was one of the borrowed Finnish roadies or one of the Germans.

"Obviously," Luka said, rolling his eyes, grabbing the handle of the door positioned halfway along the double-decker. The roadie pointedly stepped in front of the door, barring our progress.

"Right." The roadie turned to address me, puffing out his chest with importance. "You need to learn one very important thing about going on the bus. The most important thing you will ever learn. Honestly, this is the most important thing anyone will ever tell you. I don't care what they tell you about respecting people's privacy, or about noise, or tidiness, or anything else. This is the only thing you need to remember."

"Get on with it," Luka sighed. He'd obviously heard this rant before.

"I need her to realise how vital this is!" The roadie was almost petulant. "You see, nobody tells people this before they get on."

"Except you," Luka muttered.

"I heard that. I need to tell people. The thing is..." He took a deep breath. I held mine: what wondrous wisdom could he be about to impart? "It's about the toilet." Oh. "You must not – and I repeat, you *must not* – put paper in the toilet. Never. Even just one piece, one tiny piece of toilet paper, and the whole system gets clogged. I've been on buses where that has happened. It's not pretty. There's flooding, and smell, and nobody can use the bathroom at all. Do you want to make this band suffer that? It's not nice. It's really not nice."

"Er... OK?" I was keen to shut this guy up. Luka looked just about ready to pick him up and bowl him across the car park.

"So what are you not going to do?"

"I'm not going to put paper in the toilet," I said obediently, turning my best puppy eyes onto the roadie. "In fact, if I need to go, I'll go back inside. Promise."

"Promise?"

"I promise."

"That's all right then." With the kind of smile you see on serial killers, the roadie melted into the shadow of the bus. Apparently it was his job to guard it from terrifying fangirls. Fun times for him.

"He assembles us at the start of every tour and gives everyone that speech," Luka sighed, finally flinging open the door and leading me up a couple of steps.

I partially blamed – or thanked, depending on how you look at it – the toilet-obsessed roadie for the state of the bus. I got the feeling that if anyone was to leave any mess in there he'd do a psycho leap at them and start beating them with his torch.

We stepped into what I was assured was the main area of the bus – surprisingly spacious, considering it was, you know, a *bus*. Instead of the rows of seats you'd usually see on a coach, there were booths lining the curtained windows, each seating four people.

There was a TV mounted on a bracket in one corner, which I guessed came in useful on long, boring road trips, but it wasn't the massive James-Bond-style gadget I'd been expecting. Where we'd just come in was a solid partition, which led to the infamous toilet, and the stairs up to the sleeping area. This partition was partially disguised by a little kitchen area, where I could see a fridge, a sink, and a sandwich toaster. Primitive, but good enough for on the road, so Luka told me. And at least there was plenty of booze in the fridge.

It was all very tidy: practically spotless, in fact, considering how many people were travelling on there– all of Karin Cluster, and all of Karin Cluster's crew. There were a couple of pairs of large men's shoes strewn about the place, and a table covered in make-up bottles and brushes, but hey, what else could you expect?

I was just happy not to see a sea of beer cans and Max's underpants.

"It's not much, but it works when you're away from home for weeks at a time," Luka said, shrugging as he cracked open another couple of beers from the fridge. "Most nights we have hotels, but this is our base."

"It must be wonderful to travel so much," I opined, sliding into the nearest booth. "I'd love it – the open road, none of my family to drive me mad, no boss to tell me I haven't cleaned the coffee machine properly..."

"You start to miss all that, after a while," Luka said softly as he shuffled into the booth alongside me – next to me, not across the table. "Some people would do it all year round if they could. Max gets antsy after more than a week with his wife. But I'm not like that. I miss the solitude I can only get at home." He took a sip of his beer. "Being able to stand on the very edge of the island, away from all the tourists and all the people, at the place where nobody can find me. Just watching the waves crash against the cliffs, knowing that one misstep and I'd be down there myself. The power of the sea around Fehmarn is beautiful to watch. You can't get that on a tour bus."

"I suppose," I mused, pressing my back against the window, putting us face to face. "It seems like whenever I leave Guernsey, it calls me back. I don't think I'm built for a life inland. If I moved anywhere else, it would have to be by the sea. I'd still like some freedom sometimes, though," I said, not realising how true it was until I was in the middle of saying it. "Sometimes it's just too much, being trapped on such a small island. It's only about seven miles long at its longest stretch, you know. If you want to escape someone or something, there's nowhere to go. An open road seems enviable, the perfect escape."

"Some open roads can be endless," Luka pointed out. "Sometimes, you feel like you're never going to make it home."

"But no road is truly one way."

"Some can be. Should be. Must be." Luka stared into the distance across the table. I would have paid quite a lot of money to see what he was seeing: I was willing to bet he wasn't really thinking about the sandwich toaster he seemed fixed on.

"Stop getting maudlin and drink your beer!" I clapped my hands in my best schoolmarm manner, jerking him out of his little reverie. "Come on, this is my first time on a tour bus. Are you going to bore me with philosophy all night?"

"I suppose we couldn't have that." Luka turned to me, the ghost of a wicked grin starting to appear.

"Yeah, if you want to get all deep, you need to find someone else." I waved my hand dismissively. "Life's too short to fill your head with all that angst."

"How right you are." Luka raised his beer as if to toast me, those dark grey-green eyes locking onto mine.

Just at that second, my phone buzzed insistently in my back pocket. Buggeration. I shifted to pull it out, almost-unintentionally jutting my chest towards Luka as I did so. Well, I had to check the phone, didn't I? Lizzy could have been assaulted by long-haired Finns and giant Germans, for all I knew.

You'd better not have left, I'm having fun but I'm not sleeping with Udo so you can hog the hotel room! said the WhatsApp message. Well, it was nice that Lizzy was still not drunk enough to be incoherent in her messages. Still, I wasn't happy that she thought I would callously abandon her in the middle of nowhere with a load of men she barely knew.

Not until I'd had a lot more to drink, anyway.

I started to type back *I'm in the bus, I'm not going anywhere* – then reconsidered. If I let Lizzy know where I was, would she come tumbling in to drink with us? I didn't want that. I had plans for this guitarist, and none of them involved my best friend. Or any bear-like roadies.

Don't worry, not going anywhere, I decided on, and quickly sent the message.

"Sorry, Lizzy's a bit paranoid I'm going to lea-umph."

Before I could get anywhere near the end of my sentence, Luka had swooped. I dropped my phone in shock – happy shock, I'd like to point out. I had a rather sexy guitarist attached to my face, after all.

194

His breath was hot in my mouth, his lips moving quickly and urgently. I could taste beer, smell sweat, feel nothing but fire smoking inside me...

Yeah, I wasn't exactly willing to pull away. But I did; just for a second. I didn't say anything, just raised my eyebrows and let him speak.

"You said your way of solving problems involves 'pulling'. Is this what you mean?"

"Yes."

"You see, I speak English, but not *perfect* English." He was so close to me I could see the tiniest flecks of gold in his grey-green eyes. "I've not heard 'pull' before, like that."

"Well... you're doing a pretty good job so far," I whispered.

"What about if I do... this?" He reached his hand over and gently stroked my knee. Even though my jeans, it felt like his touch was made of electricity. "Is that 'pulling'?"

"It helps," I said, my voice still low. "But really, you need to be doing this, too." This time, I was the one who instigated the kiss. Not so wild this time, the kiss was slow and languid, our eyes open. Luka gripped my knee hard, surprisingly hard: so I bit his lip.

"Is that 'pulling', too?" he gasped.

"It can be," I said, raising my eyebrows again. "Though I don't think you'll find it in the dictionary."

"And...and where would a 'pull' go next?" Luka said huskily, running his fingertip all the way from my knee to my hip, skirting over the most important part. I couldn't help but have a little shudder; I leaned into him involuntarily. His hand clutched at my hip, at the top of my jeans: I was pressed against the cold glass of the window. Too cold, in fact. I wanted to move forward into the pillar of heat that was Luka.

"Well," I said slowly, biting the corner of my own lip and looking down at Luka's tight skinny jeans. More to the point, looking at the bulge in them. "It depends."

"On what?"

"On what you need." I looked back up. "See, a drunk, random pull is my cure for many things. But the level of it... if you're just a bit homesick, we've done enough to cure it. If you're *heart*sick, well then." My hand found its way to the bulge. "Things need to go a little further."

"Then, I am heartsick," Luka murmured, gathering me against him.

Chapter 15

My phone was buzzing again. Bloody hell.

"Don't answer it," Luka mumbled, pulling me closer with one hand.

We hadn't stuck around in our little booth, of course. Come on, even I've got a bit more sense than that. It would be like going home with a guy who lives in a house-share and shagging on his sofa.

We didn't go far though. In a whirl of ripping off clothes and clawing at one another's skin, we somehow managed to get upstairs, to the ever so cosy sleeping area where the band and crew members all had bunks.

Luka's narrow shelf was actually quite comfortable. For all the time we spent there, anyway. The man was like a demon on speed – he couldn't stay still. The bunk, the floor, up against someone else's bunk, against the window…

I'll leave it at that.

Anyway, my phone was buzzing. Luka and I were collapsed on his bunk, passing a bottle of beer between us. I was rather on the lightheaded side. Orgasms or booze, I couldn't work out which one had done it. It wasn't exactly an unpleasant feeling, anyway.

"Just leave it."

"No, it'll be Lizzy." I groaned. I leaned off the edge of the bunk and hung down like a monkey. Ooh, my dizzy head didn't like that very much. I plucked my jeans off the floor and hoisted myself back into Luka's arms.

Mmm. They were lovely arms. Muscled and defined, from years of pounding at a guitar. His body was beautiful. Stark black tattoos leaping from his pale skin, the tiniest smattering of blonde hair leading down to places I was becoming rather well-acquainted with…

I shook my head to clear it, and yanked my phone from my jeans pocket.

Are you on the bus? Quite drunk. Tour manager is trying to round everyone up to leave.

I really was impressed: Lizzy's WhatsApping was still coherent. My own hands were shaking – again, orgasms or beer? I didn't trust myself to respond.

"I should go and find her." I sighed heavily. "You guys have to get out of here soon." Despite being on the far side of drunk, there was still enough brain left in me to be sensible. Maybe it was something about being in another country – I couldn't exactly just stagger back to my own house at four in the morning. Homing-pigeon instincts were no use in the wilds of Finland.

"Ugh," Luka groaned, and said something that sounded rather rude in German. "I don't want to go."

"I'd rather not either, but you know." I shrugged, arching my back against his chest. "Kind of has to happen."

"Why don't you stay? Come for the rest of the tour. I can find room for you in my bunk." I turned around to look Luka in the eye. He had one eyebrow raised suggestively, but an eager, appealing look in his eyes, his hair loosely mussed all over his pillow. My goodness, he was gorgeous.

But then… no.

"Much as I'd love to, I really can't." I sighed again, ruefully this time. "You need stress relief, not a defacto tour bus girlfriend."

"Well…" I could see him trying to counter this in his head – but he knew it was true. "Yeah. You're right."

"Believe me, I'd have this night last forever if I could," I said. "Well, maybe not forever. A few months at least."

"You were right though," Luka said, grinning. He was gorgeous when he was pulling his smouldering, sulky faces, but holy shit on a cream cracker, he was even more beautiful when he smiled. "Drunk pulling does make everything feel better. At least for a little while."

"Tell me about it." I grinned back. "Now come on, help me find the rest of my clothes."

I was just smoothing down my hair and Luka was pulling on a t-shirt when I heard Lizzy.

"Cleo Weeks, you'd better be in here!" she was shouting. Rather loudly, for Lizzy. I could just about hear the toilet-fiend roadie trying to get in his spiel, but she was ignoring him.

"Hang on," I called down, giving my vest top one last optimistic straighten.

"I really wish you didn't have to go." Luka grabbed me suddenly, pulling me close against him. I could feel his muscles, taut beneath his t-shirt. God, I could have stayed in those arms of his forever, no matter how much I knew it would be a bad idea. Just for that second, I wavered...

Then pulled back. My best friend was waiting for me downstairs. We'd come here for a gig, for a bit of fun: sure, I had a little husband-hunting in mind, too. But I wasn't going to find one on this tour bus. A bit of a good time – a bit of a *very* good time – but not a husband. There were too many issues floating around in that band, and I just wasn't up to the full-time counselling.

"I tell you what," I said, gripping Luka's shirt and staring fixedly at his chest. "You lot come to the UK. Anywhere in the UK, it doesn't matter where. And if you're still feeling down and *philosophical*..." I grinned, and looked back into his eyes. "I'll be around for some stress relief."

"Everybody needs stress relief every so often." Luka nodded, smiling down at me. I reached up for one last, chaste kiss.

Of course, that was the exact moment my phone buzzed insistently, again. Bloody hell, Lizzy, I thought. I'm *coming*.

Not in that way.

That bit was over for the night.

Both me and Luka sighed at the same time.

"When I'm in the UK, I will be throwing that phone out of the window."

"You're welcome to," I growled. "Come on, let's go."

Ever the heavy metal gentleman, Luka led me down the stairs. Lizzy was waiting at the bottom, in front of the open bus door. She'd brought Udo, the bear-like roadie, and another man.

This one was certainly a better-looking prospect than his hulking compatriot: he was still muscular and tall, but in a more lithe, slender way than the massive Udo. He had a huge lazy grin practically stretching his hairline and crinkling his blue eyes at the corners – a grin that almost reached to the tunnel he had in his left ear, at least an inch in diameter. There was something... *fine* about his face. His cheekbones and jawline were almost delicate; only set off by the budding beard he was cultivating. His hair wasn't half as long as the hair belonging to every other man within a five-mile vicinity: instead, he had a shiny blonde Mohawk, a few inches tall. Quite an impressive looking man, to be honest – I kind of hoped that Lizzy had had a go of him.

At least a 'homesick' pull, if not a 'heartsick' one, if you get my drift.

"I was just coming down, there was no need to ring me again," I scolded, marching into the small space behind Luka – which of course left me pressed against him. I didn't exactly mind.

"I didn't ring you," Lizzy said, a drunkenly beatific smile on her face. "I just wanted to get you down here. Everyone's got to go home now."

"Yeah, I got your message – hey, who was ringing me then?" I whipped my phone out of my jeans, just as it started to buzz again. Gemma?

"Hello? What's up?"

"Cleo, I've been trying to get hold of you for ages!" Gem barked down the phone, almost sounding like her sister. "It's happening, I'm in labour!"

"You're what?"

"Yes, yes, contractions, contractions, waters, *mucous plug...*"

"Shite on a motorbike!" I seized Lizzy by the arm and shook her somewhat violently. "Gem's in labour!"

"What?" Lizzy gasped. I let her go with a jolt, sending her flying down the steps of the bus with a crack.

"It's way too early for this! How often are the contractions? How do we get back to Guernsey? Oh, bugger, is someone with you right now?"

"Ahh, chill out, Cleo." Hang on. Was Gem laughing? "I'm just messing with you! I'm at home, on the sofa, eating Pringles. Can't sleep. No waters, no contractions, definitely no mucous plugs. Just thought I'd check in. Shagged any rock stars yet?"

"You... are... evil!" I sighed, banging my head against the side of the bus. Suddenly I was aware of quite a commotion around the steps. Both Udo and the Mystery Mohawk Man were kneeling on the ground, Lizzy somewhere between them. Luka was peering out of the bus with some concern, saying something urgent in German. "Gemma, you berk, I've got to go. Something's happened." I whacked the red button on my screen with no small amount of violence, and shoved it back into my pocket, barging my way past all the blokes...

Just in time to hear Udo say something that made me physically chill. "I'll call an ambulance."

* * *

I hadn't *quite* killed Lizzy when I accidentally threw her down some steps. Onto a concrete pavement. While rather intoxicated.

Yeah, the guilt's still kicking me in the solar plexus every time I think about it.

We did need the ambulance: but Lizzy wasn't quite mortally wounded. When I'd heard the word ambulance, I'd expected to find her completely unconscious at the bottom of the steps, bleeding from her ears and with a caved-in skull.

Instead, I found her fully conscious and whimpering, clutching her right leg. The right leg which happened to be at a totally wrong angle from her body.

Sadly, although Luka and Udo had a very loud argument with the tour manager, they weren't allowed to accompany us to the Finnish hospital. They had a schedule to keep, and although they had the next day off, they were using it to travel the length of the country on the bus. Mystery Mohawk Man did, however, come with us.

He was soon revealed as an incredibly chatty young bloke called Wilhelm, or Vill, as I was soon calling him. He wasn't really supposed to be travelling with Karin Cluster – being Max's little brother (I say 'little' but he was thirty-three) he wanted some experience of rocking around Europe with a metal band. As Finland was the official 'Promised Land of Heavy Metal', he couldn't think of a better bit of the tour to hitch a ride on the bus. He was a guitarist himself, and was on the lookout for a band to join, having just quit one back in Germany.

He'd bonded with Udo and was spending his evenings helping him on the merch stand, which was how he had ended up having an increasingly deep drunken conversation with Lizzy.

And, also, how he was able to come and sit in a hospital with us for five hours, still being lovely and chatty despite the alcohol wearing off somewhere around hour number three.

"No, I'm not going to marry him!" Lizzy was laughing as we were waiting at Helsinki airport. We had, at this point, been hanging around for quite a while waiting for someone to find a wheelchair we could use to use to haul Lizzy onto our flight. "I don't even fancy him!"

"But he's lovely! And totally into you."

"No, he wasn't, he was exactly the same to you. And to Mel, and to Yasmin, and to Lilly, and to Laura and Sara."

"Who?"

"Two girls who had triple As too. They know the Finnish roadies."

"Oh."

"He was just generally lovely to everyone. I don't fancy him."

"Aww. But he was extra lovely."

"Cleo, to me, everyone's lovely right now. These painkillers are fantastic."

"But he stayed right to the end! Who else would do that?"

"The others would have," Lizzy pointed out, shifting uncomfortably in her seat. "Wasn't Luka still sulking when we left?"

"Well… yeah."

"And wasn't Mel nearly crying when that tour manager told her she had to get on the bus?"

"I suppose so." I smiled despite myself. "They're awesome." OK, so I was thinking more of Luka's sulky pout than Mellina's tipsy tears, but still. They *were* awesome.

At least the break in Lizzy's leg hadn't been too bad. Just a product of her landing awkwardly. A lot of medical sciencey words had been bandied about, which of course I didn't understand, but I knew it was enough that Lizzy would be in plaster for a while. Only from her foot to her knee, thankfully: if she'd been in plaster up to her thigh, I would probably have had to move in with her and help her get to the loo and other such savoury things. And seeing as it was my fault she'd broken it in the first place, I'd have had to do it with no complaints.

I did understand the part the Finnish doctor spelled out where Lizzy was told she'd heal up in about ten to twelve weeks, if she was lucky.

By which time, of course, Gemma would have gone into labour for real, and would have a baby. Wow.

Thankfully, Lizzy would only be immobilised in a wheelchair while we were powering around airports on our way home. Once we got back to Guernsey, we'd be able to get her some proper crutches of her own and she was positively encouraged to use them. Thank goodness for that, I thought. She lived *upstairs.*

I don't think any of us were particularly ready to be carrying her up and down every day.

Well, Vill might have. That is, if he'd been coming back to Guernsey with us, which he wasn't. He'd tried to: appealed to at any rate.

No matter what Lizzy said, I was absolutely convinced he had the hots for her.

I'm not going to get into the details of the journey home. No, nobody wants to hear about that. It's enough of a trial getting from Guernsey to – well, anywhere – at the best of times. Having to get to the mainland, then onwards from there, without losing any luggage or sanity... I love travelling, and it still gets a bit annoying at times.

You try it with someone wedged into their seat with a plaster cast. Someone rather drugged up on heavy-duty Finnish painkillers.

Especially when you are finding it quite hard to sit still thanks to a persistent ache between your thighs.

Hell yeah, Luka's presence was still very much known.

Not in person, of course. Despite the chaos of Lizzy's fall and the ensuing Finnish ambulance, we'd not exactly taken the opportunity to throw ourselves into one another's arms, weeping with goodbyes. That had already been well established: the occasional fuck, good. Relationship, bad. But it was rather pleasant, feeling that familiar buzz around my bits, knowing the reason why.

Plus, I was bloody well looking forward to exploiting my bragging rights among my friends. I'd just fucked a bona fide rock star. On a tour bus.

The feeling helped, at least, when I was trying to steady Lizzy on a mildly turbulent plane, trying to get her to the toilet in one piece. At least it was all worth it, I was reminded.

However, it was somewhat hard to keep so calm (and smug) when we got off the plane in Guernsey, exhausted and looking forward to home; only to encounter Flic at Arrivals.

"What the hell are you doing here?" I exclaimed, not unhappily, jamming Lizzy's wheelchair to a halt. I was a little bit touched – she'd clearly heard what had happened and had come to drive us back to Lizzy's in her fancy car. How kind of her. I even leaned forward to give her a hug.

"Oh, I was just up here anyway, I thought I might as well come and get you." Flic submitted to my hug with a pat on the back, then leaned down to do the same to Lizzy.

"What were you doing here, then?"

"I was booking our flights!" Flic gave that irritating tinkling laugh, usually saved for her superiors at work (or when she herself was feeling particularly superior). "For our department store crawl!"

"Oh, not that again," I groaned.

"Yes, I thought I might as well do it now in case I needed to put in your passport numbers while I booked it," Flic explained, taking hold of Lizzy's wheelchair and starting to head towards the car park. "And I thought I'd be able to haggle a deal if I did it at the airport, I went to school with one of the girls who works at the

Aurigny desk." Her eyes narrowed. "Useless bitch. Turns out it'd be cheaper if I did it online, I needn't have bothered."

"Charmed," Lizzy piped up. I wasn't sure if Flic had heard her, or even registered it: Lizzy was a lot more sarky than usual on those painkillers.

"When are we going, then?" I sighed. I was too tired to argue. It looked like Flic wasn't going to give in about any of this, so I might as well resign myself to my fate. "July? By then, Lizzy's leg will be back to normal and she'll be able to traipse around properly, though maybe August would be better, by then the baby will be old enough to travel, or be left with your mum."

"July?" Flic jammed the wheelchair to a halt, aghast, nearly ramming it into her own car. "August? The actual month of the wedding? Are you mad? That leaves hardly any time for alterations, for things to go wrong and be fixed, for much choice… no, no, certainly not. We're going the week after Liberation Day."

Liberation Day (Guernsey's national holiday, pretty much) was the ninth of May. Three weeks away.

"Let me get this straight." I sighed again, loudly. "You're proposing that we all trot off on this department store crawl, which we don't want to go on anyway, while your sister is… hang on," I did a brief calculation, "thirty-seven weeks pregnant. You do realise that she's not going to fit in anything?"

"You've tried all this before. It's happening, Cleo."

"Yeah, but it's mental."

"I've already lost Denise, she can't make it." Flic rolled her eyes. "She's got a family christening that week. And she's such a funny shape, I could really do with her trying things on… but no, she'll have to just go with whatever the rest of you decide on. Well, what I decide on."

"You've forgotten the most important thing." Lizzy announced grandiosely, shuffling herself into the backseat of Flic's car. "At thirty-seven weeks, Gem won't be allowed to fly."

"Yeah!" I remembered. "It's bad for the baby, or something. Or maybe the airlines just don't want people breaking their waters all over their planes. It'd be quite messy. At that time she could go into labour at any second and I don't fancy having to deliver your niece in a changing room at Harrods."

"Oh." Flic was momentarily taken aback. She slid into the drivers' seat quickly and immediately started swiping at things on her phone, leaving me to sort out the return of the wheelchair to the people at the airport.

By the time I got back, Lizzy had fallen into a painkiller-y snooze in the back of the car, while Flic was staring pensively out of the windscreen.

I'm not a big fan of silences. Too much time to think: especially now I was back at home. While Flic drove too fast down the road that ran like an artery towards St Peter Port, I tried to keep up a relentless babble about our adventures in Finland. But Flic wasn't interested. She just stared through that windscreen, seemingly focussed on the road but apparently very far away at the same time.

I couldn't help but be slightly suspicious.

I tried to put it out of my head and look out of the window instead, letting the 'conversation' peter away.

God, it was weird being back in Guernsey. Everything seemed so cramped: the granite walls at the side of the road looming over me, feeling far too tight. When Flic overtook a bus – a huge green monstrosity, way too big for the narrow roads – I thought I could hear death speeding towards me.

I didn't know whether it was my conversation with Luka, or coming back from Finland, or just the fact we were back in the land of thirty-five-miles-per-hour speed limits, but it all seemed very strange. Very small. Yes, we'd just come back from Finland. Wide open spaces are the norm over there. Wide open snowy spaces, at that.

Somehow, it felt more than that. I was positively restless, following the same turns in the road, following the same paths I'd been following since I was born. Going through the Bailiff's Cross, a junction near the hospital, I knew exactly how long it would be before the lights changed. At the top of the Rohais, one of the big hills on the way into town, I knew exactly where to turn my head to see Waitrose, and on the other side the children's home where Mum always threatened to send me when I was a naughty kid. I didn't even have to look, I could close my eyes and feel it with the incline of the hill.

I'd probably be able to navigate the way home from the airport in my sleep.

Speaking of which…

"Hey, Flic?" I spoke up as we crested the Rohais, about to go past Ladies' College. "Don't drop me off at mine, I'm going to help Lizzy when she gets home, get her sorted out and stuff."

"I'm not taking you home." Flic finally spoke up. "We've got somewhere to go, first."

"Oh, not the Jar already," I groaned. "I've got to work tomorrow, I want just a few more hours away."

"No, not the Jar." Flic shut her mouth again. I tried to raise my eyebrows at Lizzy via the wing mirror, but she was still asleep.

Things became no more apparent when Flic coasted down the Grange and straight across Guernsey's only real roundabout, past the Liberation Monument and towards the harbour.

"Oh no," I started, realising what was happening. "Flic… seriously?"

"Well, I'm not going dress shopping without my sister." Flic turned to look at me like I was the mental one. "She'll just have to come on by herself. I'll check out the boat times now, see if she's definitely allowed to travel, and see if I can wangle us a discount."

"You're just putting Gem on the boat? Not all of us?"

"Why would we all go?" Flic laughed. "Much more pleasant to fly. Gemma's the one who got herself pregnant, she's the one who can get seasick. She's the one most used to vomiting, at any rate, after that morning sickness. It's only logical."

"Gem is *so* not going to like this."

Annoying Customer of the Week, Part 7

"Hiya! What can I get for you this lovely sunny day?"

"Wow, you're cheerful. Nice for some. Cappuccino and a latte."

"Would you like big ones or small ones?"

"Medium."

"We do big or we do small, no such thing as a medium here!"

"Fine, big. And I don't want all that foam on the cappuccino."

"You want a cappuccino without as much foam?"

"Yes."

"A latte, then, I'll just change it on the till."

"No, not a latte. A cappuccino with less foam. I want more milk, don't fob me off with all that useless foam."

"OK, but that's a latte. A cappuccino is defined by the foamy milk, a latte is the one with creamy..."

"NO. A cappuccino with no foam, a cappuccino with no foam! It's a totally different thing! If you give me two lattes, I'll keep bringing it back until you get it right!"

"OK, OK, no need to get angry, sir. Gemma, can I have a big latte and a big cappuccino with no foam, please?"

I didn't even have to look at Gem to know her facial expression. And to know that the customer's two drinks would be coming at the end of the bar, both exactly the same.

My chirpiness was a total fake front. I'd have given almost anything to be back in that tour bus in Oulu.

Chapter 16

It was just... odd. That's all. It'd take a bit of getting used to for anyone, being back in the Bean Jar. It was all just so normal. Same old coffee machine, creaking alarmingly when you tried to make an extra-hot latte. Same old mural of Sarnia Chérie to stare at. Same old customers, same old soups, same old coffees.

Gemma wasn't helping.

"You fancy him."

"I do not."

"You do. You fancy him." Gem paused, then dutifully added "loser"'.

"Honestly, why would I fancy him? With his, his stupid... hair!"

"And stupid t-shirts," Gem supplied. "Yesterday he was wearing one with something from Star Trek on it. You still fancy him though."

"Gem, I do not. It's Zach. Zach!"

"Then why are you so bothered about what's-her-face?"

"Her name is Sky and I'm not bothered!"

"Like 'Sky' is a real name," scoffed the woman intending to call her unborn baby 'Cinnamon'.

"Whatever. Go and clear some tables." I turned back to cleaning the coffee machine, pretending to be bored with the conversation as Gem waddled over to the tables, mumbling to herself.

But I was still having the conversation with myself in my head. Did I really fancy Zach? *Zach*?

It had all happened so fast. It had given me such a weird jolt to see him pulling, back in Folies. Frankly, it had spoilt my night. I couldn't take my eyes off them: his hand in the small of her back, hers in his hair. Not giving the tiniest of shits what anyone thought of them. Least of all me.

Then Jonny had puked behind a sofa, Flic had gone postal, and by the time everything had been sorted out and I'd turned back to them, Zach and the girl had disappeared.

Gemma had whole-heartedly teased Zach for the next few days, but he never took the bait; just smiled a smug little smile and got back to work.

Then, of course, Finland happened.

And I hardly thought of Zach at all. Honestly.

If I did, it must have been the hangover from hell talking. Or the alcohol. Or the boredom of being stuck in a hospital.

By the time I got back to the Jar, this 'Sky' was fully installed as Zach's girlfriend. And it was weird.

I'd never really thought Zach as having such a thing as a love life. He was just... Zach. Our Zach. Always there, reliable, sometimes grumpy, part of the furniture. Not the type to go around getting a girlfriend without so much as consulting his staff. I hadn't thought he had it in him.

They'd only been together a couple of weeks and already she was practically living in the Bean Jar, despite apparently running her own business creating wedding stationery (Flic was thrilled at having a new wedding contact). She'd sit there at the bar, a sketchbook in front of her, tossing her long chestnut hair around and smiling adorably at Zach until he brought her the nicest slices of cake he could find. Sometimes she'd open up her tiny rosebud mouth and sit there with her eyes closed until he fed her the cutest little morsels.

Sickening.

To be fair to Zach, when she did that I'm pretty sure I caught him having a little grimace. But he put the bloody piece of Gâche in her mouth anyway.

I just hoped she wouldn't try and step on our toes, I thought to myself.

That was what I was stressing about, I realised in a sudden brainwave. I didn't fancy Zach at all. Of course I didn't. I was just worried about the Jar! It was my stamping ground, I'd been there since the very beginning and I didn't want some new person coming in and changing things, girlfriend or not. I was just being territorial. Obviously.

Of course I didn't fancy Zach.

Anyway, I thought to myself, polishing the coffee machine a little too vigorously, I had things to do, stuff to plan. I had Nan to try and contain, for a start.

While Lizzy and I had been partying our way through Finland, Nan had officially set up her not-WI old ladies' club. And, for reasons known only to her, she had called it the Guernsey Goats.

"Well, we are a load of old goats, dear," she'd said, with a regal wave of her hand.

They were an entirely democratic bunch; which, as far as I could tell, had so far led to them spending each of their meetings so far getting sozzled on sherry and watching Ryan Gosling movies – while wearing sparkly purple sashes, of course. There was a lot of knitting going on, but when I inquired as to *what* they were knitting I just got side-eyed and the subject changed. I dreaded to think. The only thing that was annoying Nan was that they had voted to keep the club a women-only institution.

"I'm proud of you, Nan," I'd said. "By trying to get men involved too you're striking a blow for equality! You know, feminism and all that."

"Bollocks, dear," she'd retorted. "I'm just thinking about my sex life."

Some things never change; no matter how many hip replacements they have.

Besides having to ferry Nan off on my scooter to Guernsey Goats meetings (held in a church hall on the other side of the island; I was quite surprised a religious establishment had agreed to let the old bats in) I had Liberation Day to plan.

The month of May had just sneakily rolled around, without me even really noticing; that is until Gem had hauled her increasingly enormous belly over to the table where I was drinking coffee, and plonked herself down in the most inelegant fashion possible.

"Ugh," she had said by way of greeting. "I can't believe I have to miss out on the Lib Day piss-up."

"Oh, bollocks!" I'd exclaimed. I'd totally forgotten what the advent of May meant to all us Guernsey natives.

Liberation Day is Guernsey's equivalent of Bastille Day in France – it's our national day, where everyone is allowed to be especially territorial and proud about their 'Guernseyness'. Back in 1945, the Allied forces finally got round to liberating the German-occupied Channel Islands on the ninth of May, just after the Germans surrendered and the war ended in Europe. Ever since then, Liberation Day has been a properly big deal for Guernsey.

When I was a kid it was way better, of course. I'm not just saying it because there's some kind of law about putting your entire childhood in a golden haze – it actually was. It was a bank holiday, everyone got the day off, and it used to be that everyone on the island, *everyone*, would gather in town. St Peter Port was transformed for the day. There was a parade, stalls all around the seafront, stages with people playing music, bands marching up and down the piers, beer tents, Crown and Anchor stands and, most importantly for the kids of the island, a funfair in North Beach car park.

Oh, that funfair. Just somewhere for your mum to take you, when you were little. You'd have a lovely time, then go back to school and brag to all your mates about which rides you went on. The same rides turned up almost every year – it was one of those travelling funfair things, run by a load of dodgy blokes and precariously erected with bits of string and staple guns, to look at the rides – so you'd plan for weeks in advance. You prayed to be that one lucky person the bloke on the tombola slipped the winning ticket to, so you'd get to cart around a giant teddy for the whole day.

Then you turned into a teenager, and among some groups, it wasn't the done thing to be enthusiastic. Even about Liberation Day and the funfair.

I, of course, was not part of one of those groups.

Every year, me and Lizzy meticulously plotted everything: the order in which we'd swan around the fair, which crappy local bands we wanted to see, what we wanted to buy from the traditional Guernsey market...

But as soon as we hit our teenage years, the focus changed. Instead of just aiming to ride the Sizzler and the Space Screamer until we were sick, we wanted to meet boys. That's why the 'popular' girls were so keen to appear bored by it all: a boy might be watching and they couldn't be seen to be anything but the epitome of cool.

Back then, every May I'd find myself unexpectedly popular for a few weeks. You see, I'd had the privilege of going to a mixed school for my Primary years, and back then I was still friendly with some of the strapping young lads I'd been buddies with, back when they were snotty-nosed little boys and I was a hyperactive little girl. I wouldn't touch most of them with a barge pole, of course, but some of them were of interest to the popular crowd. Particularly Connor De Jersey, six feet tall by the time he was thirteen and blissfully unadorned by the acne that plagued all the others.

Of course, the Liberation Day when I was fifteen, Connor unexpectedly gave me my first kiss under the SideWinder, and my momentary popularity was gone for good – jealous bitches. But the afternoon of long candyfloss kisses, surrounded by shrieks and screams and the occasional retching preteen... oh, it was worth it.

Liberation Days past were the stuff of legend.

The optimum word in that sentence, of course, is *past*.

It had been a few years since two things happened that would drastically change the face of Liberation Day forever. Firstly, the funfair stopped coming. Generations mourned. Secondly, drinking was banned, anywhere but licensed pubs and beer tents. More generations mourned.

It had been practically a teenage rite of passage to stagger drunkenly from Church Square to the Weighbridge taxi rank, a pint in each hand, trying not to spill any on the cobbles. It was a beloved coming-of-age tradition: taken away from us far too soon.

That first year, to replace the fair, they put on an exhibition of youngsters performing skateboard tricks in the North Beach car park. *Skateboard tricks.* An insult. Since then, it had got worse and worse. Duller and duller.

Nowadays, everyone just grouped up in pubs or houses and spent the whole bank holiday getting more and more smashed in the name of patriotism until someone attempted to start a drunken singalong of Sarnia Chérie, to which nobody knows more than the first two lines (unless they have a mural of it behind their coffee machine at work, of course). And even fewer people know the tune.

OK, so maybe that's what people have always done on Liberation Day once they've grown up. But there was always the option to do something a bit different – cavalcades, events going on in the different parishes, street parties, all kind of things even if you didn't want to be part of the huge event in town. It had all dwindled away to practically nothing.

Still, a bank holiday is a bank holiday, though the banks were making noises about stopping even that. We were making the most of it while we could. The year before, Zach had opened the Bean Jar anyway: but between confused customers looking for booze and two grouchy staff members (to be honest, also looking for booze) it had been deemed a stupid idea.

However, the advent of Sky had done something odd to Zach. He was, dare I say it, loosening up. He had actually proposed the Bean Jar as the location for the annual piss-up, inviting everyone from Lizzy to Mrs Machon (I rather hoped she had a prior engagement at the traditional pensioners' tea dance – where, incidentally, Nan and her buddies were intending to cause some havoc among the octogenarian crowd).

I wanted to go. Of course I did. No reason not to, after all.

Not that I was desperately seeking said reason, of course not.

"Come on," I groaned, draining my coffee and getting to my feet. God, my muscles were aching. I hadn't even been out on the piss for a good week and a half: why was I so sore? "Let's get you to this doctor."

It was Gemma's final MOT before the Big Event. Just to confirm all her bits were oiled and ready to go, so to speak.

214

Nothing loose in her machinery, no cracks in the windscreen... no, that's taking it too far.

Being the lovely loyal friend I am and, of course, having been coerced into being her birthing partner, I'd volunteered to go too. Besides, if I hadn't, I think she'd have punched me. She was too big now to fit behind the wheel of her mum's car (and definitely too big to go on the back of my scooter, she'd topple the pair of us), so was reduced to either lifts from other people or the bus.

As nobody with a car was currently free, we were taking the bus.

Good lord, Gem was enormous. I walked alongside her as we headed towards the bus stop, matching her slow, waddling pace to mine. We couldn't walk more than about five paces without a grin and a wink from an old lady, or even one of the infamous "not long now"-type comments. With one hand supporting her back and the other hanging onto her handbag, I was thankful that Gemma didn't have any fingers free to make rude gestures at them.

"I have a good six weeks to go," she growled. "Surely I'm not the biggest pregnant woman they've ever seen? Christ, I'm going to get bigger. Fuck."

"It's only because you're such a skinny bitch," I reassured her, for the thousandth time. "With twig-legs like that under your bump, it just makes it look even more massive than it actually is."

"If I didn't know the actual conception date to the hour, I'd think I'd made a mistake and was due three days ago," Gem groaned, not even attempting to smile at the latest cheery wink. "God, I don't know how I'm going to get through next week. Or even, like, tomorrow. It's just so uncomfortable."

"Tomorrow you can just sit in the corner and be boring and calm," I soothed. "You can steal Zach's iPad and stare at YouTube all day if you want to, nobody'll care. He'll be too busy with Sky to notice." Gem shot me a look. I pretended not to see it. "Hell, you can do the same next week. Flic will just have to deal with it. I'm going to be the one she bullies into all the dresses, I'm the only one she can. You have nothing to worry about."

"Unless I go into labour in fucking London."

"If you go into labour in fucking London, it'll all be free on the NHS. Hey, maybe we should look into this."

"That is not happening," Gem said firmly. "This baby is a Guernsey girl. Through and through."

"Apart from her Latvian father."

"He might have been Portuguese, when I think of it." Gem shrugged. It seemed like an effort. "I can't recall. He's not a *father*, anyway. You're more of the father than he is."

"Eh?"

"Well, fathers do all this bollocks." We headed leisurely for the bus that was just rolling up to the stop. "It's supposed to be the father who carts the mother off to all the boring doctor thingies, and does all the stupid breathing with Nurse of Steel..."

"Stops her from reaching for the beer on a night out when she forgets she's pregnant?"

"Yeah, that. All the stuff Jonny'll do for Flic one day, the stuff Aaron does for Meredith."

"Oh, we're not getting into him," I said, in my best warning tones. "We've been over this."

"Yeah, and I still haven't decided anything." Oh heck, she was giving me a properly Nurse-of-Steel-worthy glare.

"Have you seen him?"

"A couple of times." She shrugged again, not so much of an effort now she was sitting comfortably on the bus. "Once with Meredith – don't look at me like that!"

"He wants you to run away with him, and you're meeting up with his wife?"

"It's not like she knows anything. We weren't exactly fucking snogging in Costa."

"Traitor."

"Hey, I didn't want you peering beadily around the corner while I had a nice calm coffee."

"Decaf, I hope."

"Yes, yes. But we were fine. She talked more than he did."

I could picture it. The stolen glances across a table, the coffees steaming and the looks even more so. The oblivious wife, sitting in between them, no idea what was going on...

"We just talked about the babies and prams and changing bags, normal motherly bullshit. You wouldn't be interested."

"Hey, *father*, remember?" I pointed to myself. "What were you saying two minutes ago?"

"Yeah, but fathers aren't meant to be interested in that kind of stuff." Gem poked me. "Aaron looked bored shitless. You'd have been the same. You don't have the same investment in the humble pushchair when you've not carried the little fucker for nine months."

"Little fucker? Kind."

"She knows I mean it affectionately." Gem punctuated her laugh with a sigh, giving her bump a friendly pat. "Look, honestly, things with Aaron... well, they're not fine, but they're the same as ever. He asks, I say maybe."

"It would be better if you said no."

"At least I'm not saying yes, right?"

"You do know, right, that things will be completely different once these babies are born?" It was worth a shot. "You'll feel different, and he'll feel different. He's going to have his own baby. If nothing else, he's not going to want to go straight from one screaming infant to another. If he's serious about leaving Meredith, he'll find some nubile nineteen-year-old with no children and an intact fanny."

"I just don't know." Gem waved her hand dismissively. "We'll see what happens. Look, I don't want to talk about it, OK?"

There was something going on. Other than the obvious, I mean. Something had happened with Aaron, and it didn't look like it was just the coffee-dates Gem was telling me about. Had they slept together? Surely not. She was the size of an igloo. And if she'd made any more plans to run away – or otherwise – surely she'd tell me? She wouldn't just disappear and not tell anyone. It was unthinkable, unquestionable.

Right?

Of course, even though Gemma and I had a lot of similarities, which made us bond so quickly when we first met, we were hugely different in some respects. She kept things to herself, plotting and stewing her way to her decisions until everyone got a surprise when they finally got nonchalantly revealed. It was how we'd found out she was pregnant; she'd just announced out of the blue that she was going to have a baby. No heart-to-hearts over keeping it, or angsting over the father, or even over whether she needed to pay the Clearblue shelf a visit at Boots – the first we knew about it was when all decisions had been made. Hormones had mellowed her slightly, but it not much. I couldn't have done it myself. I'd always been the kind of person who liked to talk all my choices through, and loudly.

I couldn't pry more; it was like trying to get blood out of the granite Guernsey was made of (even more stubborn than your average stone). I'd have to regroup after the GP appointment, work out a different tack. I rued the day I stopped going to the classes with Nurse of Steel: if I'd made friends with Meredith myself, I'd be able to find out just how much she knew. And if she had any inklings of anything more going on.

But at the doctor's surgery, all thoughts of Gemma and Aaron were firmly driven from my mind.

The doctor, a jowly older woman with a streak of white through the middle of her dull brown hair, kept staring at me. Even while she was taking Gem's blood pressure and giving her an encouraging lecture about keeping off the fags after the baby was born, she was looking at me. Eyes narrowed, calculating… it was strange.

Finally, she finished poking and prodding Gem, and declared her MOT up to date and ready to go.

"Now, you," she said, turning properly to face me, for the first time not just side-eyeing me. "You need to see your doctor."

I looked around, almost expecting to see someone else sitting behind me. "Eh? No, I don't. I'm healthy, me. I'm fine."

"Really?" The doctor gave me a proper searching look. "Do you ever find yourself feeling really tired?" I nodded, slowly.

"Yes, but that's just because I go out a lot, I'm on my feet at work all day…"

"And have you put on any weight?"

"A bit, but…"

"Even with a job where you're on your feet all day?"

"Yeah, but it's just because…"

"And do you have some trouble swallowing?"

"Cleo's never had trouble swallowing," Gem started, but I punched her in the arm.

"Yes, I suppose, I'm a bit hoarse sometimes. But I'm a really loud person, I..."

"Yes, yes." The doctor narrowed her eyes again. "Your hair's quite dry."

"Thanks."

"You'll be thanking me properly before long. So how long have you had that lump in your neck?"

Chapter 17

A tumour.

No, I didn't have cancer. I couldn't have cancer. Not me.

Cancer was one of those things that happened to other people. Old people. People who had already had all the adventures they wanted to have. People who had found love, people who had had children, grandchildren… people who had travelled the world, followed their dreams, achieved things to make their families proud before bowing out gracefully.

Not me.

I had my whole life to live. I had Karin Cluster to follow, Gemma's baby to meet, Flic's wedding to attend, Lizzy's crutches to steal on a night out and use them to defend us from Folies trolls…

Of course, I was being totally overdramatic.

I'd spent Liberation Day in bed. I'd wanted a reason to avoid Zach's get-together at the Bean Jar, to not face him and Sky getting all gooey over one another in the home of island patriotism, and I'd found myself with a bloody good one. Instead of joining the party, I moped in my room and listened to Mum and Nan bickering.

"You can't go out wearing that!"

"You're my daughter, not my mother. Out of my way, girl, I've got my eye on Stanley Le Mesurier, and that Machon woman needs to learn how to enjoy herself. If I'm late, Joyce might scare her off."

"But you look like a disco ball! In a gay club! At Christmas!"

"I beg your pardon, this is from ASOS!"

I had no idea what Nan was wearing, but even speculating what sequinned and glittery ensemble she'd put together this time didn't cheer me up. I'd texted Lizzy and Gem saying that I felt like crap and didn't want to come out.

Gem had been with me at the doctor's, of course, seeing as I'd somewhat hijacked her appointment. She knew what was happening. She'd seen me go grey as the jowly doctor explained why she'd been giving me funny looks all through her appointment. She'd been reluctant to let me get the bus back to town on my own – she'd offered to come with me, but she only lived up the road from the surgery, and didn't need to be back at the Jar. I was touched she was bothered, but I didn't want anybody trying to come up with positivity or sympathies or anything like that. I just wanted some time on my own to feel numb.

I didn't know whether she'd told the others about what had happened. All I knew was that I didn't want to talk about it. My message to Lizzy was sparse at best, but she only replied with 'OK' and a string of kisses. She's always known when to bug me for information and when to leave me alone: even if she didn't know about my possible c-word issue, she probably thought that I was pining after Zach and had just come up with the world's flimsiest excuse not to go to his piss-up.

If only that was the case.

The doctor had been as vague as only doctors can be. She explained that such a prominent lump as the one in my throat was most likely something to do with my thyroid gland. It controls all kinds of stuff in your body, metabolism, hormones, all in a tiny gland at the base of your neck. What I'd thought was just an annoying swelling, what I'd joked was me turning into a man, could actually signal something very wrong.

At worst, cancer.

Oh, it could just be a benign nodule. Or a bit of swelling.

But she'd grabbed me forcefully around the neck to see what she could feel, and she'd frowned some more. And tutted. And got on the phone right away to make an emergency appointment for me with my own GP, for the day after Liberation Day. That's when the first inklings of fear hit me: it's easier to get a one-on-one afternoon tea with the Queen than to get a GP appointment at such short notice. I'm pretty sure my doctor was hungover when he examined me, but his verdict was the same.

"Yes, there's something there," he said, from the rather awkward position of behind me. I couldn't reply: he was firmly palpating my throat, pressing so hard I couldn't breathe, let alone speak. "There's definitely a nodule, on the right-hand side. It's big enough to feel." He let me go, and I gasped. "Now, I don't want you to worry." He sat himself back down in his big comfortable doctor-chair, behind a reassuringly huge desk. "Sometimes they form like this, it can be a hormonal imbalance. But the speed with which this one has come about... I don't want to leave it there."

"I'll have to have an operation?"

"Yes, I think so." He nodded firmly. "We'll do a scan first, to confirm what's there, then a quick biopsy to eliminate the possibility of anything a bit nasty being in that nodule."

He was skirting around the c-word, I could tell. But what else would they need a biopsy for? Plus, he kept calling it a 'nodule'. I knew that was just a fancy word for 'tumour'.

"When?"

"As soon as possible. I'm going to book you in at the PEH as soon as they've got an opening."

Jesus. A biopsy: an emergency biopsy. That was the moment when I knew it had to be serious: there was a definite possibility that I had cancer.

You can only get an appointment that quickly with a specialist at the Princess Elizabeth Hospital if you already have at least one leg already in your coffin. Or if your doctor thinks you're about to pre-order your shroud.

"What... what do they do for a biopsy?"

"It's very simple, really. You won't even need to be put to sleep for it. They just take a needle, insert it into the nodule, take a few cells, and analyse them." He said it in such a matter-of-fact way, I was put at my ease for a few seconds. Then I realised what he'd just said.

"Hang on, they're going to stick a needle in there while I'm awake?"

"Oh yes, it's painless. They numb the area, you won't feel a thing."

"OK." I was reassured. Nobody likes needles, of course, but I've never been phobic of them. Too obsessed with gory TV shows and books to ever be squeamish about that kind of stuff. I had had enough piercings and tattoos to not be that bothered about the pain.

Right in the middle of my neck though... I ran my hand gently over the lump. It really wasn't that big. I could feel it, yes, but surely a needle would have to go in quite far? It wouldn't be the surface-level scratching of a tattoo, or the quick punch of a piercing.

At least I'd be numbed. I held onto the doctor's reassurance like a lifeline. Thank all the deities for local anaesthetic.

My appointment with the scanner and the needle was made for a week from Liberation Day. Hooray.

Six days to wait. Seven, if you counted the time it would probably take to analyse the cells and send them to my friendly, solid-desked GP. Seven days to wonder and worry and pray.

And, of course, seven days to try and calm my friends down.

Lizzy had hobbled into the Jar a couple of days later, after a hard day back at work.

"They're getting worse, I swear," she sighed, plopping herself down onto the sofa in the window. "I gave them a worksheet to do about Liberation Day but two of them went off to Jersey, one was in Herm, and one was flown off to the mainland in Daddy's private plane. That bank holiday means nothing more to them than a free day off. Less than half the class have bothered, so we had to do it in class, and now I have to mark it tonight. God, this is ridiculous." She flung her crutches aside, then realised she'd left her capacious handbag on the bar. "Oh... bum."

"Here, I'll get it." I finished brewing her latte and picked up the handbag. "Christ on a bicycle, this weighs a ton."

"Marking," she said glumly.

"This must be killing your shoulder, we don't want that going along with your leg."

"Oh, I'll be fine." She took the handbag and pulled out a huge folder full of papers. "Hey, how are you? You didn't really miss much the other day. I don't think Zach's held a party in years. We were all just sat around watching him and Sky be all annoying and coupley until a busload of Sky's mates turned up with some more alcohol."

"Which they didn't share," said Gem, waddling over to join us, nearly sending a departing suit flying with her bump.

"You wouldn't be allowed to share it anyway," Lizzy said sternly. "At least they livened up the place. And anyway, Jonny let me share that big bottle of cider."

Gem laughed. "Yeah, that was funny, Cleo. Flic sent him to get some booze, and he came back with cider. Nice cider, that posh fruity stuff, but she wanted wine. She had a face on her for a good couple of hours."

"She was quite cruel, actually," Lizzy mused. "She shouted at him. Then went and sat on her own until Zach let her have a bottle of wine he'd been saving for Mrs Machon. Who never turned up, thankfully."

"This wedding's going to be a trial," Gem groaned, pulling out her phone and starting to scroll idly through Instagram.

"But yes, you didn't really miss much," Lizzy said from the depths of her handbag, rooting around for her red pen. "How are you feeling?"

"I didn't tell her," Gem said to me, looking up from her phone. "I thought you'd want to break that news yourself. Plus I thought I'd wait, you know, until you'd seen your own doctor."

"Yeah, OK," I sighed.

"Doctor?" Lizzy squeaked from inside the bag. She pulled it off her head, a few pencil sharpenings and bits of fluff caught on her glasses. "What's the matter?"

"Well, you see…" I explained about the trip to Gemma's doctor and her on-the-spot diagnosis. "Then I went to my own bloke today, I got an emergency appointment. He had a good root around in my neck, and I've got to go to the specialist next week. But he's pretty certain it's a tumour."

"A *what*?" Lizzy's voice had gone incredibly high pitched. Gem swore, and shuffled back towards the coffee bar.

"Yeah, he felt it and says it's a 'nodule', but that's just a posh word for tumour." I sighed again. "I'm having a scan at the hospital, then I get to have a biopsy at the specialist to see if it's cancerous. I googled. It's not impossible. And the speed they're doing this..." I let my voice trail off and ended with a hopeless shrug.

I'd hoped that, seeing as all I felt was 'numb', Lizzy and Gem would be the same. But no, I wasn't that lucky.

"Cancerous? Oh, oh, oh shit!" And so one of them burst into noisy tears.

I'm sure you're thinking it would be Lizzy. Sensitive, shy Lizzy.

But no. The one sobbing over the coffee machine was stubborn, grumpy, sharp-as-a-knife Gemma.

"Look, look, calm down, it's OK." I sped over to the coffee machine and put my arms around her – well, as much of her as I could get them round. "It might not be cancer, it might just be a nodule." Oh fantastic. I was the one who might have cancer, yet I was the one doing the comforting.

"No, it's not fair," Gem sobbed, leaning on me. I nearly toppled over. "It's fate, don't you see? My baby's going to be born, so someone has to die. One life enters, one leaves. And it's going to be yoooou." She broke off into a wail.

"Gem, you've been watching too many Netflix melodramas," I said firmly. "I'm certainly not going to die." I'd been trying to tell myself the same thing.

"No, it's true," she sobbed even harder. "My baby's going to have lost her real father *and* her surrogate father before she's even born!"

It took a while to calm Gemma down: an operation involving a big glass of Diet Coke, an even bigger slice of Gâche, and a lot of reassurances. And, of course, the reminder that she didn't want the baby's natural father around, whether he wanted to be or not. All the while, Lizzy was stalwartly helping from her position marooned on the sofa.

"Even if it is cancer, they'll deal with it," she said practically.

The colour had drained from her face, but she didn't look half as wretched as Gemma. Certainly not the weeping mess I'd imagined she'd be. Instead she was chattering nineteen to the dozen: I didn't know whether to reassure me or herself.

"They'll whip it out, maybe give you a bit of chemotherapy if you need it, and you'll be back to normal. You're young and you're strong, you can fight anything. Plus, it's thyroid, right? Metabolism? The medication they give you for that make you lose weight. My aunty had something wrong with hers, and the drugs were like diet pills. You'll be able to fit into whatever monstrosity Flic chooses for us for her wedding without a single lump or bump."

Once Gem had gone up to the toilet to compose herself, I sat myself back on the sofa.

"This is new," I said, giving Lizzy a proper side-eye. "You're being the sensible one and Gem's being over-emotional. What's up?"

Lizzy shrugged. "My therapist has been giving me a lot of advice." Lizzy was still having cognitive behavioural therapy for her balloon phobia. The last I'd heard, it hadn't been going too well and Lizzy wanted to die every time she went into the therapist's office. Things must have got better. "And I've been talking to... another friend. One with experience of this sort of thing."

"Oh?" I had a sneaking feeling I knew who this 'friend' was. One with an epic mohawk and a fabulous line in body modifications.

"Yeah. He reckons to get to the heart of my phobia I need to do a full audit of my mental health. And he thinks I need to stop worrying so much, see the good side of things. Stop thinking out all these dramatic scenarios. Look on the realistic side. And on the realistic side... you're not going to die." She gave a little hiccup, like she was trying to contain a lot. "Flic wouldn't let you, she'd have to find another bridesmaid!"

"An excellent point." I let Lizzy pull me into a hug, and I heaved another sigh: this time of relief. "I'm glad I've got you. I haven't told Mum or Nan yet."

"Is your mum still plaguing Charlie?"

"Yeah. To be honest, she probably wouldn't notice if I did have cancer and came home one day sick as a dog, as long as she could still give Charlie the daily 'this isn't how I raised you' lecture. It's been months and I think even she's sick of herself now, but it doesn't seem like she can stop. No, it's Nan I'm worried about. I don't know how she's going to take it."

"Your nan is an Amazon. She'll be fine. Your mum will weep and wail and make a scene, cut out some articles from the Daily Mail about how you've brought it all on yourself, then she'll go back to coming up with her mad punishments for Charlie. But your nan, and us – we'll look after you."

* * *

Lizzy was right. Of course she was. I told Mum and Nan as casually as I possibly could; after all, I didn't officially have anything to worry them with until after the scan and the biopsy. I just nonchalantly dropped the words 'lump' and 'nodule' into conversation over breakfast, and let them work things out for themselves. Mum barely blinked, other than to give me an absent-minded pat to the back of the hand and some trite sentiment along the lines of "Barbara from bridge had something similar and she's absolutely fine now".

Nan, however, gave me a properly shrewd look, through the diamanté-encrusted glasses she'd recently taken to wearing. She knew what my lump could mean: she could see through every blasé assurance I gave myself, and her.

But she didn't bug me. She didn't fling herself around my neck announcing my impending doom, or bravely try to justify things and make it seem like nothing. She just nodded, slowly and contemplatively, and gave me a quick, fierce hug before resuming whatever it was she was knitting at the kitchen table.

It was typical of Nan, of course, and I didn't know why I'd even thought to doubt her. I'd seen it before, on the night of Charlie's misadventure at the PEH. She'd stayed calm, never making an Everest out of the Val des Terres. She'd never go into crisis mode unless circumstances properly called for it: I'd never witnessed it, personally, but I'd heard that when my father left my mother, when Mum was still pregnant with me, Nan had been like a whirling dervish of organisation, power and revenge.

It was good to know that she, at least, understood what I was going through… but wasn't going to turn it into a drama.

All the same, even with the three levels of help – Gemma's morbid panic, Lizzy's calm analysis, and Nan's quiet support – I didn't want anybody with me when I had my trip to the specialist at the Princess Elizabeth Hospital. I was sure it would be nothing, a breeze… but I didn't want anybody to see me panicking. Just, you know, in case I did feel the need to panic.

And I bloody nearly did.

The scan was hardly pleasant: it was an ultrasound, in the very same room where I'd once seen Gemma's baby happily bopping around the grey screen. I didn't even get to look at the screen this time – after all, a tumour is hardly something to be stared at with gooey eyes. I wasn't going to be printing out a picture to take home.

I hadn't expected the scan to hurt. I hoped Gem hadn't felt it this bad, the 'wand' (otherwise known as 'huge prodding stick') shoving into my flesh, so deep it felt like it would come right out the other side. The woman doing the scanning was brusque and grumpy, and not even remotely interested in my weak jokes.

But it was the biopsy that nearly proved my undoing. I'd had my reservations, but Nice Mr Doctor had reassured me. It would all be fine. Painless and quick.

Bollocks. Absolute raving *bollocks on a stick*.

I was ushered into the room with the consultant specialist, one Mr James, according to his name badge. Great, that boded well. He was a skinny balding man about fifteen feet tall, with glasses perched precariously above the wispy white hairs blossoming from the side of his head. He looked like a doddering old elephant more than a consultant, but I'd been assured he was very good. I still took immediately against him. For some strange reason, I was still off Jameses.

"Now, Miss Weeks, what we're doing today is just a quick little biopsy, won't be a minute. We'll put the needle in here", he leaned over and prodded me, "and we'll just take a few cells to analyse. We'll have a quick look in the examining room, under the microscope, then a more detailed investigation in the lab. Right!" He clapped his hands loudly, and I nearly jumped off my seat. "Let's go through and get this done."

Meekly, I let myself be trotted down the corridor to the 'examining room' – a tiny little cell complete with a smiling nurse, a stark hospital bed, and a twitchy looking man with a microscope.

"Here you go, just pop yourself on there." Doctor Jim practically shoved me onto the hard little bed, nearly sending its scratchy paper sheet flying. The nurse was grinning away behind him as he fiddled with an alarmingly long plastic packet. The needle was in there.

Local anaesthetic, local anaesthetic, I kept telling myself. Any second now and that bit will happen…

My arse.

"Right!" Doctor Jim said again, not clapping his hands this time; he was much too busy brandishing what had to be the world's longest needle. Honestly, it was the length of my forearm.

OK, maybe it was the length of my hand. It was long, anyway, way longer than any needle had the right to be. Um, hang on. You've missed something, I thought, as he advanced.

"When do you numb my neck?" I squeaked.

"We don't."

"I'd *much* rather you did!" I sat bolt upright on the bed. Still grinning widely, the nurse gently pushed me back down. I was starting to think I was in some kind of torture-porn film.

"No, no, this will only take a second." Then before I could say another word, Doctor Jim was stabbing me firmly in the neck with his enormous needle.

It probably only took Doctor Jim's proscribed 'second', but it felt more like forever. I could feel the whole needle in my throat: it felt like I couldn't breathe, like it was cutting off my air supply. It didn't hurt, as such, but it felt so strange, so uncomfortable. It was a foreign body and I gasped to get it out…

Then suddenly it was gone, the still-smiling nurse was pressing a bandage to my throat, and I was sinking back in relief. It was done.

"That should be fine," said Doctor Jim.

"Should be?" I panted.

"Yes, we might have to do another one if we haven't got exactly the right spot."

"WHAT?"

Sure enough, after a mumbled discussion with Microscope Man and a suspicious rustle of plastic, Doctor Jim was advancing again. With a brisk "sorry" (he clearly wasn't), he jabbed me again. Again, I felt like my throat was being raped. I wanted to cry.

Then, unbelievably, just as Cheshire Cat Nurse was about to stick a nice secure plaster over the two holes in my neck, he was back. Doctor Jim, wielding yet another needle, this one seeming twice the length of the other two.

"This will be the last one, I promise." He sounded unconvinced.

"You have got to be *fucking* kidding me!" Yeah, so I was a bit rude. Quickly, the nurse grabbed my wrists. Apparently it looked like I was about to take a swing for Doctor Bloody Jim. Tempting, I can assure you.

The third stab to my neck *really* hurt, my tender skin already bruised and starting to swell. And this time, it really was in there for ages, wiggling about enthusiastically in the hunt for the elusive nodule. The pain was sudden, and sharp: for a moment, I thought I was going to pass out. I flopped back onto the paper sheet, giving the sensation as little to catch on as possible. Surely he couldn't do this for much longer.

"There we go, that wasn't so bad, was it?" It was out: Doctor Jim was packing up. Microscope Man agreed, it was done.

I wanted to kill the pair of them, and take the ever-smiling nurse down for dessert.

But it was over: weak and woozy, I could make my way home.

Chapter 18

There was one person I'd forgotten to tell about my little ordeal. Zach.

He'd been so busy running around fulfilling Sky's every whim, he'd hardly been in the Jar at all since Liberation Day. And when he *had* been around, he'd been hiding in the office, unless she was there to simper at him.

It was strange not having him properly there: he'd been coming out of his hermit cave so much more before I'd gone off to Finland. He'd been actually working on the bar or clearing tables for more than fifteen minutes at a time, and having a good natter and a banter with the rest of us. It had been fun; him not being the 'boss' for a change. And it had been fabulous having him around to placate Mrs Doubtfire every time Gem's hormonal temper hit and she intentionally over-caffeinated her coffee.

Now, Zach seemed firmly back on the 'I'm in charge' track. It was a shame.

Not because I fancied him. Because I didn't: of course not. It was just... he'd been becoming a proper friend, that's all.

His self-imposed isolation, coupled with my morose 'ill' mentality, meant that I hadn't quite got round to telling him about the tumour.

So it must have been a little bit confusing to him when I turned up at work, the morning after the biopsy, sporting a lovely great plaster over my throat.

"What's that, Cleo?" he said absent-mindedly as he handed me a bag of change for the till, spinning back to his computer screen. "Cut yourself shaving?"

"Har har har," I deadpanned. "Actually… I suppose I should tell you. I might need to have some time off work soon. Well, no 'might' about it. I've got a tumour in my neck."

"You've got a… what?" He swivelled round on his whirly office chair so fast he looked like a cartoon character.

"A tumour." I shrugged, feeling anything but dismissive. "I had a biopsy yesterday to see if it's anything serious. They want to cut it out soon, so I suppose I'll be taking time off for that. When I know more I'll tell you."

"Shit." Zach had gone white, even whiter than Lizzy had when I told her the news. He gulped. "Are you… are you OK? What am I saying, of course you're not OK." He made to get up from his chair, then sat down again. He took his glasses off then put them back on again. "You're… do they know how likely…?"

"No," I answered the question he couldn't say. "It might be cancer, it might not. It doesn't help that I don't know anything about half my family history, not having my dad around. Could be anything, really." Why did I feel like my brave face was faltering? I struggled to put it back on.

"Oh, Cleo." Zach was wringing his hands together, clasping them, pulling at his thumbs – it was like he was fighting to keep himself from leaping up out of that chair. "I – I'll do anything to help, I promise." He took another big gulp of air. "You can have as much time as you need, I'll draft in a temp if I have to. Your job will be waiting for you whenever you get back, you can take as much time…"

"Chill out, Zach," I barked. "It'll be fine. They'll just chop the thing out and I'll be back the next week. All it seems to have done so far is make me a bit tired and fat, I'm sure I'm not going to become deathly sick in the next five minutes."

"OK. OK," he said slowly. "Just let me know if you feel bad, OK? I don't want you to feel like you can't tell me. I know with Gem and the baby it's a bit difficult, but we'll manage. We will."

"Yes, Zach, I know." I smiled weakly. "It'll be fine. The only thing I'm worried about is Flic's department store crawl on Thursday."

"She can't make you go when you're ill, surely?"

"This is Flic, Zach. You know what she's like. Her sister's about to give birth and she's making her go. Lizzy's got a broken leg and she's had her orders too. A tiny little tumour on my thyroid gland isn't going to excuse *me*."

***

Sure enough, Thursday morning found Lizzy and Flic on the red-eye flight to London, while Gemma and I were already almost in the UK already, chugging our way across the English Channel on the Condor Liberation: Guernsey's favourite terrible excuse for a ferry. Lizzy and I had had a furious battle over who got to go on the plane – although both of us had been playing the martyr and trying to do the boat-and-train part of the journey.

Saying that, I wasn't so much 'playing the martyr' as 'couldn't take a whole plane journey of Flic rabbiting on about table favours'.

I finally won: broken leg trumps thyroid tumour when it comes to struggling around on various methods of transport. Plus, Lizzy has always got seasick, whereas I've got a stomach of steel when it comes to travelling. It was far more practical for me to take the seaward route.

As luck would have it, our crossing had to occur on one of those grim windy nights where the sea looks like it wants to swallow every boat whole and finish with chunks of sky for dessert. I'd say roughly three quarters of the people on the Condor were retching and squawking within about fifteen minutes of the ferry getting out of St Peter Port harbour: if I strained my eyes, I could still just about make out the Guernsey seashore.

Didn't make any difference to the pukers, though.

It helped that Gemma had fallen unconscious before we'd even left St Peter Port.

"I'm so bloody knackered," she groaned, sinking into one of the plush seats in our section of the boat (we'd decreed to Flic that if we were going to come at all, she was going to pay for us to travel 'Ocean Club' – Condor Liberation's pitiful excuse for First Class). "This little bugger was kicking seven bells of shit out of me all day. Hopefully the motion will rock her to sleep." She stared at her phone for approximately ninety seconds, a pucker on her face, and then fell into such a deep sleep I had to check she was still breathing.

So it was just me and a chorus of gawks and splutters. Couldn't people at least take themselves into the toilets? Sure, sick bags were invented for a reason… but Christ on a bicycle.

As none of the people around me seemed even vaguely aware of vomit decorum, I took myself away instead: I went and stood outside on the tipping, flailing deck. A few die-hards were gathered out there already, some smoking, some staring fixedly at the horizon, a couple clutching the dreaded sick bags. Fine, I thought. I plugged myself into my headphones, sat on a cold metal bench, and turned off from the world.

* * *

I found myself sorely wishing I could be back on that boat when we got to London. *Close your eyes and think of Finland*, I kept telling myself. But it was hard to remember the good times when I was being firmly squeezed into a satin sofa cover.

For a woman of impeccable dress sense, Flic seemed determined to make her bridesmaids suffer in the style stakes. I had a more-than-sneaking suspicion it was something to do with what Lizzy had said a while ago: Flic wanted to have all eyes on her, and if eyes were on someone else, she didn't want it to be for a good reason. I was also pretty sure that her choices were being firmly guided by whatever her favourite Instagram influencers had been trying to flog that week, regardless of whether they actually looked nice. If they were ugly recycled hemp or, I don't know, sackcloth, at least she'd be able to hashtag them with 'sustainable' and pick up some likes from the vegan crew.

Honestly, I didn't know why she was so determined that this trip had to be right that second, anyway. It was months before the wedding. In that time, Gemma would no longer have a bump, I'd probably no longer have a thyroid gland (thus hopefully less of the excess weight I was lugging around) and Lizzy would no longer have a plaster cast on her leg. The others most certainly couldn't try anything on: Lizzy's cast could hardly even fit into some of the changing rooms. She and Gem had to sit outside on a series of badly padded seats, Gem so glued to her phone that poor Lizzy was spending most of her day staring at a matching series of ugly cubicle curtains.

I was being properly squished into everything – Flic firmly maintained that I was a size twelve, even though I'd blatantly gone up to a size fourteen, minimum. The zips on the dresses were agreeing with me.

We'd already been marched around Harrods – "just to get a feel for things" – before Flic herded us onto the Tube to John Lewis for the trying-on to start in earnest. By then it was well-past lunchtime, and we were all starting to get cranky. This was *before* I'd been paraded round in what felt like every dress in London. Flic had finally decided on the colour scheme: bright oranges with flashes of yellow. It sounded horrible to my metalhead ears, but she wouldn't be convinced otherwise.

"It's summery, but with a hint of autumn," she'd said, a few weeks previously, back in a Bean Jar planning session. "Lots of gold accents. It will be beautiful."

I suppose I had to be grateful she wasn't going full-Instagram and turning the whole thing 'Millennial Pink'. With rose gold, to match her iPhone.

But shit, the dresses. There was a short yellow one with a ruffled front, cut so low you could pretty much see my nipples; a long satin one with scalloped edging that looked like the kind of nightie you might find in Mrs Machon's wardrobe (orange, my arse; it was peach); a scratchy autumnal orange one so high-necked it looked like I had an actual shelf instead of a chest; the list went on. And on. And on.

"For heaven's sake, Cleo, breathe in!" Flic bellowed, so loud that the people three department stores away could probably hear her.

"If I breathe in any more, I'll implode," I hissed back. "You're cutting... off... my blood supply!"

"Come on, come on, you can do it." She wrenched the zip so hard it snagged in my skin, and I yelped.

"Forget it." I dodged out of the way as Flic tried to come at me again, an evil gleam in her eye. "I don't like this one anyway. I feel like a Pumpkin Spice Latte. Which isn't fair when there isn't even a Starbucks in Guernsey." I glanced at myself in the mirror again and winced. "God, orange looks terrible with my hair. I look like I'm on fire."

"It's not orange, it's *burnished copper*," she spluttered. "And your hair won't be that colour for the wedding, anyway."

It was back to bright red again: I'd had it done just before the Finland trip, as a symbolic new beginning. And, of course, to cover up my truly heinous roots.

"You're right, it might be back to purple," I allowed. "Which definitely won't work."

"No, no, you're dyeing it back to brown for the wedding."

In the little seating area next to the changing rooms, I heard a simultaneous hiss of indrawn breath from both Gem and Lizzy.

"Excuse me." I put my hands on my hips, and the not-even-zipped dress strained alarmingly. "I am not dyeing my hair brown for your wedding."

"It's my wedding, and you're my bridesmaid." Flic shrugged. "You'll do what I tell you."

"It's my hair, on my head, and I don't do what anyone bloody tells me!" I whipped open the curtain. "Will you guys give me some back-up?"

"Everything will look perfect for this wedding," Flic intoned as if she was reading from a Bible. "Including your hair."

"All right, Mrs Stepford. Speaking of perfect, why don't you try and get yourself a perfect relationship to match your perfect wedding?" Gemma threw a handful of Skittles towards her mouth, glancing back towards her phone with theatrical boredom. Where the hell had this come from? "You don't really give a shit about

Jonny, do you? You just like his job and his money and his flat, and the fact you can tell everyone you're *perfect* enough to have stayed with your first boyfriend. He doesn't even love you – he's just scared of you." She took another handful of Skittles. "Oh," she said through her sweets. "Did I say too much?"

Flic spluttered semi-incoherently. "You're talking rubbish."

"No, I'm fed up, and I'm hungry, and I'm bored. That is the *perfect* recipe for me to tell the truth." With an almighty heave, Gem lifted herself to her feet, nearly crushing Lizzy as she used her as a support beam. "You've dragged me over here just to reassure yourself how much power you have. And you know what, I'm sick of it. Find yourself another bridesmaid. I'm off."

It would have been a much more dramatic storm-out if she'd been able to move any faster than a stumbling sloth. But it left the rest of us speechless, nonetheless.

"You know what," I said slowly. "I'm going with her." I started to wriggle out of the orange monstrosity – after all, I had little dignity left after the last fifteen dresses or so. "I do not need to be here."

"What? But you can't..." Flic was still spluttering.

"Yeah, I can."

"She has to," said Lizzy. Both Flic and I turned to her. "In many ways, I think she's right. Not all, maybe, but some." A brave admittance considering she had a solo aeroplane trip with Flic in a matter of hours. "I think she's right to leave. Cleo, you go with her. She shouldn't be left on her own when she's this stressed. Her blood pressure will be sky high."

"You're right." I struggled faster out of the dress, reaching for my black jeans. "Liz, are you all right staying?"

"Yes, I'd only slow you down." She smiled bravely. Flic was still opening and closing her mouth like a lost fish.

I got dressed as quickly as I could and pelted off through the department store. I'm sure the security guards thought I'd nicked something, but I didn't care.

I had my phone in my head, all ready to ring up Gem and demand she wait for me, when I saw her. The fact that she was heavily with child was an advantage for me: she couldn't exactly power-walk away. She was waddling as quickly as she could through the cosmetics hall, her phone already to her ear. Ah, I thought. She must have been calling me already.

But my phone wasn't ringing, and now she was talking to someone.

I walked up behind her as quietly as I could on the polished floor.

"Yeah, I'm out of there. It didn't take much. John Lewis. Is it? OK, I'll meet you there, I'm starving anyway. No, I don't want bloody soup!" She laughed. "All right, I won't be long. Bye."

"And who was that?" I butted in, the second she pressed the 'end call' button. She nearly jumped into the air: I hoped I hadn't startled the baby right out of her.

"Bollocking hell, Cleo, where did you come from?"

"I was taking your side," I said as icily as possible. "I was going to make sure you got back to the ferry and everything OK, but it looks like you've already got plans. Do I need to ask who that was?"

Gemma didn't even have the decency to look abashed.

"Come on, Cleo, I've got to give this a go." She rolled her eyes at me and carried on waddling. I followed, deftly avoiding a saleswoman who seemed determined to spray me with something cloyingly floral. "What fucking other chance do I have to give my baby a father? To get on with the Leap Year Pact? You and Lizzy seem pretty far from it, let's face it. One of us has got to try."

"But with Aaron?" I raised my eyebrows. "Gem, you're being mental."

"No, Cleo, I'm being realistic," she spat. "Who else is going to want me? Before, I might not have been the best catch, but at least I was sexy. Now I'm a whale – who knows how long it'll be before I'm back to normal? Aaron fancies me, even like this. He makes that pretty clear. I'm going to take this while it lasts."

"What about Meredith? His wife? Your friend?"

"She's not my friend."

"You've been for coffee with her."

"That doesn't make a friendship," she said, scornfully. "That was me, like, checking her out. Scoping out the enemy. Sensing the competition."

"Do you seriously think Aaron is 'The One'? You're supposed to *love* your Leap Year person. Not fancy them a bit and nick them from their wife."

"What's happened to you, Cleo? A few months ago, you would have found that a fun challenge."

"No." I was so taken aback I stopped in my tracks. "I've never been like that. You clearly don't know me very well, if you think I'm that kind of person."

"Well, you clearly don't know me very well, if you think I'm not."

With that, Gemma marched off as fast as she could haul her enormous belly away.

* * *

I didn't bother to follow her. Clearly she was a lost cause.

I knew Gemma could be manipulative: she called *herself* a bitch.

But I never knew how far she'd go.

Faking a friendship with Meredith. Then coming all the way to London, all the time engineering herself a way she could bugger off as soon as possible, with someone else's husband. Deliberately setting out to hurt her sister, so she had an excuse to get away. Lying to all of us.

To be honest, I was mostly miffed that she couldn't have at least confided in me. Sure, I would have tried to talk her out of it. But if she'd presented it all in a logical manner, if she'd at least tried to justify herself... no, even then I couldn't condone what she was doing. It was hurting too many people.

I got the train back to Poole on my own, stewing all the way. I sat in a McDonalds until the torturous late-night boat trip home, stewing all the way. On the ferry, I looked for Gem, hoping that she would have at least seen some kind of light after our conversation in John Lewis. But she wasn't there.

Nor was she at work the next day. According to Zach, she'd begged the day off at the same time she'd booked off the department-store-crawl day. She'd told him it was because she'd be knackered after all the travelling and traipsing around.

"I don't know if she'll be back at all," I said to him wearily. But I couldn't tell him where she'd gone. That would mean telling Lizzy and Flic as well, and I just couldn't bring myself to do it.

I could judge Gem all I liked, but I didn't want the entire island doing it as well.

Things just felt generally horrible, like all the good things in my life were unravelling bit by bit.

I had no idea where Gemma was, whether she was all right or not.

Flic was livid with the lot of us, and came into the Jar that lunchtime to hiss very loudly at me about how disappointed she was – sparking the curiosity of a whole queue of suits, of course.

Mum's hold on Charlie was loosening with the advent of his exams, and she was trying to pretend she wasn't slipping him treats behind her threats of punishment: he was recovering from being totally cowed and was starting to get smugly insufferable again.

Nan was almost totally AWOL with whatever scheme she was running with the Guernsey Goats.

Zach… Zach looked like he was about to cry every time he looked at me. He kept staring at my neck like the tumour was about to burst out and slap him in the face. Then of course he'd rush back to Sky and practically hide behind her.

Above all, I still didn't know whether or not I had cancer.

Annoying Customer of the Week, Part 8

"Who's next please? Hi there, what can I…"

"Wait one moment, you, over there – is that my decaf Americano?"

"Um, it was actually my boss who made it, but I believe so."

"NO! 'I believe so' isn't good enough. I don't trust it now. Make me another one."

"All right then, though as you're the only customer who's ordered a drink, I'm guessing it's yours. NO, don't bother kicking off, I'll get it in a sec."

"Now, there's no need to be so rude! Just get me my drink! Now!"

"I've already started serving this gentleman and in case you can't tell, I have my hands full. Give me two seconds."

"GET ME YOUR MANAGER. NOW."

"Whatever."

I didn't even bother worrying about what Zach would say. I was (mostly) in the right, and the irritating paranoid old bat was in the wrong (mostly). Plus, Zach had to be nice to me. It was Results Day.

Chapter 19

I had quite the gathering in the Bean Jar that day: Results Day. I hadn't felt so nervous since I had to go up to school and get my A Level grades. They were supposed to determine the rest of my life. In a way, so were these.

In a slightly more morbid way, I suppose.

Lizzy was in pride of place in the window seat, a position granted by her strapped-up leg. Jonny and Flic were next to her – Flic still deigning to talk to Lizzy with some degree of warmth, instead of the ice I was receiving. Still, she'd turned up to hear the news: though whether Jonny had had a part in that, I didn't know. Our irritating old regular, Mrs Doubtfire, was in her usual seat in full view of the bar. It still being opening hours, she wasn't going to surrender her favourite table... especially when there was potential gossip to be heard.

Charlie had taken advantage of his freedom from Mum's attempted tyranny and was perched on the stairs, clutching a two-litre bottle of Coke. He was still in his school uniform, claiming he had a free period and just fancied dropping by for a drink and some help with his Geography project.

"You're not old enough for free periods," I scolded him, but ruffled his hair affectionately anyway. Nice to know he cared enough about his big sister to bunk off and risk the further wrath of our mother. Not to mention whichever hell-beasts were in charge of his school.

I knew Charlie cared and it had made my heart swell to realise it. Maybe he wasn't just a rugby playing rah, king of the spoilt brats. I'd walked past his bedroom door the previous day and heard something interesting.

"Welcome to this special edition of 'Guerns Gagging For It'," he'd been saying, in quite a rush.

Well, Mum was out at Waitrose; he had limited time. I was only impressed that he'd managed to keep the thing going at all. I nearly rushed on up the stairs, eager to avoid any inferences of my little brother's love life, but something made me hang around.

"Today, we're talking about our inspirations. Well, I am. Adam and Tristan will make their own videos for this mini-series but here's mine. I want to talk about my sister."

What?

"My sister is a bona-fide slut."

WHAT?

"That's what she calls herself, anyway."

Well, true.

"But she's so much more than that. She likes to think I don't know what she gets up to with her friends at the weekend, but I hear enough that I can put the pieces together. Sometimes, she has a different man every week."

Not quite, but still.

"She's the most confident person I know, and it inspires me like nobody else. When she wants something, she gets it. When someone annoys her, she tells them. She doesn't let anyone break her heart, but she loves her friends and will look after them in all situations. And even though she might be ill, she's still carrying on, and still determined. She might be annoying sometimes, but she's my inspiration."

Well. *Well.*

I couldn't help but wipe a tiny tear from my eye.

And now here he was, pretending to have a free period so he could give me some moral support. Perhaps he was growing up.

Zach was behind the bar, ostensibly still serving – but any suits who dared to come in seemed somewhat bemused by the atmosphere of dread, and made a swift exit. Instead of doing anything productive, Zach was staring at his Sarnia Chérie mural and fiddling with the milk steamer, blurring his glasses with a hiss every fifteen seconds – even when Mrs Machon leaned out of the kitchen and told him to shut up.

Yes, Mrs Machon had turned up too, allegedly to get ahead with her cake-baking. I'd known she was feeling sympathetic when she determinedly recreated a Guernsey classic for me, the luridly pink iced Swansea Buns that had vanished from bakeries years ago. They were a mystery to anyone not from Guernsey, and nobody had the slightest idea why they claimed to be Welsh. But anyone who had grown up on the island was fiercely attached to them, even though they tasted like stale iced bread laced with e-numbers. They'd been delivered to me with a scowl, thudded onto the table like making them had been the biggest imposition of all time, but I knew she meant it with love. Well, whatever Mrs Machon's version of 'love' was.

Even Sky was there, leaning on the bar as close to her boyfriend as she could get without getting a face full of steam, scribbling on a pad and chastising Zach for getting her precious drawings damp.

"Holy bollocks in a basin, this is tense," I muttered to myself, over yet another sudden hiss of steam. I was sitting in the armchair nearest Lizzy, drumming my fingers on the leather arm over and over and over again. I was trying to nibble on my Swansea Bun but even the synthetic pink jam couldn't calm my nerves.

Everyone was pretending to drink coffee, acting as if they'd all convened by accident… but I knew full well that news had spread that the test results were expected. I knew that in their own ways, everyone was there to support me.

Except, perhaps, Mrs D, who was just always there.

The door clicked open and I nearly gave myself whiplash. I was still kind of hoping that Gemma would turn up, even though it had been three days now. I was worried about her. I'd finally confessed all to Lizzy and we had discussed trying to track her down, maybe getting in contact with Meredith to see if she'd heard anything (excuses, lies, or truth) but we were going to give it another couple of days. And another few hundred missed calls, WhatsApps, and even Instagram messages to Gemma's mobile, perhaps.

The messages were coming up as 'delivered', but not 'read'. Her phone was obviously on, at least. We decided this meant she was alive and ignoring us.

We hoped.

It was the longest we'd ever gone without Gem posting a selfie on Instagram or sending me a mildly rude picture on Snapchat, and I missed her.

Of course, it wasn't Gem coming through the door. It was Nan. Accompanied by Joyce and Pat, her two batty old mates. All three of them were wearing their purple Guernsey Goats sashes; I hoped they weren't expecting me to give them all a lift across the island on my scooter. They feigned surprise to see so many of us clustered around the seating area – but I knew why they were there, too.

They crowded round Mrs Doubtfire's table, all three giving her matching curt nods. I could see her curiosity was sparked by the purple sashes; even through my somewhat escalating panic, I couldn't help but roll my eyes at the thought of her joining the Guernsey Goats.

Zach quickly prepared a fresh round of coffees for all four of them. I pretended not to see Nan surreptitiously pouring shots of Baileys into them behind her handbag – including Mrs D's. She pretended not to see Charlie loitering on the stairs, blatantly bunking off school.

All kinds of shit was running through my head. Lizzy and Jonny were maintaining a determined conversation next to me, but it was just meaningless background noise.

I couldn't help myself: I was running through my worst-case scenario. If the test results were bad, if I did have cancer…

I'd give up my job, that was for sure. Much as I loved the Bean Jar, if I had something really wrong with me, I was going to live my life to the absolute full. I'd raid my bank account, and the modest savings account Nan had sporadically topped up since my babyhood. I'd sell everything I owned and go off travelling – not anywhere too mucky, mind. I've never been a backpacking kind of person. No, I'd go off and stay in five-star hotels all over the world, living off room service menus and Michelin starred restaurants.

Or maybe I'd get hold of Luka, take up his offer and go touring with Karin Cluster. Living in the back of a tour bus, rough rock star sex on tap, and none of the commitment: who needs commitment when you've got cancer?

Though maybe I'd been single for too long. Maybe I actually *needed* commitment. Someone to support me through the difficult months, through all the treatment and the pain. Maybe meaningless sex wasn't the answer. Maybe I was ready to find somebody to love?

Or maybe I just needed to travel alone and do that thing I've always scoffed at – 'finding myself'. I've never believed people to be truly lost. Trotting off somewhere to 'find yourself' has always seemed like the biggest pile of entitled arse I've ever heard of. Give them something constructive to do, I've always said, and then they'll find themselves quick as anything.

But perhaps that was what I needed. Time on my own, to hear my own thoughts, to help my body heal itself.

Thankfully, before my thoughts could get even more pious and ridiculous (I'd be finding religion next) we were all jolted into silence by sudden music. 'Night Owl' by Karin Cluster: my ringtone.

The conversation only lasted a few seconds, before my doctor hung up – clearly eager to break news to someone else and their clustered friends and relations. I clutched the phone to my face for another few seconds, just breathing it all in.

Then I opened my eyes and faced the Bean Jar.

"It's not cancer," I announced, my voice cracking on the last word. Everyone seemed to hold their breath, as if waiting for something worse. "It's benign, it's totally benign. I still have to have it cut out before it chokes me... but it's benign. It's *not cancer!*"

And then it felt like I was being enveloped in a thousand hugs, as everyone seemed to pile on in one great dogpile.

* * *

That evening, cleaning up the Jar by myself after everyone else had gone home, I was still on a high. Hey, I had to have surgery, I wasn't exactly *well*, and I'd probably have to take medication for the rest of my life, but I wasn't dying! I didn't have cancer!

There's nothing like the rush of finding out you're healthy (ish) after all. After a scare like that, everything seemed beautiful. The light glinting off the coffee machine as I polished it to perfection, the drizzle running down the window, the heavily pregnant woman hovering sheepishly in the doorway...

Oh. It looked like Gemma had returned.

"Don't even say it!" she hissed, as I bullied her onto the sofa, trying to dry her hair for her with a tea towel while she batted me away.

"Say what? Say that you're soaked? You look like shit? You need to drink some hot chocolate whether you like it or not?"

"Are you going to make me say it? All right then. You told me so. Yes, I know."

"I wasn't going to say that, actually." I left Gem with the tea towel to dry herself off as best she could, and started to make her hot chocolate. "I was going to ask how it all went first. *Then* say it."

"Fine, fine." She grumbled to herself while I made the drink, towelling herself off somewhat viciously. It was only drizzling: I had no idea how long she'd been standing outside watching me.

"Go on." I bustled back over, plonking two steaming mugs in front of us as I sat down. "What happened?"

"You first. Tell me straight. Are you dying?"

"No. Benign. Having it out. Boom. Now you go."

"Oh, thank fuck!" She momentarily looked like she was about to give me a hug, then stopped. We weren't quite there yet. "It's definitely, definitely not cancer?"

"They won't know one hundred percent until they whip the bugger out, but they're as certain as they can be. Not the issue right now." I blew at my hot chocolate. "Tell me."

"OK, OK." Disregarding the heat, Gem took a scalding sip. "Oh, for fuck's sake, it was a flop."

"Literally, or...?"

"Don't be so dirty. He wasn't flopping anywhere." She bit her lip. "It was me who... couldn't get it up. As such."

"Why? You were into him enough to go there..."

"Yeah, and it was lovely. He was lovely. He took me to this posh hotel, honestly Cleo, I've never been anywhere like it in my life. Plush as fuck. It was all so perfect – he was taking off my clothes, and we were kissing, and I was really getting into it... but then I just couldn't get any further."

"Oh?"

"Yeah. He got all my clothes off and I just felt... ashamed."

"That's a new one."

"It was just wrong. It felt wrong that he was looking at me like that, while I was so... well, while I was carrying my baby. It was like he was looking at her, too."

"That's creepy."

"Yeah. And it was like, shit, he's got a baby himself, the same age, still in someone else's bump. It's like he's looking at his own child like that, too. It just felt kind of disturbing. Like, what if he just has some creepy thing for pregnant women? Then I thought about what you'd said, about how maybe I'd just fancied him a bit, and was just going for him because nobody else wanted me. I just couldn't carry on with it after I thought that." She looked utterly wretched. "I've never given up on sex before."

"Gem, you can hardly walk five paces without needing to stop for a sit down and a drink. You're hardly going to have the energy for sex, let alone anything else."

"That played a part in it," she admitted. "That and realising I actually look like an egg with legs. One with stretchmarks. Oh bloody hell, Cleo, never get pregnant. It looks like I'm actually going to split apart, along the horrible little bastard stretchmarks."

"I don't have quite as far to stretch as you did," I pointed out.

"Then start eating now, and make sure you don't have to stretch at all. Horrible, horrible, horrible." Gem gave her belly a little poke. "It'd better be worth it, you hear me in there?"

"Oh, you know it'll be worth it." I pushed my hot chocolate aside. I always found it a boring drink: the comfort only lasted so long. "What did you do once you... you know. Once you didn't do *him*."

"Left." She shrugged. "I pottered around Westfield for a few hours, bought way too many baby things, sulked a bit, cursed the lot of you, then went and stayed in a manky Travelodge. I got back to Guernsey the next day, and I've been hiding at Mum and Dad's ever since. Stuck my phone on charge behind a pot plant and pretended it was the Stone Age."

"You bloody moron!" I exclaimed. "You've been stewing for three days?"

"I didn't want to face you. I just... didn't. Not after what you said. I thought you'd laugh in my face."

"Come on." I grabbed her hand. "You know me better than that."

"I'm sorry, Cleo."

"You're all right." I squeezed, ignoring her typical Gemma-like squirming. "Come on, we'll blame it all on hormones and be done with it."

Burying the issues? Maybe. A little voice in my head was reminding me about the things Gem had said, back in the cosmetics hall at John Lewis. The things she had done: entirely selfish things, there was no doubt about it. But she was my friend, one of my very best friends. Surely you forgive, you try to forget?

Though how long it would take me to do either, I didn't know.

* * *

I'd been a little bit disappointed that Mum hadn't turned up for the vigil in the Bean Jar, while I waited for my test results. Everyone else with any degree of importance in my life had bothered.

I say a 'little' disappointed. It started off as just a 'little' but as the day went on, my rage just built and built.

Even though Flic and I still weren't properly talking, *she'd* come along – and I was talking to her even less after she'd revealed that she had known Gemma was back in Guernsey, safe and sound.

Lizzy and I had been about fifteen minutes away from calling the police yet Flic hadn't bothered to tell us her sister had been safe all along. Apparently common courtesy was something that eluded our Felicity.

But she'd still sat on that sofa, waiting to hear how sick I was. And she'd still joined the melee of hugs when it turned out I was fine.

More than I could say for my own mother.

I'd been playing things down for her. Trying not to worry her too much, all that kind of thing. It's what I'd always done: she'd been through so much with her husbands, and with me being quite the tearaway teenager, and now Charlie… I wanted to keep her safe, stop her from having a mental breakdown. She'd always seemed the type, no matter what cryptic remarks Nan might make about her past and her own teenage years. It had always been like she was on the brink of a real crisis; if there wasn't an actual crisis going on at the time, she was liable to create one.

Still. Even playing things down, she had had to realise that there was something wrong. I'd not been especially close to her since I was a little girl, sure, but in the past week I'd been practically silent. She had to realise that wasn't normal. Usually I was stomping around the house making my voice heard at every opportunity.

And come on. Hearing your daughter had a 'nodule' on a kind of important gland? Any idiot could tell what that meant.

Driving up the Grange on my little red scooter, having seen Gem off on the bus, I was getting more and more riled up. This was my *mother*. She knew that today had been Results Day – Nan had been quizzing me about it over breakfast, and Mum had been in the room. Yet I hadn't even had a phone call about it.

I skidded the scooter to a halt in front of the house and yanked my helmet off. I hadn't realised quite how pissed off I was. Talk about suppressed rage. Well, it wasn't staying suppressed for much longer.

"MUM!" I hollered, stamping through the door. "Where are you?"

"Upstairs, Cleo. Keep your voice down, please."

"Why?" I stomped up the stairs, not bothering to take off my New Rocks. Sacrilege, in that house. It made a lovely loud noise, though. Every thundering stamp seemed to echo off the polished wooden steps and reverberate through the whole house.

I found Mum in her usual place: on the sofa, doing a Sudoku. She was wearing a pale blue ruffled blouse that looked like it had last been in fashion sometime in the late eighties, coupled with some fetchingly sensible brown trousers. Honestly, how she had come out of my colourful, exotic Nan, I had no idea.

She blinked up at me from behind her glasses. "How was your day, love? Did you get your results?"

"Nice of you to remember," I spat. Mum's perm twitched in shock. I hadn't spoken to her with quite so much vitriol since I was a hormonal teenager. "Tell me – would it matter to you, if I had cancer? Would you even give the slightest of shits?"

"I... of course I would." Mum blinked again. "What kind of monster do you take me for?"

"Maybe not a monster. But then, how come both Nan and Charlie managed to be with me while I got my results, and you didn't even bother with a phone call?" She started to answer, but I cut her off. "I bet if it was Charlie who was sick, you'd be all over that. He'd be helicoptered over to the best specialists on the mainland before he could even blink."

"Cleo, I..."

"Shut up." Wow. I hadn't told my mother to shut up since... ever. But the words were pouring out now and I knew I couldn't stop them. "I'm talking now. You get your turn in a minute."

Years of resentment and rage seemed to be ready to spill out of me and I didn't even bother trying to keep it all in.

"I want to know why it is you seem to..." I paused for a second. It was hard to admit this about my own mother but I couldn't help it: it seemed entirely true. "Why do you dislike me so much? You can barely look at me without sniffing and coming up with some kind of criticism. You expect me to look after you, you act like a useless kid who can't even use the Sky box by yourself, but you're not even fifty yet. You find something wrong with every single thing I do, but when something is *actually* going on, you're oblivious."

I took a shaky breath. God, it felt good to get this all out. "You go on and on about me ruining my life, you make me feel guilty for not taking Law at uni and ruling the world by the time I was twenty-one, you don't give a shit about whether I'm actually happy. And yet you barely even deign to give a shit when I might have cancer! I don't, by the way. Did I say that already? I don't have cancer. You're probably upset that I'm not going to die and leave you with your one perfect child."

OK, maybe that bit was a bit overdramatic, a bit MySpace-era teenager-y, but it was how I felt.

Mum was opening and closing her mouth like a trout. She'd twitched so much her glasses were skew-whiff.

"You can talk now. Go on, justify yourself."

"Cleo, I… don't know what to say."

"It's true then." To my shame, I was biting back a burning lump in my throat – a bigger lump, in truth, than the one on my thyroid gland. I made for the stairs, to go and hide in my room until I could keep the tears under control. To find out that your suspicions were right, that your own mother doesn't like you, it makes you feel like your heart is tearing into pieces. No matter how much you feel you've been second place since your little brother was born.

"No." Mum looked up, her voice firm. "No. It's not true at all." There was an edge of steel in her eyes that I don't think I'd ever seen before. I'd never seen her look so *hard*. "Sit down. Come on, over here." With that edge in her voice, I couldn't say no.

For once, she wasn't panicking. No dithering. No mild-mannered denying of conflict or over-the-top declarations of punishment.

It was so shocking, I sat down and stared at her.

"You listen to me, Cleo Weeks," she said. She was gripping her Sudoku book so hard, her fingertips were white. "You are talking… *bullshit*." I jumped. I don't think I'd ever heard so much as the word 'bollocks' come out of my mother's mouth, let alone 'bullshit'. I would have put money on her not even knowing the word existed. Well, unless she remembered the things I'd hissed under my breath over the years.

"Am I really?" I managed. It came out more of a plea than the sarky response I'd hoped it to be.

"Yes, you are. For a start, of course I care about your illness. I just..." She paused for a second. "I couldn't possibly believe you could be sick." She narrowed her eyes and gave me a fierce look of... pride? "You've always been so strong. It could never be anything but harmless. I wasn't worried for a second."

"Now *that's* bullshit."

"No, it's the truth. As for the rest of it... yes, I'm harder on you than I am on your brother. I admit it."

"Let me guess, I remind you too much of my father?"

"No. You remind me too much of myself."

That one rocked me. At first I was insulted. I didn't want to be like her. I wasn't like her. I didn't read the Daily Mail, I didn't panic at every opportunity, I didn't say 'yes dear' and 'no dear' to my little brother or to anyone...

Sure, me and Mum looked alike, once you took away the piercings and the perms. But that was all there was to it, I was determined.

Still, I gave her a quizzical look.

"Yes, you might not like it, but you and I are alike in more ways than just our faces," she continued, staring at me eye to eye. "I wasn't always like I am now." She gave her Sudoku book a little shake as if to illustrate her point.

"Yes, you were," I scoffed. "You were born like this."

"No, I wasn't. Do you want the truth, or don't you?"

"Yeah, I do."

"Then be quiet, Cleo, and let me tell you a story. You say I'm an old lady before I'm fifty, but there are plenty of reasons for that. If you asked your nan, she'd say I got scared. She's berated me about it enough, over the years. Calls me a shadow, a ghost, worse things. She'd love for me to go back to the way I was before, but I suppose she's right. I'm scared. Being like that got me nothing but trouble, and I don't want you to have my problems."

"I have no idea what you're talking about."

"I used to be just like you," she carried on. "You couldn't keep me still for five minutes. If I wasn't out dancing with my girls, I was drinking in the bunkers around Cobo, trying whatever drugs I could get my hands on. I dreamed of running away to India, to be a free spirit and live with the old hippies on the beaches at Goa, merrily stoned for the rest of my life."

I sat in stunned silence. It wasn't *my* mother she was talking about. It couldn't be.

"I didn't care what happened in my future, I was only concerned about the present. I didn't bother with my education, I decided that was the bourgeois path. I would take things day by day, and live for enjoying myself. A career was for someone square. I thought I was invincible, that nothing bad could ever happen to me." She gave me a shrewd look. "I was lucky, you know, that your nan and granddad had enough money that I didn't have to build a career. Just like you."

"I could have a career if I wanted."

"That's the thing though, Cleo, you don't want it, do you?" She sighed. "Just like me, you're coasting. That's why I'm on at you all the time. I was living the best life I thought I could ever have. I was free, I was having fun, loving a different man each week. Guernsey was my paradise. I had the freedom of the island – I practically lived on the beach. I talked about India, of course, but why bother travelling that far when I could have the same thing in Guernsey? What more could there be to life than sitting around a fire with your friends, getting stoned and being happy?"

I couldn't picture *my mother* getting stoned. It was quite a disturbing image. Even I wasn't into that. But she was painting a pretty good picture, all the same. Her life sounded idyllic: privileged, carefree, utterly at liberty.

"What happened? Why don't you want that for me? Weren't you happy?"

"I was." She nodded. "The best years of my life, I could say. But it was just one long, happy summer. A summer that lasted for years, but a summer all the same. Nothing lasts forever. I let myself end up in some pretty... hairy situations." She visibly winced and went silent.

We sat for a couple of minutes, both of us motionless. I waited for her to elaborate.

Come on, hairy situations? Mum? She'd just been telling me about sitting around getting stoned on a beach. How much further could it have gone?

Finally, she shook her head like she was shaking out her demons.

"I'm not telling you everything. A mother deserves some secrets."

She paused again for a long moment.

"I was out of control, there was nothing else to it. My mother tried to intervene, but I thought I knew better. The upshot was, I ran away to the mainland. Trying to get to India, or trying to get away. I'm still not sure what was going on in my head. I was gone for, oh, four months? Five? Not long. But," she gave a wry smile, "it was long enough that by the time I came back to Guernsey, tail firmly between my legs, I was pregnant with you, and with, to be frank, no idea who your father was."

It was my turn to wince. "I thought you knew."

"There was one man, the more decent of my... paramours. When he found out I was pregnant, he vowed to stand by me, whether the baby was his or not. We got married, in a registry office with two witnesses we pulled off the street." She took a deep, shuddering breath. It was the first time in her whole speech that she had shown much emotion at all. "He was the only one I truly loved, and he was the one who hurt me the most. We were married and divorced all in the space of three months."

She was silent again.

"But you don't know who my actual father is?"

Mum ignored me, and took a deep breath before starting again. "You could say that after that I was... cowed. I always knew I wanted to keep you, I never entertained a single thought of anything else. But I vowed to bring you up safely. You would never be hurt like I was. You'd never go through what I went through. That side of me, the wild side, I battered her down and never let her out again."

"And Nan didn't like it?"

I couldn't imagine Nan going all strict-mother, not for one moment.

Not *Nan*.

"She was exasperated." Mum smiled. "She loved her madcap daughter, even with her wild ways. When I came back expecting you, she told me she'd known it would happen, that it would only be a matter of time. She didn't realise that having you would turn me into someone... meek. I can see exactly what I am, Cleo. I had to try hard, at first, to batter my old self down, keep her calm. Then all of a sudden, it wasn't so hard any more. Yes, you might call me boring. But I'm safe. And if it's a choice between this and ruining your life like I did mine, I'm happy with that."

"OK..." I said slowly. "That still doesn't explain why you're so bloody ridiculous with Charlie, though."

Mum shrugged. "Aren't all mothers like that, with their sons? I'm not perfect. He's my youngest, and his father was the first man to make me feel human in years. My old self cheered at the sight of Brian, in his pilot uniform. The old me wanted that bit of adventure and when it all went to pieces, I tamped her down even further." She sighed. "Never mind Brian. I worried that if I spoiled you the way I had been spoiled, you'd turn out more like me than ever. Charlie... Charlie has always been himself and nobody else. Maybe I take it too far, but I've never felt like I had to try and shape him. He'll land on his feeet whatever I do." She gave a wry, almost sheepish smile. "Though it did hit me, after that party and the hospital, maybe I've gone too far in the opposite direction from the way I parented you."

"It makes me feel like shit, sometimes," I admitted, in a small voice. I'd not really realised quite how much that was true until that moment. "I feel like a second-class citizen in this house. Most of the time."

"I can't believe I've been that bad to live with." Mum bit her lip, and for a moment it was almost like looking in a mirror. In that moment, I could see the girl she'd been, alongside the woman she had become. "I had no idea it had gone so far."

"It has." I somehow found my voice again. "If it wasn't for Nan... I don't know how I've stayed here for so long. Sometimes, I don't know why I moved back in. If rents weren't so high over here, I think I would have moved out about twelve times just in temper."

"That's... hard to hear."

"Yeah. Hard to say, but it's true." But it wasn't hard to say. It felt so right, to be having a proper conversation with my mother. Like two adults, instead of a nagging mother and her naughty little girl. "When it's just you and me sitting here, sometimes, I feel like an unwelcome guest."

"I never realised."

"Now you do. Maybe I should move out." I tried to take a steadying breath, but it was coming in bursts as the impact of our conversation properly hit me. "If it hurts you so much to look at me, if you think I'm going to mess up the same way you did. I don't want to feel guilty for my existence." I thought for a second, and that burning lump rose in my throat once again. "You just told me your life would have been better if I'd never been born."

"Again, *bullshit*," Mum said sternly, grabbing hold of both my hands in hers. "Maybe if I hadn't had you, I would have gone down that path so far I would have destroyed myself. You were nothing but a blessing. I just don't want to see you stumbling down that same path when you're capable of so much more. I've always thought that if I'm strict with you, maybe it'll be less likely to happen."

"You've got to get over this." I tore my hands away and blundered into the middle of the living room floor, like I was about to give a speech. "Can't you see how much you've pushed me away? This house is toxic. And you know what? I'm not you. I'm not going to get hurt. And if I am... I'll learn from my *own* mistakes. You only had to tell me about yours, you should have done years ago. You didn't need to hide it away."

"Well then, that can be step one." Mum clapped her hands together, almost sounding like Nan. "We're a healthy house, you found that out today. And we're going to make this a happy house, too. Step one will be no more secrets." She stopped to think for a second. "Well, not *no* more secrets. You're still my daughter, and I'm still your mother. I simply don't want to hear what you and your friends get up to on a Saturday night, as long as you keep yourself safe."

"Can step two be that you stop treating Charlie like the new messiah? Frankly, it was refreshing when you were torturing him." I leaned on the fireplace, crossing my arms.

"I wasn't torturing him, I just wanted to punish him for what he did." Was Mum blushing? "All right, I think I went a bit far with it."

"You've spoilt him so much that you don't know how to discipline him properly," I suggested. "Maybe try a bit of mild punishment once in a while. Then you won't have to go all-out."

"I'll… I'll bear that in mind." She looked a little bit sickened at the thought of having to actually be fair about her precious little prince. But she nodded gamely anyway. "I don't want you to hate your brother."

"I don't hate him. As he's growing up, he might actually be turning into a decent person." I hated to admit it, but his behaviour in the last few days, over my tumour… he was showing some good colours, colours that I thought had been long buried under layers of Hollister and Jack Wills. "Well, sometimes. Did you know he's been bringing me cups of tea every night since I found out about the thyroid thing? I mean," I giggled in spite of myself, "I hate tea, can't bloody stand it, but he's got it in his head that tea will help. He's going to be a good human being, even if he does cause a bit of havoc along the way. He probably doesn't need you to make his life hell every time he disappoints you. I mean, he's bound to do it at some point."

"I suppose so. It's just a bit difficult, you'll have to appreciate that."

"I'll do my best."

"And I'm going to do my best to support you in whatever you want to do, I'll stop nagging you." She paused. "Well, as much as I can. Sometimes you might need it."

I couldn't help but laugh, a little bitterly. "I might have to disagree with you there, we'll see how it goes."

"I'll start with this operation of yours. I promise you, I'll be there for you through all of it. Right by your side. Like a mother is supposed to be."

"Ahh, you don't need to do that. I'll be fine."

"No, no," she insisted. "You've never had an operation before. I'm your mother. I'll make sure you get through it all right. I'll be there when you wake up, I promise."

Chapter 20

My mother was kind of wrong. She wasn't with me when I woke up from my operation. That proved a bit too difficult to manage.

She did visit, of course.

But she wasn't the only one.

* * *

I got into hospital at an utterly antisocial time of day, roughly seven o'clock in the morning. Even for a Monday morning, it felt grim.

It was spring, pushing on for summer, and the sky was clear and sunny even at that hour. Everywhere I looked, flowers were in bloom, tiny blossoms peering from the cracks in the granite walls. Guernsey was at its summery best.

I still felt rather melodramatically like I was on my way to my death.

Of course, I was being ridiculous all over again. I was one of four people having exactly the same operation that morning – well, not exactly the same operation, perhaps. One woman was unlucky enough to have had the results I'd been praying to avoid, full blown thyroid cancer, or so I gathered from waiting room whispers. It so easily could have been me; I felt lucky.

Mum had been stoically by my side since our frank discussion. In some ways, it was a bit irritating. It felt like she was trying to make up for the past few years in a matter of weeks, and it was a little smothering. But I appreciated the sentiment.

However, she was surprised to have her way barred by a nurse at the door to the surgical ward.

"You can come back later," the nurse said firmly. "No relatives on the ward at this time. Thank you."

"But she's my daughter!" Mum's perm twitched in horror.

"And this isn't a children's ward, so off you pop."

With that, I was hustled in, and Mum was hustled out. It was all very smooth: I hardly knew what was going on. I made a mental note to get some tips – it would be a useful skill to have when trying to get rid of unwanted suits from the Bean Jar.

Somehow, from that moment on, I was calm. Everything just seemed surreal. Everyone was quiet, drifting past in their own little world – patient or doctor, it didn't matter.

The nurses were gently herding me from place to place: to a cubicle to put on a paper hospital gown; to a waiting room filled with uncomfortable chairs and a TV showing the breakfast news; to a little windowless room to have some blood taken; to a different windowless room because my veins were too dehydrated to accept the needle and I needed a nurse with more expertise; to another windowless room to an actual haematologist who finally succeeded in extracting a few teaspoonfuls of blood; back to the waiting room to be given the time for my operation – eleven o'clock.

Eleven o'clock! By this point, it was barely nine. Why they'd dragged me in from seven, I had no idea. Maybe to make sure I didn't have a last minute attack of the nerves and make a bid for freedom. It would be far too difficult in a paper nightie.

I thought I'd be bored stupid, but I wasn't. Those two hours passed in seconds, or so it felt. Before I knew it, I was being ushered into another little room – that hospital was like a rabbit warren – with nothing but Jeremy Kyle on the telly and a snoozing old lady for company, her paper nightie fluttering open at the knees with every twirl of the ceiling fan and giving me a view I didn't really fancy, thank you very much.

I still wasn't freaking out. Now that the operation was finally properly upon me, I wasn't scared. Even though it was going to be my first time under anaesthetic... hey, it could have been so much worse.

And now I was actually in the hospital, I was fascinated. As I was summoned into a room full of machines with an ominous set of double doors at one end, I couldn't stop staring at everything. I had no idea what anything was, of course, but it was interesting anyway.

"I'm just going to put the mask over your face," said a soft voice – one of the nurses, I guessed. "Breathe deeply." Ooh, this was exciting, I wondered what...

* * *

And then I woke up. Dizzy, confused, disoriented. Where was I? Where was the nurse with the soft voice, where were all the baffling machines?

I felt sick. Oh, my stomach felt like it was twirling in unhappy little circles, round and round my abdomen.

And my *neck*. The pain. The pain was ridiculous. It felt like something had been ripped out of me – which, in a way, it had – but instead of cutting me open and gently snipping it out, the surgeon had just reached a meaty hand down my throat and tugged.

The lights were far too bright: couldn't hospital management realise that people waking up from an operation don't generally want blindness to add to their problems? I closed my eyes and eloquently expressed all these sentiments by giving a pathetic little whimper.

"Hello, Cleo," said a soft, gentle voice somewhere above me. "Are you awake?"

"Eurgh," I said. "Feel sick."

"Don't worry, dear, that's normal." I opened my eyes a crack to see a uniformed nurse hovering next to me, taking my pulse while a blood pressure cuff squeezed at my arm. "Here, put this on." She carefully fastened a plastic oxygen mask onto my face.

Everything felt so strange. I was adjusting to the light, but my head was still spinning. I could just about make out that I was on a ward, surrounded by other groggy people, all of whom had their own personal nurse. I wished I was lying flat so I didn't have to see them. I wished I could just go back to sleep.

"Your operation was a success," said my nurse. "We'll take you round to your ward in a bit, dear. How would you rate your pain from one to ten?"

"Eight," I managed to croak. Though, of course, I had no idea. Have you ever tried rating your pain? It might be a ten to you, but someone else might be struggling manfully with way worse in the next bed and only calling it a four. And the powers that be might give you a massive dose of medicine and knock you out for the next week, just because you you're being a wimp.

Still, it felt like an eight to me.

"That's OK, dear, we'll get you some more morphine."

I closed my eyes and groaned pathetically. I desperately wanted to roll over onto my side and go to sleep, and wake up when this was all over. But, of course, I couldn't. I didn't really notice the tube coming out of my neck and into a canister at the side of the bed, something disgusting draining out of it. Not until I tried to turn over and nearly yanked it out of myself, anyway.

The nurse must have been a bit shocked at the noise I made: even to my own ears it was reminiscent of someone stepping on a dog's tail. And I was the dog.

"Now dear, careful. You don't want to pull out your drain."

I lay rigid on the bed, trying not to move, waiting for the morphine to kick in.

And oh, it was beautiful. It was only a matter of hazy seconds, or so it felt, before the pain dulled and a wave of warmth spread through my body. I felt all the breath leave my body in a sigh, and I floated away on a happy cloud.

Then the happy cloud started to pitch and toss in a storm. My stomach was rocking and rolling like I was jumping up and down in front of Karin Cluster, but not in a good way. Up and down, up and down, round and round…

"Feel *really* sick," I managed to squeak, before giving a massive burp that echoed horribly round my oxygen mask.

"Here you go, dear." The helpful nurse whipped the mask away and thrust something under my face just in time for me to hit it with a wave of vomit. I felt almost like it was going to burst open my surgery-wound and come leaking out of my neck in a stream of revolting fluid. I'd never had such a disgusting puke in all my life, and I've had some crackers of hangovers. This even beat the black Salmiakki-sick in Finland.

I sunk back onto my papery hospital pillow and closed my eyes, not even bothering to wipe the crust of vomit from the side of my mouth.

"Don't worry, dear, just a reaction to the morphine," came the soothing voice again. "Some people are just unlucky that way, we'll get an anti-emetic in you."

Of course, before that happened, I had to puke again. Twice.

Then when someone finally managed to inject the anti-emetic into my arm, it burned all the way up my vein, in a pain even worse than the one in my neck.

I felt utterly wretched.

* * *

Before the operation, I'd hardly imagined my recovery period at all. I'd pictured a bit of wooziness, maybe a slightly sore throat, then sitting up in bed eating ice cream within the hour.

Instead, I just wanted to go to sleep for the next week or so. The anti-emetic had stopped me puking, at least, but it was making me extra dizzy. It seemed to be zapping the precious morphine, too, and I was feeling every single movement in my neck: when a porter wheeled me out of the recovery room and into a normal ward, I genuinely wanted to die.

It was only a little nodule, not even cancerous. I had no idea it could cause so much pain.

Mum had wanted to come in, but had been firmly told at the door that morning that she'd have to wait until visiting hours. Another interchangeably friendly nurse told me that she'd been on the phone to check up on me, but I didn't really care. All I wanted was to fade out of existence until I felt better.

I must have done, at least for a while. I can vaguely recall having some distinctly odd dreams – at least, I assume that Luka and Max from Karin Cluster hadn't actually come into the ward and done a waltz, nor had my year nine maths teacher wandered in and started preaching about aliens and their ability to take on GCSE trigonometry.

I woke up gradually, warily, sniffing the air before I opened my eyes. Was the pain still there? Yes. Was the dizziness still there? I opened my eyes to check. Wonderfully, it wasn't so bad. I had had the curtains drawn around my bed, so I didn't have to look at anyone else, but there was just enough of a gap in the floral fabric that the nurses would be able to see me if I started doing Exorcist impressions again. I liked having the curtains shut: it dimmed the bright hospital light. It didn't do much for the faint whiff of sick in the air, but I'd already got used to that.

For the first time, I felt brave enough to touch where the tumour had been taken away.

I was lucky, I suppose. Lucky that the operation had been done in 2016, not 1992 – it was only in recent years that they'd stopped having to cut your throat from ear to ear to be able to get to your thyroid gland. They used to have to staple you back up, and you looked like Frankenstein's monster for months. I already had the green skin, after the morphine incident.

I'd been told I'd only have the tiniest of cuts – just at the base of my throat. It would fade quickly and be barely visible within a year, just the faintest line that could easily be mistaken for a little fold in my neck. Not bad at all. I didn't even have to have any embroidery done; just one long stitch to hold everything together for a week while it got the worst of the healing process out of the way.

What I was not expecting, however, was that that one long stitch was being held in place by what felt like a washing line, two little posts protruding out of my skin by about a centimetre. I could pull them out a tiny bit – they were held in by the stitch. Good lord, it felt strange: painful as hell when I pulled at it, of course. I could feel a bit of a crust around the wound. I hoped it was blood, not some kind of horrific pus. *That* was busy leaking into my drain, which someone had helpfully hung off the bars on my bed. I gingerly felt along the tube, which ran under my skin for the length of the scar. It felt enormous. I was already dreading them pulling it out.

I hadn't noticed the drip before, either: a bag of fluid was leaking into me through the cannula in my hand. I didn't have the slightest idea what it was. I hoped it was painkillers, nice juicy painkillers to take me back to the happy cloud of numbness – without making me sick this time, I hoped.

Visiting hours had to be starting: I could hear sudden loud voices passing through the ward. And sure enough, my curtains were being whizzed open.

But it wasn't Mum. It was Lizzy.

"Wow, you're speedy," I croaked. "Wasn't expecting you till tonight."

"Cleo, you look awful," she squeaked, hobbling over and flinging her crutch aside so she could grab my hand – before recoiling in horror at the drain and whatever was floating in it. "Oh, my goodness."

"Don't you start vomming, I've had enough of that for one day."

"You poor thing." Lizzy sat down next to the bed and stroked my hand sympathetically, letting her crutch drop onto the floor with a crash that reverberated through my skull. "Does it hurt?"

"Yes. Lots." Suddenly, I realised something. Lizzy was not supposed to be there. Why was she not in school? And why was she biting her lip in the same way she always does when she's working something out? "What? Has something happened?"

"Um… I'm not sure whether I should – you should probably just rest for a while yet…"

"What's happened?" I couldn't really do what I'd usually do – grab her by the cardigan and shake it out of her – but instead I gave Lizzy my very best glare. "Don't make me hit you with my bottle of pus."

"OK, OK. Well, this morning, Gem was feeling a bit funny. She was at mine again, while her mum and Flic are in London. She woke me up at about three o'clock this morning, I could hear her pacing up and down, then when I was about to leave for school, she asked for a lift up here because, um, she's in labour."

"What?" I nearly fell off the bed. "Already? It's not supposed to be until next week and they always say first-timers go overdue!"

"It's definitely not a false alarm. I've been at work this morning, but I promised her I'd come in on my lunch, she thought it'd be to take her home because it's not real labour… but it is."

"Holy bollocks on a biscuit." I thought for a second, trying to get past the dizziness that was still persistently hanging around my head. "Gem's having the baby now?"

"Not right this second," Lizzy said quickly. "She's still got a long way to go, but she's in, what do they call it, active labour?"

"Yeah, I've heard of that." I tried to fight past my fuzzy head to remember anything, anything at all about the classes with Nurse of Steel. "It means it's really happening, the contractions will be for real and she'll be dilating… I think… oh hell, my *head*." I hit myself in the forehead, trying to clear the clouds. I only succeeded in nearly pulling my drain out again. "Is there anyone with her?"

"I told you, her mum's with Flic in London, Flic's having a wedding dress fitting." Lizzy started wringing her hands together again. "I don't know if Gemma's even bothered to ring them. Her dad's out on the boat, he's halfway to Sark at least and has no phone signal. I've told her I'll be back after work, there's nobody to cover me this afternoon…"

"No, don't worry about it," I said, trying not to croak. I pulled myself (painfully) to a full sitting position. "I'll go and look after her."

"Don't be silly, Cleo." Lizzy put on the special teacher voice that could thwart a whole uprising of eight-year-olds. "You're only just out of surgery."

"So? I'll get them to push me down in a wheelchair or something. I've been helping Gemma prepare for this for months. I'm her birthing partner! No tumour is going to get in my way!"

* * *

A noble statement, perhaps. But not one easily fulfilled.

"You cannot leave this bed!" The nurses had stopped being quite so gentle and lovely, and had brought out the battle-axes. Not metaphorical. They'd been storing up all the old bats from Nurse of Steel's era for exactly this moment. Maybe they kept them in a cupboard. Or a cryogenic freezing facility. "No patient under my care will be gallivanting off over this hospital."

"I don't want to *gallivant*," I protested. "I just want to be with my friend. I'm her birthing partner. It's kind of a big deal."

"Let the father of the baby be there," said the nurse dismissively. I say 'nurse' but she looked more like an old-fashioned matron: tall, strong looking, a bust like a battering ram and a face like the back end of a Guernsey donkey. "That's his job, not yours."

"But she doesn't know who it is, he definitely doesn't know he's about to become a 'father'," I said, trying to maintain a veneer of reasonability. "I'm all she's got. Even her mum's off on the mainland. Come on, have some human compassion!"

"I only have human compassion for my own patients," she said. "And you, young lady, are still far too sick to be out of bed. Especially with anti-emetics in you, you're more likely to faint than not."

"I've got to get up at some point," I said. "Like, the amount of water you've made me drink, I'm going to need to wee soon."

"And you'll use a bedpan."

"Woah, hang on." My eyebrows raised so high they must have disappeared into my hair. "Bedpans are for old people. I'm perfectly fine to walk to the loo."

"No, you're not. You will use a bedpan."

"I'll hold it in for the rest of my life rather than do that!"

Not long before, one of the other women on my ward had requested the bedpan. They'd closed the curtains around her bed, but I'd still heard everything. Every tinkle, every fart. Revolting. I wasn't having the entire ward listening to my ablutions, thank you very much.

"Do you want to make yourself even more ill?"

"I'm not ill, I'm recovering. And if you don't let me get out of bed, I'll bloody well do it anyway. What are you going to do, tie me down?"

I would have stormed off with grace if I'd not been the one marooned in bed. Instead, I folded my arms and glared my best glare across the battle lines – well, across the cubicle. The matron just stared back at me unflinchingly, before shaking her head and stalking off herself.

My mum, of course, chose this moment to turn up for visiting hours.

"Oh, Cleo, you're awake!" She rushed to my bedside and attempted to hug me around my drain and the drip. It didn't really work. "I phoned before and they said there was no point coming in until evening visiting hours, you wouldn't be yourself, but I wasn't going to let them stop me… Nan's just downstairs, we didn't want to crowd you so she's gone to visit Stanley Le Mesurier, he's in for a knee replacement."

While Mum babbled happily away, clearly content that I wasn't dead on an operating table, I calculated. She could be useful… Lizzy had already gone, rushing to make it back to school before the end of her lunch break. But I'd need someone to help me if I was ever going to get to Gemma – why not Mum?

"Shut up a sec, Mum, I need you to do something for me."

Ten minutes later, we were ready to go.

"I don't care what you say, I am here to help my daughter, and that's what I'm going to do." Wow, Mum could have a bloody loud voice when she wanted to.

"But we must leave the curtains open in case…"

"Don't be silly, I'm getting her into her own pyjamas. Your recommendation, if you recall." She could sound quite beautifully haughty as well. Almost like Nan. "She doesn't want all the other visitors looking at her."

With a satisfying whizz, Mum swished the curtain closed.

"Right then, if you can just get me into these…" Together, with relatively little dignity, we wriggled me into a pair of tracksuit bottoms and an oversized Karin Cluster t-shirt. It was a bugger trying to navigate the drip and the drain, but somehow, between the two of us, we managed it.

I only nearly yelped in pain, just the once when I snagged my washing-line-stitch on the neck of my t-shirt. I slipped my phone into my pocket, and slid into a pair of huge leopard print bootee slippers, especially purchased for the occasion by Nan.

"There we go, love," Mum said, her voice wobbling a bit. This was more up Nan's street, to be honest. Mum's usual line would be somewhat in line with Matron's – keep me in bed for the rest of my life, if possible. But in the spirit of our great reconciliation, she was eager to please me. And even she could see that Gem needed some help. She was giving birth, for heaven's sake.

"Right, here we go." I braced myself. Getting my feet free from the sheets had been dizzy-making enough: I wasn't quite sure how actually getting off the bed would work. "Oh, bollocks." My legs felt less like jelly than like custard: thick and slippery, yielding but not wobbling. I nearly crashed straight onto the floor.

"Careful, love," Mum whispered. "Do you want to get back on the bed?"

"No, no, I'm doing this," I said through gritted teeth. "Let me just go slowly." I got up again, holding firmly onto my drip stand.

Over the next few minutes, I managed to circle the cubicle a couple of times, my drain under my arm. I still felt a bit fuzzy – my head was doing tiny little spins – but I could feel myself getting stronger just from being out of bed. I didn't feel half as wretched while I was on my feet.

"OK, I think I've got it."

"Shall I…?"

"Yep. Now's your big moment, Mum. Please don't screw it up." I attempted to give her a hug, but with a canister of pus under my arm, it was kind of difficult. "If you do, they might actually strap me to the bed."

Mum took a deep breath, and left the cubicle. I listened closely.

"Yes, you, are you in charge of this ward?"

"Yes, I'm just coming onto my shift but I'll be in charge for the rest of the day – yeah, see you, Trixie."

"Goodbye, Emma."

I recognised that voice – this couldn't have been more perfect! Matron was leaving. And was called… Trixie? Good lord, she didn't look like a Trixie. Maud, Ethel, Dolores perhaps, but not *Trixie*.

"Yes, all right then," Mum said, not even a tremor in her voice. "The thing is, I'm worried about the state of this ward. You hear about it all the time nowadays, I've read the Daily Mail. MRSA, is it? Everywhere! And yet this place is filthy!"

"I'm so sorry, madam, I can assure you the wards are cleaned thoroughly, and we've got hand sanitizer at every station, so we really are trying our best to keep bacteria at bay. Honestly, you don't have anything to worry about-"

"Really? I'd like you to come and have a look at this."

I heard determined footsteps march past my cubicle, towards the window at the end of the ward. The window opposite the way out.

I peeped out of the floral curtains.

"Look! Look at the smudges on this window!" Mum was really getting into her little bit of drama. "Can you tell me that's clean? Don't bacteria live on windows?"

Shuffling as fast as I could in my slippers, I made for the door, making sure the curtains were still firmly closed around my cubicle, and Mum was still keeping the nurse turned away. None of the other patients paid me the slightest bit of attention. Most of them were still too woozy or sick themselves to bother.

God, my head was still dodgy. Whatever was in that anti-emetic, it had done a beautiful job of stopping me puking; but an equally beautiful job of making me fuzzy as fuck. I was proud of myself, though. Matron had predicted I'd faint before I could even get to the loo, and look at me! Hobbling at top (ish) speed past the empty nurse's station. I'd cunningly engineered my great escape to be at the same time most of the nurses were on a blood-pressure-and-pills round.

At the main entrance to the ward, I encountered my first suspicious nurse.

"Where have you come from, dear? Aren't you supposed to be in bed?" I didn't recognise this one.

"No, I'm allowed to be up," I explained. "I'm a smoker. I had a bit of a fight about it, but I'm allowed to go down for a fag." I patted the pocket of my tracksuit bottoms, hoping the shape of my phone could pass for a packet of cigarettes.

"How long have you been out of surgery, dear?" The nurse was eyeing my canister of pus with some suspicion.

"Since yesterday," I lied. "I'm having this all taken out in a couple of hours, but I need a smoke to calm my nerves."

"Go on then, off you go," the nurse said, shaking her head in mock disapproval of the post-surgery 'smoker'. Ha, I could smell her breath from a mile away. She'd totally just come back from a sneaky puff herself.

As soon as she got out of my way I was off again, through the door and into the main corridor. Ha, freedom! Now I just had to get shuffling again. Stopping hadn't been good for my head. I could just about cope when I was in motion, but when I stood still things started to swim a bit.

Plus, I didn't know how long Mum could keep up her tirade about germs and bacteria and smudged windows. Or how long the nurses would leave the curtains closed on my cubicle before they insisted on opening them for a blood pressure check or some other pretence to make sure I was still in there.

Right, a lift. Bingo! I shuffled painfully down the corridor, avoiding eye contact with the few people bustling by.

I scanned the notice at the side of the lift, not entirely sure where I was – or, for that matter, where I was going. I knew I had to get to Loveridge Ward, the maternity wing… but that was the limit of my knowledge. Gemma had had a tour of the place a few weeks previously, but she'd gone with Aaron and Meredith while I was at work.

I called the lift, and leaned heavily on the wall as it took me downstairs. On the other side, nobody seemed to look at me twice, even hauling my drain under my arm and trundling a drip stand behind me. It was a hospital, after all – people taking their various fluids for a walk had to be a common sight.

I paused and tried to work out where I was.

"Cleo!"

It was such a shock to hear my name, I jerked wildly. Then of course I proceeded to nearly pass out with the pain of my drain shifting. I leaned against the wall, panting.

"Nan, what are you doing?"

"Coming up to see you, my darling, but by the looks of things you've decided to come to me." Nan raised one eyebrow – one deftly painted-on arch of an eyebrow, of course. In fact she raised the eyebrow so high it nearly disappeared into her sequinned purple beanie. It matched beautifully with the glittery purple shawl she had wrapped around herself like a toga, offset by sparkly purple stilettoes and… purple jogging bottoms. All different shades of purple, but a pleasing combination nonetheless.

I quickly explained about Gemma.

"Mum's trying to keep them occupied but I need to get settled in there before they work out where I've gone and tell Loveridge Ward to bar me."

"They will find you," Nan mused. "But they can't move you by force. If they catch you on the way, though... here. I wore this because it's your favourite colour, it only seems correct that you should have it instead."

With a flourish, she whipped off the voluminous shawl and wrapped it around both me and my drip stand.

"Here you go, tuck that under there... *there*." She stood back to survey her work. "They'll be looking for a girl in a t-shirt with a drip stand. You can hardly see the stand at all, now!" She ceremonially took the beanie off her head and plopped it on my own.

"Are you not going to freeze?" Luckily Nan was wearing something under the shawl: a black studded vest that had definitely been swiped from my wardrobe. I was going to have to put a lock on the door.

"I'll get your mother to part with her cardigan." Nan pulled herself up to her full height and sniffed pompously.

"Nan..." I said slowly, suddenly taking in something about her that I'd missed. "Why is your lipstick so smudged?"

"Oh." She rolled her eyes. "Stanley might be getting over an operation, but he's certainly amorous. His wife is threatening to leave the Guernsey Goats." She shrugged. "I can't help it if he prefers me."

"Oh, Nan." I gave her a quick hug, trying not to whomp her with my drip stand. "And I wondered where I got it from."

Nan sniffed, her imperious expression still strong... then winked. "Go on, my darling, you go and look after your friend. I'll see if I can help your mother stall that nurse."

I managed to not get lost between Nan and the maternity ward, and I faced the video intercom with an iron will.

"Hi, I'm Gemma De Carteret's birthing partner," I said as nonchalantly as possible, trying to hide my drip stand deep underneath Nan's shawl, away from the little camera. I grinned nervously at it.

"Name, please?"

"Cleo Weeks."

"Ah yes, you're on her notes. Come in, she's in room two."

Yes! Entry granted.

With just a few shuffling steps, I fell into room two, hardly noticing Gem sprawled on the bed. All I saw was an armchair next to the bank of beeping machines – I collapsed into it with a sigh.

"Right, it's OK, I'm here, you can give birth now," I announced.

"Cleo?" The mountain that was Gemma rolled over and stared at me. "What the…"

"Hey." I closed my eyes and leaned back against the chair, willing the room to stop spinning. "Now I'm here, I'm not bloody moving." I opened my eyes again and started to unwrap my various fluids from swathes of purple glitter. Gem's eyes were wide. "Yeah, meet the drip and the drain. Now what's this about you having a baby?"

Chapter 21

They tracked me down, of course. It took them a while, though, at least half an hour. Mum and Nan came down to Loveridge Ward, trailing behind a small contingent of nurses. I'd never seen Mum and Nan look so alike, their expressions of haughty pride properly uniting them for the first time in my life.

"I kept her talking for ages," Mum whispered to me. "They didn't even notice you'd gone until they came round with the tea urn."

"Then I pretended to have a spasm of the heart." Nan grinned and gave her chest a good thump.

"Now, Cleo, you've got to come back up to your bed at once." Ha. Emma-the-nurse was no match for Trixie-the-matron in the menacing stakes. She didn't have a chance in hell of getting me to budge.

"Nope!" I said cheerfully. "I'm not moving. Couldn't if I wanted to, I think I've fused to this chair."

"And I'm not letting her go," Gem growled from the bed. "She's my birthing partner. That's more important than some stinky wound in her neck."

"Yeah, what she said." I put my most stubborn face on. "I'll rest tomorrow. For now, we've got a baby to have."

"I really don't think this is a good idea."

"Look, this is my wound, in my neck," I pointed out. "And I'm fine in this chair. If I feel really bad, well, I'm still in hospital, aren't I? I'm not trying to piss off home. I promise you, if I feel like I'm about to drop dead, I'll just get someone to take me back up to my own bed."

"This isn't just about you, Cleo," said Emma-the-nurse, trying to match my stubborn face and failing miserably. "You're giving us a lot more work, too. We've got to keep coming up and down the stairs to check on you..."

"Take the lift," I suggested.

"On your head be it," she said, throwing up her hands. "I'll send someone down to give you some painkillers in a couple of hours. And if you feel the slightest bit worse, call up immediately. The midwife will know the extension."

"Yeah, yeah, whatever." I grinned. Battle won! The nurse stomped out of the room, looking rather sour-faced.

Nan gave me a high-five.

OK, maybe I was being kind of selfish. The nurse would probably get in all kinds of shit with her superiors, letting me escape like that.

But it wasn't *properly* selfish. Gem didn't have anyone else. Well, not until Lizzy was finished at work anyway. And then she'd have marking to do and all sorts of lesson planning stuff, it being midweek. Plus, even though she was down to just the one crutch now, her leg was still giving her twinges of pain while it healed. She didn't need to haul herself all the way back to the hospital while I'd just be sitting upstairs in a hospital bed drumming my fingers. Totally not happening.

Nan volunteered to stay as well – I think she appreciated the drama of the situation – but Mum insisted she go home and have a rest. She left me with the purple shawl and beanie, though. I was becoming quite attached to them.

I'd won my battle. I'd made it to Loveridge Ward. And honestly, it was ages before I started to regret it.

I'd been warned a lot about poo, puke, blood, guts, gore – all the usual things that go on when someone's squeezing a human out of their private parts.

Nobody had warned me that quite a lot of labour is actually a bit… boring.

I mean, boring for the person that isn't doing the painful bits.

Gem was in proper labour, that had been confirmed. When I got down there, she was already five centimetres dilated. Five! She was, apparently, speeding along, especially by most first-time mothers' standards.

But that didn't mean the baby would be coming out any time soon.

All it meant was that every few minutes, regular as clockwork, Gem would start making a noise like a cow stuck in a fence, would suck on a plastic tube like it was Ryan Gosling's penis, and would grip her pillow extremely tightly. Then she'd stop and resume normal conversation.

"Honestly, it's not that bad," she panted after one contraction. "I thought it would be worse than this. Like, way worse. Horrible worse. *Doom* worse. But this stuff is great." She took another suck of Ryan Gosling, even though she wasn't having a contraction.

The tube (Ryan) was, of course, the famous gas and air. And Gem was absolutely loving it.

"Are you sure you don't want a go?" she said, her voice muffled by the tube that she was never taking out of her mouth.

"I'm sure, I'm on my own painkillers," I said. Though after the first couple of hours, I was starting to consider it. Despite Emma-the-nurse's promise, it was three hours before my painkillers were delivered to me. By that time, I was eyeing plastic Ryan Gosling with no little jealousy.

"Really, it's like being on a little cloud," Gem said dreamily. "The pain is still there, but it doesn't matter as much. Are you dressed up as a plum?"

"It's Nan's," I explained.

"Your nan's a plum? I like the sparkles, though. Here, sparkly plum, can you hear that herd of cows? Are they trying to break into the hospital? I don't need any milk. Or cheese."

"What cows?" I listened for a second. "No, Gem, that's not cows. That's the woman next door howling in pain."

"Ooh." Gem contemplated for a second. "Maybe I should give her some of this?" She waved Ryan Gosling for a second, then bit down firmly on it as another contraction struck her. "Oof."

I was pleased to notice that Gem hadn't given into any of Flic's ridiculous ideas for 'birthing wear' – of course she hadn't. This was Gem after all. She'd diligently packed her labour bag weeks ago, but it didn't contain any of Flic's preferred floaty monstrosities: she was clad instead in a giant grey t-shirt with a picture of a pink elephant on the front. Classy. It made her look the tiniest bit like an elephant herself – an elephant with increasingly wild hair, of course. Not particularly amenable to being tamed at the best of times, Gem's curly ponytail was frizzing determinedly out of the top of her hairband and giving her a fuzzy brown halo.

Of course, she didn't care and neither did I. Despite my purple sparkles lending a nightmarish disco-effect to my ensemble, I wasn't exactly looking my best either; I had a kind of vague sense of gratitude that there was nobody beyond nurses and midwives around to see us both looking like crap. Though, in the great scheme of things, there couldn't really be a more justifiable situation to look so bad.

However, I hadn't realised that visiting hours counted for people in labour as well as the women who'd already had their babies.

So I was somewhat surprised when, at some point that evening, there was a timid knock on the door of the room, and Aaron stuck his shaved head around it.

"Hello?" he said in a small voice. "Gemma? Can I come in?"

"AARON!" she bellowed happily, her beloved Ryan Gosling falling out of her face. "You're here!" Of course, he had to come when she'd just finished a contraction, didn't he? Therefore Gemma was very much high on a recent dose of eau de Ryan Gosling.

"Of course I'm here," Aaron replied, grinning as he came into the room. I rolled my eyes, knocking back the last of the pills that Emma-the-nurse had left for me. I didn't know what it was, but it had to be good enough to get me through this.

"Aah, you're not bad, are you Aaron?" Gem said, grabbing him by the hand as he crossed the room. "I mean, you might be bad. You've got a wife. But you're not bad?"

"I'm only bad when you want me to be," he promised, smiling. Ooh, I didn't like that smile. Not what I wanted to see. But Gemma, gassed up to the eyeballs, clearly didn't notice it herself. I couldn't say anything, though. I was staying out of this.

"Maybe I'll actually want to have sex with you when this is over," Gem explained, enthusiastically. "I like sex. Just maybe not in London. Pregnant. You know."

"I do," Aaron said, leaning closer to Gem. "I want to be with you, Gemma. Not just for sex. Forever."

Ugh. I was starting to feel a little bit sick. I didn't know whether that was the painkillers or the faux declaration of commitment, mind. I wasn't sure what was *in* my painkillers – I just hoped that Emma-the-nurse had been told about my violent reaction to morphine.

"Forever?" Gem burped a little bit. "Forever? Let's think of forever later."

"No, we'll think about it now," said Aaron, forcefully. Not in the *violent* forceful way, though. Just the perfect level of forceful for a romantic hero. Which I'm sure he thought he was. I did my best snort of derision, but neither of them seemed to remember I was even in the room. I didn't think Aaron had even noticed me.

"I can't think about it now," Gem whined. "I'm too cold."

Ten minutes ago she'd been too hot and trying to strip off her nightie, but never mind.

"Put my fluffy socks on," she demanded. "They're somewhere at the bottom of the bed. Can't do it myself, too much bump."

"Anything for you, love," Aaron murmured. I rolled my eyes again, feeling really sick now. He bent down to find Gem's socks and started to manoeuvre them onto her feet.

"Are you painting my toenails?" Gem mumbled woozily, just as another contraction hit. "Oh bloody hell." She started to suck furiously on Ryan Gosling, mooing all the while. She didn't seem to appreciate Aaron's presence around her feet at that moment, and got in a good kick to the side of his head. I sniggered to myself.

"Ow." Aaron looked affronted. But what can you say to a contracting woman who's just kicked you? They're allowed to do whatever they want, there's some kind of law about it.

"Oh, bloody bloody hell, they're getting worse," Gem panted, gripping onto her tube with fury. "Why is it getting worse?"

"It has to get worse, but then your baby will be here," Aaron said tenderly, surfacing from the bottom of the bed and gripping Gem's hand again. "Your beautiful baby."

"No, I'm going to die before then," Gem said blithely. "If it's going to get worse than this, I think I'd better make the most of life while I can."

With that, she yanked Aaron down to her and gave him a massive sloppy kiss.

It was too much.

"Oh, bollocks," I managed, before I had to reach for a horrible hospital cardboard tray to puke into.

"Oh, shit," said Aaron, pulling away from Gem and looking at me as if I was the most revolting thing he'd ever seen.

"Oh, yuck," Gem said, burping again – then reaching for a cardboard tray herself.

"Oh, *shit*," Aaron said again, pulling a truly hideous face and running from the room.

All I could do was retch again.

Which set Gem off.

Aaron, sadly, hadn't quite run for the hills. He came back in a second later, trailed by an anxious midwife. "There's vomit everywhere!" he said in a pitiful voice.

It was, of course, perfectly normal for a woman in labour sucking up lots of gas and air to be doing a little sick every so often. And it was also perfectly normal for someone with an apparent morphine intolerance to do the same, having been mistakenly given a morphine-based painkiller.

It wasn't quite normal to have the two in the same room at the same time, but hey. People had to deal with that.

The medical staff weren't pleased, and I had another lecture from Emma-the-nurse when she was called downstairs to inject me with some more anti-emetic, but I didn't really care as long as I could get my drugs.

I was, however, starting to wonder whether I could deal with this whole labour malarkey. The anti-emetic, having burned all the way up my arm again, was making me all dizzy and fuzzy – just as I'd started to come out of the last lot. Gemma was just as bad on her gas and air, but she was in a lot more pain now, too. Mine was getting slightly better: hers was getting a lot worse.

Plus, despite all the pain, things seemed to be getting slower rather than faster. It had only taken an hour for each centimetre before: it took more than two hours for Gem to get from six centimetres dilated to seven.

And in those two hours, I had to put up with Aaron.

Yes, he was still around. I'm pretty sure the midwives had mistaken him for a father, and were quite actively permitting him to be around. He knew better than to go in for any more kisses, but he was always there. Holding Gem's hand, whispering words of encouragement, helping her up when she wanted to totter around the room for a bit "to let gravity have a go at getting the little bugger out".

All *my* jobs, I would have announced dramatically, if I hadn't been slumped over an armchair, clutching my bottle of pus in one hand and trying not to feel quite so shit.

It wasn't going to last forever, though, and the tide soon turned.

"Do you want me to rub your shoulders?" he was asking.

"No. And stop stroking my hand." Aaron was making one of the fundamental mistakes in the world of Gem. Those of us who'd known her for years were well-versed in Gemma-etiquette, but he'd clearly not done his homework. Gem really didn't like being touched, definitely not hugged, and most certainly not 'rubbed'. Unless she was in massive emotional turmoil, or having sex with you, and then only when she was at exactly the right temperature and the stars were properly aligned: you just couldn't be skin to skin.

I only hoped her baby would be the exception.

"Sorry, love."

"I'm not your fucking 'love'," she hissed. "Oh, *oh*, here it comes again, bloody bloody bloody hell." Gem clamped the mouthpiece of the tube between her teeth and sucked like her life depended on it. "Ohhh. Fuck."

"Just breathe, breathe, remember to breathe," Aaron said 'soothingly'.

It clearly wasn't very soothing to Gem.

"I. Am. Fucking. Breathing," she mooed in between breaths. "Fuck. Off. With. Your. Breathing!"

"What?"

"I said, *fuck off.*" The contraction started to die off, and Gem relaxed back into her pillow. "Holy shit, that was a big one. Now, you. No, not you, sparkly plum Cleo. Aaron. FUCK OFF."

"But... you're not thinking. I thought you wanted me here?"

"I never asked you to be here, did I?"

"But your baby is coming, Gemma. Your beautiful baby, and we're going to raise her together..."

Gem laughed, a wild, high-as-a-kite laugh. "No, you're going to raise your own baby. Meredith's. Go on, fuck off. Stop trying to touch me and fuck off."

Without another word, Aaron stalked out of the room, holding his head high in what was probably supposed to be a dignified stance. It was somewhat lessened by the flecks of sick on his shirt from Gem's most recent vom-bomb, and the fact that his head was starting to get a five o'clock shadow in a ring around the bottom. He didn't quite have the heroic good looks to be able to pull off a 'stately storm-off'.

"About time," I piped up from my armchair.

"Oh, I was getting sick of the sight of him." Gem groaned and rolled over onto her side. "I can't get bloody comfortable, and this gas isn't helping anymore."

I had to ask it. Totally not the right time, but I had to ask anyway. "Is that a permanent 'fuck off', or...?"

"I haven't decided yet. I just don't want him in this room. Don't want anyone. Just you. Oh, this is so uncomfortable. And it hurts. Oh, bloody hell, bloody hell, that's another one. Fuck, fuck, *fuck.*" Gem howled for a couple of minutes, then stopped abruptly. "Cleo, I can hear those cows mooing again. Why are the cows mooing?"

"Gem, that's you."

"Oh. Oh, fuck, fuck, bloody hell."

* * *

It got worse. Of course it got worse, it was labour. It was meant to get bloody worse.

I, of course, was getting better by the minute. By eleven o'clock that night, I was no longer dizzy or sick, just sore. But I was getting through on just codeine, instead of the morphine-laced puking pills they'd been throwing at me. Emma-the-nurse had come down at the end of her shift for a last-ditch attempt to get me back to bed, but I cheerfully and wholeheartedly refused.

Gemma was now at nine centimetres – so close, but so far. Every contraction was evil agony, and she was howling for an epidural. But the only anaesthetist on call was with an emergency caesarean, and he had a budding queue of screaming women to get through before it would be Gem's turn. The epidural train didn't look like it would be arriving in the station any time soon.

Her waters hadn't even broken yet, mind. Every time the midwife came in and stuck her hand up for a feel, she could apparently feel them 'bulging'. Even without the painkillers of doom, I still felt a bit sick when I heard that. 'Bulging' is not a good word, when it's in reference to something up your chuff.

I'd rolled my armchair and drip stand painfully across the floor, and was now positioned right at the head of the bed. Gem had finally reached that stage of emotional turmoil when she actually wanted someone to hold her hand and reassure her. Lizzy was a lot better at that than me, of course, but although she'd turned up as soon as she'd escaped work, she'd been turfed straight out when visiting hours ended. It was all up to me.

"Cleo, I'm getting hot," Gem would whine, and I'd press a cold flannel onto her forehead.

"Cleo, I'm cold," she'd wail, and I'd quickly throw the sheet over her and turn up the heating in the room.

"Cleo, I'm going to be sick," she'd burp, and I'd thrust a cardboard tray in front of her.

See, I wasn't entirely useless. Though I had to hide my neck drain behind the arm of the chair. After all the gas and air and a bit of pethidine (which didn't seem to help the pain at all), just the sight of my lovely canister of yellow pus was setting Gem off with the stomach-contents and the cardboard trays. I was only happy that my own stomach was behaving itself.

Not that there was much in there to puke up, of course. I'd been brought a revolting hospital 'roast dinner' (definitely microwaved: quite exceedingly soggy with very lumpy gravy) but Gem had had such a temper tantrum when I started eating it that she made herself sick. Again. I'd had to make do with a sneaky Snickers bar while she was in the bathroom, nicked from her own labour bag.

"Let's have another look at you," said the midwife, bustling into the room. This was the second midwife we'd encountered, thanks to a shift change: her name was Amelia, and she was absolutely stunning, with a pretty pink hair bobble in her glossy chestnut hair and a face full of make-up. She seemed about fifteen, fresh-faced and innocent underneath the make-up. I wasn't sure how wise it was to be wearing that much slap on a maternity ward, but hey, she knew best.

"I want an epidural," Gem panted – her common greeting now for anyone who happened to pass by the room. Or the hospital. I'm sure half the island must have been able to hear her.

"Oh, now love, you know that's not possible. You're almost there!" Amelia wasn't shy – she'd been in the room thirty seconds and already had one blue-gloved hand firmly up Gemma's bits. "You're so close to ten centimetres now, this baby will be with you very soon!"

"Don't care," Gem grunted. "Want. My. Epidural!"

"Sorry, love." Amelia smiled some more, starting to free her hand.

But that wasn't happening: in anger or desperation, I wasn't sure which, Gem clamped her legs firmly together. Amelia's hand was well and truly trapped.

"Now, hon, come on," she said, looking a tiny bit terrified. "You have to let me have my hand back."

"Not until I get my epidural!" Gem flexed her still-enviable thigh muscles, holding onto the poor midwife even tighter.

"Give her back her arm," I said, having a horrible vision of Gem's baby having to be c-sectioned out of her, the poor midwife's arm still attached. Amelia's impeccable hair was coming loose, as she tried to reach the 'call for help' button with her free hand.

"No! Epidural! Oh… oh God!" Gem's legs flopped open and Amelia's hand was washed free by what seemed like a tsunami of fluid.

It went everywhere: in her hair, on her beautifully made-up face, all over her pale blue scrubs, soaking the bed…

"Ah," she said, wiping a damp strand of hair off her face. "That'll be your waters."

You don't say.

Things seemed to happen very quickly after that: it was like the waters breaking had forced Gem's cervix to open that infinitesimal couple of millimetres and the baby was finally ready to start the journey to the outside world.

Gemma, however, appeared to have changed her mind, and was pacing around the room as fast as a woman in the latter stages of labour could go, stopping every few steps to grab whatever she could and have a good moo. Amelia had tried to persuade her to keep still, but it wasn't happening.

"I don't want a baby," she wailed, gripping me tightly by the arm and trying to pull me to my feet. I winced as she jogged the cannula in the back of my hand, nearly yanking my drip out. "I'll have a guinea pig instead. Let's go down to the GSPCA and pick one out. Come on."

"I don't think Amelia's going to let us do that," I explained, as patiently as I could while I detangled Gem from Nan's purple shawl.

"Shh, we won't tell her," Gem whispered, loudly. About two feet away on the other side of the bed, Amelia raised her (now dry) eyebrows, but didn't say anything. I suppose she was used to it. "Shh. You see that window? You distract her, I'll climb out. I'll meet you at the main entrance in ten minutes."

I gave the tiny vented window a glance, followed by a covert look at Gem's still-considerable bump.

"Yes, Gem, we'll do that," I promised. "Let's just have this baby first, eh?" I gave her a gentle shove and she sunk back onto the bed, big tears falling down her face.

"But it hurts!" she wailed, gripping her sheets. "Oh *shit*, oh *shit*, oh *shit*. WHO IS THAT?"

I turned to the door. A bespectacled man was being led into the room by a nurse in scrubs. "It's that one," she said, pointing to me.

"Ah," said the man, marching purposefully over to me. "Cleo? Yes? Now, I'm the consultant on call for your ward, and I must insist on you coming to bed immediately."

"GET OUT!" Gemma hollered, lunging at me. Of course, she missed, and grabbed my drip stand instead. She looked momentarily confused as to how I'd suddenly got so skinny, but still didn't let go. "Cleo is my birth partner and she's staying here!"

"Honestly, it's really not…"

"GET OUT!"

"GET OUT!" I hollered, joining in. It hurt my throat, but I didn't care.

Amelia looked briefly like she wanted to join in with the hollering, but mercifully didn't.

"Cleo is doing just fine here," she piped up instead. "And as this baby's definitely on her way, I'd suggest you leave, now, Cleo will be up when she's ready."

"I really must insist," the doctor attempted again, but Gem chose that moment to scream so loudly I wouldn't have been surprised if people had felt the aftershocks in the depths of Torteval.

"C'mere!" she yelled at Amelia, then grabbed her by the scruff of the neck, pulling her close. "The baby's coming out," she hissed, looking around furtively at the consultant and the nurse. "But it's *coming out of my bum*. I can feel it!"

"Now let's have a look, shall we?" Amelia said, wriggling free. "I'm sure she's not coming out of your bottom."

"She is, I can feel it!"

"No, no, but she is coming. I can see a lovely head of hair."

"Grab hold of it and pull!"

"No, hon, I don't think that would be wise."

"She's not shit herself, has she?" I had to ask.

"No, she's doing really well," Amelia said. "Now come on, Gemma, *push*!"

"Aaaarghh." Gem let out the world's most inhuman noise, still clutching my drip stand in one hand. I was glad the tube connecting it to me was rather long.

"Another one, there's a good girl!"

"AAARGH." Gem closed her eyes and strained. I was practically pushing along with her.

"Nope, she's gone back up," Amelia sighed. "This happens sometimes, don't worry. We'll have her here soon."

"NO, we will have her here *now*," Gem insisted, pulling herself up the bed and glaring around the room with a regal expression that somehow managed to transcend her sweaty face and wild hair. Even my consultant was caught in her glare and hovered by the door, holding his breath. "Be. Quiet."

Gemma pushed again: in absolute ice-cold silence.

And within a few moments, just after midnight, there was a horribly slippery squelching noise, and Amelia was holding a sticky, blood-stained puppy in her arms.

At least it sounded like a puppy, those pathetic little squeaking cries.

But it wasn't a puppy, it was a baby. Gemma's baby girl.

"She's here," I whispered, tears rolling down my face.

"She's... she's..." Gem couldn't get the words out, as Amelia wordlessly placed the tiny, squirming bundle onto her chest. "She's got gel in her hair!"

"No, Gem, that's blood," I had to point out.

"Oh, whatever." Trembling, Gem kissed the top of the baby's dark little head. "Oh, she's beautiful. Look, she's looking at me. She's beautiful, and she's mine."

Annoying Customer of the Week, Part 9

"Good morning! What would you like today?"

"Two coffees please, love. Cappuccinos."

"Would you like those big or small?"

"Medium, please, love."

"We do big or small. See, here are the two cups."

"Medium please, love, those ones there. Ooooh, Marian, aren't they big? Bigger than the medium at that other place we go to."

"Ooh, you're right there, Mavis. Huge. I'll be widdling all night!"

"Me too, Marian!"

"That's four... sorry, that's four... hello? Ladies? Sorry, that's four pounds twenty, please."

"I'll get this, Mavis."

"No, I'll get it, Marian, you got the last one."

"No, Mavis, it's my turn..."

"Don't insult me now, Marian, I'm getting these..."

"Here love, quick, don't take her money!"

"No, look, my card's already in the machine!"

"Take the cash, love! No, Mavis, put that card away!"

"You paid last time, Marian, it's my turn!"

As the old ladies squabbled hopelessly in front of Sky, the queue of suits tutting in outrage, I breathed a happy sigh. It was good to be back in the Bean Jar – especially as it wasn't me having to deal with the battling old bats.

Chapter 22

"If you wake her up, I will claw at your face until you bleed."

Technically, Gemma was on maternity leave, and I was off work to recover from my operation.

We were, of course, in the Bean Jar anyway.

Zach had drafted in Sky to do a few shifts (did she *ever* do her own job?), and had summoned in one of the teenagers we used over Christmas, practically on bended knee considering it was almost the summer holidays and thus 'getting drunk on the beach' season. He'd even, in desperation, got Mrs Machon to do a couple of shifts out front, cleaning tables and sweeping the floor and generally bossing everyone around. Fun for the whole family.

Whether it was the purity and innocence of her, or the symbolism of a new life and a blank slate, or just the fact she was adorably cute, Gem's baby seemed to heal a lot of wounds. For a start, Flic was there in the Jar with us, already besotted with her tiny niece. A bit too besotted, some of us privately thought, seeing as she was trying to monopolise the baby at every moment.

Though, let's face it, we were all spending most of the time bickering over who got to hold her.

"Aww, look, she's sucking her thumb in her sleep!" Lizzy cooed, provoking a chorus of 'aww'.

"I said shh," Gem hissed, clutching her baby close to her. "She's a little ratbag when she starts screaming." But she said it with affection.

"How are you managing with your parents?" Zach said, leaning over the sofa to get a better look. He took his glasses off and dangled them absently from his finger, grinning goofily.

"They're, like, so in love with her, of course." Gem stroked the baby's hair, an astonishing mop of black. "But shitting hell, they're annoying. Mum wakes up every time she starts screaming in the night, but won't be useful. She gets up and makes a cup of tea, then sits reading a book. Next to me. While I'm feeding her. Practically unconscious. I don't know why she doesn't just offer to do some herself." She shifted and winced uncomfortably. "Oh holy hell, I need a wee. Here, hold her." She gently tipped the sleeping baby into Lizzy's arms.

Flic made a grumpy noise. "I'm her aunty and I haven't held her all day!"

"Shut up. You're *all* her aunties." Gem limped gingerly off towards the toilet.

It was only a week since the baby had been born. Gem was, of course, still feeling a little bit tender. After it was over, she'd acknowledged along with everyone else that she had had a comparatively easy time of things: we all knew someone with a horror story about tears and c-sections and poo to tell. But she was still left very sore, of course she was, she'd just pushed seven pounds of baby out of her bits. Going to the loo was still a bit of an ordeal.

I wasn't exactly in the best shape myself. It could have been a lot worse: leaping out of bed three hours after waking up from surgery had probably helped me, getting me moving instead of hanging around in bed for ages feeling sorry for myself. I couldn't exactly get back in the bed and start feeling sorry for myself once all the birth stuff was over.

However, I still wasn't right. More than anything, my surgery scar was irritating the hell out of me. It was itchy, occasionally it was a bit weepy, and I had another two days before my washing line could be removed. I had a perfectly round hole by the side of it where the drain had gone in (I'd been right: getting it out had felt hideous) and it was deep and sore, more so than the main cut.

More than anything else, though, I was self-conscious.

It was such an ugly scar: well, wound. It was still too fresh to be called a scar, really, considering it was still crusty and brown. I couldn't even cover it up, it got so itchy when it came anywhere near any kind of material, and the washing line got jiggled and made me squeak. Plus, it was June. The sun was shining all the time already, and it was over twenty degrees every day. I didn't want to be covered in layers just to hide my neck, even a floaty scarf was unthinkable.

But walking down the Grange (I was forbidden by Mum to go anywhere near my scooter while I was still on strong painkillers) and then past the shops on Smith Street, I noticed more covert looks than I was happy with. And in the Jar, there had been a family with a little boy who just wouldn't stop staring. Eventually he'd asked his mum very loudly about it.

Zach had intervened, though, before I could get upset.

"Oh, I'd be careful around her," he said to the little boy. "She got in a fight with a ninja, down the back of Albert Pier. He had his knife at her throat, just enough to cut it just a tiny bit, but she threw him off and chucked him in the marina."

"Really?" said the little boy, wide-eyed.

"Absolute truth," said Zach, solemnly, turning to flash me a crooked grin. "She's a superhero."

I still felt a little bit wobbly, though. I wasn't looking forward to going back to work. Zach had told me to take as long as I had to, but with Gem off for the foreseeable future, I thought it would be best to go back after two weeks.

Zach had been the perfect boss: I didn't think he could be anything *but*. He was the first person barrelling into the hospital as soon as visiting hours hit, bearing two huge bunches of flowers. One was for Gemma and one, surprisingly, was for me.

"I've had a tumour out, not a baby," I'd laughed, accepting the bunch of purple freesias anyway.

"Ahh, you've been through a lot," he said shyly, running his fingers through his hair.

He'd been incredibly helpful to Gem and the baby, too. He'd been the one to help them home from the hospital, sorting out a particularly plush taxi when Gem's dad managed to reverse his car into their own gate post in his enthusiasm to meet his new granddaughter. And Zach was just as smitten with the baby as the rest of us.

Now, as she was just making 'waking up baby' noises and starting to wriggle on Lizzy's lap, he reached down and eased her away.

"I've got a bottle cooling down, I'll give it to her before she cries," he said, before Flic could protest.

Lizzy tactfully turned her attention to Flic. "Did get your dress sorted in the end?"

"Oh, yes." Flic sighed heavily and rolled her eyes. "The seamstress didn't want to alter the lace insert, but I told her..." She launched into some interminable rendition of the Wedding Dress Blues, but I wasn't paying attention.

I was busy watching Zach. He was feeding the baby like it was something he was born to do: she hadn't even had the chance to start crying before he'd soothed her and got the bottle in her mouth. And, being Gemma's baby, she wasn't one easily soothed once she got going. Despite all her earlier aversions, Gem was making attempts to breastfeed: it wasn't working as well as she'd like, so about half of the baby's milk was coming out of a bottle. But we were all pleased – and relieved – that while Gem still shunned physical contact from the rest of us, her baby was exempt.

Sky was watching Zach too, I noticed. She was standing behind the coffee bar, allegedly being the barista for the day, though her coffees were so bubbly they were practically undrinkable. She didn't seem to find Zach and the baby as mesmerising as I did. Her expression wasn't the usual gooey one most people couldn't help getting at the sight of such an adorable tiny human. She just looked... disgusted.

In fact, Sky had been the only person we knew who hadn't been completely enchanted by the baby. She'd had a little cuddle with her, the first time she'd met her... but she gave her back pretty quickly when she woke up and started her cranky crying routine.

It was a bit weird, but I put it out of my head. Not everyone could be a baby person. I'd not exactly considered myself one, even just a week previously.

Gemma came back from the loo, still wincing.

"My bits are like a warzone," she announced to the café in general. Nobody batted an eyelid. We'd all heard worse from her in the past week. "Cheers, Zach."

"No problem," he said, grinning down at the greedily sucking baby.

Gem plopped herself back down on the sofa, as gingerly as she could manage. "Oh, fuck, I hope I'm back to bloody normal soon."

"You practically are," I pointed out. "You'd hardly think you'd had a baby at all, to look at you." Apart from the bags under her eyes, I supposed, but then Gem often had those after a weekend in Folies. And thanks to the breastfeeding, she had managed to retain a decent-sized pair of boobs, instead of the pancakes she'd had back in the day.

"I don't know what you're looking at, I'm fat as fuck."

"Gemma," Lizzy chided, trying to cover the baby's little ears over Zach's shoulder.

"She's a week old," Gem pointed out. "I've got a good few months left before I have to worry about her repeating anything. Besides, it's true. I'm fat as fuck."

"No, you're normal-person sized," I said. "You're just not skinny as a drip stand."

"Will you stop about that drip stand? I wouldn't have thought it was you if I wasn't drugged up to the eyeballs."

"Oh dear, oh dear, silly baby," Zach said suddenly, as the baby made a bit of a spurting noise. "Eww, it's all over me." Lovely milky baby puke, all over his t-shirt (which had a picture of a velociraptor on it: everyone's favourite nerd as always). He was still laughing, though. "That was a bit silly, wasn't it, little one? Wasn't it?"

"Will you stop talking like a twat?" Sky bustled over from the bar, a scowl on her face and a wodge of blue roll in her hand. "We're supposed to be having dinner with my mum in an hour, and you're covered in vomit." She tried to dab around the baby to get to the puke. I seized the poor kid quickly before she could get slapped with the blue roll.

"Chill out, Sky, it's just a bit of milk." Zach submitted to his wiping anyway, passing me the bottle with a roll of his eyes.

"I saw that!" Sky glared at him and tossed her glossy hair. "It's vomit, it's revolting, and you know it."

"It's milk, from a baby, it's not a big deal."

Suddenly, the atmosphere was so tense we could all feel it. Even the baby seemed to slow her sucking, and I swear she raised a tiny eyebrow. Thankfully, Flic had enough perception somewhere deep in her to change the subject.

"Anyway, never mind about that – when is this niece of mine getting a name?" she demanded. "It's been a whole week."

"She's right." I hastily agreed with Flic – hey, circumstances called for it. "We can't keep calling her 'the baby' forever."

"Nothing I thought about before she arrived seems right," Gemma moaned, dropping her head into her hands. "She doesn't look like anything – not a Laila Mae, not a Lacey. She's definitely not an Angel or a Honey. She's stronger than that. She's not even a Cinnamon."

"Thank heavens," Flic said, grinning.

"What about something classic? You could call her Amelia, after that midwife," Lizzy mused. Gem made a puke face. "But then you could shorten it to Amy, or Milly. Or Alexandra, for Alex or Lexie."

"Or how about something to do with Guernsey?" My eyes had drifted to the mural behind the coffee machine and I had a sudden thought. "Guernsey's flower is the Guernsey lily, you could call her Lily."

Gemma mused for a second, following my gaze, then she grinned widely and held out her arms for her daughter. "You have just had the best idea you've had all week."

"Oh, really?" I was quite proud of myself.

Gemma took her baby into her arms, newly full of milk and staring up at her with big blue eyes. "Your Aunty Cleo has just named you. Not Lily, though. Boring. You're a Guernsey girl, through and through. Your name is Sarnia!"

* * *

Flic's eye-rolling may have been practically propelling the world around its axis, but the name 'Sarnia' was sticking. Gemma was determined, and besides, she was right. It was the baby's name: you only had to look at her to know it.

Sarnia Daisy Blue De Carteret. A bit of a mouthful, but it worked.

Well, we were all a bit unsure about the 'Blue' part, but Gem was adamant.

"Her eyes are just so blue," she said, stubbornly.

"All babies have blue eyes," Lizzy pointed out.

"No, her eyes are going to stay this colour. I just know it."

Flic really wasn't pleased, of course. We could practically see it flashing before her eyes: she'd have to tell her colleagues she had a niece called *Sarnia*. None of her posh English friends, most of whom had moved over to the island for the job opportunities in finance, had a clue that 'Sarnia' was the Latin name for 'Guernsey'. Most of them wouldn't have the slightest idea what the Sarnia Chérie mural in the Bean Jar was all about, let alone been able to drunkenly sing along to the song on Liberation Day.

The De Carteret parents – now grandparents – were just plain old gobsmacked. Mrs De Carteret had timidly suggested some names that she thought would be more appropriate.

"How about Sandra?" she proposed. "Or Sarah? They're close to Sarnia..."

"*Sandra*. Mum, it's 2016." Gemma was having none of it. "She's Sarnia and that's that."

It was not long after that particular altercation (well, as far towards an altercation as the cowed and meek Mrs De Carteret would get) that Gem decided she had had enough.

Over the space of two days, and far too many trips for Lizzy's little yellow Micra, Gem and Sarnia had moved out of the crowded family bungalow in the Castel, finally leaving Mr and Mrs De Carteret to enjoy their retirement entirely daughter-free.

Of course, she couldn't afford a flat of her own, not at Guernsey rates.

So she moved in with Lizzy.

"Let's face it, you've been practically living here anyway," Lizzy had explained when she had made the suggestion. "Why not make it permanent? I'd be able to help you with Sarnia, and it gets lonely sometimes when I'm on my own in that big flat."

It was true that Lizzy was almost more adept at handling the baby than her own mother. Although we were all still fighting over cuddles, Lizzy was the only one who volunteered to do the nappy changes. And, within the space of a week, she was doing night feeds too.

"Aren't you a bit worried she's... taking advantage?" I dared to ask, one Saturday morning when Lizzy tottered into the Jar, still held up by one crutch and red-eyed with tiredness. "You're still not in the best shape yourself."

"I wouldn't do it if I didn't want to. Plus, she does plenty herself." Lizzy gulped back a black coffee, the first properly strong coffee I'd ever seen her consume. "She hasn't asked me to do anything, really. I just want to be of use."

* * *

Still, Gem didn't put up much of a fight when I determinedly set out to bully her into a night on the town. Three weeks after she'd given birth and she was skinnier than me by a long way, fitting into a dress she'd owned since she was nineteen. Apparently, back then it had been her 'fat' dress. I kind of hated her for that.

"I'm enormous," she whined, determinedly trying to stuff a boob into Sarnia's face at the same time as putting mascara on. It wasn't really working. "I haven't been this big since before I started smoking."

"Get used to it," I said sternly. "You're not going to start again, are you?"

"I'm going to try not to." She looked a bit sheepish. "You know what happens when I'm pissed."

"You've gone months and months now without a cigarette, you can keep it up."

"I only really stopped because fags made me want to puke."

"And you'd hurt your poor little baby?"

"Well, yes. That too." Gem looked down at Sarnia, her face lighting up at the little chubby cheeks, even after weeks of sleepless nights. "But anyway." She tore her moony gaze away. "I am ready for a night of debauchery. It is well overdue!"

And so Sarnia was handed over to her Aunty Lizzy, stuck at home anyway with a pile of marking, and given instructions to behave (the baby, not Lizzy).

"I am going to get trashed," Gem said, with no little satisfaction.

But after a single JD and Coke and a mere half pint of Fosters, Gem was ordering a taxi to go home.

For once, not with a man. We hadn't even reached Folies.

"My boobs hurt every time I think of her. Maybe I'm not ready for a night without her after all," she said, practically sprinting out of the door towards the taxi rank.

I'm going to be honest: even after all we'd been through together in that hospital, I still didn't one hundred percent trust her.

There was the tiniest bit of me – OK, maybe not that tiny – that was expecting her 'must go home to my darling baby' story to be an outright lie. I hadn't heard anything about Aaron since Gem's labour, when he had turned up declaring his love.

Of course, I didn't know whether Gem herself had heard from him or not. I hadn't really thought to ask, there had been so much going on. I couldn't help but think that maybe now she was bumpless, she'd got hold of him and was heading off for a sneaky shag.

Hovering between the White Hart pub and the taxi rank, I watched Gem rush into her waiting taxi. It sped off towards St Sampson at once. Well, that meant nothing. Just because it was the right direction didn't mean Aaron didn't live somewhere around there too.

I sent off a speedy WhatsApp to Lizzy, demanding to know if Gemma had arrived back. Fifteen minutes later and the reply came: yes, she had, and was currently sitting on the sofa with Sarnia on her lap, squeezing the baby so hard Lizzy was genuinely concerned she would pop, her top off and offering each boob in turn with no concern whatsoever that Lizzy was watching.

Curiouser and curiouser.

I had a sudden rush of self-consciousness. This was supposed to be my first night out since my operation, my tentative 'getting back on the horse', so to speak. Getting drunk and daft with Gem, like old times. The pair of us hammered and going a bit mental.

But here I was, two drinks down, a practically raw wound open on my neck for the world to see, and not a friend in sight.

Maybe I should just go home, I thought. Everyone else was being so *grown-up*: Gemma with her baby, Lizzy with her career and stable mental health, Flic with her fiancé. I was the last one up for a good night of string-free sin and fun.

"Cleo!" Suddenly, a disembodied voice called my name.

"What... where...?" I made a couple of incoherent noises then spun around in a little circle.

"Here, you berk." Zach loomed out from the White Hart doorway, Sky at his side. They were both dressed to impress: I think Zach had even attempted to brush his hair. Sky was in a floaty little cream dress that would have looked like toilet roll on me, but somehow looked ethereal and beautiful on her.

Bitch.

"We've just been for dinner, what are you doing here?" Zach punched me lightly on the arm. He seemed a tiny bit drunk. It was strange to see him without his glasses – his eyes seemed startlingly blue. I knew he had to be practically blind; he was almost phobic about contact lenses. I didn't want to know how Sky had convinced him to leave the glasses behind. "Hot date?"

"Hardly. Gem just stood me up."

"Aww." Zach sounded distressed; Sky made a noise that I think was supposed to sound sympathetic. Hard to tell when she was looking determinedly in the other direction.

"Yeah, she's gone back home to the baby. Couldn't spend the whole evening without her."

"Well, we're just going for a drink. Fancy it?"

Sky looked up, horrified. Zach didn't notice: there was a puppy-like eagerness in his eyes. At the prospect of a drink, or at some company other than his sulky girlfriend?

"Erm..." I stole another quick look at Sky. Yup, some strong pouting game going on there. Perfect brows lowered, she stared at me coolly. Yeah, didn't take a genius to work out that she really didn't want me hanging around.

It would have been lovely to say "yes, I'll join you" and annoy her all night. Maybe get Zach shitfaced and leave her to deal with him. Or flirt outrageously and watch her face get grumpier and grumpier until it consumed itself. Or until she ran off in an even bigger sulk. Then I'd have Zach all to myself...

I had to remind myself that I didn't fancy Zach. Just for a second there, faced with his best puppy-dog eyes and his best (only a little bit crumpled) shirt, I was starting to forget that I didn't have a thing for him. Oops. Damn those three drinks in my just-off-painkillers system.

"No, I'll just get on home." I smiled at the pair of them (yes, even at Sky). "I was all geared up for a night of madness and I don't think a quiet drink will cut it."

"Who says I don't want a night of madness?" Zach sparkled.

At me. Not at Sky. He was sparkling at me. Just for a second, I felt my entire insides melt and turn into goo. I hadn't felt something like that since... since ever.

Don't be silly, Cleo.

"Zach, come on, she said no." Sky spoke up while I was momentarily struck dumb. "You can have your night of madness with me."

With that, she tugged him off towards the pub. He waved sheepishly behind her back, powerless to resist the tiny tidal wave yanking him along.

Odd times, very odd times.

I refused to think about that strange gooey feeling I'd just got. Must have been the JD, not my usual tipple after all, I told myself firmly. I resolutely stamped towards the Grange and home.

Chapter 23

"CLEO WEEKS!"

I rubbed my ear, wincing, and held the phone away. "Christ on a bicycle, Lizzy. What's up?"

"Oi, no phones on the café floor!" Zach had appeared as if by magic – I'd thought he was lurking in his office. He was in a right grump, I didn't want to ask why. I was skulking around near the stairs, pretending to clean tables while surreptitiously trying to answer my phone, which had been ringing insistently in my back pocket.

"It's Lizzy!" I protested. "It might be an emergency with the baby!"

"It's the middle of the day, Lizzy's at work." Zach scowled, his glasses balanced on the end of his nose like a Victorian schoolteacher. "Two minutes and that's it." He stomped back up the stairs. What had got into him? Suddenly deciding to play the big boss. Arse.

I was getting tired of Zach's personality flips when it came to the Bean Jar. One minute everyone's best mate, the next the boss from hell. It was a right pain in the arse, and I never knew which Zach I was going to get when I rolled into work.

June was soon to float into July: baby Sarnia had just smiled for the first time (the first time that we'd ascertained wasn't wind, at any rate), and Guernsey was starting to get a bit feverish

– what with the heat, and the summer holidays looming. Every time a schoolchild came into the Jar you could practically feel the excitement bubbling off them.

Even Charlie and his mates, supposedly too cool for anything but nonchalance, had been in the Jar requesting frappes and excitedly sitting down to plan their exploits for the summer holidays. It seemed like 'Guerns Gagging For It' was still going, despite Charlie's ban from all online life for the last few months. I wasn't going to go looking for their videos – I was still suffering residual trauma from the thirty seconds or so I'd watched back when they first came up with the idea – but I was glad they'd be doing something fun over their holidays. Something that, hopefully, would keep them far away from any alcohol and a repeat of the 'house party to end all house parties' (that had, I suppose, effectively ended all house parties for the time being).

I'd been back at work for almost two weeks, and I was settling back into the swing of things. My coffees were still delicious – if I do say so myself – and my customer service was still served up with a beaming smile. Well, most of the time.

Zach had nothing to complain about, honestly. But he'd still morphed into a grouchy harridan, seemingly out of nowhere. Again.

All of a sudden, everything had to be dealt with by the book; no phone calls during working hours, breaks only when he allowed them, no helping myself to slices of cake when the café was quiet. He'd stopped acting like a friend, and was acting like a... well, like a boss. Impersonal, direct, firm. All good qualities when you're running a team of thirty people; not so great when your team consists of three staff members, one of whom is your grandmother and another of whom is on maternity leave.

I'd expected things to be good in the Bean Jar when I returned to work; I'd expected the chaos and the drama of the past couple of months to bring us all closer. I even wanted Sky to be a part of it, I'd kind of hoped that she'd soften towards us all and start acting like a proper mate (and stop giving me excuses to dislike her).

No such luck.

She was still hanging around the Jar a lot more than I liked and, nine times out of ten, had a pout on her that would put most of Instagram to shame. Whether at Gemma and Sarnia, the state of the coffee, or the non-vegan-ness of the sandwiches, she always had something to glare at. I thought she might bond with Flic at least, over their mutual passion for #cleaneating and similar such bollocks, but she wouldn't even be friendly to her.

It looked like the same sulkiness had rubbed off on Zach. Maybe that went some of the way to explaining his sudden professionalism? He had enough on his plate with one emotional woman – he wanted to keep his distance from the others.

Either way, it was bloody irritating and I wished he'd get back to normal.

"What is it?" I hissed into my phone, ducking into the shadow of the stairs.

"Have you been on Twitter?" Lizzy squeaked, clearly trying not to scream.

"No, Zach's being an arse about my phone," I hissed back. "What's happened?"

"It's Vill!"

"Who?"

"Vill. Wilhelm. Max's brother!"

Oh yes. The trip to Finland seemed like years ago; it took me a couple of seconds to remember Max-the-hairy-drummer's fit little brother, the one who seemed to have taken quite a shine to Lizzy when she broke her leg.

"What about him?"

"You know he was looking for a band?"

"Yeah."

"Well, he found one. Joined last week. *Last week*. Pay attention, that's a big deal."

"Yeah?"

"They have ONE British date."

"London?" I sighed. "Always the case. Boring sods. I can't take time off work to go to London, Zach'll kill me."

"No." Lizzy's voice reached a pitch where barely even dogs could hear her. "Guernsey."

I was momentarily struck dumb. "You... what?"

"Guernsey."

"*Guernsey*?"

"*GUERNSEY.*"

"Are you… are you serious? As in this Guernsey? As in where we live?"

"Yes!" I could practically hear Lizzy punching the air.

"How… how?" My brain was whirring. No decent bands came to Guernsey. Ever. Especially not when they could have their pick of all of Europe, including London.

"It must have been Vill," Lizzy said. "The date was only added after he joined the band. As in, last week. He wants to come and see us!"

Well, *us* might have been putting it a bit strongly. I had a funny feeling about this; a funny feeling that Vill wasn't all that interested in seeing *me* again. After all, during most of the afterparty, while Lizzy was making friends, I was getting rather busy in the tour bus.

"When?"

"It's in two weeks. They've been booked for everywhere else for ages. They're coming here! Two weeks, Cleo!"

"Holy crap," I murmured. "Look, I've got to go. This is epic news, but Zach's going to beat me with Mrs Machon's oven gloves if I don't get off the phone. I'll talk to you later."

Well. That was something to think of.

I was directionless with the Leap Year Pact; Flic and Jonny were boring as hell; Gemma had lost all interest. Maybe Lizzy would be the next one to get her future husband? And an interestingly be-mohawked one at that.

"What's going on?" Zach appeared at my elbow as if he'd been summoned by magic. I nearly jumped several feet into the air – usually of late I'd been able to hear him coming from miles away, he had such a stamp on him. "Is it an emergency?"

"No," I admitted. "Well. Maybe. One of the guys we met in Finland is coming to Guernsey."

"That guitarist?" Zach scowled.

"Er, no, and no need to make that face." I turned back to the table I was meant to be wiping and rolled my eyes. "The roadie who helped us in the hospital when Lizzy broke her leg."

"Sorry." There was a thump as Zach sat down heavily on the ancient sofa.

"Huh?" I whipped around to look at him.

"I said sorry." He wasn't looking at me, but was staring at the ceiling, running his fingers through his hair. It looked like Mrs Machon had been at him with her forty-year-old hairdressing scissors again, but instead of calming it down, it was sticking up even more than usual. "Just a bit stressed at the moment."

"Everything all right? It's not the Jar, is it?"

"No, no." He dropped his gaze back to me and smiled his crooked smile. "Ahh, it's nothing really. Just a bit of, you know, personal stuff." He sat up. "Actually, Cleo, you might be able to help me. You know about this stuff."

"What stuff?" I gave him a wary look and scooted back round the bar. "You're not about to ask me about your love life, are you? Because in case you didn't notice, mine's hardly rosy."

"Hey, you have a... well, you..." Zach blushed.

"Are you trying to say 'Cleo, you're a bit of a slut' without actually calling me a slut?"

"No," he said haughtily. "I'd never use that word. Just... oh, forget it."

"No, tell me." I abandoned my sanitiser and cleaning cloth on the bar and vaulted over to the sofa, sinking into the creaky leather. "I might be able to help."

"Don't worry, Cleo." Zach smiled, the left side of his face dimpling as always. The smile definitely didn't reach his eyes. Definitely not. "I'm just being daft. You see, Sky..."

But just as he was about to get into the good stuff, the door clattered open and our peace was smashed into pieces by the arrival of Mrs Doubtfire... trailed by, of all people, Mrs Machon.

"Afternoon, all," Mrs D trilled.

"Get up off that sofa, Zachary." Mrs Machon grabbed him by the scruff of his Harry Potter t-shirt and hauled him to his feet. "You're supposed to be in charge of this establishment. There's nobody behind the bar. What will customers think?"

"You're right, Gran." Zach brushed off his t-shirt, shot me another smile, then trotted obediently off towards the coffee machine. "Drinks, both of you?"

"And you, madam." Mrs Machon narrowed her eyes and, thankfully, decided to haul me up by the elbow rather than her usual trick of grabbing me by the apron – I didn't fancy having it yank on my still-sore throat. "What are you doing sitting down when you're being paid to work?"

"We've got a couple of customers upstairs but we're mostly quiet…"

"I don't care, can't you be cleaning something?"

For the first time, I realised that both Mrs Machon and Mrs Doubtfire were – oh, God – wearing purple Guernsey Goats sashes over their respective sensible jumpers.

"So what are you up to this afternoon, ladies?"

"Knitting," Mrs Doubtfire said, grandiosely settling herself into her usual seat. Mrs Machon followed with a thump.

"Yes, we have a deadline," she said, puffing up her not-inconsiderable chest with importance. "We have a task."

"We can't speak too much about it, of course," Mrs D put in, cheerfully, already whizzing some knitting needles from her capacious handbag. "But it's very important. Commanded by the Guernsey Goats."

"Don't ask, don't ask, don't ask," I hissed to Zach as I fled to the kitchen. "Whatever it is, we won't like it."

"Agreed," he whispered back, rolling his eyes as he got Mrs D's pathetically weak latte to her desired temperature of 'tastebud-boiling'.

I slipped into the kitchen and hoped neither of the resident old bats would follow. I had a very important night out to plan.

* * *

With two weeks until the gig, we didn't have all that long to plan and plot. Which, I reasoned to Lizzy, was probably a good thing. It was hardly the Karin Cluster trip – we only had to travel to the Rohais, not to Finland. There wasn't much to plan, which felt immensely weird. I'd practically written a novel's worth of planning and lists for Finland – I barely needed a post-it note for this gig.

But we held a summit anyway, as soon as Lizzy got home from work.

I'd barely parked up my scooter and hauled myself up the fire-escape-style stairs when she burst out of her flat, bouncing on the balls of her feet.

"Isn't it exciting?" she squeaked. "Vill's coming here!"

"So much for you not fancying him," I muttered, rolling my eyes and grinning.

"I don't fancy him, and he doesn't fancy me," she insisted, shepherding me into the flat.

"She keeps saying this, but I don't believe her," Gemma butted in. I followed her voice into the airy living room. The windows were open, looking out onto the sparklingly calm sea, letting in a slight salty breeze. Summer in Guernsey really is perfect, and it was made especially so by the presence of the tiny baby wriggling her arms and legs on a playmat on the floor. Gemma was bending over her daughter, waving a squeaky teddy.

"I don't believe her either." I plopped onto the floor next to Sarnia, stretching out in the patch of sunlight.

"I *don't*," Lizzy insisted, parking herself primly on the sofa. "How come you're out of work so early?"

"Don't change the subject," I said sternly. "I'm not skiving. It's dead in there today, if people aren't at work, they're at the beach. Zach's managing on his own, told me to sod off early."

"Is he still being an arse?"

"Kind of." I sighed. For some reason, I didn't want to tell them about how he'd nearly confided in me. About how I was pretty sure something was stewing in his relationship with Sky. "He said I might as well go because I'm not going to do my job properly until I've gossiped about Vill with you two. Which is true, I suppose."

Lizzy didn't look happy that her subject-changing hadn't exactly worked.

"Come on." I propped myself up on one elbow. "Do we have any more details?"

"Details?"

"Come on, Elizabeth. Details. What this band is like, are any of them hot, will you be having sex with Vill afterwards, what kind of music do they play, usual questions."

"Excuse me," Lizzy spluttered. "I will not be having sex with Vill afterwards."

"We'll see about that." I leaned over and lazily tickled Sarnia under her chin.

"Anyway." Lizzy coughed pointedly. "The band is called Cinyras. There's Vill on second guitar, two Greek guys on lead guitar and bass, and another German on drums. None of them are particularly good-looking, as far as I can tell."

"Aww," Gemma and I chorused together.

"I haven't heard their music yet, though. I only found out they exist while I was on my break this morning, Vill sent me a message on Facebook to tell me all about it, and to look out for him."

"See!" I exclaimed, pointing at Lizzy. "See! He sent a message to *you*. Not me. I've got him as a friend on Facebook too."

"But you never go on Facebook," Lizzy pointed out. "He could have sent you twenty-three messages and a dick pic, and you wouldn't know."

"What can I say?" I shrugged, lying back down on the sunny carpet. "I'm old-fashioned."

"We've been talking a fair bit, actually," Lizzy said. I could tell just from her tone of voice that she was trying very hard not to blush.

"I knew it!"

"No, not like that," she chided, busying herself with her phone so she wouldn't have to look at me. "It's just... oh, you wouldn't understand."

The bang on the front door made us all jump, including baby Sarnia, who started to whimper softly.

"Ahh, no, none of that business, please." Gemma swiftly hoisted the baby onto her lap for a cuddle. "I'm having such a nice, chill afternoon. Let's not spoil it with crying."

"I'll get it." Lizzy hopped up and went to the door.

She was back a few seconds later.

Trailed by Aaron.

"Gemma," he said, sounding almost hoarse and running his hand over his stubbly head. "We need to talk."

Gem eyed him for a second. "Yeah, we probably do, don't we?"

I raised my eyebrows so high I thought they were going to fall off my head and onto the carpet.

I'd hardly been keeping tabs on the great saga that was Gemma-and-Aaron. I was satisfied when Gem and I tried to go out on the piss that she hadn't skulked off to be with him. As far as I knew, she hadn't seen him once since Sarnia was born. She certainly hadn't mentioned anything.

"I just…" He gulped, then looked around the room. Lizzy was standing in the doorway; I was still lying on the floor. Sarnia was eyeing him beadily from her mother's lap. "Is there somewhere we can talk privately?"

"No," I piped up, just as Gemma and Lizzy both said "yes".

"Come on, Cleo," Lizzy said, reaching over and giving my arm a yank. "We'll take Sarnia for a walk. Come on, Sarnie-love." With no resistance whatsoever from Gem, Lizzy plucked up the baby and marched into the hall. "*Cleo*. Come on."

Mutely, I followed. Gem refused to meet my eye as I left the room, giving the door a pointed near-slam behind me (I couldn't properly slam it – I didn't want to shock the baby).

"Are we really going for a walk?" I hissed. "Aren't we going to eavesdrop?"

"No, Cleo." Lizzy sighed, strapping Sarnia to her chest in some sling contraption. "Here, you carry this." She thrust a heavy messenger bag at me.

"What the hell is this?" I nearly buckled under the weight.

"Changing bag."

"How long are we going for, a month?" I followed Lizzy as she marched out of the building towards the breezy seafront.

"She's a baby, she needs a lot of stuff."

"Remind me not to have one of these until I have a muscly man to carry all this crap." I hoisted the bag onto my shoulder.

I gave the big white house behind us a longing look, namely the open windows facing onto the seafront – too high up for me to see what was going on inside. "If we stand on the grass in front of the beach, do you think we'll be able to see in?"

"No, Cleo," Lizzy chided, grabbing my shoulder with one hand and propelling me along the road away from the house. "We need to let them work it out for themselves."

"But they'll just end up shagging," I almost whined. "And we all know that's not right."

"It's not right," Lizzy said, turning up the hill towards Delancey Park. "But if that's what Gem wants, and if that's what they decide to do, then we just have to leave them to it."

"But why?" I actually did whine this time. "They're not right for one another. He's not the right dad for Sarnia. He has his own baby." I paused for a second. "Well, he should do by now. I wonder if Meredith has popped it out yet." I had a sudden rush of hope. "Maybe that's what they've got to talk about! Maybe he's become a proper father to his own baby and he's realised the error of his ways." I was warming to my theme. "Whatever this is, he's come to break it off."

"I don't know." Lizzy shook her head as she walked. "He's been awfully persistent."

"Nobody's heard from him for weeks!"

"Yes, we have," she said quietly. "He's been round a couple of times."

"Seriously?" I gasped. Not so much at him going round, but at Gem not telling me.

"Gem's not seen him," Lizzy explained quickly. "She wasn't here. I told him… I told him he should stay away." She busied herself adjusting the baby in the sling, refusing to meet my eyes. "I shouldn't have tried to interfere, but he wouldn't listen to me anyway. I think it's up to Gemma now."

"Yeah, but…" I sighed. "We should be there. We're her best friends. We're supposed to give advice."

"We've tried that." Lizzy sighed too. "We've told her how we feel. She knows exactly what we think." She gave me a wry look. "Especially you. Now, we just need to keep out of it."

"I just don't like him," I blurted. "I just hate the thought of them getting together. He just… he thinks he's some kind of leading man, and he really isn't. He's smarmy. And he gets a daft five o'clock shadow on his head."

"That doesn't matter if you're in love."

"They're not in love," I scoffed. "They just fancy one another. It's just hormones. Pheromones. Whatever. You know Gem's not mentioned him once since she gave birth, it was probably just pregnancy hormones."

"She didn't mention him much when she was still pregnant," Lizzy pointed out. "She doesn't exactly broadcast her feelings."

"I know, I know." I sighed again. "I just don't want her to get hurt, I suppose that's what it boils down to. Her and that little one you've got round your neck. And Meredith and her baby, I guess. If this happens, a lot of people could get hurt."

"Or a lot of people could be made happy," Lizzy said. We bypassed the new play area – all shiny and metallic, nothing like the demolished death-trap further up the hill that we used to play on when we were kids – and headed towards the viewing point, on top of one of the old concrete German bunkers, sticking incongruously out of the hillside amongst the greenery of the park.

"Those two getting together won't make anyone happy," I said stubbornly.

"It might," Lizzy countered. "Just think. If Aaron and Meredith's marriage is as bad as he thinks, and if Gem and Aaron really love each other."

"God, you need to stop looking on the good side."

"Maybe you need to stop looking on the bad side."

We walked in silence for a few minutes. Sarnia had fallen asleep, strapped to Lizzy's chest. We ambled slowly up to the viewing point and stared out over the islands. Although it was getting towards the evening, the islands were still swathed in a foggy heat-haze, sunlight glinting off the still sea. A lone speedboat bounced its way towards the blurred spectre of Castle Cornet, just about visible in the distance.

"When did you get so bloody wise?" I sighed at last, breaking the silence. "You're like an owl. A big blonde owl."

Lizzy shrugged, giving Sarnia a little jiggle. "I've had my heart smashed into pieces in the past year. First Dan, then… Dan again. I really thought we were it, me and Dan. And we weren't. And it broke me. Even more than I ever let on." Her voice caught a little and she bit her lip. "It gave me a lot of perspective."

I reached out and rubbed her shoulder – I could hardly give her a hug with a baby round her neck, I'd squish the poor thing.

"Has… has a certain man with a mohawk helped you with this perspective?"

"He might have done." Lizzy sighed, gently bouncing the baby up and down. "We've been talking a lot. He's… he's good at this sort of thing. He's had a lot of experience."

"I wish I had perspective," I mused, staring towards the distant islands. "Maybe then I'd…" I trailed off.

"Face up to what you really feel?"

"I don't know what you're talking about."

"You will," said the wise old owl in glasses. "Give it time. And maybe he'll work it out too."

"Now I *really* don't know what you're talking about."

"Of course you don't." Lizzy laughed softly.

We stood side by side at the railings for a few minutes longer, watching the speedboat bounce around the bay. A bigger, slower fishing boat trundled in the other direction; I wondered if Gemma's dad was out there, happily making his living while his youngest daughter got up to whoever-knew-what just a matter of miles away.

I couldn't hear the rush-hour traffic on the road below, just the faint shrieks and laughter from the children playing on the playground, the well-meaning shouts of their mothers; of course, interjected with the occasional sleepy gurgle from Sarnia while Lizzy rocked her gently in the sling.

"Have we given them enough time yet?" I said eventually.

"Come on then," Lizzy said, bracing herself against the rails and shifting Sarnia into a more comfortable position. "We'll go the long way back. Down the steps and along the beach. Give them plenty of time to work things out."

"But not so long that Gem will need us and we're not there," I said briskly, scooping up the gargantuan changing bag and pulling it back onto my shoulder. "Honestly, does Gem keep bottles of vodka in this thing?"

* * *

We got back at the perfect time. We were just climbing the fire-escape steps back to the flat when Aaron burst out of the door and barrelled towards us, still running his hand over his bristly head.

"Hi," he mumbled, pelting hell for leather towards the seafront.

Lizzy and I exchanged a look, pausing on the landing before the flat.

"Did he look a bit... flustered? To you?" I ventured.

"A bit," Lizzy admitted. "I think... I think his shirt was on backwards."

"Oh, bollocks."

I burst through the door first.

"Gemma!" I called softly. If I could have, I would have bellowed bossily, but you know – sleeping babies and all that.

"Shit," I heard her hiss from upstairs. From her bedroom.

"Christ on a bicycle," I sighed, and stomped up to the attic.

"I thought you'd be a bit longer," she called from the bedroom. "You're not great at tact."

"We wanted to make sure you were all right." I flung the bedroom door open and crossed my arms, glaring over the threshold.

"I'm fine, obviously." Gem pulled a t-shirt over her head and glared back at me.

"At least you're dressed," I sighed. "Just." I uncrossed my arms and strode across the room, flopping onto the bed. Then I realised that two people had very probably just had sex on it, and I jumped up again. "Go on. Tell me."

Gem scowled. "We shagged. Obviously."

"Yeah, I got that. Your hair's a haystack."

"Happy?"

"Why would I be happy?" I snapped, putting my glare back on. Then I took it off, remembering what me and Lizzy had just been talking about. "Are *you* happy? Because, you know, that's all that matters... even though I don't like him, if he's going to leave Meredith and come to you, if you're in love with him then..."

"I'm not in love with him," Gem snapped, wrestling her hair into a ponytail and refusing to meet my eyes. "Whatever's happened with us is... over."

"Wait, what?" I shook my head. "But you just shagged him. Like… five minutes ago." I gestured futilely to the crumpled duvet and Gem's frizzy hair.

"Come on, Cleo." Gem laughed grimly. "You know as well as I do, that's hardly a guarantee of a relationship."

"Woah, what's happened here?" Lizzy exclaimed, arriving in the doorway minus Sarnia.

"Did you lose my daughter on your walk?"

"No, she's in her Moses basket." Lizzy brandished a baby monitor almost threateningly. "I think you need to tell us what's going on or Cleo's going to explode."

"True story." I nodded violently.

Gem sighed deeply. "I just said it. Me and Aaron, whatever's been going on… it's over."

Lizzy eyed the bedcovers too, but said nothing.

"What happened?" I pressed.

"He came over here, to 'talk'." Gem laughed again, just as bitterly. "As soon as you two had buggered off, he kind of flew across the room and we were kissing. We were up here in about five minutes."

"Thank you for not having sex on my sofa," Lizzy said solemnly.

"You're welcome. Anyway, yeah, sex, bang bang bang, done."

"Was it that bad?" I couldn't help but ask.

"Had better, had worse." Gem shrugged. "It felt a bit weird, I mean come on, it's been nearly a year. The last thing that went up there stayed for months."

"Not the nicest way to put it," Lizzy said, wincing.

"Whatever." Gem rolled her eyes. "We did the deed. It was OK. I thought, cool. This is nice. Ish. I mean, everything down there has kind of shifted, but never mind. I thought, it'll be better next time." For the first time since she'd even met Aaron, her voice caught in her throat. "I thought, for like five minutes, maybe this was actually going to work, it was going to be a proper thing." She took a deep breath and pulled herself together. "Well, nope."

"Nope?"

"Nope." She laughed bitterly. "Do you know why he came here now? Not weeks ago? It's because Meredith is in labour. Right now."

"Eh?"

"Yeah. She's having their baby right now, maybe right this second, and he knows full well that when it's born, he won't be able to play away. He'll fall in love with it." Gem's voice got a bit high-pitched. "He'll love it, he'll rediscover his love for Meredith, and he'll never be able to leave. And he knows this. So he thought he'd have," her voice got even higher, "*one last fling*, before the baby came out and he couldn't do it again." She paused for a second to compose herself, then nearly growled. "Fucker thought he was doing me a favour. Letting me have a piece of him before he disappeared for good. Thought he'd get a thank you."

No wonder Aaron had looked so flustered when we ran into him on the stairs. It sounded like he'd just got a grade-A bollocking. And so he should.

"What a…" Lizzy shook her head, unable to think of a word suitably strong enough to describe Aaron.

I filled in. "Cunting bastarding bollockless wanker?"

"Something like that," Gem said, her voice low again. But she was smiling, albeit shakily. "Clearly, that's the end of that."

"Are you… sure?" I couldn't help but ask.

"Of course I'm sure," Gemma spat, recoiling from the gentle pat Lizzy was trying to administer. "He's had his chance. He could have left his wife today, well, maybe after she's not in labour any more, and I would have had him. But this is the end of it. He's messed me around now. He's shown he's a prize arsehole. And I don't want him anyway."

And with an extra-fierce scowl, she burst into tears.

Chapter 24

I'd noticed something rather useful since the great thyroid removal. Well, to be technical, since the great tumour removal – it wasn't my fault the surgeon had to take half the gland with him. They told me it was necessary, but I still kind of believed it got caught on his Fitbit and he couldn't shake it off.

The something-rather-useful was related to the pills I'd been put on: seeing as I couldn't work my own thyroid gland very well any more, I had to have medication to do it for me. And it was doing a bloody brilliant job.

For the first time in at least two years, I was losing weight. And I wasn't doing a thing to facilitate this off my own back. Mrs Machon's selection of cakes was as vast as ever – I wasn't going to be cutting down any time soon.

It was amazing. My jeans weren't tight for the first time in months. If it carried on for much longer, I was going to have to start buying size ten trousers, something I hadn't done in many years.

More to the point... all my scraggy old going-out dresses were not only even more scraggy than ever, they were starting to sag. They were actually *too big*. That beautiful sequinned dress Flic had chosen for me to 'woo' James, months ago? I tried it on, and it stood out about four miles from my boobs.

Gemma jumped at the chance to come shopping with me.

"I have the opposite problem," she said glumly, grabbing her chest with both hands. "Boobs! Boobs, boobs, bloody boobs. They're huge."

I eyed her sceptically.

"They are," she insisted. "I'm a *C* cup."

"Whoop de doo." I raised my eyebrows. "I've lost weight and I'm still an E."

"I'm not complaining, really." Gem gave her left boob a quick fondle with a grin. "It's... interesting. Weird, but interesting. But. BUT." Her face turned sour. "They're no bloody use if I can't go out to use them!"

"You do use them," I reminded her. "You know, for their intended purpose?"

"I mean their other use," she said, a familiar wicked grin emerging. "I might not want anyone but Sarnia touching them at the moment... but they can always do a fabulous job of catching some attention."

Of course, Gem's plan to resume her social life within fifteen minutes of giving birth had hardly gone to plan. Little Sarnia had been far too demanding for that; Gem had been perfectly happy to submit to those demands.

She didn't admit it, but part of the reason she'd not been going out on the town with me was that she had been waiting to see what would happen with her personal pet married man. The whole debacle with Aaron was only a week old, and where most people would be raw from such a confrontation – emotionally and physically, when you'd given birth less than two months before – Gem cried for ten minutes, sniffled for a further five, then pulled herself together and started plotting.

Sex with Aaron may not have been that fantastic, but it had woken Gemma up again. Between that, and Sarnia's latest weigh-in at the health centre – during which a doctor felt up Gem's bits and proclaimed them fully raring to go – our favourite new mum was ready to get her sex life properly back on track.

Sarnia was to be left with Flic and Jonny, to give them a nice premonition of their own future surrounded by babies. Gem was going to come to Vill's gig with me and Lizzy.

And for this, new outfits were desperately needed.

I've never been particularly good at shopping. Anyone who calls shopping a hobby needs their head fixing, in my personal opinion. I can make a heroic effort for approximately half an hour, then I get bored. Plus I don't like trying on clothes in changing rooms – the mirrors are always horrible and the lighting makes my skin go from 'pale' to 'green'. Not a good look on anyone.

I'm one of those people usually to be found snoozing on the stool where you try on shoes, waiting for everyone else to finish preening themselves in front of the mirrors.

Thankfully, Gem had a similar mindset, being too impatient to stare at more than three things in any one shop, and so we planned our shopping trip with military precision. The Wednesday before Vill's gig, I worked the lunchtime rush with Zach in the Jar, then Gem came in to go over our strategy.

"We'll start with New Look," she said, lining up a row of sugar packets on our table to represent the high street. "It's out of the way, and it's where we're most likely to find stuff."

"Agreed." I took a slurp of my Americano and tried not to meet Zach's eye. He was in a thoroughly bad mood – again. Just because he had to run the café on his own for a few hours.

Come on, I needed an afternoon off occasionally, and Gem wasn't going to be back from maternity leave for months. He could keep his dark looks to himself, or hire someone else. Or, of course, he could make Sky come and do some actual work for a change instead of fannying about with wedding invitations.

"Then if we move down through the Arcade…"

"Coffee at Dix Neuf?" I raised my eyebrows in an exaggerated glare at Zach's back as he retreated into the kitchen.

Gemma barked a laugh. "Maybe. Or some chips. You know those little bowls of fries they do…"

"Mmm. Fries." I raised my voice. "So much nicer than soup!"

"Shut up or you'll get sacked," Gem said briskly, returning to our battle plan. "Right, we don't want anything else around there, too expensive. Miss Selfridge? Are we too old for Miss Selfridge?"

"What about Warehouse on the way up?"

"Too expensive. And too respectable." Gem gave a shudder. "Just because I'm a mum doesn't mean I'm going to stop dressing like… like…"

"Are you trying to say 'dressing like a hooker' without saying 'dressing like a hooker'?" I supplied helpfully.

"Yes." Gem shrugged. "It's me. So maybe yes to Miss Selfridge… Dorothy Perkins?"

"Flic orders almost everything online nowadays," Jonny put in not-very-helpfully. "Though I suppose you don't have enough time."

"Not really, not for this weekend," I agreed. Then nearly jumped off my chair in fright. "*Jonny*? Where the bloody biscuits did you come from?"

He wasn't actually at the same table as us – pulling that off without us noticing would have been quite impressive. Hell, it was impressive in itself to be sitting on the sofa without us noticing. This was the Bean Jar after all: titchy.

He must have just been there all along, sitting so unassumingly that we didn't even notice. That, or he'd been hiding behind the laptop that was open on the coffee table, eavesdropping.

"I decided to work out-of-office this afternoon," he said, smiling shyly.

"You could have said," Gem huffed. "I could have been talking about *intimate* things."

Jonny blushed. "Sorry."

Gem narrowed her eyes. "Flic's not got you spying on me, has she?"

"No, no! Nothing like that." Jonny's blush receded. "I just… like it in here."

Gemma and I exchanged a disbelieving look. Every time Flic and Jonny had ever come into the Jar, poor Jonny had had to sit quietly in the corner while Flic held court. If Lizzy was around she'd usually take pity on him and have a chat, but if not, he'd have to sit there until Flic formally allowed him into the conversation.

Come to think of it, this was probably the first time I'd seen Jonny on his own since the night he'd got incredibly drunk with his mates and ended up in Folies, just before me and Lizzy had packed our bags and buggered off to Finland. The same night Zach got together with Sky.

I hadn't asked how that night had turned out – Flic flirting with every vaguely presentable-looking man she laid eyes on, Jonny drunkenly clinging to Lizzy as the only possible way he could stay upright. After I'd seen Zach more or less chewing at Sky's face, and watched Jonny puke into a corner, I'd gone home with Gem, who'd felt thoroughly incapable of dealing with Flic's sick-related hysterics while hauling her bump around.

I couldn't help but wonder how that night had ended for the future Mr and Mrs Jonathan Rabey.

"Does my sister know you're here?" Gem asked, leaning back in her chair and doubling the intensity of her piercing grin.

"No, no," Jonny stuttered. "She's at work. She doesn't…" He gulped. "She doesn't need to know I'm not in the office."

"Then why come in here, you goon?" I rolled my eyes. "If you want to hide from your fiancée, go to Café Emilia, go to Costa!"

"Yeah, don't go where you know you'll find in-laws." Gem pointed to herself with a 'you're a moron' expression on her face.

"I just… ah." Jonny was turning red again. "Never mind. You can tell her if you want. It's just an out-of-office day."

Both sets of eyebrows raised almost to the ceiling, Gemma and I took a brief look at one another and decided now was the time to leave.

* * *

"This is it, this is *so* it," I almost squealed. "Look at my stomach!"

"Look at my boobs!" Gem practically walked into the mirror trying to see down her own dress. "Sound the gong, I have a cleavage!"

It was as if we'd swapped places, clothes-wise. Normally I was the one draped in layers of black, showing off my boobs. Gem was usually in bright colours, showing off everything else.

It was clearly the season for change.

For once in her life (someone had to say it), Gemma looked classy. The simple strappy black dress, embellished along the low-cut neckline with tiny glinting diamantés, came to just above her knees, hanging in floaty folds.

"I'm still not wearing heels."

"But…"

"Number one, it's a heavy metal gig. I'll be jumping up and down, right? Number two, I plan to be off my face, and I don't want to fall over. Number three, if I've got any chance of finding a husband, I can't dwarf every man in there."

"Oh, you're back on your Leap Year Pact, then? Silver pumps are the way to go, in that case." I gave a little twirl, balanced on my tiptoes. "What about me? Would heels be too much?"

"Wear those big gothy boots of yours," Gemma suggested. "The Doc Martens, not the New Rocks. Heels might say 'hooker'. Boots say 'contrast'."

"Look at you, going all fashiony," I mocked.

"I've been spending far too much time on Instagram while I feed Sarnia."

I wasn't wearing a dress, which felt a bit weird for a non-spontaneous night out. But I wasn't wearing jeans either, which was even weirder.

"It's summer," Gem had insisted when she strong-armed me into the changing room. "Give it a try!"

I was wearing shorts. Not only shorts, but black leather shorts, so short they were practically hot pants. I think they *were* hot pants, but being a short-arse, I managed to escape them going all the way up my bum.

Somehow, said shorts made my legs look slim and long. Quite an achievement on someone my height.

On Gem's insistence, I'd teamed the shorts with a floaty t-shirt, pale pink and embossed with black roses. It was overlarge, and hung from one shoulder – only the slightest hint of cleavage was exposed, rather than my usual in-your-face boob action. It felt weird, but apparently that was how it was supposed to go. At least it showed off the tattoo on my right shoulder.

Even a few weeks back, it would have looked like maternity-wear with my super-sized stomach. But thanks to the good old thyroxine pills, it actually looked rather flattering. The exceedingly girly top seemed to work with the leather shorts, and I felt Gemma might be right when she said my old Docs would contrast nicely. I hadn't worn them in at least a year, favouring the New Rocks... but hey, it was summer. Time to take the boot-action down a notch.

I'd taken my hair to the hairdresser for the first time in months, and treated myself to a professional dye job instead of a packet from Boots. I was now the proud owner of a glossy purple bob, a few shades darker than usual, with a fringe that cut across my forehead with ruler-straight precision. At least, it did when I attacked it with the straighteners.

"We scrub up rather well," I said smugly, preening some more.

"We do indeed," Gem murmured, plucking a stray eyelash off my cheek. "Make a wish."

"I don't believe in that kind of bollocks."

"I don't care. Make a wish. Wish for sex, that's what I'm doing. And I don't even have an eyelash."

"OK." Obediently, I blew the eyelash away.

"What do you make of this thing with my future brother in law?" Gem started shimmying out of the dress.

"What thing? Him turning up in the Jar?" I shrugged my way out of the beautiful new top and reverently hung it up on the changing room door. "He's just bored."

"Of what, though?"

"I don't know. Being bossed around?"

"At work?"

"Maybe. Or by Flic?" I pulled my own usual black t-shirt over my head and started to struggle out of the tight shorts. "I think he realises if he wants to see any sign of proper life, he's got to come to the Bean Jar. I think he needs to get his fix or he'll shrivel up and die."

"That's my sister you're talking about."

"You say it all the time."

"It's different when I say it." Gem heaved a deep sigh. "I know it's nothing, of course it's nothing. It's just a bored dude going to a café for the afternoon. But that thing about not telling Flic... what if he was meeting someone?"

"A girl? Jonny?" I laughed. "Where would he find one of those?"

"Come on, you've seen what Flic's been like recently. She hardly lets him out of her sight. What if there *is* a girl? What if he's having secret assignations with that, what's her name, Denise? Flic's other bridesmaid?"

We still hadn't met the elusive Denise: she'd gone to school with Flic and Jonny, and nowadays was working in Jonny's office. They were apparently very good friends, good enough for Denise to be nominated as a bridesmaid, but not good enough for Flic to drag out to London, or to any of the interminable wedding-crap meetings. I got the feeling she was definitely Jonny's choice of bridesmaid: I wondered why he'd obviously put his foot down over her.

"Then why would he go to the Jar?" I hoisted my jeans up, pleased at how I had to tie my belt a lot tighter than I used to. "Like you said, his future sister-in-law is always in there. He knows word would get back to Flic if he was doing anything dodgy. Doesn't matter if we'd recognise this Denise or not, we're still not blind enough to miss him with a *woman*."

"Maybe that's the point!" Gem said with a flourish. "Maybe he *wants* word to get back to Flic. He's too much of a, like, wet blanket to break up with her, even if he's got someone on the side, ready to go. He needs *her* to make the break, so if I tell her he's acting weirdly…"

"You're massively overthinking this, Gem," I said as we headed towards the tills. "This is Jonny. *Jonny*. He's not bright enough to think of something like that."

"I don't know," she mused. "I've known him as long as Flic has, and he's definitely up to something. More to the point, so is my sister."

"You've heard her, she just wants everything to be perfect," I said, clutching my collection of hangers with reverence. "Like always. Come on, she's getting married in just over a month. She was always going to be a stressy cow."

"But she's being worse than a stressy cow," Gem insisted. "She's always been possessive, yeah, but she's being practically evil. Did you know, she's told Jonny he can only have a single stag night, and it's got to be in town, and she's got to be in town at the same time?"

"Seriously?" I laughed. "With her…"

"Yeah." Gem nodded grimly. "With all *that*."

Flic's hen parties were looming. And yes, that is indeed the plural. She'd booked herself and a few friends on the much-maligned spa holiday in Tuscany, to have a good old relax the weekend before the wedding. That was supposed to be part of the hen celebrations. Of course, only one of her actual bridesmaids could go – the aforementioned Denise. Nice to see she'd been included on the 'fun' bit of the wedding planning, while she'd managed to miss the hellish trip to the department stores.

Lizzy technically could go on the spa holiday, seeing as she'd be in the middle of her summer holidays, but it coincidentally fell on her dad's sixtieth birthday and she'd fallen upon the excuse with open arms. I couldn't get the time off work – and didn't want to go anyway – and Gemma refused to either leave Sarnia or have to deal with her on a plane.

So Flic planned part two of the hen celebrations – an emulation of the Tuscany trip, just in Guernsey instead. Those of us who weren't 'committed' enough to bugger off to Italy for the weekend were being 'treated' to an afternoon at the St Pierre Park hotel, getting our pores squeezed and our faces washed, or whatever else a spa treatment day consists of.

I say 'treated' because, Flic being Flic, we were expected to pay for this ourselves.

Then there was part three of this epically self-centred hen party – a 'big night out' in Guernsey. I say 'part three', but we'd managed to convince Flic to have this part first, so that at least all the spa treatments and forced relaxation could deal with the inevitable post-drinking terrible skin and bloating.

From the early stages of planning it seemed like Flic was just about aiming for one of the nights out me and Gemma would have had, back in the day. A tame one, at that. Of course, even though it's supposed to be the bridesmaids who organise the hen activities, we were all banned from anything but attendance.

Apparently we'd make it too 'tacky'.

I can't imagine why she'd think that.

I mean, yes, I organised a tequila ice luge for Gemma's last birthday and the two of us ended up stuck to it by our tongues but that can't be a premonition of *anything*.

"Oh well," I said, handing over my debit card with a tiny prayer it wouldn't get rejected. "At least Flic's hen gives us another excuse to wear these clothes. Silver linings, you know."

Annoying Customer of the Week, Part 10

"Hiya, what can I get for you today?"

"Hello. Yes, er, which one of those muffins is lowest in fat?"

"That'd be the low fat blueberry muffin. Hence why it says 'low fat' on the label."

"Oh yeah. One of those then, please."

"Here you go. Anything else for you today?"

"Yeah. I'd like a… hot chocolate please. A skinny one."

"Sure thing, what size? Small or big?"

"Medium."

"We do small or big."

"Oh, OK, a big one, yeah? And… can I have that skinny?"

"Yes, you said that."

"Yeah. Skinny, please."

"That'll be three pounds and…"

"Wait! Can I have a caramel shot in that?"

"Yes, if you want."

"And marshmallows? And, like, whipped cream?"

"Yeah… if you want."

"But… it'll definitely be skinny, right?"

I had a momentary urge to recommend thyroxine to the poor deluded dieter, but decided to keep the secret to myself instead.

Chapter 25

The leather sofa felt almost sticky on my naked back. I couldn't so much slide up and down it as bounce my way along, the ancient cushions squeaking in a rather threatening manner.

Dignified? Hardly.

Caring? Even less.

"Take these off," he said, the edge of desperation in his voice almost brushing my skin. True, the leather shorts weren't exactly helping with my squirming against the sofa. Plus, they were far too tight for him to get his hand in... a hand I never thought I'd see like this, a hand I thought I no longer had a chance with.

Obediently, I wriggled the shorts down my thighs. Slowly. I couldn't do any more, not with the leather sofa to contend with.

He leaned further over to kiss me once again, his hair brushing my cheeks. I sighed contentedly, and relaxed back into his arms, skinny but laced with muscle.

These kisses were like nothing else.

Could there be a more perfect end to the evening? I thought, as he almost reverently eased my knickers down my legs to join my shorts. I was naked, and so was he. The twinkling lights of Guernsey's harbour winked at us through the huge curtainless windows, as if giving me the go-ahead. Somewhere above, the pale light of the moon helped cast an eerie glow over the room, making even the spindly chairs stacked on the tables look magical: more than anything, the man sprawled on top of me on the battered leather sofa.

The Bean Jar had never before been witness to such a display.

* * *

"I'm not standing at the front!" I said stubbornly, crossing my arms in front of my beautiful new t-shirt and glaring.

"Come on," Gemma whined. "It's my first heavy metal gig! I want the full experience."

"If you wanted the full experience, you should have come to Karin Cluster with us," I said, shaking my head. "This place is too small." I waved at the tiny little stage, loaded up with so much equipment I genuinely worried that it would collapse. "If we jumped up and down, we'd clonk poor Vill in the nose."

"She's right." Lizzy turned back from the bar, where she'd finally commandeered the barman's attention and managed to get a round in. "We're best off here. He'll still be able to see us, and we'll still be able to have a good time."

"I suppose so." Gemma sighed. "Next time, though!" She wagged a finger. "Next time, I'm coming with you to see Karen Carpenter or whatever those Germans call themselves. I'm coming to everything." She grinned, evilly. "I want a bit of what Cleo had."

"Just because Cleo had the best sex ever..."

"Hey, I never said that!" I protested, grabbing my pint of beer in its plastic cup and taking a dramatic gulp. "I said it was *some of* the best sex ever. Top three, maybe, but to be upgraded to number one it would need to be missing the constant possibility of being invaded by a toilet-obsessed roadie."

"Anyway," Lizzy carried on. "Just because Cleo had 'top three sex' doesn't mean all rock stars are like that."

"Like you'd know," Gemma mumbled, raising her eyebrow. "Yet."

"Oh, shush." Lizzy put her teacher-face on, taking a demure sip of her vodka and orange. "I don't fancy Vill. Vill doesn't fancy me. The rest of the band are hairy and weird-looking."

"Don't say that too loudly," I hissed, peering around. "We don't want them to hear us, we want to befriend them. Imagine if they end up supporting someone really good, like Nightwish or Slipknot or someone. I've had a taste of the Triple-A passes and I want more!"

We might have been at a very small and slightly scuzzy venue, more of a pub than a concert hall, but at least it had a very well-stocked bar. To be fair, it didn't even really need it: we'd been having a good old-fashioned pre-drink at Lizzy and Gemma's place before the gig, the only difference from the old days being that Gem had to break off her getting-ready routine halfway through to hand her daughter over to Flic and Jonny.

After that, the Vopple Juice had flowed with wild abandon, and we were already well on the way towards 'tipsy' before we'd even arrived for the show.

"I wouldn't mind a hairy man," Gem said, her eyes flicking maniacally around the bar area. "I wouldn't mind any man."

"No," Lizzy and I chorused firmly.

"You're not jumping back in the game with any old troll," I said.

"Think of the Leap Year Pact!" Lizzy chided.

"Screw the Leap Year Pact." Gem took a gulp of her JD and Coke that swallowed almost three quarters of the drink. "Stupid idea. Like any of us are going to get married!"

"You were all for it the other day! Besides, it spurred Flic and Jonny on," I pointed out. "At least they're getting it out of the way sooner rather than later."

"It won't work for us though, will it?" Gem sighed deeply. "My chance was Aaron, and he turned out to be a dick. Your chance was James, and he turned out to be a boring banker bastard. And a dick. And *your* chance..." She paused, giving Lizzy a critical eye. "Well, OK. Maybe your chance is this Vill bloke. Because before you say it, it wasn't Dan!"

"I know it wasn't Dan." Lizzy rolled her eyes. "I'm over that."

"Are you sure?" I'd been so wrapped up in my own trials and tribulations, I hadn't really thought much about whether Lizzy still had feelings for her ex. I just assumed that although she wouldn't take him back, and for all her brave sentiments while we'd been peering out at the sea past Delancey Park, she was still nursing a long-lost hurt for him, or something Mills-and-Boon-esque like that.

"Totally over him." Lizzy waved her arm in a very dismissive way, almost Gemma-like. "But I still don't fancy Vill."

"Yeah, we believe you." Gem rolled her eyes again. "Which one is he, when this band comes out? I don't want to fancy him by mistake, I'm not leaping in on your territory."

"I *don't fancy him*," Lizzy cried plaintively.

"He's the tall one, I would bet you money that he's the tallest one there, he's about nine feet tall," I explained. "Blonde, has a Mohawk, big tunnel in his ear. Quite muscly, in a skinny kind of way – guitarist-skinny."

"Does he play the guitar?"

"Yeah, I think so. Lizzy?"

"He plays guitar and bass, but he's second guitar for this lot."

"A man who can use his fingers." Gem nodded slowly, contemplating. She tried to take another swig of her drink, but realised she'd drained it already. "You could do a lot worse, Liz."

"Oh, shut up." Lizzy blushed. "I don't fancy him, I don't want to think about his fingers."

* * *

The music fans of Guernsey must have been pretty perturbed to see a rather fierce Greco-German metal band come clumping onto their favourite stage. Mostly, the little venue played host to various local indie bands, lots of acoustic stuff. When a metal band did appear, it was usually of the metal-lite kind of genre – not like Cinyras.

They were good, I suppose, in their own special way. Lots of growling, lots of pounding at guitars. The skinny little singer, one of the Greek guys and probably the least hairy of the whole lot, seemed to spend most of his time howling incomprehensibly in the general direction of the microphone, almost ripping his hair out with angst. It was the kind of music I'd probably listen to when I was in a really, *really* bad mood.

The crowd was good though: whether through copious amounts of alcohol or just a happy spirit of change, they really got into the music and soon enough there was a makeshift mosh pit going on in front of the stage. I was quite proud of them. I wouldn't have been surprised if half the people in the building had never been in a real mosh pit in their lives, but they were throwing themselves about with wild abandon in no time.

Vill, on the stage, so tall he made his guitar look like a toy – he was having the time of his life. I didn't know whether this was something to do with Lizzy being in the audience, or if he just had a proper love of performing; but he had the most massive grin on his face, and was practically bouncing off the walls.

Not that he had much choice, of course. The stage was so small, every time he tried to get in a good headbang he almost *had* to rebound off the back wall. Let's just say the bass player – with the fall of black curly hair almost down to his arse – was lucky to avoid getting his hair caught in a ceiling panel.

"This is fun!" Gem squealed in my ear, trying to jump up and down in her elegant black dress without sloshing her latest drink all over herself and the floor.

"It's not bad," I said, going for the 'voracious nod of the head' approach rather than the actual headbanging or jumping. I wanted to keep my nice clothes looking *nice* – and I had a beer in one hand and a Jägerbomb in the other. Preserving the alcohol at all times, that was my game plan.

Plus I was still feeling like the tiniest bit self-conscious about the wound on my neck. It still hadn't really progressed from 'wound' to 'scar': it was healing, and it wasn't seeping any more, but it was still very, very red and very, very obvious. I'd already had a couple of drunken-eyed stares that evening, and I didn't really want to draw any more attention to myself than I really had to.

A definite first, for me.

"Nobody's looking at your scar," Lizzy whispered in my ear, reading my mind as ever. "If they're staring at you, it's because you look hot."

"Ahh, shut up." I punched her gently in the arm as a song came to a close. The room erupted in – somewhat intoxicated – cheers and yells. "You don't look half bad yourself."

"I've not made a *special* effort!" Lizzy protested hastily.

"Yeah, yeah, you don't fancy him." I rolled my eyes to the ceiling.

Whether she admitted to it or not, I was damn sure Lizzy *had* made a special effort. She'd been ready for the evening before either me or Gemma, polished up to the eyeballs even before Jonny and Flic had turned up to collect baby Sarnia. Her hair was loose and positively golden in the laser-esque gig lighting, and she'd put in her contacts instead of wearing her glasses, all the better to show off her new eyeliner (she'd spent twenty straight minutes in front of the mirror swearing like a sailor while she tried to get the perfect cat-eyed effect – thankfully, after all that effort, it had worked).

I'd noticed, too, that I hadn't been the only one losing weight in the past couple of months: Lizzy was only wearing an old faithful yellow one-shouldered top, one that floated out at the waist, but she'd put it with a pair of tight, dark-blue jeans that I was certain she wouldn't have gone anywhere near a few months previously. She would have claimed they made her thighs look like tree trunks, or some other unflattering analogy. But now she was wearing them with pride (and a pair of shiny silver heels, celebrating the fact that the cast had finally been removed from her leg), and even passing my most critical eye over her, she looked hotter than she had done in years.

"I'm just nipping to the loo." With a swish of her hair, Lizzy disappeared.

The band was just starting to segue into a fairly slow song – I wouldn't call it a *ballad*, but it was a lot more gentle than anything else we'd heard so far. Gem took the opportunity to turn to me.

"There's a man looking at you," she said, leaning down to murmur in my ear. "No, no, don't turn around. He's been watching you the entire time."

Of course, when someone says something like that to me, I get a proper itch in my neck to spin around and stare out whoever's got their eye on me. But Gemma almost had me in a headlock.

"He's not staring at your scar, don't panic about that," she said, peeping over my shoulder. "He's been grinning at you for at least half an hour."

"What does he look like?"

"He's hot," she whistled. "Not my type. But definitely yours. Bit older than us. Long hair. Stubbly. He's got a black shirt on, but he's got it unbuttoned almost to his waist, show off. A few tattoos, not too many that I can see, pretty tasteful... he's got to be a proper metal fan."

"Sounds nice," I said, feeling a tiny bit of excitement building in me.

"He's *really* grinning at you." Gem sounded the tiniest bit put out that she didn't have a hot metal fan smiling at her from across the bar. "At least, I think it's at you, he hasn't made eye contact with me once, and believe me, I've tried."

"Hey." I punched her lightly in the arm. "Get your own hot metal fan."

"Where's he come from, though?" Gem mused in my ear. "Surely if there's a hot metal fan in Guernsey, you'd have come across him by now?" She paused. "Literally."

I punched her again. "Give me time. Can I look yet?"

"No. Oh, shite." She stood up straight and brushed down her dress, taking the Jägerbomb out of my hand and giving it a quick slurp while simultaneously straightening my t-shirt. "He's coming over."

I made a noise that could probably be best described as "eep". Hey, it had been a while since I'd had some bona fide male attention. I didn't want to mess it up – especially if this guy was as hot as he sounded.

From the frozen half-smile on Gem's face, I guessed the guy was standing right behind me. That, and I could feel the slightest hint of warm breath on the back of my neck as he bent down. I felt tingles start to buzz in the top of my head, and I started to almost pant in spite of myself.

"I've been finding myself rather stressed, recently."

I knew that voice.

A deep, slow, accented voice.

Sexily German.

I closed my eyes and let the smile break out across my face before I turned around.

I found myself looking into a pair of slate-green eyes, a wide smile across a pale face.

"Hey, Luka," I said.

✳ ✳ ✳

The beautiful moment of me and Luka's reunion was, of course, ruined in approximately three seconds flat. Not by the gobsmacked Gemma, of course; she was far too busy being shocked into silence for probably the third or fourth time in her young life.

No, it was instead broken by a high-pitched shriek as Lizzy barrelled into me, clutching Max Wolf by the hand.

"Look who I found outside!" she squealed, all decorum forgotten. Then she spotted Luka, and nearly fell over. "And Luka! Christ on a bicycle!"

"Hello, girls," said Max with a wide grin on his pockmarked face. Bless him, he sounded like a horny Father Christmas.

I put my hands on my hips and grinned at the pair of them. "Have you got Mel and Yasmin hidden under the bar, or is that it for the surprises?"

"Just us." Max laughed and tugged me into a bear hug. I didn't protest – though of course, I was far more interested in finding my way into Luka's arms. "Surprise!"

"What are you doing here?" I freed myself from the hug and took a deep slurp of my beer to steady myself. Out of the corner of my eye, I could just about see Gem shaking her head in disbelief and downing the rest of my Jägerbomb.

Max shrugged. "I wanted to come see my little brother perform. Didn't like any of the German dates."

"And I thought I'd come along for the ride," Luka said, his voice soft, barely audible over the pounding music still coming from the men on the stage. "I wanted to see your little island."

My gaze was on a bungee cord – I kept meeting Luka's amused eyes, then blushing and staring at his half-exposed chest instead, then bouncing back up to his hypnotic stare.

Parts of me that had been rather neglected of late were suddenly buzzing and ready for action.

We'd been reunited for about five seconds and already I was trying to work out how to get Luka alone. If he'd pulled me into the dirty venue bathroom, I probably would have gone for it.

If he'd pulled me onto the dirty venue *floor*, I probably would have gone for it.

But there were rather too many people watching to just pounce on him right there and then – even though I could see in his eyes, on his face, in his entire body, that he wanted me as much as I wanted him.

Come on, he'd come all the way to Guernsey.

* * *

Somehow, within a couple of hours, we had ditched the sticky venue entirely.

Not just me and Luka, sadly. I was itching to run away with him, to pull him out of the group and drag him to somewhere, anywhere I could get his clothes off.

But in spite of that, we were having a good night.

After the gig, we'd picked up Vill and the lead singer of Cinyras – the skinny little Greek guy called Niko, who was very much up for a few drinks – and we'd piled into a taxi to town. Vague noises were made about taking the boys to Folies, but we started out in a big pub just down the road from the Bean Jar. A good place for cheap Jägerbombs, that was all I really knew it for – I only seemed to go in there when I was already good and tanked.

I still wasn't quite there yet; the shock of seeing Luka and Max had thrown me into a state of near-sobriety, and I needed to fill myself up again.

Thankfully, we set to this at speed. I was pleased to see that not only were our metal boys well practised at drinking plenty of booze, they were also very keen to get the rounds in for everyone else, too.

Lizzy was being ladylike and sipping on a glass of water between her bottles of cider. Such a good girl. Gemma and I, on the other hand, had two drinks each on the go and were alternating between them at very unladylike speed. Not such good girls.

I was very aware of Luka sitting on my right-hand side. *Hyper* aware. We were all crammed into a round-tabled booth, all seven of us squished onto the long banquette. Gemma practically had the little Greek guy sitting on her lap, on my other side. Every time Luka so much as shifted, I felt tingles shoot down my right arm, spreading up my neck and making me shiver.

He was just sitting still, being very proper and polite, only moving his arm to raise his beer to his lips and back again.

But every one of those movements was an agony of what I knew was to come.

When he rested his left hand on my thigh, casual and totally matter-of-fact, I thought I *would* come.

But I had to try and ignore the tingles; I had to stop myself from exploding all over the floor of the pub. Or dragging Luka into the bathroom and pouncing on him like a horny teenager.

Instead, I watched the others, trying not to focus solely on the hand on my leg.

Even through the budding fuzz of alcohol and the bigger fuzz of desire, I could see something happening that I hadn't predicted.

Lizzy had been right: she didn't fancy Vill, and he didn't fancy her.

Yes, she had made a special effort for the night. Yes, she'd been so excited that he was coming to the island. Yes, they were bantering and joking like they'd known each other for years and years.

But Lizzy wasn't treating him any differently than anyone else sitting round the table. Not Max or Niko, or Luka, or even me and Gemma. Watching her chat with Vill, all I could see was friendship. Maybe a deeper friendship than I'd have anticipated, for someone she'd only met in person once... but definitely just friendship.

I'd seen Lizzy fancying people countless times. I'd seen the way she lost her voice entirely and just stared, big-eyed, until she could work up the nerve to speak. I'd seen the way she'd simpered at Dan like half her personality had been sucked away by a giant personality hoover.

None of this with Vill.

And he was the same. I'd not spent all that much time with him in Finland – most of our acquaintance had come from Lizzy's brief stay in the Oulu hospital, where we'd spent our time desperately trying to translate all the Finnish medical words being thrown at us. I'd been far too busy with Luka on the tour bus to make friends back at the drinking stage of that particular evening – I hadn't had much chance to see how he behaved in a crowd. I'd just seen the uber-attentive way he'd looked after Lizzy, and assumed he was after her.

Apparently, he was just a nice guy who wanted to help.

There was something in the way he treated Lizzy, with guru-like reverence, that made me feel like there was something else in their relationship... but still nothing romantic. A different level of friendship, for sure. I suddenly remembered how Lizzy had admitted (under duress) that she'd been talking to him a lot on Facebook – and that he had 'experience' in dealing with matters of the heart.

I could deal with that. I was a tiny bit miffed at the thought that she had been taking her problems to someone who wasn't me, but if the result of it was this new, serene Lizzy, I couldn't complain.

Besides, I couldn't think about it too hard, because I was witnessing something else.

I could see that Vill was just being nice and not flirting, because he was behaving just as nicely and non-flirtily with everyone at the table.

Everyone except one.

He was leaning across the table, nearly sticking his Mohawk up his brother's nose, purely so he could stare at Gemma and hang off her every word. His usual big happy grin had changed into something far more suave, far more focussed. And he wasn't just being *nice*: he was properly flirting his little heart out.

Gem was trying her very best not to respond. I remembered her words from earlier: she still thought Lizzy was after him and she didn't want to tread on any toes.

But I knew Gem. And I knew I hadn't seen *that* look in her eyes before.

She really, properly fancied him. There was no calculating, scheming look on her face – the look I'd seen so many times before when she was trying to lure a potential conquest into bed. She wasn't pretending to laugh at his jokes – she was actually laughing.

Bloody shocking. Especially as she kept glancing at Lizzy – busy across the table laughing at Max – with a particularly tortured gaze.

"I'm going to the loo," I announced abruptly, standing up and shunting Gemma along with me. I was loath to move Luka's hand from my leg, but it had to be done. "Come on." I grabbed Gem with one hand and yanked Lizzy out of the booth with the other, and stalked towards the bathroom.

"How cool is this?" Lizzy said happily, as we joined the long queue for the two toilets. "We're drinking with rock stars again!"

"Yeah, yeah, old news," I said loftily, crossing my arms and staring at the two of them. "Right. I'm getting laid tonight. Obviously."

"Obviously," the two others chorused, Gem leaning glumly against the hand drier.

"Don't you look so bloody depressed," I chided, giving her a glare. "You're getting laid too."

"I suppose I might find a troll in Folies," she sighed.

"No." I shook my head violently. "With Vill."

"He's Lizzy's," Gemma said immediately, shifting her stare to the somewhat sticky floor.

Both Lizzy and I spoke at once. "No he's not!"

"Eh?"

"She doesn't fancy him," I supplied. "He doesn't fancy her. He fancies you."

"Well, I got that," Gem said, with a raucous bark of a laugh that almost sounded like her old self. "But I'm not getting in Liz's way. I've been… I've been shitty lately. The whole Aaron thing, London… I'm not doing it again." She narrowed her eyes and drew herself up to her full height in a particularly noble, if pointless manner. "Not this time."

"We appreciate the speech, but seriously, Gem…"

"Honestly, I don't fancy him!" Lizzy said eagerly, grabbing Gemma by the arm. "Thanks for finally believing me, Cleo."

"It was obvious," I said, shrugging. I had a sudden thought. "You're not going to sleep with Max, are you?"

"Why the hell would I do that?"

"Because he's come all this way... politeness..." I shrugged again. "I don't know. You're a very polite person."

"Shut up and get back out there." Lizzy giggled, giving me a little shove. "You have a rock star to play with. And," she shoved Gem, too, "so do you."

"You're not messing with me? You're not just being some kind of, like, martyr about all this?"

Lizzy looked affronted. "I am a lot of things, but I'm not a martyr."

"Come on, come on." I realised that time was ticking on and there was a rather beautiful German man waiting for me a matter of feet away. "Let's get out of here."

"Wait!" Gem panted, squinting into the dirty mirror. She was reapplying her eyeliner at superhuman speed. "Now I know I can flirt, I need to adjust! Are my brows on straight?"

* * *

Less than half an hour away from straightening things out in a toilet queue, we were hit with a rather disappointing realisation: the pub was closing. Damn the early Guernsey licensing laws – it wasn't even one o'clock yet! If we were in Finland, we'd be able to drink until the early hours. The *properly* early hours, not just the two o'clock Folies closing time.

The others seemed to flow seamlessly from the door of the pub to the door of the club, regardless of the fact that they'd be chucked out in just over an hour. Max had the idea in his head that he wanted to go dancing, and Lizzy was giggling beside him, flanked by little Niko who was already making noises about holding an afterparty in his hotel room. Gemma and Vill were ahead of them, storming towards the queue in a rather hysterical race. Flirting was in full flow.

Luka and I dawdled behind.

"I don't feel like drinking anything else," he said softly, taking my hand in his. "Show me some more of Guernsey?"

"OK," I said, powerless to resist.

Of course, I was far more interested in getting his clothes off than giving him a guided tour of St Peter Port. But I had issues: I could hardly take him back to my place and shag him stupid in full earshot of Mum, Nan and Charlie. I wasn't seventeen any more.

The sensible solution would be Luka's hotel room. But he was bunked up with Max, and I knew *he* wasn't getting lucky. Depending on how successful Niko's plans for an afterparty would be, Max would be staggering back to his own room, potentially in just over an hour.

Nowhere near enough time to do everything I wanted.

It would hardly be an aphrodisiac to have a large, hairy German come barging in, off his tits at half past two in the morning.

We walked almost aimlessly towards the twinkling lights of Castle Cornet, not saying much. I was very aware that we were hand in hand. I'd never thought that just hands could be so sensitive. Every time his thumb made the slightest movement against my palm, I could feel it through my entire body.

I didn't want a romantic walk with heartfelt conversations.

I just wanted sex.

"I've got an idea," I said, stopping dead in the middle of the seafront.

"Yes?" Luka turned to face me, brushing his loose hair out of his eyes, then reaching over to cup my chin with his hand.

"You don't need a tour," I said, breathlessly. "Why don't you come and see where I work?"

"The famous café?"

"The very same."

Before I could take another breath, Luka had almost dived at my face, smothering me in a kiss so powerful I nearly sank to the ground.

* * *

We made it back to the high street – and the Bean Jar – in what was quite possibly record timing. I'd never powered along the cobblestones so quickly before, least of all with that much booze flowing through my veins.

I was shaking so much that I could barely get my key into the lock. Then I could hardly remember the code to stop the alarm from howling at us.

Finally, we were in: the dim café eerie in just the light from the emergency exit sign, pulsing fluorescently in the corner.

"Well, this is… small."

"No," I said firmly, throwing my keys on the bar and turning back to Luka, putting my hands firmly on his chest. "No small talk."

And that was it: we were off. None of the sexy banter of last time. No, now we just tore at one another, me clawing at his hair, him pulling up my top and scrunching it desperately between his fingers.

"No," I said again – well, panted, pulling away momentarily. "Not down here." I still had just enough presence of mind left to realise it wouldn't be the best of ideas to start going at it on the sofa in front of the window, not so close to club chucking-out time. We'd have an audience in less than half an hour. "Upstairs."

Kissing all the way – which, believe me, is more difficult than you'd think on steep and narrow staircases – we staggered our way up to the top floor of the Jar.

"Wow." Luka pulled away from me for a second, staring out of the huge windows.

The top floor of the Bean Jar has always been my favourite: it's everyone's favourite. More room than anywhere else in the shop, comfy sofas aplenty, and above all, the huge floor-to-ceiling windows along the back, looking out towards Castle Cornet and the marina if you looked in one direction, and the distant islands over the breakwater if you looked the other way.

It was a beautiful view: especially at night when all you could see was a mass of sparkling lights; flickering reflections on the still sea.

I didn't care.

"Yeah, yeah, how beautiful, I get it." I pushed Luka towards the sofa in the window.

* * *

The draught was starting to annoy me, but I didn't want to move.

I didn't even want to open my eyes.

Clearly I'd drunk a lot the night before. More than I'd planned to, anyway. I had the feeling that if I opened my eyes, my head would fall off and roll across my bedroom floor.

Hang on: was it my bedroom?

I let my nerve endings do an exploratory investigation.

No, it wasn't my bedroom, nor was it Lizzy's sofa. I was well acquainted with both of those, and this was new.

This felt strange and almost tacky, like... leather?

I was very cramped, and apart from the draught blowing from somewhere, I was warm. I realised that was because someone was holding onto me tightly, someone who was breathing softly and regularly into my ears; someone who was asleep.

I had the sudden, somewhat shocking revelation that I was stark naked.

Then I relaxed.

Luka. The Bean Jar. The gig, the night, the drinks.

Of course.

I smiled to myself and snuggled back into Luka's arms.

Bloody hell, it had been a good night. If possible, even better than the last time. The only thing spoiling my glow was the hangover that was pressing at the edge of my brain, ready to come storming in like an invading storm cloud if I so much as opened my eyes.

It had been a while since I'd drunk so much: of course I was going to be hungover as fuck. I'd made sure I had the day off work as a precaution, feeling very proud of my prescience and responsibility.

I took a deep breath, and closed my eyes even tighter.

I didn't want to ruin this moment. I didn't want to lose my post-sex haze of sleepy happiness by going back to reality – hungover reality, at that. I knew full well that Luka and Max were flying back to London that afternoon to catch their connection on to Germany. We only had a few more hours left together, and, well, I was probably not going to be in the state to do anything fun for those few hours. Not once I'd opened my eyes, anyway.

I just wanted to lie still, encased in Luka's arms, feeling my personal pet guitarist breathing slowly in my ear, savouring my moment.

Of course, I was under no illusion of what was going to happen, again. We'd made promises last time this happened that we weren't going to get involved, we were just a useful bit of stress relief. A bit of good sex when the opportunity arose.

Yeah, maybe it was different with him having travelled miles and miles – two flights, no less – to come and see me. He'd admitted, in that fuzzy post-sex time between orgasm and sleep, that he'd only come to the island to see me.

Not that I hadn't worked that out for myself, mind you, but it was nice to be told.

I still wasn't considering Luka in any way a sensible choice for the Leap Year Pact. Too many issues, too much touring – I knew full well what happened on those tour buses. I wasn't going to go falling in love with him.

But that didn't mean I wasn't going to enjoy the moment while it lasted.

I didn't want to open my eyes to see what time it was. I hoped that the overwhelming silence meant it was still really early – of course it was, my head hadn't started properly pounding yet. It couldn't be later than seven o'clock.

I let myself drift back into that place somewhere between sleep and awake, where hangovers are held at bay.

The footsteps on the stairs barely registered.

"What the fuck, Cleo?"

My eyes shot open, the light instantly piercing my retinas and activating the full force of the headache.

I focussed just in time to see Zach's horrified face, before he turned on his tail and clattered back down the stairs.

Chapter 26

I was on edge.

More than on edge: I was living in a permanent state of the horrors.

I'd never felt like this after a one-night stand before. Other people felt like this, I'd heard it a million times before: guilt, longing, shock at their own depravity.

But most people didn't have their entire livelihood threatened by their one-night stands.

When Luka and I scrambled out of the Bean Jar, Zach's office door was firmly shut. He didn't emerge. And, coward that I am, I didn't seek him out.

I had just about enough adrenaline in my system to sit with Luka while he had breakfast in one of St Peter Port's other cafés – I couldn't eat anything myself. I tried to maintain a normal conversation, but between the hammering in my head and the churning of my stomach, it took everything I had just to keep my eyes open.

"Tell me about him," Luka said suddenly, somewhere in the middle of his full English.

"About who?"

"That man. Your boss."

"I told you. He's my boss." I shrugged somewhat desolately, picking a bit of fat off my bacon roll. "He's just... he's Zach."

"I saw your face," Luka said softly. "It was written on there, as plain as anything."

"Can't think what you mean," I mumbled, like a sulky teenager.

"Look, Cleo." Luka reached across the table and grabbed my hand, stroking gently down my thumb with his. Just that delicate, soft touch made tears come to my eyes that I struggled to hold back. "I've seen that look before. In the mirror. Even if you won't admit it yet... this is hurting you, isn't it?"

"Did it hurt you?" I still didn't confess to anything. Even to myself. But I had to know. "Did it... did it feel like you were breaking?"

"Every day," he said, his voice low. He still held onto my hand, gripping tightly, but he stared at the glass-topped table like it was playing his life-story back to him. "It still does." He looked up at me suddenly, panic crossing his sharp features. "I don't mean I don't feel... what we've been doing..."

"Chill, Luka." I barked what may have been close cousin to a laugh. "We have sex occasionally, we're not about to march off down the aisle. I'm not stupid."

"No. Of course." He sighed in relief.

"Tell me, then," I ordered.

"I don't know if I can," he said with another sigh. "It's not my story to tell. But... there was a girl. And I loved her. Love her."

"Go on."

"I thought she loved me too. I still think she might. But..." He shook his head, tossing his ponytail somewhat violently. "It's hard to put into English. She couldn't cope with me, with my life."

"Did you cheat on her? On a tour bus?"

"No. Never." He gave me a cross look. "I don't do that kind of thing."

"Sorry. Had to ask."

"I understand." He nodded with the ghost of a smile. "After all, look at how we met."

"Exactly."

"But no, I've never really been like that. A different groupie after each show. That's much more Yasmin's department."

"*Really?*"

"Has to be seen to be believed." He gave a proper smile this time, then sighed again. "The thing with my girl... I get these periods of depression. A real black dog, I think they call it in English. Not very often, but when I do, it's big." He paused, and shrugged. "It can be good for the song-writing, but not much else."

"And this happened with your girl?"

"Lots happened with my girl. Lots. But she had her own problems back home, family problems. She couldn't look after me, and her family, and herself. Something had to give way." He gave a funny little hunched shrug that looked almost painful. "That something was me."

"You couldn't make it work?"

"Maybe one day." He looked me in the eye. "We've gone no-contact for now, it's been a while. It's better for her. But I think about her every single day. I raged, for ages. I was so low, I couldn't deal with the pain. I was out of my mind. Vill helped a lot, actually."

"He really is the world's agony aunt, isn't he?"

"Just a bit. He's studying psychology in his spare time, and he's good at it. He made me realise it wasn't my fault, it was the depression, and the timing of things, and all the other things that went on around the same time." He winced. "Still, I always think, if I'd been better, if I'd been less selfish, if I'd been more assertive in the first place... we could have overcome all our problems together. But instead, they drove us apart." Luka gripped both my hands tightly. "If you even have a chance of happiness, you need to take it. Don't let anything get in the way. Don't ruin it for yourself."

"I think I already have."

Around midday, I put Luka in a taxi to the airport, leaving him with a kiss and a tight hug. I never wanted to stop hugging him, to be honest: I could have disappeared inside his skin and let him carry me along to Germany, clinging to a kidney. I had the feeling that if I asked him, he'd take me with him in an instant. Mystery love-of-his-life or not.

But realistically I didn't want that: deep down, I knew *he* didn't want that. Even if he didn't know it himself.

He had issues, and thanks to his confession, I was starting to piece them together: an episode of burn-out, the girl who had broken his heart, something to do with Lilly's jealousy, a rash wedding... I didn't want to find myself with a starring role in the ongoing drama.

And I knew I had to face the consequences of our night in the Jar..

I had countless messages on my phone from Lizzy and Gem, and one from a foreign number I didn't recognise: I assumed either Max or Vill, looking for Luka. I didn't look at any of them.

Instead I staggered groggily up the Grange, hardly even glad that there was nobody around to see my blatant walk of shame, still in my party clothes. All I wanted was to fall into my bed, sleep for twelve hours, and pretend I didn't have to face Zach the next day.

* * *

I was first in the Bean Jar on Monday morning: I even beat Mrs Machon. It was my turn to open up the shop – that is, if the locks hadn't been changed. That's what I feared. I didn't want to face the humiliation of turning up at seven in the morning only to find Mrs Machon glaring at me from the other side of the door; Cerberus, only meaner.

If I was going to be shut out and sacked, I wanted to be the first to know about it.

But my key slid neatly into the lock, and my code still worked in the alarm.

Clearly I hadn't been given the boot.

Yet.

I set up the café as usual, keeping out of Mrs Machon's way as soon as she stormed into the building.

Of course, the storming wasn't unusual – I couldn't tell whether she was just in her normal grump, or whether her grandson had let on what I'd been up to at the weekend.

Monday morning was always busy in the Bean Jar. All the suits who'd spent the weekend getting happily pissed at Folies and Barbados were on their traditional Monday comedowns. The beautiful morning sunshine only made things worse, and they were queuing at the door by eight o'clock.

It was a bit of a rush, a bit of a stress, trying to deal with the morning riot without Gemma to take control of the coffee machine and bark at the suits to shut up when they got too whiny. But I was happy, or as close to it as I was going to get. When I was busy, when I was being moaned at by Monday-hating suits, I wasn't remembering that look on Zach's face as he stared at me, frozen at the top of the stairs.

Every time I thought about that face, it was as though I'd necked eighteen shots of espresso in half an hour, and my heart was on its way to pounding its way out of my chest: every time I thought about that face, I had to stare very hard at the cloudy mural of Sarnia Chérie and try not to cry.

Having to listen to a suit practically weeping because he'd put brown sugar in his skinny latte instead of sweetener? Far preferable, for once.

I'd done such a good job of burying my head in the sand for the entirety of Sunday that I should have expected Gemma to turn up before the door was even open. As it was, she trundled her way in just as the last breakfast-suit bolted from the café, almost late for work.

"Right, you, why are you hiding?"

I was on the floor at the time, restocking the fridge under the coffee bar with plenty of skimmed milk (it was beach-diet season, apparently, and about eighty percent of the people I'd served that morning wanted 'skinny' drinks).

"I'm not hiding, I'm getting milk," I piped up, trying my best to sound plaintive.

"You know what I mean."

I looked up towards the coffee machine: Gem was standing right in front of it, arms crossed and eyebrow raised.

I hauled myself to my feet and tried to busy myself with the cupboard above the sink.

Sadly, it was so packed with bags of hot chocolate powder, I nearly got brained as soon as I opened the door.

"You deserved that."

"I know I did." I sighed deeply and rammed the offending bags of powder back into the cupboard.

"Eh?"

"I deserve everything I get." I sighed even more dramatically and leaned on the sink.

"Woah, hang on. I meant about hiding from me and not telling your sex stories. Did something else go on the other night?"

"Um. Yes."

Gem leaned over the bar and pressed all the espresso buttons at once, manoeuvring cups underneath the nozzles with professional speed. "This calls for caffeine. And cake. I thought you were just pining because you didn't want Luka to leave... this looks like more."

"It is." I sighed yet again, and trotted obediently around to me and Gem's usual table by the stairs, dragging Sarnia's buggy behind me as I went. The baby gurgled happily, so I pulled her onto my lap and gave her a cuddle – I felt like I was the one who needed it.

"Right." Gem plopped herself down at the table with a bucket of coffee for each of us. "I have plenty of stuff to tell you myself but for once in my life, I'll let you go first."

"Did you shag Vill?" I said eagerly, forgetting my own woes for a second. "How was it? Lizzy didn't get with Max, did she?"

"Lizzy didn't get with anyone." Gemma rolled her eyes. "And yeah, I had Vill in my bedroom until Max came and physically dragged him to the airport. But that's not what we're talking about, is it?"

"Well..."

"What happened?"

"I had sex with Luka."

"No shit, Sherlock." Gem slurped her coffee and yawned. "I think even the fish in the bottom of the marina could see that one coming. So what, was it bad? Did he piss you off?" She gasped. "Oh God, could he *not get it up*?"

I poked her with a coffee stirrer. "No. It was lovely."

"Bollocks on a biscuit, you didn't fall in love with him, did you?"

"Number one, it doesn't happen like that. I don't believe in thunderbolts. Number two, no. I didn't. But…" I let out my biggest sigh yet. It sounded like the tide going out. "We kind of got… caught. Naked. In the morning."

"Your mum? Nan? Come on, they must have seen it a hundred times, I can't see your nan batting an eyelid…"

"No. We didn't go back to mine. We came… here."

"Wha-a-at?" Gemma sounded exasperated. "You fucked a rock star in the bloody Bean Jar?"

"Yeah. Upstairs. But we must have slept too long, because… Zach came in."

"Ah."

I stared at the table. Gem stared at me.

For at least a minute, the only noise in the café came from the kitchen, where Mrs Machon was listening to BBC Guernsey on the radio at a very high volume. I doubted she'd hear us talking.

Not that I planned on saying anything more.

To be absolute horror, there was a lump in my throat that hurt.

For a second, I thought my tumour was coming back with super-powered speed – then realised it was actually the onset of tears. I swallowed fiercely, fixing my eyes on the happy baby making cooing noises on my lap.

"Give me that," Gem said firmly, plucking her daughter away from me. "No distractions. We need to discuss this."

"Why?" I managed, squeaking pathetically. "That's it, really. He's probably going to sack me. I'll see if there are jobs going in Costa, or maybe one of the kiosks."

"Don't be thick," Gemma said sharply. "He won't sack you."

I took a scalding gulp of coffee, trying to drown the prospect of tears. "Would *you* keep an employee who'd used your business as a place to have a shag after hours?"

Gem shrugged. "Probably. You can't exactly do it anywhere else. I'd be especially benevolent." She gave me a piercing look. "You're really fucking upset about this, aren't you?"

"Well, obviously!" My voice was coming out about an octave higher-pitched than usual. "This job is my life. I love it here. It's perfect for me. I'll never love working anywhere like I love it here."

Gem just stared at me for another couple of seconds. "Yeah. It's the *job* you're so attached to."

"It is!" I squeaked. "You'll be back here soon enough. I have so much fun here, we have a laugh. I love you, I love the coffee machines, I even love arguing with the bloody suits."

"And you love Zach."

"I love Zach in the same way I love you." I pointed an emphatic finger. "Don't make this into something it's not."

"Something it's not? Come on," Gem scoffed. "If I'd walked in on you, or Mrs M, you wouldn't give a shit."

"Because I know you wouldn't tell, and if it was Mrs M I'd be too busy being thrown out of the window."

"No, because we're not Zach. It was always going to get back to him, you know that. This place is his baby…"

"Exactly! This place is his baby. He's going to sack me because I've defiled it."

"God, I wish I still smoked." Gem rolled her eyes dramatically. "I think I need the nicotine to get this through to you. Yeah, he might still sack you. But it won't be because he loves this place so much and you got sex all over it. It'll be because he loves *you*."

"He doesn't fucking love me."

"Like hell. If he's angry about finding you shagging Luka on a sofa, it's because it's you. If I'd brought Vill back here and shagged him on the sofa, he'd probably have found it funny. This is Zach, we're talking about. He's not as lacking in the sense of humour department as we like to make out. And if he sacks you, it's because he can't bear to look at you after he's seen you starkers with another man."

"You're talking bollocks," I scoffed. "I think we've been over this. I don't fancy Zach and he doesn't fancy me."

"It's beyond fancying now. It's more than that."

"You're talking shite." I shoved my chair back from the table and marched back to the bar. *You're thinking shite too*, I told myself in my head. Maybe I'd come close to admitting something to myself, that conversation with Luka… but I had to push the feelings away as far as I could. "He's with Sky now anyway. He's in love with her, if he's in love with anyone."

Gemma had to shuffle around in her chair to keep berating me.

"Have you managed to miss how much they've been fighting lately?" she said, exasperated. She didn't even need to raise her voice for me to hear, it wasn't like I'd gone particularly far. "Jesus Christ, I think they're only still together out of stubbornness. They were a random pull in Folies that just happened to stick for five minutes. You and Zach… you've known each other years. You spend half your lives together. You two need to talk this out."

"What's up with you?" I countered, ignoring the memory of Zach sitting on the sofa, looking broken, about to tell me all about the rot in his relationship. "Talking it out? You'd usually be telling me to pounce on him and talk later."

Gem shrugged. "Mellowed by motherhood, maybe."

"Mellowed by *love* more like." Shamelessly, I tried to turn things around. "You and Vill. I've never seen you so into someone before."

"That's not love!" Gem wagged her finger, almost dislodging poor Sarnia. "That was a good shag, nothing more!"

"Did he add you on Facebook?"

"Yeah, so?"

"Instagram?"

"Yeah."

"Snapchat?"

"Cleo."

"Have you Skyped him yet?"

"That's besides the point!"

"That's a yes." I grinned. "You're blushing."

"I don't bloody blush," Gem said, blushing more. Even Sarnia was giggling.

"I'll be watching that space with interest," I said primly, sticking my tongue out as a group of women barged into the café, three buggies between them, already braying that they needed more high chairs than we possessed.

"Well, I'm going to sit here to watch *your* space." Gemma stuck her tongue out in retaliation. "What time is our boy Zach due in?"

Throughout the rest of the morning, I tried to push everything that Gemma had said out of my head. It was all rubbish; of course it was. Gem knew about as much about relationships as that baby daughter of hers: how could she possibly be right about all that 'love' bullshit?

I'd almost convinced myself she was entirely wrong, that she couldn't have the slightest clue, that it was all bullshit, bullshit, bullshit.

Then just as the lunchtime rush kicked in, Zach marched through the door.

I felt dizzy. *Dizzy*, like some kind of fainty princess in a fairytale, swooning as her prince pranced up on his horse.

And I'd always thought the concept of 'heartache' and 'heartbreak' was a whole load of old bollocks, a convenient way for card shops to sell buckets of heart-shaped cushions on Valentine's Day. The 'heart' in the romantic sense was just a notion, something that happened in some bit of your brain, not in the rather unattractive organ that pumped blood around the body.

Well if that was the case, why the hell was my chest suddenly tight? Why did it feel like something was about to jump up out of my throat, pounding so hard it physically hurt?

Oh, I was in trouble.

Zach nodded curtly at me and headed straight for his office, swinging his satchel-like man-bag behind him.

"HI ZACH," Gem almost bellowed from the bottom of the stairs, but he barely acknowledged her. She swung around to give me a knowing look.

The rest of the day was hardly pleasant: but I didn't get sacked.

In fact, Zach hardly spoke to me at all.

I wondered if he just wanted to get his money's worth out of my shift before he booted me out.

The day passed in a blur of suits and soup, coffee cups and cakes. I mopped up puddles from where toddlers threw things on the floor, I swept up an endless stream of crumbs, I made latte after latte and didn't even judge when a potential Annoying Customer of the Week tried to convince me that a macchiato should automatically have caramel in it.

All the time, I felt like I was just two steps away from having a heart attack.

Gemma watched me knowingly for literally hours, sticking around until Lizzy turned up after school. Lizzy didn't even get the chance to talk to me – Gem yanked her down to her table and explained everything to her in a stream of hissing whispers. The two of them had a frantic little conference, then left together with nothing more than a wave.

Great. I could sense the implication: Zach and I were supposed to have a Conversation.

A blissful distraction came into the Jar only about ten minutes after the girls had buggered off: Jonny. I know, I doubted anyone has ever referred to him as 'blissful' before, but truly, that's what seeing him felt like. Bliss. I could pounce on someone else about their problems!

"Jonny!" I cried, as if I hadn't seen him in weeks. "You're finished work early!"

"Um, yeah." He cast his eyes around shiftily. "Have you seen Flic?"

"Nah. She hasn't been in in ages. Coffee?"

"Yes please. Latte, please."

"Skinny?"

"No." He smiled. Shiftily. What was with all this shiftiness? "I don't like skimmed milk."

"Good man!" I dashed to the coffee machine, sliding past Zach as he headed into the kitchen, trying my best not to touch him. "Where's all this come from? Flic always makes you have skimmed milk."

"But Flic's not here." Was that a wink? From *Jonny*?

"She'll find out, you know," I said. I was almost joking. "She'll probably test your fat levels or something."

"I don't care." He smiled, glancing around again and seeming to relax. "Did you know skimmed milk is actually more fattening than whole milk?"

"Really?"

"Yes. The fats that are skimmed off are actually good for you, they help you digest the natural sugar. Without them, the sugar just gets turned into body fat. Or something like that, anyway."

"Have you told your fiancée this?"

"She doesn't believe me." Jonny smiled again, tightly. "If it has 'skinny' in the name, she's going to believe in it."

"Sounds about right. So, the wedding's only a few weeks away, you excited?" I pushed the latte across the bar to him, and waved away his proffered pound notes.

He shrugged. "Yeah. I mean, definitely. I'm marrying the love of my life. My childhood sweetheart." He sighed, then tried to smile bravely at me. "I'm just going to sit down for a bit and do some work."

"OK. Enjoy your coffee, Jonny."

He spent the rest of the afternoon on the sofa with his laptop on his knee, typing furiously, only stopping to peer nervously out of the window.

What *was* he hiding? I'd promised Gemma I'd keep an eye on him. Her sister might have been a pain in all our arses, but she *was* Gem's sister, and my friend. I was honour-bound to find out if her fiancée was having it off with someone else.

But unless he was having an affair online, there didn't seem to be another woman in his life. Just his laptop, and his rebellious full-fat latte.

It had to be something work-related, whatever it was he wanted to hide from Flic. Had he been sacked? Was he job-hunting? Spending most of the day hiding in St Peter Port's ample selection of coffee shops?

Pondering the dynamics of Jonny and Flic's relationship took up welcome space in my head to keep out the inevitable Conversation I was supposed to be having with Zach. And Jonny's actual presence helped, too: I couldn't have the Conversation with him listening. He helpfully stayed in the shop right until Zach swung the 'OPEN' sign to 'CLOSED', when he left with a sad little sigh.

But even then, the Conversation wasn't happening. Even if I'd been able to get three words out to him without turning bright puce – he didn't want to string things out.

Eventually, like he'd just had a stern word with himself, he marched himself in front of me while I was wiping down coffee splashes from the Sarnia Chérie mural. The coffee bar was a physical barrier between us: intentional, to stop him from wringing my neck?

"About Sunday," he said stiffly. "Consider this an official warning. That kind of behaviour won't be tolerated, I don't expect it from my employees."

"OK," I managed to get out, looking at the floor. "Got it." I took a deep breath. "I'm sorry, I mean, I was very drunk and it was a stupid…"

"I don't want to hear it." Zach cut me off, turning his back to me and heading towards the stairs. He paused, then spoke quietly. "I don't want to hear anything about it."

Chapter 27

If you'd asked me back in May or June what would be the most unthinkable thing to see in Folies, I'd probably have been a bit stumped. After all, we'd seen almost everything in there: our old schoolteachers getting down on the dance floor, the most snobby bully from my old school vomming up alcopops over the bar, Sky and Zach's dramatic first kiss in front of everyone...

Yes, all of that had been unthinkable.

But nothing compared to what happened at Flic's final hen party, at the end of July.

***

We'd expected it to be totally yawnsome, and it started off just as we'd thought. Lizzy, Gemma and I sat together in a little clump at the edge of the table full of tediously boring friends of Flic, yoga buddies and work mates, all talking about their dull husbands, their dull jobs and their dull diets. The three of us seemed to be passing a roll of the eyes between us – even Lizzy, who was better equipped than me and Gem at blending in with the accountant-types, due to some kind of inbuilt politeness I still hadn't managed to drum out.

We were in a cocktail bar near the marina that, if we stayed there for long, was threatening to bankrupt me within about an hour. Beautiful drinks at horrendous prices. I had a creamy, fat-filled White Russian in front of me that had cost me over an hour's work at the Jar: the boring accountant-types all had fruity, low-calorie concoctions, and they'd all screamed about how 'naughty' they were being before we'd even got to the table.

"We've got to liven things up," Gem mumbled. "I haven't got enough money, we need to pool resources and get some fucking shots."

Lizzy and I eagerly complied, and sent Gem up to the bar with a fistful of notes.

A few minutes later, and she was back, holding a tray aloft.

"Come on, you boring bitches. These won't make you fat, and they'll make your night *so* much better!" she called, setting the tray down in the middle of the table. The accountant-types gasped as one at the shiny array of shot glasses.

"But... what are they?" one piped up bravely. Gem fixed her with a scathing look.

"If you don't know, that's probably for the best. Drink up, girls!" She seized a shot glass in each hand and knocked them back in an almost professional manner.

I was proud. "Cheers!" I hollered, and knocked mine back at once. I shuddered happily as the Sambuca eased its way into my stomach. It was no Salmiakki, but it would do.

The accountant-types eventually followed suit, after a fair bit of bullying.

Two absolutely refused to go near the shots – one was pregnant, so we allowed that, but the other one was just interminably boring.

Coincidentally, she was Flic's fourth bridesmaid, the ever-dull Denise who worked with Jonny. Yes, we finally had the pleasure of her company, and trust me, she definitely couldn't be counted on for a good time. With her demure houndstooth shift dress and sensible flats, she looked like she was off to the office. She shied away from the tray of shots like they were poison (not entirely off the mark, to be fair).

Surprisingly, Gemma didn't even get the chance to swipe up the unwanted booze, which was most unlike her.

She was beaten to it by her sister.

"Oi, I was going to have those!" Gem squawked in horror as Flic piled shot after shot into her face.

"It's my hen night." Flic stuck her tongue out. Half the accountant-types were staring at her in horror. "If I can't have a good time now, when can I?"

"Fair enough." Gem raised an empty shot glass. "Cheers."

Gemma's plan had been a good one: if anything was going to rouse the pack of accountant-types into something resembling 'wild', it was a couple of shots of tongue-loosening Sambuca. Sure, the night hardly compared to some of our own classic occasions: the accountant-types seemed to think they were being incredibly daring when two of them shared a toilet stall.

"Imagine if they knew about the time I had sex with a policeman in an empty cell," Gem mused, shaking her head sadly. "I think they'd have a collective cardiac arrest."

"When was *that*?" Flic butted in as she swung past on her way to the loo. "Why didn't I know about it?"

"Ahh, you wouldn't be interested." Gem waved her hand. "There was quite a lot of Sambuca involved, though."

"Sex in a cell." For once, Flic didn't sound disapproving. She sounded interested. Instead of heading towards the toilets, she flopped onto her sister's lap and stared at the ceiling, musing. The Sambuca shots had clearly been a direct hit. "What was that like?"

"Ew, like you really want to know?" Gem shoved Flic's bony bum onto Lizzy's lap instead. "I'm your sister."

"Only in the abstract." Flic waved her hand. "I mean, it sounds so... hot."

"Yes, very, but I'm not telling you the details."

"Was it on the little mattress thing? Or..."

"I'm NOT LISTENING." Gem scooted off her chair and away from the table. "I'm going to the bar!"

"Seriously, though." Flic swivelled on Lizzy's lap to turn to me. "Do you lot really do things like that?"

"*They* do," Lizzy pointed out.

"I don't!" I protested. Then remembered the sofa in the Bean Jar, and blushed. "Well, sometimes."

"I wonder what that's like," Flic said dreamily, staring at the ceiling again. "Really wild sex. You can't wait to get back to a bed, you don't have time to change the sheets or light candles, you just have to *do it*, right there, anywhere..."

Lizzy and I exchanged alarmed looks. Where was Flic going with this? More to the point, did we really want to know about her making Jonny get up and change the bed sheets as soon as they'd finished?

Luckily, one of the accountant-types chose that moment to blunder past, heading for the bar.

"Francesca!" Flic squealed, leaping off Lizzy's lap and grabbing the hapless Francesca around the neck. The pair of them nearly fell to the floor, but staggered against the wall instead.

"Felicity!" Francesca brayed back. The pair of them were smashed. They started to have an earnest discussion about their boss.

"This is weird." Lizzy shook her head fervently. "They've had, what, three cocktails each? And a couple of shots? Even I'm not this much of a lightweight!"

"They're all so skinny," I opined. "And too worried about their diets to ever drink more than a glass of low-cal wine. They're just not used to people like us."

Clutching a fresh drink, Gem sat back down. "One of them just barged past me," she said cheerfully. "She's puking in the street. First casualty down!"

* * *

By the time we actually got to Folies, we were four accountant-types down – sour-faced Denise had been dispatched each time to put them in a taxi and send them home. At least her boring houndstooth dress did a good job of hiding the little splashes of other people's sick.

The rest were still going strong, and Flic was in the thick of it.

I was drinking a lot – come on, of course I was – yet somehow I couldn't seem to get drunk.

I still wasn't feeling right. Even in the middle of laughing at one of the accountant-types attempting to 'get low' on the dance floor, I still didn't feel like I was *really* laughing. The laugh wasn't reaching all the way down.

I didn't even perk myself up when I was approached by a vaguely-hot man who tried to flirt with me. He followed me all the way upstairs to the bar on the balcony, and determinedly asked to buy me a drink. I took the drink, but was hardly up for conversation, and certainly not up for the kiss he tried to land on me.

"What is up with you?" Gem hissed after the man had trundled off, looking disappointed.

"I think I've slept with him already," I said, trying to put a proper smile on my stiff face.

Gem peered at him for a second. "You might be right. Can't remember. But that's not it, is it?"

"Hey, after sex with Luka, nobody else is going to come close!" I tried to put on my best swaggery bravado.

Gem merely raised her eyebrow.

Lizzy scooted over from where she'd been helping an accountant-type stagger to the loo.

"Casualty number five!" she giggled. "This one didn't puke, but she's weeping all over her mate and refusing to come out of the toilet. I think we can safely say that's another one down." She took one look at my glum face and stopped in her tracks. "Oh dear. I've seen that look before."

"What look?" I grinned like a clown. Garish and fake.

"No, I know what that means." She crossed her arms in front of her and looked positively Gemma-esque. "That's your unrequited love face. You're still mooning over Zach and he's not even here!"

"It's not even unrequited, either," Gem put in, reaching out to grab a passing bottle of Smirnoff Ice from one of the accountant-types, who didn't even notice. "He loves her too. They're just both too stubborn and arsey to admit it to one another."

"He doesn't give two shits about me." I grabbed the proffered Smirnoff Ice and gulped it down in three glugs, gasping as the iciness froze my throat, fizzing down to my stomach. "I'm his employee."

"And his friend, and the love of his life!" Lizzy said, practically stamping her foot on the floor. "You two were meant for each other!"

"Oh, give it a rest," I sighed, wiping sticky vaguely-vodka-ish liquid off my lips. "We're completely different. He's geeky, and calm, and knows what he wants to do with his life. I'm *me*."

"You balance one another out," Lizzy said solemnly. "You fill in one another's gaps."

"I bet they'd love to fill one another's gaps."

"Shut up, Gem. They do." Lizzy's face lit up. "Maybe this is your shot at the Leap Year Pact! Not James, not Luka – Zach! He's been here all along!"

"That only happens in fairytales." I rolled my eyes. "And certainly not ones set in Guernsey. The only one of us who's going to actually make this stupid pact is Flic."

"Speaking of the bride to be, where is my darling sister?" Gem peered over the balcony towards the dance floor. "God, this feels so wrong. It's not even half eleven yet, I'm nowhere near off my tits, and I'm having to make sure she's not wandered off and fallen in the marina. Not normal."

"It's her hen night, she's supposed to go a bit crazy," I pointed out. "To her, having six shots and puking in the taxi at the end of the night will be practically rehab-worthy."

"Believe me, if I do ever get married, which is looking less likely by the day, I'd like to point out – we're not having any of this bollocks." Gem leaned further over the balcony, squinting crossly. "We're going to go somewhere properly tacky, like Blackpool or somewhere, and we're all going to get so drunk we can't remember who I'm marrying. And ride rollercoasters."

"I'm not going on rollercoasters when I'm pissed," I said hastily. "There was this time at uni when they brought Waltzers to the end of term ball..."

"We'll do the rollercoasters first." Gem stepped back and sighed. "Where the fuck is she?"

"Guys," Lizzy said softly. We could barely hear her over the pounding, cheesy music. I turned to see where she was pointing first, then Gemma.

We'd seen signs of it before. The last time we'd brought Flic out, she'd behaved like this – only marginally more restrained.

Last time she'd flirted. She'd almost leaned in.

This time, she was being kissed, and enjoying it.

Right up against the back wall of the balcony, in full view of everyone at the bar. Her hands clearly grasping the arse of the man nibbling at her face like she was his first hot meal in months.

The man who was very much not Jonny.

It was officially the most unthinkable thing we'd ever seen in Folies.

* * *

What could we do? Gemma could hardly go and yank her sister off her conquest, it was too late for that. The few accountant-types still standing had been clustered around the bar, they couldn't have missed the spectacle. Plus, half of the young (ish) population of Guernsey was in that club: Guernsey's a small island.

Gem was all for going over and literally shoving Flic away from the mystery man, then giving her a very stern talking to. But Lizzy and I managed to talk her out of it – and when I say 'talk her out of it', I mean 'grab hold of one arm each and physically hold her back'.

"If you start yelling at her, you'll create even more of a scene," I hissed.

"But she's lost it! She's really lost it this time." Gem struggled fruitlessly.

"If we just try and, you know, block her out…" I suggested, and started inching towards the pulling pair as if they were a couple of dangerous wild animals who would bite me if I got too close.

"We'll just look like bodyguards," Gem pointed out. "Or like we're condoning it. We need to stop her."

"Maybe we just need to keep out of the way and hope she realises what she's fucking doing."

"She knows what she's doing." Lizzy's voice was surprisingly hard. "She's betraying her fiancé. You don't do that without knowing *exactly* what you're doing."

Before we could decide what to do, the decision was taken entirely out of our hands.

The man pulled away, and looked down into Flic's elfin little face with what had to be a suggestive look. She peeped back at him from under her eyelashes, looking coy.

Then Denise appeared.

She'd been in the toilet, looking after the weeping accountant-type. Come on, she was sober by choice – all the accountant-type care had been firmly left up to her. It could only be expected. She'd gone along with it as docilely as could be expected, though she was hardly lacking in sour-faced glares at the rest of us.

Now, the sour-faced glare was wiped off her face in one fell swoop, to be replaced by one of absolute horror and shock.

"What do you think you're doing?" she shrieked.

"There goes keeping this quiet," I muttered.

"Felicity, I never expected this of you!"

Flic was frozen, eyes wide. The man mumbled something to her and tried to put his arm around her, but formerly-dull Denise leaped forward and batted him away.

"After all these years, after all this time!" Denise hollered, elbowing her way between Flic and the man. "You took Jonny from me, you knew I fancied him. And he might have wanted me too, but you couldn't deal with someone preferring plain old Denise, could you?"

Was that why Denise had been made a bridesmaid? Appeasing Flic's ten-year-old guilt? We'd all known the great love story of Flic and Jonny had begun with teenage-Flic nabbing Jonny right from under someone else's nose... we hadn't known it was Denise.

"I've tried to kid myself you loved him, you almost had me convinced, Felicity. But this is too much, too far. You have the most lovely man in the world..." Denise was sobbing now. "And you just don't care!"

"I... I..." Flic was trying to pipe up while the man sidled away, looking like he was trying to pretend he was anywhere else.

"Don't you start!" Denise's voice reached ear-piercing proportions, her hysteria reaching such a point it looked like she was about to slap Flic right in the chops.

"Come on, I'm not having this," Gem growled, attempting to roll up her sleeves before she remembered her dress didn't have any. She strode across the balcony, shoving innocent bystanders out of the way. "Oi. OI. Denise. Shut the fuck up and bugger off." She turned to her sister, who was more or less cowering against the wall. "And you are coming home with me."

As Gem led her newly-passive sister past me towards the stairs, I realised that Flic really was totally out of it. Her eyes were unfocussed, and she was permitting Gemma to manhandle her roughly out of the building.

With a shrug, Lizzy and I followed, the sounds of Denise still shouting down the stairs behind us fading into the distance.

* * *

By the time our taxi had reached Lizzy's little bit of seafront, Flic had passed out. Not before vomming directly into her own handbag, of course.

"That cost her nearly a grand," Gemma said grimly. "I remember her practically tattooing the receipt on her forehead." She tossed it into the parking space in front of the flat with an expression of disgust.

We managed to get Flic up the stairs and into Gem's bed, Lizzy's mop bucket by her side.

"What are we going to do about this?" Lizzy piped up, boiling the kettle to make herself a cup of tea.

"Do?" I flopped into a chair at the kitchen table, yawning. "Come on, we've all done worse."

"None of us have ever had a fiancé." Lizzy dropped her mug onto the worktop with a lot more force than I thought was necessary. "He loves her. He shows her every day how much he loves her. And she's ignoring that and going after some loser in Folies."

"She *is* very drunk," I thought I should probably point out.

"So? Do Sambuca shots wipe your memory? Make you forget you've got a ring on your finger?" Lizzy slumped into a chair, her face dark.

"Look." I put my hand on top of hers. "I know you're a bit raw about cheating stuff, after Dan..."

"This is nothing to do with bloody Dan!" She yanked her hand away and scowled. "It's just... oh, never mind." She blushed. "I just don't like people who cheat. Especially on decent guys like Jonny." She took a deep breath and stared at the table. "He'd never do anything to hurt her."

"Yeah, but maybe he's just as much to blame. All these weird visits to the Jar, acting like he's hiding something..."

363

"He's probably just hiding from *her*." I'd never heard search vitriol from Lizzy, not directed towards Flic. She'd always been able to tolerate her so much more than I had, more so than even her own sister. And yet now she was the one sitting at the kitchen table with her arms crossed, looking like she'd be quite happy to punch Flic in the nose if she came into the room.

Instead of Flic looking for a fight, Gem marched into the kitchen.

"She's been sick again, and is once more unconscious." She thumped into the chair next to me and pulled her hair loose, running her fingers through the tangled strands. "I'll sleep in with her, make sure she doesn't choke to death. Thank God Mum's got Sarnia, I wouldn't want her to witness this."

"She's hardly old enough to be influenced," I laughed.

Gem raised her eyebrow. "You never know. I always thought I'd be the bad example, I didn't count on it coming from Flic."

"She's a bad example in plenty of other ways." I took an absent-minded gulp of Lizzy's tea, and nearly puked. I hate tea.

"This is the worst, though. I always knew she could be a bitch, but she's my sister." Gem ran her fingers through her hair again, looking horribly close to tears. "I always thought if she fucked up like this, I'd find it funny. I've been saying her and Jonny are wrong for one another for years. But to actually get off with someone else..." She shook her head firmly. "I never thought it would happen."

I stroked her arm. Yep, the situation was bad: instead of flinching away at being touched without permission, Gem let me give her some reassurance.

"We have to tell Jonny." Lizzy banged her cup again. "He needs to know."

"I can't fucking do that." Gem sounded more despondent than angry. "It'll ruin her life. He's all she's ever wanted."

"No, he's not!" Lizzy shoved her chair away, her hands shaking. Gemma and I were both knocked speechless. Talk about violent overreaction. It wasn't like Flic had cheated on *her*. "She wants the money, and the posh flat, and the nice handbags. Jonny was just a convenient boy for her to pick when she was a kid, like Denise said, she probably couldn't deal with someone showing an interest in her friend when she thought she was the better option. Especially with Jonny, he's so clever, he was always headed for security. That's what she's always wanted. And now she's on track to seal the deal, she's decided she wants a bit of excitement too. Well, she can't have both!"

With that, Lizzy stormed into her bedroom and slammed the door.

Gemma and I looked at one another, mouths open.

"When did she get so principled?" Gem stared towards the bedroom door as if hoping Lizzy had written the answer on it.

"She's always been principled, but this is something else," I said slowly. "I thought it was because of the whole thing with Dan, but it's not. She couldn't be less bothered about him. I know she's always wanted security and the happy-ever-after, but I didn't realise she was so jealous of Flic."

"It all comes out when you're drunk," Gem said wisely, stretching her long limbs and popping her joints. "She's probably right. My stupid sister thought she could have her cake and eat it too. Do you think Lizzy'll really tell Jonny?"

"Nah." I shook my head. "She'll have changed her mind by morning, when she's sobered up. But even if she doesn't..." I sighed. "Half the bloody island saw Flic with that bloke. If Lizzy doesn't tell Jonny, someone will."

"My money's on screamy-Denise," Gem said sagely. "She really went for it. And if she really did have a crush on him when they were teenagers..."

"When they were teenagers?" I laughed. "She works with Jonny, remember? It's got to still be a thing. She's totally having an unrequited office love situation."

"Like you and Zach?"

"Oh, bugger off."

* * *

If we'd actually had a bet on, Gemma would have been significantly richer by Sunday afternoon.

Flic's hangover was so spectacular, there was no way she was leaving Lizzy's flat without puking all over the carpets. Even though Lizzy herself was still sulking in her room and refusing to talk to Flic (I had my suspicions that that was also hangover-related) she was far too polite to turf a suffering person out onto the street when it was likely they'd pass out halfway along the seafront.

There was a knock on the door at around three o'clock, just as the very ropey Flic had managed to work her way to the living room, where she was sitting in the armchair nearest the window, peering out at the sparkling sea through bleary eyes.

"I'm never drinking again," was all she could seem to say. None of us had confronted her about the man yet: as Gem pointed out, we needed her to be fully sober and clear-headed before we quizzed her on her emotional state. Particularly as we privately decided she needed to feel a good hard bit of guilt building up in her, first.

"That'll be Mum," Gem said. "Cleo, go and get my baby."

"Piss off and go yourself," I said, from the other end of the sofa. I'd slept there under Lizzy's spare duvet, and at some point Gemma had joined me, claiming her bedroom smelled like sick and she was too tired to clean it.

"I've got it," Lizzy called, suddenly appearing from her bedroom. She briefly stuck her head into the living room. "I thought you two didn't drink enough to be hungover?"

"We're not," we chorused.

"We're just lazy," I added helpfully.

Flic didn't say anything.

Lizzy clucked and rolled her eyes, but grinned at the same time. Even in the depths of her sulks, she was still always happy to see that baby. She was pretty much her second mother.

But as soon as Lizzy opened the door to the flat, there was the sound of violently stamping footsteps on the wooden floor, and an imposing figure burst into the living room.

Yes, I just said imposing, and I don't mean baby Sarnia (though she could be pretty bloody imposing when she needed her nappy changed).

It wasn't Gem's mum with the baby.

It was Jonny.

"I just had a really interesting phone call from Denise," he said, marching over to the window and crossing his arms, right in front of his fiancée. "And then I looked on Facebook, and I had an equally interesting message from Lorna. And one from Jack, who I haven't spoken to since we left school. He even kindly attached a photo."

"Shit," Gem whispered, pulling the duvet up under her chin. "Here we go."

"I don't know what to say," Flic said hoarsely, still staring out of the window. "I really... I don't know what to say."

"Makes a fucking change," Jonny spat.

Jesus Christ fire-eating on a unicycle. I'd never heard Jonny speak like this before: I'd never even heard him swear. He looked a mess – his hair was on end, as if he'd been running his hands through it, and his face was twisted in pure rage. He didn't look like the passive pushover we'd all come to know: he looked like a very, very angry man.

"I can't believe you've done this to me," he carried on, pacing up and down. He didn't seem to register Gemma and me on the sofa, or Lizzy standing in the doorway with her jaw almost on the floor. "I've supported you so many times, I've, I've..." He paused, as if building up for a proper tirade. "I've stood up for you when you've been bitchy to everyone else in the world, I've gone along with you acting like I'm worth less than a fucking handbag." He took a deep breath as if to steady himself. "This is what I get back? And don't even bother trying to say it was just a drunk thing." His voice shook. "Just a kiss. Because how am I supposed to know that? How am I supposed to know there haven't been others? You know, this is too much."

"You think this is too much?" Suddenly, Flic snapped into action, swivelling in her chair to glare at Jonny. "You've had enough? What about me? You're such a... such a doormat! Maybe I've gone and kissed someone else, but did it ever occur to you it's because you hardly ever bother, nowadays? That maybe if I goad you into enough of a reaction you might actually be interesting for a change?"

"If I'm a fucking doormat, it's what you've made me." Jonny's voice was getting louder. "You've worn me down and worn me down, you've taken advantage of me..."

"Well, maybe I have," Flic retorted. "It's not like you don't know where the door is. You could have left me at any time…"

"Love doesn't work like that!" Jonny was properly shouting now. "I told myself I loved you, I couldn't live without you. Even when you were treating me like I was something that belonged to you, like I was something you could carry around and wheel out for special occasions… even then, I told myself I loved you. I couldn't picture myself with anyone else…"

"Like anyone else would have you," Flic sneered. "You're so bloody boring."

"Then why have you stayed with me?" Jonny crossed his arms again and stared. "Go on. Why didn't you bugger off before and find someone more exciting?"

Flic was silent again.

I couldn't help but think that Lizzy's analysis of the night before was true: Flic only stayed with Jonny because he was her teenage dream, and she couldn't bear to admit to herself that that dream had died before her teenage years were even a memory.

"It's all about you, isn't it?" Jonny was quieter again. "It's all about what you want to do, where you want to go, who you want to see. It's about your dreams and your ambitions. Whenever I want something, you shoot it down."

"Oh, are we on that bloody book again?" Flic sighed overdramatically and turned her head back towards the view of the sea. "Berate me for one little kiss all you want, fine, but don't bring up that fucking book."

Gemma and I glanced at one another, then at Lizzy, still marooned in the doorway. Nope. We didn't have a clue what they were on about.

"It's perfectly OK for you to spend thousands flying all over the place looking for a wedding dress, it's fine for you to have a hen weekend in Tuscany, but it's not fine for me to go to London to meet a literary agent?" Jonny laughed, hollowly. "It's not fair, is it?"

"Maybe if you wrote something decent," Flic scoffed. "I read that pile of crap. Dragons and elves and whatever. You're not exactly Tolkien. Waste of time, waste of money. And to think you want to quit your job…"

Well. It was all coming out of the woodwork now.

But it looked like Flic had finally pressed Jonny's berserk button.

"That's it." He took a deep breath, then shouted. "That's it, Flic. I'm not doing this. No more wedding. No more us."

"What?" Flic's voice picked up about four octaves and she clucked like a chicken with a frog in its throat. "What?"

"Oh, like you even care." Jonny made a derisive snort. "You kissed someone else. In front of everyone in fucking Folies."

"A drunken mistake, and you know it!"

"It's just a symptom." As if suddenly exhausted, Jonny leaned against the window, staring out towards the sea. "Whatever sickness is in this relationship, you very publicly pulling someone else is just a symptom of it. It's probably a symptom that I've been keeping secrets from you, too."

"Secrets?" Flic perked up again.

Gemma and I gave one another a significant look. Finally, Jonny's business in the Bean Jar, peeping shiftily out of the window – he was going to explain it.

"You think I'm still working, don't you?" He laughed drily. "Hardly. I do a bit of consulting in the morning, if someone's willing to pay me, then I write all afternoon. No more nine-to-five, Flic."

"I knew you'd do something like this," Flic hissed, leaping out of her chair, the hangover forgotten. She stood in front of Jonny, fists balled at her side like she was trying to stop herself from punching him. "You're so stupid. This, this, *novel*, it's not going to get you anywhere. You're going to end up crawling back to that company on your knees within the year."

"And if I do, I'll have spent a year of my life doing exactly what I wanted," Jonny said quietly.

"How are we supposed to pay for the wedding now?" Flic shrieked, vibrating on the spot with the effort of not smacking Jonny directly across the face. "We've got the hotel, the registrar, the flowers, the food..."

"I'll help you out with what I can, any deposits that you can't get refunded." Jonny turned away from the window and looked

Flic in the eye. "But I don't think you got it the first time. The wedding is off."

As if he couldn't bear to look at his now-ex-fiancée for a single second longer, Jonny turned on his heel and made for the door.

It slammed behind him with a resounding bang. Like the full stop at the end of a sentence.

Annoying Customer of the Week, Part 11

"Hello. What can I get for you?"
"Two teas."
"Sure. Big or small?"
"Medium."
"Big or small?"
"Medium."
"Big. Or. Small."
"Oh. Small."
"Three pounds, please. Ready on the end, milk's on the side."
"Wait, what? I've got to put my own milk in?"
"Yes. It's in those jugs. Skimmed or full fat."
"WAIT. No semi-skimmed? And I've got to put it in myself? This is hardly the most customer-serving idea, is it? Putting the milk in myself! This is why I've come out! I could have stayed at home. Putting the milk in myself... and what are these? Plastic spoons? PLASTIC? So I've got to press my teabag against the side of the mug to make it stronger, by myself, and put the milk in... ALL BY MYSELF? Unbelievable. You should have teapots. And teaspoons. And proper milk jugs that you come around and put in for me. With semi-skimmed milk. Don't you know how to run a teashop?"

I just let the rant wash over me. Usually my snappy reply would have earned me a place in some kind of sarcasm awards ceremony, but at the moment... I just couldn't be bothered.

I couldn't be bothered with any of it.

Chapter 28

Surprisingly, life went on.

We all had our suspicions that despite his sudden and unexpected backbone-growth, Jonny would realise after fifteen minutes that he couldn't live without Flic to prop him up, and we'd find him floating face-down in the Model Yacht Pond. That, or Flic would bar the door to their flat and refuse to let him claim any of his possessions until he married her there and then.

But nobody died, and there were no dramatic reconciliations.

Flic was the one to move out, seeing as she'd been the one to technically commit the adultery, even though we could all see the rot that had been lurking beneath the surface of that relationship, now exposed for all to see.

She moved into her parents' bungalow, taking Gemma's old place. We all thought Flic might need some TLC: a fair few of the accountant-types had deserted her in the wake of the pulling-in-Folies scandal, and she was lucky that her boss wasn't supposed to judge her based on her extracurricular activities. We all knew that things in that office were chilly, to say the least.

Lizzy was still behaving in an alarmingly principled way, so it was left to me and Gem (and Sarnia) to provide the aforementioned TLC. To our surprise, Flic didn't seem to want it.

We turned up at the bungalow the Saturday after the Great Break-Up, armed with a pile of girly DVDs as tall as me, a bucket-load of low-fat popcorn and a couple of bottles of wine – Flic's ideal night in. But she just laughed in our faces.

"I'd have thought better of you!" she said, letting us into her bedroom. She was wearing just a bra and pants, and as we stood there somewhat dumbfounded, she pulled a very short, very sparkly dress over her head and stepped into a pair of vertiginous heels. "Wanting a quiet night in on a Saturday. I'm off out with some of the girls from work."

"Some of…?"

"Not the ones from last week." Flic made a noise like an amused horse. "Come on. Now I'm single, I've been having lunch with a couple of the secretaries, they're single too. We're going to go out and look for men."

"Look for…?"

"Oh, close your mouths, you're causing a draft." Flic turned her attention to her own reflection in the mirror. "If last week showed me anything, it's that I haven't been living enough. I'm still young! I'll be beating you at your own game soon, in those world-famous pulling contests you used to do, Cleo."

And with that, Gemma, Sarnia and I were abandoned, our bottles of wine clinking sadly in their Waitrose bag.

"Well." Gem looked totally flummoxed. "OK. I'll admit, I've never seen her go through a break-up before, seeing as this is her first one… but she's handling it well."

"Are our pulling contests really world famous?"

"They used to be." Gem shrugged. "Remember that time I tried the bouncer and he threw both of us out?"

"That was a special night," I mused.

"Especially when he chased me down the street and we ended up fucking in the back of his car on North Beach. I definitely won that night."

"And now Flic's at it."

"Don't worry." Gem patted me on the shoulder. "She'll never beat your record."

"Dump the baby with Lizzy and go and watch the madness unfold?"

"No." Gem shook her head slowly. "For once, no. She needs to get through this on her own… she needs to make her own mistakes and not have us lot to pick her up afterwards." She sighed deeply. "Let's go back to Lizzy's and watch the X Files."

Jonny was coping equally well. I'm not saying that he was throwing himself into the clubbing scene and pulling as many women as would have him. At least, not that I knew of, and I counted myself as pretty in-tune with those goings-on on the island.

No, Jonny was taking full advantage of his sudden freedom, both from Flic and from work. He was in the Bean Jar most afternoons, tapping merrily at his laptop. Within two weeks of the break-up, he had flown to London, met a prospective literary agent, and been welcomed onto their books with open arms.

"Another latte, Jonny?" I only needed to lean over the coffee bar to ask him – he'd taken over the table by the stairs where Gemma and I usually sat, taking full advantage of its position near the plug socket. He was in the Jar for hours at a time, now that he didn't have to disguise his writing-time in every café in town.

"Black Americano instead, please Cleo." He beamed over at me. "My agent seems to think I work better with lots of caffeine in me, he was talking about some of his favourite scenes in my book and, well, they were written at four in the morning when Flic was asleep and all I had for company was the Nespresso machine."

"Whatever you want," I said, grinning at him.

Bless him, every other sentence out of his mouth began with "my agent".

Being free had already transformed him. Well, that, and his evident adoration for "my agent", who by all accounts was a bit of a hipster. No more tailored, boring suits; no more monthly haircuts to keep his sensible hair sensible. He was even experimenting with a pair of huge hipster glasses, instead of the contact lenses Flic had insisted on throughout their relationship.

He seemed to look at Zach as his mentor in this new life of his. After all, they'd both been the same, once: dull office jobs that brought in plenty of dough, but no chance to be themselves. Jonny's breaking point had just come at him and he was trying to follow his dreams. Zach had reached his breaking point long ago and become the geeky café-owner we all knew (and some of us loved).

Yes, as July trickled warmly into August, and most islanders seemed to all fall into a lazy summer routine of dividing their time between the beach and the Bean Jar, I admitted it to myself.

I was in love with Zach.

And let's face it, I had been for months.

I'd known, really, that time I'd seen him kissing Sky in the middle of Folies. The jolt it had given me, the horror I had to choke back... what else could it be?

I had tried to block it all out by buggering off to Finland and finding myself a nice rock star to occupy my time. By the time the trip was over, Sky was officially Zach's girlfriend, and I'd lost my chance. I'd been too stubborn to let those feelings in, to dare to admit to myself that I could want something as pedestrian and domestic as a relationship. Me, a relationship? The very thought!

But it was what I wanted. And I knew exactly who with.

Whether he'd had the reciprocal feelings or not, I'd well and truly fucked it up now. Even if I'd waited for the whole Sky thing to fizzle out – which, by the looks of things, it was doing at quite some speed – I'd ruined any chance I may have once had with Zach by going and shagging my rock star on a sofa in his beloved café.

I'd been lucky enough to hold onto my job: I was hardly going to hang onto any romantic possibilities too.

Zach had warmed up a bit in the few weeks since my tryst with Luka, but not much. He wasn't quite looking at me like I was a piece of dog poo that had wandered into the Jar and bought itself a coffee, at any rate.

I was getting on with things, but no matter how hard I tried, I felt like I was only pretending to be the person I'd been just a few months earlier. Even though on the surface I was trying to be as bossy and opinionated as ever, it just wasn't coming across: I was more like a sad pining teenager, dreaming of a pair of bright blue eyes and tousled brown hair with no way of stopping myself. I couldn't even bring myself to be properly bitchy with the Annoying Customer of the Week, for at least four weeks running.

For the first time in a long time, my solace was at home. Mum had mellowed so much that she didn't nag me, or question me at all. She just provided home-cooked meals, and tried to keep

Charlie away from me while I was still obviously looking like hell. She didn't even ask why – I guessed she thought I was getting used to my new thyroid meds. We'd been warned that fluctuating thyroid hormones could lead to depression. Well, I didn't need any physical problems to help me along with that.

Yes, home was peaceful, and calm – most of the time.

Charlie had learned from his little incident of alcohol poisoning and Mum's overreaction to it, and if he was getting up to crazy stuff with his mates, he was keeping it very quiet and far away from the house.

Mum was just Mum, pottering around in her Per Una, the Daily Mail under her arm. Far more pleasant in her attitude than a few months previously, but, let's face it, nothing was going to metamorphose her from drab to fab any time soon.

If any excitement was going to hit us, it was going to come from Nan.

Since my hospital stay, there'd not been anywhere near enough drama in her life, apparently. The WI and Age Concern meetings just weren't cutting it for her and her two cronies, Joyce and Pat, and they were restless. Even Nan's beloved Guernsey Goats were having a bit of a calm phase, with half of them off on their summer coach trips or visiting their numerous grandchildren. The poor remaining Goats couldn't even get a decent poker game going, let alone the Lady Gaga theme night Nan wanted to get off the ground.

Never mind that it was so hot half the elderly population of the island was dropping dead from heat exhaustion. Nan, Joyce and Pat – they wanted adventures.

The sad thing was, they were getting them.

Mum and I may have called our truce, and we understood each other a lot more than we used to. But Mum wouldn't truly be Mum without someone to nag, and Nan was helpfully providing the crazy teenager antics.

Getting brought home by the Age Concern bus because she'd turned on Nicki Minaj at the tea dance and caused a riot among the pensioners? Check.

Getting brought home in a police car because she got herself stuck on top of the German fort at the Guet forest while looking for somewhere to sunbathe in the nude? Check.

Not getting brought home at all until four in the morning because she had been to a party on a yacht owned by a spry octogenarian? Check.

At least trying to keep up with Nan's exploits was keeping me from turning completely in on myself and disappearing into a pit of angsty misery. I could have done without her dragging Mrs Machon into things, of course.

I knew Mrs Machon had been strong-armed into the Guernsey Goats a while back, but I didn't realise she'd joined their central, mischievous core. I'd known that she'd been a witness to Nan's disgrace at the most recent Beau Sejour tea dance – when Nan danced far too provocatively with old Stanley Le Mesurier after a few too many sherries, while his wife watched angrily from the sidelines, immobilised because Pat had hidden her zimmer frame. I'd heard about that one in the Jar for a while; in particularly disapproving tones. I'd been idly wondering if she was going to quit the Goats entirely.

I certainly didn't think I'd end up finding her clutching a bottle of sherry at the bottom of my back garden late one night, one arm around Joyce and one arm around Nan, all three of them singing something about the White Cliffs of Dover. One of them – I believe it was Joyce – was trying to beatbox.

I'd just come home from Lizzy's myself, where we'd spent a happy evening with Gem and Sarnia, admiring the baby's newly found ability to roll over. Of course, this had been discovered when she'd rolled neatly off her changing table into a conveniently abandoned pile of dirty washing in Gem's room.

I stood at the French windows and peered into the back garden, shaking my head. I wondered if I'd have to teach Nan to roll over herself as she toppled over backwards laughing, being hauled back up again by a near-hysterical Joyce as the three of them finished singing.

"I'd expect this sort of behaviour from you, not from my elderly mother." Mum had appeared silently behind me.

"If I'm having half as much fun as them when I'm that age, I'll be a happy old girl," I pointed out. "Though since when has she been such good friends with Mrs Machon?"

"God knows." Mum sighed, squinting into the dim garden. "Is that Pat, lying on the ground?"

"Maybe she's fallen and hurt herself and they're too pissed to notice," I said, alarmed. Mum was already reaching for the door handle.

"Cleo! And Janet!" Nan boomed authoritatively. "Come and join our little soirée."

"What's that smell?" Mum stopped in her tracks halfway down the garden. "Is that…?"

"Marijuana, dear," Nan said pompously. "I put some in the cake I made for the Guernsey Goats meeting tonight. Livened the place up a treat!"

"Oh shit." I buried my head in my hands. Nan had got Mrs Machon stoned.

"We brought the rest home and Pat here's had a bit too much of it," Nan said sadly, reaching over to prod Pat between the ribs with her toe. "She's stargazing."

"I think I can see the Orion Nebula," came Pat's dreamy voice. Joyce giggled.

"What about this one?" I thumbed Mrs Machon, who was gripping her bottle of cooking sherry like it was her first-born child. She was very busy maintaining a stony glare at me across the garden.

"She wanted to know my recipe." Nan winked naughtily. "I brought her back to show her. She pinched the cooking sherry out of the kitchen and has been at it ever since – I think you girls would say 'necking' it."

"Oh, shit on a *biscuit*." I groaned. "Zach's going to kill me."

"My grandson will do no such thing," Mrs Machon piped up haughtily. "If he's not killed you yet, he won't start now."

I raised my eyebrows, wondering quite how much Zach had confessed to his grandmother. Or what Nan had confessed to her: she'd been following the saga of me and Luka with quite some passion, though she didn't know that I was actually somewhat in love with Zach. At least, I hadn't quite spelled it out. She probably knew anyway.

"I do like that grandson of yours," Nan said, waving her hand regally. "He loves my Cleo."

There we go.

"More's the pity," Mrs Machon growled, taking a deep swig of her sherry.

I raised my eyebrows even higher, so high they must have vanished somewhere behind my fringe.

"These waitresses," Mrs Machon tutted, a tiny stream of sherry dripping down her chin. "Oh, sorry, 'baristas'. Waitresses, we called them in our day. Neither of them can make a cup of tea worth drinking, and still he loves them."

"Is he still with that hippy girl?" Nan asked innocently, giving Pat another kick to make sure she was still alive. "Rainbow? Sunshine? Whatever she's called."

"Sky." Mrs Machon gave a hiccup and shook her head violently. "I don't like her. But I don't think he likes her either." I think she was trying to sound mysterious and important. It didn't really work.

"On the road for disaster." Nan sounded wise. Well, as wise as a woman in her eighties can sound when she's off her face on weed. I dreaded to think where she'd even got it from: I worried for a second that it had been Charlie, then realised that after the trouble he'd been in earlier in the year, he wouldn't dare be in possession of such a thing. At least not anywhere Nan could get at it.

"I hope you ladies realise it's nearly midnight," Mum barked.

"Lighten up, Janet," Nan commanded. "I feel like some more cake is in order. I'm finding myself quite alarmingly hungry."

I never thought I'd see four elderly women stampede towards the kitchen like their hip replacements were distant memories: but then again, I never thought I'd see four elderly women with the munchies.

Mum and I stood in the light from the patio doors just staring.

"Why do I feel like I've suddenly aged about forty years?" I said, wearily, sitting down heavily on the little stone wall that cut across the middle of our garden.

"Well, it certainly takes me back." Mum sat down next to me, a wistful smile on her face.

I looked at her side-on. "Do I want to hear this?"

"I'd never have bothered hiding my stash, back in the day, if I thought she'd like to share." She shook her head, but carried on smiling. "How things could have been different."

"But Nan wasn't strict, was she?"

"Oh, no. Not properly." Mum grimaced. "Not like me. I was her miracle child, she adored me. Spoiled me. But she tried to crack down a bit when I started to get out of hand."

"And when I came along you thought you'd nip me in the bud before I could get to that point?"

"More or less." Mum put her arm around me and gave me a squeeze. It was weird, but it felt nice. We sat quietly for a minute or so and I tried, for the approximately nine thousandth time in the past few weeks, not to cry.

Then Mum spoke. "I wonder if they have any of that cake left?"

"No." I giggled in spite of all my overdramatic malaise. "It's bad enough that we've got four old ladies off their tits in the kitchen, I'm not adding you to the mix too."

"Then we'd better go back in there and make sure Charlie's not found any leftovers."

Our stampede back to the house was nearly as swift as the old biddies'.

Chapter 29

"You're not going to believe this!" Jonny burst into the Bean Jar, waving a piece of paper aloft and practically skipping past the queue of summer-weight suits waiting to pay for their sandwiches. They all glared at him, clearly not recognising that he used to be one of their own. Well, I wouldn't either – the baggy shorts and t-shirt, Jesus sandals and hipster glasses, none of it was really up the street of a suit.

"Busy, Jonny," Gemma called from the coffee machine. She wasn't officially back from maternity leave yet, nowhere near, but it was getting so busy during these summer holidays that she'd offered to man the coffee machine for a couple of hours each day while Sarnia slept in her pram in the kitchen.

"This is too important!" Jonny waved the bit of paper in front of him, panting, nearly giving the tall suit huffing next to him a paper cut on the nose. "I've got a meeting with a publisher!"

"For real?" I abandoned the suit brandishing a twenty pound note at me and rushed around the bar to give him a hug. "An actual face to face meeting?"

"Usually they send standard rejections, so something must be good!" I'd never seen Jonny's face so animated. "This is so exciting!"

"Proud of you, Jonno." Gem waved a cup in his direction. "I'll get you a coffee. Or, you know, a sedative."

A couple of suits huffed their way out of the shop at the blatant display of favouritism as Jonny got very obviously shoved to the front of the queue.

"We have to celebrate!" he said, trying to hold onto his coffee with shaking hands. "I think I'm going to have a party…"

"Go and sit down and think about it," I suggested, steering him towards his usual seat. There was a lonely suit sitting at the table too, but I decided neither of them would care. "We'll chat after the lunchtime rush."

By the time the crowd of suits had departed, Jonny had calmed down a bit. Gemma and I cleaned up the bar, picked up Sarnia from the cool kitchen, and parked ourselves on the freshly vacated sofa.

"Come on, then, what are you planning?"

Before Jonny could reply, Lizzy came bounding through the door.

"I just got your text!" she squeaked, hugging Jonny fiercely. "Well done."

"I thought you'd be here too," he said, almost in his old, shy tone of voice. Hang on, was he blushing? Suddenly he shook his head, as if pulling himself together. "Yes, we need to have a party. Or something. The meeting is next week, and I want to send myself off to London with the best vibes possible."

"I'm a bit stuck for babysitting at the moment," Gem sighed, jiggling Sarnia on her lap. "I feel a bit bad using Mum and Dad all the time, and Flic's in Ibiza."

"Ibiza?" Jonny looked confused.

"In case it escaped your notice, it's supposed to be your wedding day next week," Gemma laughed, but not bitterly. "This week she was supposed to be off in Tuscany or somewhere getting her spa on with the accountant bitches. She decided that'd be too dull, and she's gone off to Ibiza with her new mates instead."

"Wow," Jonny whistled. "She's really taking back the years, isn't she?"

Funnily enough, he didn't look concerned in the slightest. In fact, he looked immensely cheered by the fact he could avoid all awkwardness and not have to invite his ex-fiancée to his party.

"I could always get Mum…" I started, but Lizzy cut me off.

"Why don't you just bring Sarnia? We could have a barbecue on the beach!"

"Excellent plan," Jonny said, nodding like a dog in the back of a car. "Perfect."

"For a Guernsey girl, she's not been to the beach very often," Gem said, nodding at her content little baby. "Good plan."

With a clatter of the door, Zach marched into his shop. Conveniently having missed the lunchtime rush, as usual.

"Why are all my staff sitting on a sofa?" he sighed.

I leaped up and hopped over to the bar, nearly careering into one of the spindly chairs and bumping my hip on the corner of the worktop.

I could hear Gem giggling, but ignored her.

"Zach, we're having a party," Jonny piped up eagerly. "I might be getting published!"

"Well done, mate." Zach clapped Jonny on the back. "Count me in!"

* * *

I hadn't had a proper beach barbecue since I was about seventeen. Back then they'd been exercises in not setting one another on fire while still managing to flirt across the sausages. Well, I suppose both of those skills are still vital when you maintain the practise as an adult.

We'd stopped doing the traditional beach barbecues when we'd all got old enough to appreciate the simple joy of drinking beer in an abandoned German bunker – far easier to hide than when you were in plain sight of the police, on a crowded beach.

Of course, now we were old enough to have our beers out legally.

Considering it was technically a party, there wasn't really that many of us, but it didn't matter. A few of Jonny's boring accountant-type mates, who had already been deemed 'not hot' by Gemma; Jonny's younger brother, who seemed mightily relieved that he wasn't going to have to deal with Flic telling him to behave.

Plus, of course, me, Lizzy, Gemma, Sarnia and Zach.

No Sky.

In fact, word on the grapevine was that Sky was no more: I don't mean that she'd dropped dead, just that she and Zach had officially split up. No big loss, was the common consensus.

Of course, now I'd ruined everything in a dramatic fashion, I knew that even with Sky out of the picture I didn't have a chance with Zach myself. But I was still happier than I had been in weeks: at least I could enjoy the party without having to worry that Zach and Sky would be slobbering all over one another, just out of my eye line.

It was the perfect lazy day, down at Cobo. We'd parked ourselves right against the sea wall, spreading all our towels and umbrellas strategically close to the steps that led towards the chip shop – come on, we didn't hold out much hope for our little disposable barbecue. Plus, the Rockmount pub was conveniently just along the road, for when our cool-boxes of booze ran low.

The sun was hot, and the sea was sparkling. All right out of a cheesy postcard. The wide curve of the bay was dotted with families, groups of teenagers, people like us: but, being a Friday lunchtime, wasn't as bad as it would have been at the weekend.

"Do you think the suits are banging on the door?" Zach asked, sprawled on a beach towel wearing only a pair of shorts and sunglasses. I was very busy helping Sarnia 'build' a sandcastle (if you can call flopping about and staring with wide eyes 'building') and most certainly not looking at Zach's half-naked body.

"They've probably broken the door down by now," Gem said, slathering sun cream onto Lizzy's back with expert slaps, between swigs from a can of cider. "When was the last time you closed in the week? Or, you know, ever?"

"Um." Zach squinted up at her. "Never?"

"My goodness, Zachary, you're loosening up."

"I have my moments." He stretched his long legs so that his bare heels were digging in the sand at the end of his towel. His back arched. I stared determinedly at Sarnia, who was flailing her tiny fists so much there was a mini cyclone of sand around us.

Gem giggled. "You're blushing," she whispered in my ear, so quietly that nobody else could hear.

"Fuck off," I whispered, equally quietly.

"I think the burgers are done!" Jonny called over. He was having the time of his life, playing with the disposable barbecues with one of his old office buddies, neither of them with the slightest idea what they were doing. Come on, would Flic have ever let him do anything as undignified as a barbecue on the beach? With cans of beer freely available, not a bottle of dry white wine in sight? Unless it had linen napkins and a fashionably shabby chic vintage picnic basket, and the possibility of some good hashtags, she would never have been interested.

A whole batch of sausages had already been binned, due to a slight mishap with some lighter fluid: nobody had the prescience to tell Jonny that gasoline-based substances don't make great condiments.

With some trepidation, I took the paper plate that Lizzy handed me. She'd been oddly subdued all day: she'd put a face on for Jonny, but she'd spent most of the day already sitting under an umbrella staring sadly at the sea.

A bit like me, to be honest. Only she wasn't eyeing Zach while using a baby as cover.

I made a mental note to talk to her later. But for the moment, I was more interested in not dripping barely-cooked burger juice all over myself. I'd made enough of a fool of myself in front of Zach in the past few weeks. I didn't want to extend it to needing a bib.

I kept catching him glancing in my direction, frowning and looking away each time.

Then I realised my stupid mistake of the day: I was wearing a pair of shorts and a Karin Cluster t-shirt. Admittedly, the t-shirt hardly had a big grinning picture of Luka's face on it – it was just a copy of their album artwork, a couple of releases ago. But it was still very blatantly Karin Cluster. And although Zach wasn't exactly what you'd call into them... he'd been my employer long enough to know what their logo looked like.

Every time he looked at me, he must have been reminded of what I'd done in his café. I could have slapped myself round the chops.

Once we'd given up on the barbecue – and Gem had made a fervent promise to go up to the chippy later in search of proper sustenance – Jonny and his mates produced a football from somewhere and started thwacking it about. Zach joined them, leaping around with gusto.

"You're mooning," Gem said, as soon as they'd bounded out of earshot.

"No, I'm not," Lizzy said immediately.

"I know *you're* not." Gem peeped into the buggy where her daughter had fallen asleep, happy and shaded. "You, however…" She poked me between the ribs.

"I'm not." I sighed in a manner that was blatantly 'moony' and took a contemplative sip of my cider.

"One of these days, honestly." Gem shook her head slowly.

"One of these days, what?"

"I'm going to pretend I'm in a cheesy film and lock the two of you in… in…" She paused. "Liz, help me out?"

"It depends what kind of cheesy film," Lizzy said pragmatically. "If it was a cheesy horror film, you'd lock them in a cellar and one of them would end up cannibalising the other."

"Cheesy romantic film, come on." Gem gave Lizzy a poke. "I don't want them to finish one another off. Not yet." She gave me a quick glare. "Not unless they keep mooning."

"Well, in a cheesy romantic film, you wouldn't lock them anywhere," Lizzy mused. "You'd send them off on an important road trip during a snowstorm. They'd bicker in the car all the way and decide they were never going to speak to one another ever again. And then the car would break down and they'd have to snuggle to keep warm."

"Then it'd all come out," Gem said, satisfied. "They'd cuddle up and tell all their lovey-dovey secrets."

"Few problems there." I flopped backwards onto my towel, shielding my eyes from the sun. "Number one, it's the middle of summer. Number two, if we went for a road trip in Guernsey, we'd just be driving round and round the coast road until we got dizzy. Number three, neither of us can drive, and I don't think it's possible to snuggle on my scooter. Number four…"

"Oh, that's enough numbers." With a soft thud, Gem landed on my towel next to me. "Point remains. You two need to have, like, a proper talk about this. Especially now hippy-dippy Sky has buggered off."

"Does anyone know how it happened yet?" I asked, trying to sound very much like I didn't care and failing miserably.

"Nope. Word is, it's been a couple of weeks... he's kept it quiet. Bet it was him who did the chucking, though." Gem nodded enthusiastically.

"Really? I thought it would have been her, she was always picking on everything." I almost growled. Zach was perfect just the way he was, annoying habits and all. "She just didn't seem to like him very much."

"No, listen to your wise Aunty Gem. He's quite the catch. Owns his own business, and his own flat. He's got plenty of qualifications if he ever wants to go back to the boring career track. And he's just about passable on the eye. Seeing some reasons for her to want him?"

"Come on," I scoffed. "Gold-diggers don't go after guys like Zach. His t-shirts are too goofy."

"What do you think, Liz?"

"Lizzy?"

Gemma and I both shoved up onto our elbows.

"You OK, Lizzy?" I reached out and touched her arm, but she didn't respond. She was staring determinedly at the sea, taking deep breaths in and out. In through her nose and out through her mouth: typical anxiety control.

"Ah, bollocks." Gem flopped back onto the sand with her arms over her head. "They've always got to bloody spoil it."

We'd been so busy bitching at one another about Zach that Gemma and I hadn't noticed the group of people making their way down the steps and onto the beach, only a few metres away from us. Three adults were unloading Waitrose bag after Waitrose bag of sandwiches, crisps, fruit and cake – with a big birthday cake taking pride of place on their little fold-out table. At least ten children in swimming costumes were already racing around like crazy things, batting one another with balloons.

Who the hell brings balloons to the beach? Beaches are sandy. Sand is basically glass. It's not good for balloons. Nor are the rocks and stones and jagged crab shells which are usually scattered around; unless you're on honeymoon-white sands in the Caribbean, I suppose.

"I'm OK," Lizzy said, in a very small voice.

Sure, she'd been coping with her phobia a lot better since her cognitive behavioural therapy. We'd all noticed how she could even walk through town at sale-time without flinching, nowadays – as long as the balloons weren't waved in her face, of course, and they didn't pop.

Having them flying about in a frankly precarious situation a matter of metres away? It was hardly going to be easy for her. I could tell that even with all her deep breathing and careful self-control, all she wanted to do was run.

Suddenly, Jonny came barrelling over.

"I'm bored of football," he announced brightly – overly brightly. 'Distraction' levels of brightness. "Liz, do you want to come for a wander over to the rock pools?"

"Yes please." Lizzy was on her feet in seconds, not so much 'wandering' as 'power walking'.

As he followed her, Jonny turned to me and Gem and gave us a little wink, then nodded in the direction of the children's party.

"Since when has Jonny known about Lizzy's phobia?" I wondered aloud.

"Never mind that – since when has Jonny cared enough to be the first on the scene to look after her?" Gem pointed out.

We looked at one another for a second. Then we were both struggling to our feet, staring off down the beach with our mouths open. Jonny had caught up with Lizzy and the pair of them had slowed down dramatically, ambling towards the rock pools. They were both nattering at top speed. It was as if Lizzy had completely forgotten about all the balloons: I hadn't seen her so animated in weeks.

Gemma and I looked at one another again.

"Holy fuck." I said. "Are they… do they…?"

"I think they fancy one another." Gem's voice was hoarse. She sat back down on the towel as if her legs just couldn't hold her up any longer. "How the bloody hell did we not see this coming?"

"I have no idea." I thumped down next to her, squinting towards Lizzy and Jonny.

"All this time…" Gem shook her head slowly. "I thought Liz was being nice to him just because she's polite."

"We're all nice to him! I certainly don't fancy him!"

"No, didn't you ever notice? She goes out of her way. Like, whenever Flic was ignoring him…" Gem paused for a moment of drama. "He'd always turn to Lizzy! And she'd always be there!"

"Look how she's perked up." I craned my neck. "Never mind perked up, she *lit* up as soon as he came and talked to her, and not just because he was rescuing her from the balloons. She really likes him!" I could see Lizzy throwing back her head in laughter at whatever Jonny was rattling on about. "She's been a bit down the past couple of weeks…"

"So have you," Gemma felt the need to point out, as one of the balloons burst somewhere off to our right. I flinched automatically, then remembered Lizzy was well out of earshot.

"Shh. We're not talking about me. But I suppose…" I gulped, guiltily. "I suppose I've not been paying as much attention as I could have. Too wrapped up in my own stupid head."

"Ahh, you're allowed." Gem patted me absently on the arm. "But it looks like you've both been mooning over, you know, similar things. Men. Conveniently located lanky buggers who happen to feature in ninety percent of our bloody lives."

"Oh, will you shut up." I paused for a second. "You're right though. Oh my God, they *so* fancy one another!" The two of them had reached the rock pools in the distance, and we could just about see them gambolling over the rocks like a pair of clumsy mountain goats.

"I think they're chasing one another," Gem said in a monotone. "This is getting a tiny bit sickening."

"Come on, it's sweet!" I took another good squint. "Oh God, I think he's tickling her. All we need is the billowing orchestral soundtrack and we've got ourselves a chick flick."

Gem made a vomming noise, and glugged on her can of cider. "Too sweet for me, I can't watch."

I couldn't tear my eyes away. "God, this is more than just fancying one another. They're into one another. Properly. Why has she been so bloody upset?" I felt a pang of jealousy. Why couldn't *my* conveniently-located-lanky-bugger feel like that about me?

"Flic's sloppy seconds?" Gem put in.

"Probably…" I said slowly. "Ish. You know what Lizzy's like. Moral compass of a Victorian. She probably thinks she's going to, I don't know…"

"Piss on Flic's chips?"

"That's one way to put it." I shoved Gem gently in the arm. "Christ on a bicycle," I mused. "They really work, don't they?"

"Time will tell," Gem said, her tone business-like. "If she's got that much guilt it's sending her into a moony depression, she might be best staying away."

"Or being with him could cure everything." The two of them seemed to have settled down now, and had perched themselves on a rock facing the sea. I could only see their heads, close together, almost touching.

"We're going to have to have words," Gem sighed. "Aren't we?"

"When have you ever known me to keep my mouth shut?"

Another balloon burst with a resounding bang.

* * *

Thankfully, the kids managed to destroy all their balloons within half an hour, and Lizzy and Jonny came ambling back across the sand towards us.

I was only glad the children's party managed to stop being a threat before the sun started to set. Sunset over Cobo bay, while staring at it from a romantic rock formation on a beach? God, the romance of the whole thing may have sickened poor Gem to the point of actual puking, and we'd had more than enough of that in the past year.

I wanted to leap up and hug Lizzy as soon as she came close enough for me to see her face. It was a picture of misery and elation all rolled into one. It was as if she'd just been offered the most beautiful, enormous, chocolate-sprinkle-covered bowl of ice-cream in the entire world… then a kind soul had informed she was lactose intolerant. She could still appreciate the beauty of the ice-cream, but she knew she'd have horrible stomach cramps if she ate it.

Oh, come on, it was the best analogy I could think of at the time. I hadn't seen that look on her face since her ill-advised attempt to go on a diet when we were eighteen, right before Nan had made me a birthday cake taller than I was and instructed me to share.

"Um, OK, I'll…" Jonny hovered around for a second, while Lizzy peered with great 'interest' into Sarnia's buggy. "I'll see you in a bit?"

"Come on, Jonny," Gem said snappily. "We're not going anywhere. Go and join the football game before Zach gets murdered by those teenage boys."

"What?"

"They tried to steal your ball," I said. "We think they've been digging traps for Zach since he gave them a lecture." How come just saying the word 'Zach' was giving me a little buzz? I was almost shy of saying it. God, I was pathetic.

Jonny bounded off to join his mates, with a fleeting glance at Lizzy as he went. She was still staring determinedly at the baby, as if trying to stop tears from welling.

"Sit down," Gemma and I chorused. Lizzy looked up, startled.

"Come on." I patted the edge of my towel invitingly. "Down you come."

"Can't I just… stay here?"

"Nope," Gem said briskly. "We're not giving you the chance to bolt. Sit."

Lizzy sat.

To my great surprise, before I could even open my mouth to gently goad Lizzy into confessing all, Gem took both Lizzy's hands in hers.

"Look, we know what's going on with you and Jonny," she said softly. Lizzy opened her mouth, but Gem didn't let her speak. "No, listen to me. It's fine. My sister is merrily screwing her way around Ibiza. You only need to look at her Instagram to know she's having the time of her life. If she even dares to kick up a fuss about this, she's done much worse and she knows it."

Lizzy looked somewhat thrown.

"Nothing… nothing's going on," she said, her voice quivering.

Gem raised her eyebrows so high they disappeared into her hairline – no mean feat, with her hair scraped back in her customary tight ponytail.

"We could see it from a mile away," I pointed out. "Well... whatever the distance is between here and those rock pools."

Lizzy blushed. "We were just talking. And... talking."

"You've gone very red," Gem said tartly. "Did you catch the sun while you were leaping about like kids over the local sea life?"

"Look." Lizzy dropped her voice, and stared at her lap. "Even if... if I, if we wanted to do anything, be anything... you're wrong about Flic. She's so possessive. If Jonny ever wants another relationship, he's going to have to leave Guernsey. Or Europe." She gulped. "And even if he did find a girlfriend in Guernsey, if that girlfriend was one of her best friends..."

"She'd be glad that her friend was happy," Gem butted in. "She's not a monster." She paused. "Well, sometimes she is. But not about this. She'll be fine, honestly. And if she isn't, she'll have me to answer to." She frowned. "You two are so into one another, it's sickening."

Lizzy's blush got deeper. She was silent for a few seconds. "He's asked me out every time we've met for weeks. Since just after he dumped Flic, actually."

"Knew it," I crowed.

"Shut up, Cleo." Gemma poked me, then turned back to Lizzy. "And you haven't said yes? Not even once?"

"No." Lizzy's voice got even lower, even more despondent. "I can't hurt Flic like that. When she hurt *him*, I thought I wanted to strangle her. But I can't..." She had that look on her face again, the ice-cream look. Her head was so low I thought she was going to tunnel through the towel and make an escape route under the sand. "We kissed."

"You kissed?" I squeaked, as if we really were fifteen again. "When? Where?"

"Day before yesterday," Lizzy whispered. "When I was helping you out in the Jar. He was writing, upstairs, and I sat with him for a bit. And... he kissed me." She let out a cry of shame. "And I let him!"

"Elizabeth," I said firmly, pulling her distraught face up to meet my eyes. "Stop being so bloody dramatic. It's not the nineteenth century any more. Or wherever else these values of yours are bloody coming from. You and Jonny would make each other so happy."

"Sickeningly so," Gem supplied.

"Yeah. We could practically hear the emotional soundtrack when you were walking down the beach. Flic's moving on with her life. It's not a crime for Jonny to move on with his."

"If you two get it on..."

"Gem!" I clucked. "Get it on? It's far more romantic than that. We'd have to say 'make love'."

"Give over," Gem scoffed. "Whatever. If you two 'make love', yeah, maybe Flic'll be a bit upset. For approximately five minutes. If you don't..."

"You'll be depressed for a lot longer," I finished.

"For fuck's sake, think of yourself for a change." Gem hauled herself to her feet to pluck the stirring Sarnia out of her pram. "That's an order."

Lizzy sat in silence for nearly five full minutes while Gem fussed with the baby, and I pretended not to be sneaking stares at Zach – who, despite Jonny's intervention, had been lured into a craftily-hidden freshly-dug trench by the teenage boys and was now firmly stuck.

"I've fancied him for months," Lizzy eventually said, her voice soft, stealing a glance across the sand. "Since before we even went to Finland. Every time Flic was mean to him, or ignored him, or left him feeling unloved, it just broke my heart. I couldn't believe that he was still with her. Then when we were in Finland, when I met Vill... we got talking and it all spilled out of me. You didn't know, but I cried all over him that night."

"Oh, Liz."

"You were busy." She smiled. "It was such a relief to get it all out, though. And he's been helping me through for weeks. I thought I was getting there, I thought I might finally be over this stupid daft crush. But then Flic ruined it all with that other guy, I couldn't believe how angry I was with her."

"I thought you were just being, you know, moralistic," I said.

"No." Lizzy shook her head slowly. "It was because it was Jonny. I couldn't bear to see him in so much pain. Even though I knew I couldn't have him myself, it hurt me so much to see him feeling like that."

"You can have him yourself." I squeezed her hand.

"If I'm not mistaken, I just gave you an order," Gem said, trying to change Sarnia's nappy and hold her nose at the same time. "Think of yourself for a change. Do you want me to be more specific?"

"I do," I said quickly.

"OK." Gem snapped Sarnia's babygro shut with a flourish, and hauled her daughter onto her lap. "Here's your orders. On your feet, please."

Ever compliant, and with the faintest inkling of a smile on her face, Lizzy stood up

"Well done. Now, walk over there to the lads. Our lads, not the teenagers. Grab Jonny, and..."

"I'm not going to snog him in front of everyone," Lizzy said sharply.

"Who says 'snog' nowadays? It's twenty bloody sixteen." Gem rolled her eyes. "I wasn't going to say that. I was going to say – grab Jonny, and ask him to come up to the Rocky with you for a drink. Talk to him."

"Kiss him again," I said, eagerly.

"Shag him, if you can."

"Gem," I sighed. "These two aren't us. They'll leave it for a few dates yet, I'm sure."

"Whatever. Do you accept your orders?"

Lizzy looked towards the rowdy game of football, teetering for a second. "Yes. Yes I do."

With that, she obediently trotted off, and within minutes, she was marching up the steps towards the pub and out of sight, Jonny trailing behind her with the biggest grin I'd ever seen plastered across his face.

"Have I missed something?" Panting heavily, Zach landed in a heap next to me on the towel, brushing sandy hair out of his face. "I haven't run like that in years. Little buggers. Yeah, what did I miss?"

"Jonny and Lizzy are in love," Gem said, very matter-of-factly. "They're going to the pub to discuss it."

"Oh." Zach looked like this was old news. "Well, he's been pining after her for months. About time they got round to it."

"He's been pining after her?" I inquired, while Zach pulled a handful of beers out of the nearest cool-box, spreading them between the three of us. "I thought it was the other way round."

"Oh, he's fancied her for ages." Zach glugged back his beer. "I think he'd have left Flic a lot sooner if he'd known Lizzy would go for him."

"Bloody hell, how have I missed all this? How do you know it all?"

"I have eyes." Zach shrugged. "Every time they've been in the Jar at the same time, I've noticed." He stretched out on a towel, popping his joints. "They're perfect for one another."

* * *

The day started to meander towards the evening, and our little party started to drift apart. For a start, Lizzy and Jonny hadn't returned from the pub, and we'd accepted that they were gone for good. For the evening, at least. The accountant-types had spotted a group of women with a picnic just down the beach from us, and were on some kind of exploratory expedition to flirt with them – well, perve on them, but we all knew the eventual aim. Jonny's brother had made friends with the teenage boys and was halfway down the beach letting them share his coolbox of beer.

Gemma, Sarnia, Zach and I were left on our own with the remnants of the barbecue, and the rest of the beer.

Understandably, conversation was taking a turn for the weird.

"I'm not choosing between those," I giggled, clutching Gem's arm in horror. "Neither! Never! The horror!"

"Come on! Be married to John McCririck, or have a penis for a nose?"

"But would it be an actual penis? Like, functional?" Zach wanted to know.

"No." Gem shook her head firmly. "It would just be a nose. But it would look exactly like a penis."

"Big or small?"

"Average size." Gem shrugged.

"I'd marry John McCririck," Zach said, shaking his head sadly. "Repulsive. But he's got quite a bit of money, right?"

"I'd probably go for the penis," I sighed. "At least it'd be a talking point at parties."

"Here, have we run out of beer?"

"We have." I peered into the cool-box. "Yup."

"I'm bored." Gem twitched on her towel, staring around her as if expecting suitable entertainment to leap out of the sand in front of her. "Let's go for an adventure!"

"We've all lived in Guernsey all our lives," I pointed out. "Not much scope for adventure nowadays."

"Come on," Gem scoffed. "Your nan's still having adventures and she's a hundred and seventeen. Let's go to the Guet!"

'The Guet' meant the woods just behind the beach, up on a hill. We all call it a forest, everyone does, but that was just a relic of Guernsey childhoods. In reality, it's just a hillside covered in pine trees, with twisting walkways winding their way around to an old German fort. I'd loved to go there with friends when I was a kid, to play hide and seek and make 'dens' among the trees and bushes: then, of course, when we were a bit older, there were rumours that the cool kids used to go up to the fort to get clandestinely drunk.

It's also the place where Nan nearly got arrested for her naked sunbathing incident.

With a few beers in me, a little visit seemed like an excellent idea. "Yeah! The Guet!"

"What about Sarnia?"

"Ah, Zach, don't be a party pooper. I'll phone my mum, she'll come and get her. Then we can go exploring!"

Chapter 30

"I'm going to kill her," I mumbled, almost incoherently. Well, I assumed it must have been incoherent: I was pressed against an iron gate that smelled like mould.

"I'll help," Zach said grimly, giving the gate a kick. "We're not getting out of here without the fucking fire brigade. She's properly wedged us in."

"She threatened this kind of shit. I thought she was just messing about."

"What? Why would she threaten this?" Zach gave the bars a rattle. For a gate of pensionable age, it was doing a great job of staying firm. "GEMMA!"

She wasn't going to hear us.

Gemma was long gone.

I'd honestly thought she was being genuine when she said she wanted to go off for an adventure, a bit of random tipsy exploring. I hadn't thought for a minute she had an ulterior motive.

Of course, Gem is Gem. She *always* has an ulterior motive.

She'd bounded up the shady path to the German fort, giggling hysterically, me and Zach stumbling behind her. The trees kept out what little light there was left, and the concrete fort at the top of the hill was almost entirely black against the moonlit sky.

"Calm down!" I hissed. "Come back! There could be anyone in there!"

"It's empty!" she called back down the hill. "Come on!"

"You're a lunatic!" I was laughing, nearly stumbling as I tottered up the path. Zach was just as bad, grabbing onto the back of my t-shirt more than once and chuckling away.

"Come on. Ooh, look at this, the gate's open. We can get inside!"

We tripped and tottered our way into the fort, still giggling.

"I don't want to go in there." Zach stopped dead at the entrance to one of the old prison cells. "It smells weird."

"Don't be such a baby." I gave him a shove, and followed him into the dark hole.

I'd thought Gem was in there too, lying in wait to make us jump.

Wishful thinking.

She *was* lying in wait... she was just doing it behind the old iron bars, timing her attack with precision. With a triumphant cackle, the gate slammed behind us, echoing dully through the old cement.

"Woah, woah, hang on." I leapt into action, whipping around and reaching out to give the door another good shove. But my reflexes were dulled by the beers I'd been drinking, and I didn't manage to grip the door before Gem had heaved a sizeable piece of loose cement against it.

"I'm going to leave you two to chat," she said. In the dim light from the moon I could just see her eyebrows waggling maniacally. "I'm sure you have a lot to talk about."

And with that, she was off. Bounding away like a mountain goat over the heaps of old concrete and gun emplacements.

Bitch.

"I'll ring her," I said, when I came to my senses, pulling out my phone. "Threaten her with twenty-three different types of death... oh, bollocks."

"What?"

"I've got no signal." I stared blankly at the lack of bars on my phone. "Have you?"

Zach dug around in a pocket of his shorts. "Nope."

"Emergency calls only... do you think this merits 999?"

"Obviously." I could feel Zach's eye-roll more than I could see it. "Fire brigade. I've never called 999 before."

"Oh, I have," I said breezily. "They're nice. Do it."

"When did you have to phone them?"

"Couple of times." I shrugged. "When Gem was so drunk I thought she'd stopped breathing. Admittedly, I was off my face too. All very fun. Ran into the dispatcher in town a couple of weeks later, turned out I went to primary school with her. Bought her a drink. Will you just dial?"

"I am dialling." I could hear Zach was gritting his teeth. "I'm not getting anything."

"Maybe all the concrete blocks the signal?" I sighed. "Even for the emergency calls."

"Stupid bastard network." Zach threw his phone onto the ground. Temper.

He regretted it, of course.

Throwing an iPhone rather dramatically onto a concrete floor never really goes well.

"Oh, bollocks." He flung himself to the floor after his phone, and mewed sadly at its smashed screen.

"Serves you right for throwing a paddy," I said snippily, turning my back on him and trying to use the light of my own phone to find a corner of the bunker that wasn't covered in dubious-looking dirt. Animal poo, bird poo? Something like that.

At least it was the summer holidays, meaning that the bunker had probably had its fair share of teenage piss-ups to clear out the place. It would have been a lot worse if this had been going on in the middle of autumn, with a nice covering of rotting leaves to go with the mould.

Using the toe of my shoe, I managed to sweep myself an almost-clean bit of concrete, and sat down with a huffy sigh.

"My battery's low," I said, after a couple of seconds of staring blankly at my screen. "Not that I have any signal, either."

"Someone'll come by in the morning." Zach flopped backwards into the opposite corner of the bunker, sighing deeply. "Dog walkers. Joggers."

"Or Gem will decide we've been in here long enough." I paused. "OK, no she won't. She'll leave us in here forever."

"What was she on about?" I could hear Zach shuffling about to make himself comfortable. The moonlight wasn't bright enough to see him properly, in that far corner. I was kind of glad: I didn't want to know what he'd sat on. "Why does she think we have a lot to talk about?"

"Oh, come on," I scoffed. "We both know what she's on about. Unless, of course, you're a twat who's just been an arse with me for the past few weeks because you're a grouchy sod."

Somehow, it felt safer talking about this in the dark. Almost as though it wasn't really happening.

"I don't know what you're talking about." Zach was speaking through his teeth. That was a pretty good indicator that yes, he did indeed know exactly what I was talking about.

I took a deep breath. Darkness. He couldn't see me. I could say it. "You've been pissed off with me ever since my... thing. With Luka. In the Bean Jar."

"Well, obviously," Zach blurted. "You had sex in my café! On my best sofa!"

Maybe everyone else was wrong. Maybe I'd been right. Maybe that was the only reason he had been pissed off. But if so... I had to get it out in the open anyway.

"The others, Gem in particular, obviously..." I tried not to let tremors into my voice. "They think you... fancy me. And that's why you got so pissed off but still didn't sack me."

Zach didn't say anything.

My heart was trying to throw itself out of my mouth.

Either it was true, or he was laughing at me, or he was just so angry he couldn't say a word.

"It doesn't matter why I was pissed off," he said eventually, his voice even and low. "I'm not annoyed anymore." He was silent for a few seconds more. "I'm over it. Whatever 'it' was. It's gone."

My heart stopped trying to abseil into the bunker and slid down to my toes instead.

I wanted to curl up in a ball on the dirty floor and bury myself in my own misery.

He didn't want me.

Maybe he had, once upon a time. But that was gone.

I'd ruined it all.

Neither of us spoke for a while. I was too busy trying to keep the lump in my throat from coming out as a noisy storm of tears. Zach was embroiled in his own thoughts. That, or falling asleep. We *had* consumed quite a lot of beer and cider.

It was so quiet, I could almost hear my own heartbeat. I concentrated on keeping it regular, calm, in control. That way I wouldn't start howling. Or screaming.

I wasn't expecting Zach to be the one who screamed.

I suppose I'd been concentrating so hard on my own heartbeat, I hadn't been listening to the rustling and pattering going on in Zach's corner. If it had crossed my mind at all, I'd just thought it was him making the sounds.

Not the local wildlife.

"Rat, rat, rat!" Zach squawked, flinging himself across the bunker and almost landing on my lap. "Ow!"

"Ew!" I shot up to my feet, yanking Zach behind me and clinging to his arm. "Ugh. I don't like rats."

"Ow." Zach gripped me, hard.

For a fleeting moment, I thought that maybe he fancied me after all, and this was going to lead to a lovely clinch in the middle of the dingy bunker.

But then he sank to the ground, whimpering faintly.

"What's up?" I dropped next to him, trying to see his face in our little bit of moonlight.

"My ankle," he gasped. "I just twisted it when I got up. Oh, heck, it bloody hurts."

"Shit." I stared down at the ankle in question. Zach was clutching it like it was about to fall off.

"I think it's swelling up," he whispered, wincing dramatically. "Ow."

"Let me have a look." I fumbled for my phone and activated its pathetic little light. "Oh, there's nothing sticking out of it, that's a good sign. And I can't see any swelling."

"But it hurts so much."

"Believe me, this is nothing." I switched off my light before it could completely drain my phone's battery. "I saw Lizzy's leg when she broke it. *That* was swollen. Pretty much purple, too. It was gross. Yours is fine."

"Doesn't feel fine."

"Don't be such a wuss."

"I'm not being a wuss, I'm wounded."

"Drama queen." I doubted he could see my eyes in the dark, but I rolled them anyway. "Walk around, shake it off."

"I'm not walking around in here," he snapped. "I might step on a rat. And it hurts too much."

"Whatever." I leaned against the mouldy wall, no longer bothered if any of it rubbed off onto my Karin Cluster t-shirt. "What time do you think the sun will come up?"

"I don't know. I don't care." Zach flopped back onto the ground with a groan. "Oh, this hurts so much I don't even care if I get ratted."

I'm pretty sure I know how this next bit would have gone in Gemma's imagination.

Damsel in distress (in this case, Zach): "My ankle hurts. I'm so upset and scared here in the dark. Oh, woe is me. I need a cuddle."

Handsome prince (in this case, me): "Never fear, o beautiful damsel! I am here to provide the love and affection you need."

Prince sinks to the floor, clutching Damsel to bosom.

Prince: "This moment is incomparable."

Damsel: "I will love you forever."

Prince: "Let's talk about our feelings until the sun comes up, then trot happily into the distance on my fearless stallion."

They kiss, and credits roll.

Yeah, that didn't happen.

Instead, Zach curled up in a ball on the floor clutching his ankle and occasionally having a little moan, while I propped myself up against the wall and tried not to either burst into tears or kick him in the ribs while I thought up more and more torturous punishments for Gemma.

We hardly fell asleep in one another's arms, clutching each other and promising to be true.

It could have been a couple of hours: it could have been a couple of bloody minutes. Of course, stuck in my own stupid head, going round and round in circles, it felt like we'd been stuck in the bunker for several decades. I fully expected to look in the mirror when I finally got home and see deep crevasse-like wrinkles and grey hair.

"Do you hear that?" Zach rasped, his whisper tearing through the darkness.

"No." I must have been actually starting to fall asleep.

"There it is again! Listen!"

"What?"

Suddenly, I heard it – a snatch of laughter that sent a chill right down to my bones. I'm not kidding: it was the kind of cackle you only hear in bad B-movies and usually heralds the arrival of a mad axe murderer.

"Oh shit," I hissed, shuffling back against the wall and trying to make myself as small as possible. "It's a homicidal maniac."

"Or a drug gang," Zach whispered frantically, dragging himself over to me at top speed. Clearly the ankle wasn't bothering him anymore. "We've landed in the middle of a deal gone bad and we're going to get caught in the crossfire."

"Not if we keep quiet." I clapped my hand over the general area of his mouth and listened, hard.

There was silence for a few seconds before we heard the voice again.

"YOUR ANUS!"

Er... what?

"Is it... doggers?"

"What?"

"You know... people *dogging*." His whisper got even lower, as if even in this particular moment of potential peril, he was blushing. "Public sex."

"Hey, maybe they won't kill us." I shook my head and tried to clear the sleepy, mouldy fog away. "Let's attract their attention."

"No!" Zach fumbled to cover *my* mouth. "Drug deal! Murderer!"

"Hardly," I hissed again. "This is Guernsey." I took a deep breath. "*Is there anybody out there? Hello?*"

"Bloody hell, you've got a loud voice."

"Did you not realise that before now? *Hello? We're trapped in here! Hello?*"

There was a brief silence, then it seemed like whoever was out there lost their heads entirely.

"OH MY GOD, IT'S THE ALIENS!"

"Shut up, Pat." Hang on, I knew that voice. "Hello?"

"*In here!*" I yelled again. "*In the bunker!*"

"Charlotte! Where are you going?"

"To the fort! Are you with me, Joyce?"

"DON'T DO IT, JOYCE, IT'S THE MEN FROM MARS!"

"Oh, do be quiet, Pat, and put down that sherry."

I buried my head in my hands. Of all the bloody people...

"Cleo," Zach said slowly, in a very measured tone of voice. "Is that your grandmother?"

"Yes. Yes it is."

"WAIT FOR ME. What's happening? Joyce, Pat? Where's Charlotte going?"

I giggled as Zach groaned. "And that, Zachary, is yours."

* * *

It turns out the team of intrepid grannies had been at the sherry since the evening, when their meeting of the Guernsey Goats had deteriorated into what can only be described as a piss-up. Most of the other old biddies had hobbled home hours ago: but Nan, Joyce, Pat and Mrs Machon had kept on it. Somewhere along the line they'd decided that seeing as the Guet was so close to their meeting hall, it would be a lovely idea to do a bit of stargazing.

That did manage to explain why Pat had been yelling about anuses. Not anuses: Uranus.

"What are you doing here?" I demanded, the second Nan poked her nose through the bars of the bunker.

"Cleo? Cleo!" She sounded utterly delighted. "What are you doing here?"

"Gemma locked us in," Zach said grimly.

"And Zachary! How delightful. Clementina! It's your grandson!"

Clementina? I'd never really thought of Mrs Machon having a first name before. I'd certainly not expected it to be something quite as exotic as 'Clementina'.

"My grandson? Here?"

"In the bunker!"

With a thunder of footsteps, Mrs Machon arrived. In the dim light, I could make out that she was wearing her purple Guernsey Goats sash threaded through her perm like a very sparkly tiara.

"Zachary! What are you doing in there?"

"It's not intentional." It sounded like Zach was speaking through clenched teeth.

"Where's Joyce with that torch? JOYCE!"

"I'm here, I'm here," Joyce panted. "Pat's dropped the sherry bottle and we can't find – Cleo! Is that you?"

"Hello, Joyce." I sighed, blinking as Joyce shone a heinously bright flashlight directly into my face. "Can you lot get us out of here? Or at least call for help?"

I didn't really have all that much faith in four intoxicated old biddies managing to wrench open the door that Gemma had jammed quite so lovingly, but surprisingly, they made short work of it. To be fair, that was mostly down to Mrs Machon's bulk. They managed to shift the brick of cement that Gem had hauled in front of the door, and wrenched the bars open with surprising ease.

I stepped into the cool, starlit night, drinking up the fresh air.

Pat was singing merrily to herself somewhere in the distance, and Joyce pottered off to find her.

"Zachary!" Mrs Machon gathered him into her arms like he'd been missing from her life for several years. "What have those terrible girls done to you?"

"Get off, Gran," he said, wincing dramatically as he hobbled out of the bunker. "Ow, that bloody wrecks."

I tried not to look at him. Now we were out, I could feel the ridiculousness of the situation washing over me in waves.

Why the hell had Gem decided to play at chick flicks? It had only made things worse.

"I won't ask why Gemma decided you two needed some time alone in the bunker," Nan said pompously. "But I do believe we should all go home. I shall ring for a taxi."

Chapter 31

There was a new tourist attraction in the Bean Jar.

At least, that's how it seemed.

Lizzy and Jonny had overnight become an established couple. Sitting in the Jar together, gazing moonily at one another across their coffees, gooey grins plastered firmly on their faces, it was like something out of a very cheesy fairytale.

People were coming in from far and wide to have a gawp. Nobody could quite believe that Jonny Rabey, firmly under his fiancée's thumb for as long as anyone could remember, had a bona fide, living and breathing new girlfriend – people kept coming in for 'coffee', just to make sure he hadn't just built one in his attic. Or had a lobotomy.

To be fair, to anyone who hadn't seen him in a while, that's what it must have seemed like. Gone was the shy, nervous man sitting in the corner trying to blend into the background. Now we had a near-hyperactive hipster desperately trying to grow a beard while proudly showing off his new girlfriend to everyone who passed by.

Dull Denise had even been in, her eyes tragically swollen. I was willing to bet she'd been crying ever since the news hit her, and in spite of herself, she had to come and see things for herself.

I felt sorry for her. Let's face it, we'd all treated her pretty badly: we hadn't made any effort to get to know her in the months before the wedding-that-wasn't; and if we had, things might have been sorted a bit sooner. She'd seen that Flic and Jonny's relationship had been faltering – she had her vested interest to spot such things, of course. She was clearly still crazy about Jonny herself. But he looked through her like she was a piece of the furniture: he only had eyes for Lizzy.

Let's face it, to Jonny, we could all have been totally inanimate objects, the attention he paid us. Lizzy had him eating out of her hand already… though the feelings were very obviously mutual. I'd not seen Lizzy so happy in years.

They hadn't even had sex yet, and it had been over a week since the beach party.

"We're taking things slowly," Lizzy said firmly when I cornered her about it in the Jar's kitchen, when she was helping me load the dishwasher. "We've waited this long for one another, we want to get to know each other a bit better first."

"But come on." I raised my eyebrows. "Don't you want to?"

"Yes." She blushed. "But we're waiting."

A thought suddenly struck me. "You're not waiting for Flic, are you?"

"No." But she blushed even more.

"Jesus and the apostles on the Travel Trident to Herm, you are, aren't you? You're waiting for her blessing."

Lizzy stared at the floor. "Yes. Because I know that once we sleep together… that'll be it. I won't be able to turn back, even if she wants me to."

"Look at me, Elizabeth," I growled, swatting her with a tea towel. "You are not to be bollocking bothered by Flic and her demands. If she throws a tantrum over this, you're going to ignore her. Right?"

"It's not that simple…"

"Yes it is. Come on, you're the happiest I've seen you since… ever. There's no way in hell I'm letting Flic fuck this up for you. There's no way *you're* letting her fuck this up, seriously. Do you really think you'd be able to say goodbye to Jonny now?"

"Well… no." She grinned in that gooey way again. "I don't think I could."

"And Flic's not going to cause any bother anyway," I pointed out, turning back to the dishwasher. "She WhatsApped me from Ibiza yesterday, something about how I was always right about Jägermeister and why had she deprived herself for so long. She's happy. I think even if Jonny wanted her back – which he doesn't – she wouldn't even take him now."

"But this week was supposed to be her wedding... this Saturday. I'm just a bit scared that the first thing she finds out when she gets back from Ibiza is that her ex-fiancé is already, you know..."

"Balls deep in someone else?"

Lizzy winced. "Come on, Cleo, do you have to be so disgusting?"

I shrugged and wrapped my tea towel absently around my wrist like a bandage. "Sorry, force of habit. I get what you mean, but you know what? I think she'll be relieved."

"Eh?"

"Relieved that Jonny's not going to come knocking on her door the day of the wedding wailing that he's made a big mistake. If nothing else, she can use it as an excuse to get absolutely beautifully plastered with her new friends."

"You're probably right." Lizzy sighed deeply. "We don't want her to find out from anyone other than us, though, so we're going to meet her at the airport when she comes back tomorrow. But you're probably right."

"I am." I flicked the dishwasher closed with a satisfying thud. I didn't point out to Lizzy that news had very probably already reached Flic, thanks to Dull Denise and her unrequited crush and the magic of social media. She didn't need anything else to worry about. "So go and shag that man of yours."

"Give me five minutes." Lizzy laughed, and blushed, but I knew. It wouldn't be long.

* * *

That very same afternoon, Gemma and Sarnia came into the Jar after hours with some surprising news.

"Bloody hell, this thing is a monster," Gem grumbled, dragging Sarnia's enormous behemoth of a buggy through the door. "Why did I let you talk me into this one?"

"It's cool," I called over from the bar. "I wasn't letting you get that bright pink thing with the frilly bits on the hood."

"At least I might have been able to get that one through doors," Gemma muttered, plucking a cooing Sarnia out of the offending pram and plopping onto the sofa.

I waved at the baby and carried on sanitising my coffee bar. "Drink?"

"Nah, thanks, just need to feed this one before we wander back to Lizzy's." Gem was already pulling out a boob and wrestling with the jiggly baby to get it in her mouth. How times change.

"Beware." I thought I might as well point out what was probably going on. "There's a slight possibility Lizzy and Jonny are going to be having an emotional first shag when you get back."

"Eurgh." Gem rolled her eyes. "They're lovely, but I don't want to listen to that. That's why I'm moving out."

"You what?" I squawked. "I thought you were loving it in that flat!"

"I am." She shrugged, expertly managing to not dislodge Sarnia from her boob. "But they're a couple now. Any fool can see they're in it for the long run."

"It's not even been a week yet," I felt I should point out.

"Still, come on." Gem beady-eyed me. "You know as well as I do that it'll take a miracle to split them up now."

"True."

"I just feel a bit like I'm treading on their toes. I don't want to have to, like, wear headphones to go to sleep every night so I don't hear them shagging. And I feel a bit bad about Sarnia interrupting the shagging by starting to screech right in the middle of it."

"They've not even done it yet!"

"But they will." She raised her eyebrows. "You just told me they're probably doing it right now. And it's not just about *their* sex lives. It's mine too. Have you any idea how hard it is to have

Skype-sex when those two are being all couple-like and sickening all over the flat?"

"You and Vill are having Skype-sex?"

"We're *trying* to have Skype-sex," she corrected. "Between Sarnia deciding to howl right in the middle of it, Lizzy's dodgy broadband connection cutting out just at the good bit, and trying to be quiet so Jonny doesn't come running in thinking I'm being murdered... it's quite hard."

"And not in the good way," I supplied.

"Obviously."

"How does Skype-sex even..."

"Never you mind." Gem glared at me over her daughter's head. "Point is, me and Sarnia are fucking off. I've never been properly on my own before, I've always been propped up by Mum and Dad, and now by Lizzy. It's time for me to grow up, for the sake of this little one at least." She gave Sarnia a little jiggle; then, of course, regretted it as milk shot out of the baby's mouth at high velocity.

"Where do you think you'll go?"

"Where *are* we going, you mean." She grinned, quite a feat seeing as she was mopping baby sick off herself. "We were just looking at flats. Found a one-bedroom ground floor place at the top of the Grange. Mum and Dad have agreed to help me out with the rent for a couple of months while we get furniture and stuff sorted. I think they're terrified I'm going to move back in again."

"Hang about. Top of the Grange? As in, right near me and Zach?"

Gem shifted on the sofa, a quick flash of guilt in her eyes. "Um, actually Zach's the one who suggested the flat. It's in the same building as him. He's in the attic, I'm on the ground floor."

"Oh."

Things with me and Zach hadn't exactly been fantastic since the whole locked-in-a-bunker business. He'd been wearing a giant support bandage on his ankle, for a start, and had been giving me pathetically baleful stares every time he caught me looking at it. Not to mention a properly theatrical limp.

Other than that, though, things were strained and incredibly over-polite. I couldn't decide whether I'd preferred it when he was being Mr Big-Angry-Boss or whether this impersonal politeness was an improvement. It was as though he was trying really, really hard not to say anything that would give away any emotion whatsoever, or that would provoke any emotion in me.

I just wanted things to go back to the way they used to be. Back when we were friends, when we could take the piss and have a laugh. Before I'd challenged him on his 'feelings'. Bloody feelings. When I could get up the gumption to feel angry, I rued the day that 'feelings' had ever been invented.

Most of the time I just felt too sad to muster up anything beyond pathetic mooning, of course.

I didn't quite know what to feel about Gemma practically moving in with Zach.

"Well, you'll be closer to me, at any rate," I said eventually. "I'll be able to help you out with Sarnia more, and I'm sure Mum and Nan will be happy to give you a hand, too. Hell, we can even bribe Charlie to babysit when we go to Folies."

"Excellent plan." Gem nodded firmly. "Or when I've got Skype dates."

"So you and Vill, then…" I leaped on the subject-change with more vigour than I'd been able to rally for days. "You're having Skype-sex, you've had real sex… what's occurring with you two?"

"Give me a piece of that Gâche and I'll tell you. Breastfeeding mothers need sustenance to tell their stories."

Obediently, I sliced off a chunk of Mrs Machon's latest loaf of Guernsey Gâche and ceremonially presented it to Gem on a plate with a huge stack of butter.

"Go on then, tell me." I perched on the end of the sofa and watched Gem expertly feed herself and Sarnia at the same time.

"I think… fuck, this is hard to admit. I think I *like* him." She practically spat the word as if it was worse than any of her (copious) collection of swear words.

"Yeah, I think we all worked that one out." I rolled my eyes.

"No, like, really like him." She looked almost sick. "I want a relationship."

"You know that's not a bad thing, right?" I raised my eyebrows. "You were all ready to jump into a 'relationship' with Aaron, and he already had one."

"Yeah but…" Gem sighed, and wiped a dribble of milk from Sarnia's chin. "It all seemed like a game. Like it was all part of that stupid Leap Year Pact."

"Hey, you're the one who made up the stupid Leap Year Pact."

"And clearly I was stupid." She raised her eyebrows right back at me. "Why the fuck did you let me come up with that thing? Throwing ourselves into relationships that we wouldn't ever consider if we didn't both have a stupid need to win everything?"

"Speak for yourself."

"Come on, Cleo, you're as competitive as I am. So's Flic. The only one who isn't is Lizzy, and look who's the only one left in a real relationship."

I shrugged. I didn't want to admit that I only took things as far as I did with James because I wanted to beat the others to the altar. In any other situation he would have been a nice one-night stand, then thrown to the kerb. I wouldn't exactly say I got 'in too deep' – more like I paddled in the shallows – but usually I'd only be sticking a toe in the water then running away.

"Hey, give it five minutes and *you'll* be in a relationship," I pointed out.

Gem looked slightly sick again. "Hang on. I said I wanted it, not that I was going to actually do it."

"Come on," I scoffed. "I saw the way you and Vill were looking at one another that night. I've never seen you look at anyone like that." I paused. "Except perhaps Sarnia. And I know you love *her*."

Gem looked down at her black-haired scrap of a baby and smiled. There it was: the gooey look. Previously seen on Lizzy and Jonny, and Vill.

Then she let the smile drop. "But it's just too difficult. He lives in Germany, he's going to be on tour a hell of a lot. It wouldn't work out. Plus, I know what goes on behind the scenes at these metal gigs."

Fleetingly, I thought of Luka. "It's true." I got up off the sofa and picked up my sanitizer and kitchen roll again. "But I never saw Luka look at me like Vill looked at you. Just… give it a go and see what happens." I turned back to the sofa. "What have you got to lose?"

"If I've got nothing to lose, neither have you." Gem's eyebrows were disappearing into her hairline. "Why didn't you go with Luka when he asked you?"

"You know why." I squirmed. "I'm not in love with Luka."

"Then pounce on Zach." Gem shrugged. "You've got to do something, you're stagnating here."

"Hey, this isn't about me." I gestured a bit violently with my sanitizer. "This is about you wanting a relationship with Vill. Zach doesn't even like me anymore, we've already established this."

"OK." Gem nodded, turning back to her baby. "You keep telling yourself that."

* * *

I power-walked up the Grange after I'd cleaned and locked up the Jar, falling through my front door with a sigh that probably shook the house to its foundations.

I'd had enough of couples.

Lizzy and Jonny and their immeasurable cuteness. Gemma and Vill and their potential. I was going to have to start hanging out with Flic and her batch of single secretaries if I was to have any chance of regaining my usual clubbing-and-pulling lifestyle.

The question was – did I want it?

I had no idea what I wanted, and it was driving me mental. Did I want to declare my undying love to Zach and refuse to take no for an answer, potentially settling into a functional relationship? Did I want everything to go back to the way it used to be, sleeping with a different man every weekend and pulling my way around every randomer on the island? Did I want to run away from it all and jump on Karin Cluster's tour bus?

None of it made sense in my head, so I did what I've always done: I buried my head in the (metaphorical) sand.

I slumped onto the sofa and stared at the TV.

"Evening, my darling," Nan said, peering beadily at me through her diamanté glasses. "How was your day?"

"Ugh." I shrugged hopelessly, teenagerly. "Where's Mum? And Charlie?"

"Your mother's at bridge club, and your brother's with his father."

"Oh yeah, I forgot he was here this week."

"You look a bit lacklustre, my dear." Nan put down her stack of knitting and crossed her arms. She was wearing a Disneyland Paris t-shirt that I faintly recognised as being from our family holiday circa 2003, teamed with cut-off denim shorts and purple tights. Fairly reserved, for a change – at least it would be if it wasn't for those sparkly glasses.

"Eh." I shrugged again. "Don't know what I'm doing. Usual."

With an audible creak of her joints, Nan stood up and snapped off the TV.

"Do you want my advice, my Cleo?" She gave me her best glare through the glasses. "Anyone can see that Zachary is as mad about you as you are about him, but it might take something special for him to admit it. To himself and to you."

"What, take off all my clothes and sprawl on the coffee bar waiting for him?" I raised my eyebrows.

Nan giggled, sitting back down on the sofa. "Oh, that would make him come around quickly, darling. Reminds me when I first met your grandfather…"

"I'm not sure I want you to finish that sentence," I said quickly, burying my head in the sofa cushion.

"Don't worry," Nan clucked. "I'll save that story for another time."

"Or never."

"You never know, I might have some tips for you."

I poked my head back up from the cushion. "Maybe. But I think I need a few drinks in me before I listen to them."

"Anyway." She clapped her hands together. "I meant give him some space. In a big way. Why don't you go and find that nice rock star you've told me about? I'm sure he'd appreciate your company for a while."

"But I'm not in love with him," I found myself saying for the second time that afternoon. "He was fun, Nan, and I do like him. But with Zach…" I gulped, and found I couldn't finish the sentence. I buried my head back in the sofa cushion again instead.

I felt a thud as Nan landed next to me. She started stroking my hair – it felt nice, it was almost like being a child again, sitting on her lap listening to stories.

"Listen to me, my girl," she said softly. "I know you love him. You know it. Half the island knows it, my love. But maybe if you go away for a while, leave him to be by himself, he'll realise he can't live without you. And if he doesn't... then *fuck* him."

"Nan!" I sat up straight. "Language!"

"Like you can talk." Her eyes were sparkling nearly as much as the diamantés on her glasses. "I've heard you swearing like a sailor plenty of times. I'm telling the truth. If he can't work out how wonderful you are, my darling, then he doesn't deserve you."

I dropped my head back in her lap again and sighed.

"Don't you sigh at me, Cleo Weeks." Nan picked my head back up and made me look her in the eyes. "You're wasted on this island, my love. You need to get out and see the world. There's more to life than just this place. Enjoy your life while you're young."

"Mum did," I pointed out. "And she came back pregnant with me."

"But at least she went." Nan stared at me over her glasses. "Don't waste your life moping over young Zachary. You're too young for that."

"Maybe." I felt exhausted all of a sudden, and drooped onto Nan's shoulder.

Nan knew it was time to let the subject rest. She gave me a squeeze, and pottered back over to her chair and her knitting.

"Nan, what *are* you making?" I snuggled back into the sofa. "You and the Goats have been at it for months... are they socks?"

"No." Uh oh. The mischievous look was back on her face. "Well, yes, actually, in a way."

"Eh?"

"I'll tell you, if you promise not to tell your mother."

"OK..."

"Running the Guernsey Goats has been quite expensive." Nan picked up her needles and started clacking away at something striped in pink and purple. "We need some way to fund our activities."

"And bottles of sherry," I supplied.

"Yes, quite. So we thought we'd be a bit enterprising. It was while I was talking to Stanley Le Mesurier that I got the idea..."

Nothing involving Nan's married paramour could be a good sign. I'd met the spry old bugger a few times, and he was the most dirty-minded pensioner I'd ever come across.

"Well, he used to complain that every time he wasn't getting some *relations*..."

I groaned. "Do I really want to hear this?"

"If you want to know what I'm making, then yes." Nan waited for me to nod a queasy assent. "Whenever he wasn't having relations, his *parts* were too cold."

"Eurgh." I buried my head again.

"It was his way of trying to get either me or his wife into bed more often," Nan said. "Cheeky old sod. Going for the sympathy tactic."

"That's the worst pick-up line I've ever heard," I said through the cushion. "'My wrinkled old dangly bits are chilly, can you come and warm them up for me?' Ugh."

"Quite. So just as a little joke, I knitted him a willy warmer."

"A willy warmer?" I turned over and stared at the pink and purple knitted 'sock' with more than a little horror. "Oh heck."

"Believe it or not, he loved it," Nan said briskly. "And his wife appreciated the peace. So we've gone into production. We've been sending Guernsey Willy Warmers all over the world. We're on Etsy."

"Bloody hell, Nan." I had a sudden thought that made me shudder. "You're making wank socks!"

Nan shrugged. "It pays for our sherry. And we're going to have saved enough to get in a proper DJ for our Christmas party."

"That's kind of gross." I paused. "But I'm quite proud of your ingenuity."

Nan nodded. "We spotted a gap in the market. It's proving quite lucrative. Would you like to help? Take your mind off your love life, my darling."

"I think I'd rather drown myself in the Model Yacht Pond than knit wank socks for old men, but thanks for the offer."

Chapter 32

The first week of September saw the island's kids shipped back off to school after their long summer in the sun. Charlie, for one, was practically kicking and screaming when Mum shoved him out of the door, a bag full of new folders and pencil cases, and ears ringing with stern warnings about his GCSE year.

Nan denied that she'd slipped the box of liqueur chocolates into his bag as a lunchtime pick-me-up, but we all knew the truth.

The Bean Jar was absolutely dead. With the kids back at school and their parents at work, and the weather still stunning enough to keep everyone else on the beaches, we were left with just our lunchtime suits and the occasional afternoon regular.

This, of course, led to plenty of occasions where me and Zach were left on our own for hours at a stretch.

He was still being frosty: so frosty I could almost make ice-cream from his half-drunk cappuccinos. The veneer of politeness was still there, but I missed how he used to be – having a laugh, taking the piss, even losing his temper and throwing a shit-fit if something didn't go to plan. This cold stranger could have been an empty clone.

It had reached the point where we were starting on the monthly stocktake mid-afternoon rather than have to talk to one another.

Thankfully, Gemma and Sarnia were visiting, Gem occasionally barking questions at Zach across the room about the lease on her new flat.

"When the landlord says I can't smoke in the flat…"

"You're not smoking again, are you?" I threw myself out from behind the bar and made to grab Gem by the neck and throttle her.

"No." She looked at me with scorn. "I'm not, but what if I have a bloke round who does? Can he lean out of the window or do I have to boot him outside?"

"I don't think this is an issue that needs to go in your contract, Gem," Zach pointed out, sticking his head out from the cupboard under the stairs where he was making a start on counting packaging. "And surely you wouldn't let any random man smoke anywhere near Sarnia?"

"I mean if she wasn't there." Gem rolled her eyes. "I'm not bringing guys back when she's asleep next to us, that's gross."

Zach nodded and dropped to his knees, pulling a stack of soup cups behind him. I could hear him counting out loud.

"Did you know my flat actually comes with a Henry Hoover?" Gem called to me. "A real one! And I can keep it, for free! The last tenant left it behind…" She trailed off. She had the same look on her face that I'd seen her make when Sarnia had done a particularly fearsome poo. "Oh bloody hell. Fuck. I'm excited about a fucking hoover."

"You said you wanted to be a grown-up." I shrugged and turned back to counting individual packets of brown sugar.

"OK." Zach sighed, standing up from the cupboard and cracking his back. He ran his fingers through his hair and stretched.

I tried not to look at him. His hair was getting a little bit too long; Mrs Machon would be threatening him with her scissors soon if he didn't get it cut. I suppressed the urge to jump on him and run my fingers through it, turning his face to mine…

That would probably come under the definition of 'pouncing', as Gemma continued to advise me.

No. That would be stupid.

I focussed on my stack of sugar packets.

"I'm going to start putting these figures into the system." Zach grabbed the first sheaf of paper from the clipboard and made for the stairs.

I heard the click of the office door closing just as my phone started to ring.

* * *

This wasn't like the last time. I wasn't filled with panic, imagining ninety-nine different scenarios, worse and worse until I'd worked myself up into an anxiety attack.

This time, I stayed calm.

As if another entity had possessed my body, an entirely poised person existing on a cloud of normality, I carefully put my sanitizer down on the bar and marched up the stairs to Zach's office.

"I need to go," I said quietly. My voice was measured. It sounded like it was coming from very far away.

"What?" He turned around in his swivelling office chair, his expression cross.

"I need to go," I repeated. "My nan's in hospital. She's had a stroke."

I watched the colour drain from Zach's face as if I was a disinterested observer.

This had to be some kind of dream. Nightmare. It couldn't be real. But I had to go along with it anyway.

Without another word I grabbed my jacket from the hook behind the door and strode back down the stairs.

"Cleo, wait!" There was a thundering noise as Zach sprinted down behind me. "I'm coming with you."

"What's going on?" Gemma stood up, juggling the baby under one arm while she fought to get an explosion of nappies back in the changing bag. "Where are you going?"

"Nan's in hospital," I said. It still felt like someone else was saying the words; like I was on a different plane altogether. "She's had a stroke."

"Shit. Fuck. I'm coming with you."

"No." Zach was already on his phone, trying to get hold of a taxi. "I'm going. You stay here and mind the Jar."

"But…"

"No. I'm going."

I stayed in my passive coma until the taxi came, allowing Zach to shepherd me out by the arm, placidly sitting in the back of the car while he barked instructions at the driver.

He slid onto the backseat beside me. The taxi had only just screeched off from the kerb when, with an audible gulp, Zach grabbed me by the shoulder and pulled me close to his side.

Even a few minutes ago it would have flooded me with hope, but I barely even registered him.

I started speaking in a low voice, as if the words were falling straight out of my head. "I can't believe she's had a stroke. It's just not possible. I had breakfast with her this morning and she was fine. She's going to hate this. What if she can't talk? What if she can't move properly? What if she's paralysed? She's going to hate it. My nan."

"Shh, Cleo." Zach gripped my hand hard, but it felt like he was hardly touching me. "She'll be fine. People bounce back from strokes all the time… and you know your nan better than anyone. She won't let anything keep her down."

He shook me slightly to hammer in his point, and somehow the words trickled through my numb outer shell, breaking into the nightmare with absolute rationality.

Zach was right.

Nothing could knock Nan down for long.

She might be sick for a while – she might have some paralysis or whatever, but she'd leap back into action by the force of will alone. We'd all help her out. It might be hard, but we'd get there.

She'd be fine.

* * *

Nan died four hours later.

Joyce and Pat had noticed she was having problems speaking at the Guernsey Goats meeting – they'd been putting together their latest batch of parcels for Etsy and of course, Nan had been holding court with her latest round of bawdy stories. Pat's husband had had a stroke ten years before and she knew the signs; she had her phone out within seconds.

But Nan had fallen unconscious before the ambulance even arrived. She never woke up.

"She'd want it like this." Mum seemed determined not to let me and Charlie see her cry. Determined to be the strong one, for the first time in our lives, even though every part of her was shaking. "She wouldn't want to suffer."

I sat on the hard plastic chair in the hospital corridor, letting everything wash over me. It was over; it was done. The doctor was in with Nan, doing whatever it is doctors do after a person has died. We had been told to go home, go and sort ourselves out so we could grieve in private, but none of us could bear to leave.

Charlie had his head in his hands next to me, looking very small; Zach was pacing the hall, running his hands through his hair and stealing the occasional glance in our direction. Mum stood in front of us, gripping her own hands so tightly I could see her nailbeds turning white.

I couldn't focus on anything.

Mum was still talking, as if by rattling on she'd be able to block out reality.

I stood up. I couldn't sit there for five seconds more.

"Cleo?" Mum made to grab me, but I dodged and power-walked right out of the hospital.

Somehow, I found myself alone, sitting on the low wall along the seafront, staring out at the islands across the choppy sea. I had no idea how I'd got there, no idea how much time had passed. I could hear the traffic pootling by somewhere behind me, the wind picking up and whipping my hair into knots, but I didn't care.

I still felt numb.

Nan couldn't be dead. Not my nan.

She was so full of life. Who else would organise the old ladies of Guernsey into a crack-force of willy-warmer knitters? Who else could ever mobilise Mrs Machon into letting loose and getting high, of all things? Who else would there be to get the Guernsey Goats rave off to a banging start?

But never mind all the old biddies... what would *I* do without my nan? Rolling our eyes at one another behind Mum's back, laughing at stupid programmes on the TV, even going shopping together and talking one another into more and more ridiculous outfits.

Where else would I go for advice? Who else would accept me just the way I am, without expecting anything in return? Who else would steal all the hats out of my wardrobe and customise them with sequins?

I would never again see Nan sweeping by on the stairs, swathed in purple and glitter, on the way to her next madcap scam.

It seemed ridiculous. Improbable, impossible. The world wouldn't be able to keep going without her. The island would crumble into the sea. I would fall apart.

The sun was coming down over Guernsey, turning the island sky into swirling eddies of purple and orange, the sea a roiling dark chop.

I didn't notice Zach until he put his arm around me. I jumped so much I nearly fell off the wall.

"How long have you been here?" My voice was hoarse.

"A couple of minutes." He shrugged, shuffling backwards on the wall in case I knocked him off. "You seemed lost in thought."

I shrugged back. Somehow, Zach's arm around my waist was making a lump rise in my throat.

He pulled me closer into him, and I sighed. With his arm around me, I could feel my whole body relax. For the first time, I could let tears leak out. Zach let me turn my head into his shoulder – he didn't even pull away when I cried all the way through his t-shirt.

Eventually I managed to pull myself back together and hold back the sobs. More tears would come, I knew they were just behind the curtain, but with an audible snotty sniff I managed to suppress them for a bit longer. Zach didn't even flinch.

He pulled back a little bit, keeping his arm tightly around me, and gave me a small smile.

"Do you feel a bit better now? I mean, obviously you don't feel better. I mean… oh, I'm crap at this."

"You're doing really well." I managed a small smile myself. "Sorry for getting your shirt all wet."

"You can get my shirt as wet as you want," he said, his voice low. Then he blinked. "That sounded like a really shit come-on. Sorry. Told you I'm really bad at this."

"You're fine." I couldn't help myself, and snuggled right back into Zach's shoulder.

He gripped me tightly.

All of a sudden it seemed like all the drama of the past few months just didn't matter. All the backwards and forwards, love-hate relationship bollocks... it was all just pointless. Now something real had happened, something truly horrible, and through the fog of grief it hit me: Zach was right there for me. The way it was supposed to be. And I knew he always would be.

I pulled back again and looked up. He was looking down at me, his eyes scrunched against the wind but still peering at me with concern.

I could see right then that he'd give me anything I asked for. That the frosty exterior of the past few weeks had just been a veneer, his way of protecting himself from me hurting him again. And now I was broken-hearted, he'd open up for me in a second.

I had a flash of my future. If I took this opportunity right now, right this second, I could have Zach. I could have the true love I'd dreamed of. We could be properly together, and it wouldn't just be a random one-nighter. It would be real. It would be forever. I'd be happy, we'd both be happy.

If I just reached up and tugged his face down to mine, it could all happen.

But Nan would still be dead.

I pulled away and jumped off the wall.

"I've... I've got to go home."

"Are you all right?"

"I'm fine." I sighed and steadied myself. "I just want... I just need to be alone for a bit."

Chapter 33

The next two weeks were a jumbled nightmare. The funeral. Comforting Mum when she finally broke down, clearing out Nan's room. Arguing over where to scatter the ashes.

All the while, I was fighting with myself.

But eventually, I made my decision. And it didn't take long at all to put my plan into motion.

I didn't tell anyone while I was getting myself organised. This wasn't something I could do with a committee. It was something I had to do all by myself.

A week after the funeral, I was ready to confess, and I summoned them all to the Bean Jar after hours.

Gemma and Sarnia arrived first, having just marched down the hill from their new flat. Gem was bubbling over with the joy of being on her own for the first time, marvelling at having her daughter all to herself.

Lizzy came next, Jonny trailing behind her. Both of them were still wearing slightly bemused expressions, as if they couldn't believe it was possible for them to be so happy.

Flic swanned in a few minutes later, even giving her ex-boyfriend a beatific smile. I'd seen her photos on Instagram from the past few weekends, and she was having the time of her life getting plastered in Folies. She was finally letting loose, and was making the most of having no regrets.

And above all, there was Zach – hovering behind the bar with a nervous smile on his face. He'd been entirely respectful for the past couple of weeks; keeping his distance from my grieving family, but always there to help us out whenever we needed him. He was giving me space, but I knew he was waiting for me to come to him.

None of them had really known how to treat me. Lizzy had vacillated between tying herself round my neck in back-breaking hugs while her own tears spilled forth, and giving me the cryptic 'space' that grieving people apparently need. Gemma and Flic had both been determined to act as if everything was normal, occasionally blushing in the middle of some raucous tale or other as they remembered they were talking to the recently bereaved. Zach was just... Zach. At his best.

And it made what I was about to do even more difficult, but even more necessary.

They spaced themselves out around the Jar, staring at me expectantly. Lizzy and Gem were fussing over Sarnia on the sofa, with Jonny perched on the arm, never out of touching distance from his new girlfriend. Flic was sprawled elegantly over the spindly table almost under the stairs, scrolling idly through Instagram and crunching some vegan snacks. Zach stayed behind the bar, allegedly wiping down the coffee cups fresh from the dishwasher, but keeping his eyes on me all the same.

"Are you about to make a life-changing speech?" Gem said, trying to be as flippant as usual. Lizzy elbowed her in the ribs, her best serious-face on.

"Kind of." I shrugged, and pulled myself up to sit on the coffee bar, adjusting Nan's sequinned purple beanie on my head as I turned to face my friends. I wanted to keep Zach behind me. If I looked at him while I said this, I'd crumble. "You've all been so good to me since Nan... Since Nan. I don't... I don't want any of you to think I'm doing this because of you. Any of you." I stared at my own knees.

"Doing what? Spit it out." Gem could always be relied on to be impatient.

I took a deep breath and looked up from my knees. "Most of Nan's estate went straight to Mum, of course, but she left a chunk of money explicitly for me. She didn't leave instructions, like what she wanted me to do with it, but I've got a pretty good idea." I tried not to let my voice wobble. "She stayed in Guernsey her whole life to raise her family. She loved it here, but she always told me she missed a lot of chances. She always encouraged Mum to get out and enjoy her life, and then when Mum lost her nerve, she did the same to me. And I've been letting her down my entire life."

"You've not been..." Lizzy started, making to get up from the sofa, but I cut her off.

"I think I gave her a bit of hope when I went off to uni. She thought I'd get a taste of freedom and go off exploring the world, doing all the things she wished she could have done, but I didn't. I lost my nerve just like my mother did, and I came back here where everything was familiar. But now..." I sighed. "She always said I was wasted here, and I'm not going to keep letting her down."

"You're leaving?" Lizzy whispered. I heard Zach drop a cup on the bar with far more force than strictly necessary, somewhere behind me, but I refused to look round.

"Yes. I'm leaving."

"Like a holiday?" Flic piped up. "Oh, go to Ibiza, it's fabulous."

"No, not a holiday." It was hardest to say this bit. "I don't know when I'll come back." I sighed again. "I mean... I'll always come back, of course. Guernsey is my home. But I need to get out for a while. I need to do all the things Nan never could. I need to be on my own, in places where nobody knows me. Where I've not got you guys or my family as a security blanket. I need to grow up, and I can't do it here."

I stared at my knees again, waiting for someone else to speak. But nobody did.

"You probably all think I'm being really stupid," I said in a rush. "Like I'll come back in a month or something with my tail between my legs." I looked up, trying to sound tough and defensive. "And maybe I will, but at least I'll have tried."

Gemma stood up suddenly, depositing Sarnia into Jonny's lap.

"I think you'll be fine," she said softly, and strode over to the bar to grab me in a skinny-armed hug. "You go and have your adventures. We'll keep this place warm for you."

I felt another two bodies join the hug as I was swept off the bar into Gem's arms, knocking Nan's beanie off my head. I was shocked to realise it was Flic stroking my hair. Lizzy was sobbing unabashedly into my shoulder.

"What'll I do without you?" she sniffled.

"You're bloody brilliant, Liz," I choked. "You don't need me."

"I do. You're the only reason I've ever done anything, if you didn't bully me I'd just be sitting in the corner shaking all the time."

"Bullshit." I managed a smile, from somewhere under Gem's armpit. "I just started to drag it out of you. You've done the rest perfectly well by yourself. Especially this year."

"And I was just looking forward to having you as a pulling partner." Flic stepped back and grinned at me. "I hope you won't mind if I take over your crown as Pulling Queen of Guernsey."

"I pass it on to you with good intentions," I said solemnly, then smiled and punched Flic on the arm. "I'm sure you'll do very well."

I detached myself from Lizzy and gently propelled her towards Jonny and Sarnia, then unhooked Gem's hands from around my neck.

"What if you're gone forever?" she said, her voice oddly small. "You're practically Sarnia's dad, what if you're not here to see her grow up?"

"You'll be fine without me," I said, my voice threatening to break again. "You've probably got plenty of adventures coming up without me anyway. Vill's bound to summon you over to Germany soon..."

"Maybe I'll run into you on a tour bus."

"Maybe." I pulled her forward for another squeeze.

"When are you going?" Lizzy said through her tears. "*Where* are you going?"

"I leave for Gatwick on Thursday," I said.

Lizzy gasped. "So soon?"

I shrugged. "There's no point in hanging around. If I wait any longer I might change my mind. I'm not sure where I'll go first. I'll probably hang around in London for a bit, maybe go up to Manchester and rediscover a few of my old haunts, look up some of the old uni crowd. Then…" I shrugged again. "Who knows? I want to try Australia and see what all the fuss is about. Nan's brother emigrated to New Zealand about forty years ago, I might go and see if I can look up that side of the family. No idea where I'll end up."

One by one, the girls left the Bean Jar, promising to come and see me off at the airport, Jonny and Lizzy already discussing a scrapbook they could put together for me, Gem and Flic squabbling over whether Flic could come back to Gem's pristine new flat for dinner, and whether or not it would be gluten-free.

The door shut behind them, and it was just me and Zach.

Finally, I turned around to look at him.

"Shall we go and sit upstairs?" he said, his voice low.

"Yes."

We sat on the sofa in front of the floor-to-ceiling windows. I ignored the rush hour St Peter Port traffic rumbling below us, pretending the busy port with all the cranes wasn't spoiling the view, and stared out at the bay instead. The sky was so bright and blue it could have been a summer afternoon, instead of heading into a chilly autumn. Just the tiniest touch of fog – or heat haze – made Herm and Sark seem like spectres rising from the far distance, across the sea. From high over the harbour, the water looked like glass, like it could be smashed by the speedboats bouncing idly between the islands.

In just a couple of hours it would be dark out there, the lights of St Peter Port spilling onto the water and lighting my path across the sea.

From the other end of the sofa, Zach took my hand, and we sat in silence. I wanted to memorise everything about the moment. I had to remember the touch of his hand, the feel of him breathing softly next to me, the electricity that seemed to be tingling from him to me.

I didn't know if I'd ever feel it again.

Eventually, he spoke.

"I'd ask you if you're sure, but I know you are."

"Yes."

"I'd ask if you wanted me to wait for you, but I think I know your answer to that one too."

"Yes."

He was quiet for a couple of minutes more. A couple of minutes that seemed to stretch months into the future, if not years.

"I will, though."

"Zach, don't." I sighed, but I didn't take my hand away. I kept my eyes on the distant hazy islands, telling myself they were only fuzzy because of the fog. Just some fog in my eyes, that was all. "I'm doing this because I want to be alone, but I can't guarantee I'll be alone for my whole time away."

"Especially if you go to Germany." His voice wasn't angry, just deflated.

I squeezed his hand, suddenly acutely aware of what had happened on this same sofa and realising that yes, I probably would find myself in Germany at some point.

"I don't know where I'll go. But I'll come home. One day I'll come home."

"I can't say what I'll do while you're gone," Zach admitted, almost as if he was talking to himself more than to me. "But I'll be here for you if you come back."

"I'll come back." I turned to look at him for the first time, and let my eyes meet his. A pair of bright blue searchlights – I sighed inwardly thinking of all the times I'd avoided looking past the glasses and messy hair, afraid of loving what I'd find there. I'd denied what I'd felt for too long, and now it was too late. For just a second, I wavered. I knew that if I fell into Zach's arms now, I'd never leave.

But I had to go. I was teetering on the edge of the rest of my life, and if I put it off for any longer, I'd never get to experience it.

"I'll come back," I said yet again, and leaned forward to let my lips gently brush Zach's.

His arms were around me in a second, gripping me tightly to him as we kissed, kissing as if we were the last two human beings in the world.

He pulled away first.

"We'll be waiting for you," he said hoarsely. "Me, and Guernsey. We'll be here."

And I knew that wherever I went, wherever I ended up, whoever I ended up with, Zach was right.

People might change, relationships might come and go. I might become an entirely different person. For all his intentions, so might Zach.

But the quiet island in the English Channel would always be waiting for me. When my heart ached, the home of my childhood, that little gem of the sea, would always call me back in the end.

As I left the Bean Jar, I went behind the coffee bar to pick up my bag and the mural caught my eye. I'd always loved it. Zach had painted it with his own hand, and I loved him. But more than anything else I loved the words, the song that has been sung for so many years, and should never be forgotten.

I would certainly never forget it.

Sarnia Chérie. Gem of the sea.
Home of my childhood, my heart longs for thee.
Thy voice calls me ever, forget thee I'll never.
Island of beauty. Sarnia Chérie.

Acknowledgments

Thank you to everyone who has had this forced upon them to read over the last few years: Tash, Sara, Frances and Hannah, your constructive criticism has helped immensely! Thank you to Naomi for going on many adventures with me and inspiring a good chunk of this book. Thank you to Lee for letting me vent, often. And most of all thank you to Kev and Teddy, for putting up with me through writing, editing, and banging my head repeatedly against the desk.

Printed in Great Britain
by Amazon